✝The
Curse
Keepers

By Denise Grover Swank

The Curse Keepers
(Urban fantasy)
THE CURSE KEEPERS
THE CURSE BREAKERS
THE CURSE DEFIERS

Rose Gardner Mysteries
(Humorous southern mysteries)
TWENTY-EIGHT AND A HALF WISHES
TWENTY-NINE AND A HALF REASONS
THIRTY AND A HALF EXCUSES

Chosen Series
(Urban fantasy)
CHOSEN
HUNTED
SACRIFICE
REDEMPTION
A CHANGE IN THE WIND (short story collection)

On the Otherside Series
(Young adult science fiction/romance)
HERE
THERE

Off the Subject Series
(New adult contemporary romance)
AFTER MATH
REDESIGNED

✝HE CURSE KEEPERS

DENISE GROVER SWANK

47N◉RTH

Published by 47North
P.O. Box 400818
Las Vegas, NV 89140

ISBN-13: 9781477808627
ISBN-10: 1477808620
Library of Congress Control Number: 2013939859

Cover illustration by Larry Rostant

To my son Trace, who always believed in the impossible. And still does.

⌒ Chapter One ⌒

The moment I laid eyes on him, I knew he was trouble.

He stood in the doorway of the New Moon restaurant, filling the space with his tall, slightly muscular frame and sucking the air from the room. Literally. As I focused on inflating my chest with the limited air supply, I tried to ignore the warning bells ringing in my head.

Always listen to your instincts.

My instincts had been honed by years of working as a waitress in a tourist town. You learn a lot about people working with the public.

From the beginning of May until the middle of September every year, my town of Manteo on Roanoke Island, North Carolina, was overrun with tourists. They came to see our quaint little town but mostly to see the alleged site of the first English colony to settle in North America, the Lost Colony of Roanoke. Everyone had a theory about what happened to the colony that settled on the Roanoke Island shores over four hundred years ago, from a massacre by neighboring Indian tribes to alien abduction. My family had their own take on what happened. A version I'd forgotten fifteen years ago, except for the very basics.

The late lunch crowd was clearing out so it was that rare period in the summer when we got a breather before dinner. Marlena seated the guy in her section, but I could tell she did so grudgingly. She tried to fix me up with any man who walked in the door without a wedding ring.

I nearly groaned when I realized that I'd checked.

I hurried out the back door and leaned against the building, gulping deep breaths as the brick pricked my arm. *How can I be having an asthma attack? I don't even have asthma.* I'd never experienced anything like this before. No matter how much air I sucked into my lungs, I still felt short of breath.

After about five minutes, I got control of my panic and made myself go back inside.

Marlena had already taken the guy's order, and he sat brooding over a beer, staring out the window onto the tourist-filled street. I only had two tables left and Marlena had rung both of them out while I was hiding out back. With nothing to do for the moment, I picked up a towel and wiped the bar counter in tiny, mindless circles. My chest felt tight, but my breathing was manageable. *I must be coming down with a sudden summer cold.* Finding a rational explanation settled my frayed nerves. Slightly.

"You rub that spot any more and you're liable to wear a hole right through it." Marlena winked. She seemed to be breathing without any problem whatsoever. "Someone got you shook up?"

I shot her a scowl, then looked around the small restaurant. No one else seemed to be having issues either. Except for the guy Marlena had seated. His chest rose and fell at a slow, even pace, as if he were concentrating on the movement.

A small part of the back of my brain screamed that it knew what was going on, but I shushed it, pissed off the thought had even crossed my mind.

The curse was a fairy tale. It wasn't real.

"No," I said to Marlena.

"Then good. I'm due for a break and the only one left in my station is that one." She shot a thumb in his direction. "You won't mind finishing up Mr. Hottie for me."

I knew I'd gotten off too easy with her putting him in her own section. Shaking my head, I turned my back to the dining room, just as I saw the man give me a quick glance. "Nope. No way. He just sat down, and he hasn't even ordered his food yet. *You* take his order, *then* take your break."

"He doesn't want any food, just the beer." Raising her eyebrows, she lowered her face to mine. "He's a fine-lookin' man close to your age, and he's been eyeing you since he walked in the door."

"That's what worries me." But truth be told, that wasn't all that worried me. My difficulty breathing worried me. The fact that this guy dredged up all kinds of ugly, terrifying memories full of curse nonsense, the kind that drained the life out of my soul—that's what worried me. The sooner "Mr. Hottie" walked out the door, the better.

Marlena nudged me with her shoulder. "You should give him your number, Ellie."

My mouth gaped, and I quickly shut it, glaring. "I'm *not* giving him my number!" I spat. "I don't even *know* him. Besides, I'm dating Dwight. And tonight is date number five. Tonight's *the night*." I really needed tonight to be the night.

"Dwight the insurance adjuster from Michigan? You're still dating him?" Marlena crossed her arms over her ample breasts and shot me a stern look. Marlena was an intimidating woman, standing nearly six feet tall with the body of a small linebacker. When Marlena put on that stern look, most people cowered in fear. Unfortunately for her, I'd learned she was mostly bark. But she still scared me a bit. I just tried not to let her know it.

I put a hand on my hip and tilted my head in defiance. "Of course I'm still dating him. Why wouldn't I?"

To my surprise, Marlena refrained from commenting on my tumultuous dating history, despite the fact that she'd been forced to endure four years of listening to me complain. Sometimes in excruciating detail. Maybe she was worried if she pushed too far, I wouldn't give Mr. Hottie a chance. Releasing a sigh, she put her palm on the counter and leaned forward. "Look, sweetie . . ."

I groaned, rolling my eyes. Every time she uttered "Look, sweetie," I knew a lecture was coming.

Her mouth puckered in disapproval as she pointed a finger in my face. "Don't you be rolling your eyes at me, Miss Elinor Dare Lancaster. You respect your elders."

Elders, my eye. Marlena was barely fifteen years older than me.

"I know good and well that Dwight's here on a temporary assignment. Which means he'll be leaving soon, and you'll be all alone."

"So?"

"So, give that warm-blooded American man over there a chance, Ellie."

I pursed my lips, shooting a glance at the customer at table five. He took a sip of his beer and continued watching the crowd outside the window. His short-sleeved T-shirt showed off his muscular arms—not solid enough to make him look like a bodybuilder, but just enough to show that he was a man accustomed to working with his hands. Suddenly, my mind took a detour to forbidden territory, thinking what he might do with those hands. I shook my head to snap out of my stupor. It had been too long since I'd had sex, and I wasn't entirely immune to an attractive guy. My defenses were weakening.

Sighing, I shook my head. "For all you know, he's a tourist, so what makes him any different than Dwight?"

Something about my demeanor signaled Marlena's victory, and she grinned. "He's ten times better looking, for starters." She thrust his bill into my hands. "You'll thank me for it later. Now go." Turning with a laugh, she walked out the back door, calling into the kitchen, "I'll be back in fifteen, Fred."

I studied the dining room after she left. People often lingered at their tables, seeking refuge in the air conditioning from the humid heat outside. Only two of the twenty tables were occupied: the table where the man I'd tried to avoid for the last fifteen minutes sat, and a table with an older couple in my station. The couple, obviously tourists based on their camera sitting on the table and their "Outer Banks" T-shirts, had rung out with Marlena. They studied pamphlets while discussing where to go next and ignoring their half-full glasses. I took a pitcher of sweet tea and Marlena's bill folder and stopped at the couple's table first. "Would you like a refill?"

The woman smiled, pulling her reading glasses off her nose. "Oh, no, honey. We were about to leave."

"You all are welcome to stay as long as you like," I said, shifting my weight, trying to calm my increasing anxiety. I was getting light headed and I fought the urge to gasp for air. My blood pounded in my head. The man and woman in front of me seemed fine. "No need to hurry off." If they left, I'd be alone in the dining room with the stranger. Sure, Fred was in the back, but little good that did me.

The older gentleman stood and grabbed his backpack. "Thanks for the beer recommendation. That was the best draft ale I've had in a long time."

"You're welcome," I forced out with a smile, my heart racing as they headed for the door. "Thanks for coming in. Have a great day."

They waved as they walked into the summer heat, and I turned to table five, trying to force air into my lungs. *This is stupid. He's just some guy. Give him his ticket, and he'll leave and that will be that. This has nothing to do with him.*

But I knew he was different. Deep, deep down in the pit of my soul. One of the few things I remembered from Daddy's story floated into memory, begging for attention. My shoe caught on the edge of a table foot, and I stumbled, sloshing tea over the side of the pitcher and onto a nearby table.

What in the hell was *wrong* with me?

The man turned his face to watch me. His dark eyes burned into mine. Marlena was right. He was an extremely good-looking man. His dark hair was closely trimmed and stubble covered his face, like he'd forgotten to shave for a few days. But the hint of dark circles underlined his eyes, giving him a weary look. He clutched his beer bottle, his knuckles white, as though he were nervous even though his expression suggested otherwise.

Alarms rang in my head again, my instincts pinging every nerve along my spine. I needed him to leave. Now.

I set the pitcher on the sticky table and took two steps toward him. The hair on my arms stood on end as though I'd become electrically charged.

What the hell?

The man's eyes widened as he turned to me, his lips parting slightly.

I thrust the folder toward him from several feet away, and flopped it on the table with a dull thud. "You can pay whenever you're ready," I said in a rasp, the air sticking in my throat even more than before. My panic rose and I stomped it down, frustrated that after all these years, the fucking curse was the first place my mind leapt to in this situation.

The corners of his mouth lifted into the barest hint of a smile, giving him a ruggedly handsome look. I was sure most women around the world swooned at the sight. I, on the other hand, was close to passing out from lack of oxygen.

His chest rose and fell in heavy gasps. He was having a hard time breathing as well. It should have made me feel better. Instead, it made my near-hysteria worse.

Don't let him touch you.

I took two steps back and put my hand over my heart. Maybe we were being overcome with carbon monoxide poisoning. Could you get that from air conditioning? There had to be some logical explanation what was happening to me. Happening to *us*. I just couldn't seem to find it at the moment.

He reached into his pocket, pulled out his wallet, and hastily removed some cash, tossing it on the table. The hair on his arms stood on end.

My eyes widened in fear as he got to his feet. He took a step toward me and stopped as I backed into a table. His dark, almost black, eyes held my gaze. "I didn't catch your name." His breath escaped in short bursts.

My face tingled from lack of oxygen, and I felt dangerously close to passing out. The closer he came toward me, the more difficult it was to breathe. I knew I should move away from him but everything around me slowed, and I couldn't seem to get my muscles to work. Not to mention I was trapped by the table and two chairs on either side of me. The hair on my head felt electrified. "I didn't give it." My words came out slurred.

His face had paled and his eyes moved to my name tag. He grinned, but it wasn't friendly. "Thank you, *Ellie*." My name sounded like the answer to a riddle on his lips. "Until next time."

He started to walk away, then stopped, spinning around and grabbing my right hand with his, as though he meant to shake my hand. An electrical shock ran from my palm into my chest.

For one brief moment, the entire world seemed magnified and microscopic all at once. The room faded and I was no longer me. I was the waves in the sound off the pier and the clouds in the sky. I was an ant outside on the parking lot. I was part of every tree on the street.

Before I could marvel at the vast connectedness of the universe, I felt a tear in the veil separating the earthly world from the spiritual, and the screams of hundreds of things, ugly and foul, filled my head.

The man's mouth opened, and he dropped his hold with a start. Stumbling backward, he hurried out the door, not even casting a glance back.

My lungs expanded, as though some invisible band around my chest had burst loose. I sank into a nearby chair and sucked in gasps of air. My head spun, grappling to make sense of what had just happened, sure that I'd just had a hallucination, further proof that there was a logical explanation. Maybe I'd been poisoned. Or drugged. People didn't sense bugs or plants. People didn't feel like they were one with the water a hundred feet away.

The door creaked, and I jumped out of the seat, worried that he'd returned. Instead, a young family entered the restaurant. The mother pulled off her sunglasses and squinted at my startled reaction. I forced a smile and snatched up the pitcher off the nearby table. "Welcome to the New Moon. You all can take a seat wherever you'd like. I'll be right with you."

I hurried to the back and washed the now dried, sticky tea from my hand, trying to calm down. Never in my twenty-three years had I experienced anything like that. Yet part of the story Daddy had recited since before I could talk echoed in my head.

"*When the two Keepers meet for the first time, the seam separating the spirit world and our world will be ripped apart and the gate will be opened. Your chest will tighten, and you'll have a hard time catching your breath. It will be as though the very air you breathe is sucked out of you. It is. The Keepers watch over the seam dividing the worlds. They alone will feel the tear. That is when the curse will be broken. Then God help us all.*"

My palm tingled and I glanced down at my hand, gasping at the faint pink mark I saw there—but that wasn't all. The outline of a square surrounding a circle, their lines intersecting, covered my palm.

"*Once the mark of the Keeper appears, you have until the beginning of the seventh day to make things right.*"

Oh shit.

I had to talk to Daddy.

⁊ CHAPTER TWO ⁊

Another rush hit within minutes of the man running out the door. It was as though he'd been keeping everyone away. But when I thought about it later, it was probably the two of us combined. He and I were polar opposites, like magnets when you try to stick the wrong ends together and they shove each other away. Not only could we not occupy the same space without repelling one another, but we flung off the people around us.

Until you flipped the magnets and set them right.

But then again, to my irritation, I'd hardly been repelled at all. Nearly suffocated, sure. But repelled? No. Marlena was right. He was extremely good looking, if only I could get past my sudden asthma attack. My reaction had to have been some kind of breathing episode exacerbated by my overactive imagination, because for some reason, he triggered a resurfacing of all the hocus-pocus I'd left in the past with my middle school Tamagotchi and *NSYNC posters.

The curse was make-believe and nonsense.

Still, something stirred deep inside, setting me on edge and making me clumsy the rest of the afternoon. What the hell had I experienced when he touched my hand? And how did I explain the scorch mark on my hand and the thing that looked like a tattoo?

"What's gotten into you and more importantly, why are you still here?" Marlena asked. "You tryin' to get out of your date with Dweeb tonight?"

Her question shook me out of my thoughts. I'd forgotten all about my date. I forced a scowl. "*Dwight.*" I rolled my eyes. "And no, I'm not. If anything,

I'm late for my shift at the inn. But I can't leave because I'm covering for Lila. She had to run up to Norfolk."

Marlena tsked. "That's twice in two weeks that girl's sloughed off her shift." She snagged my shirt and pulled me backward, untying my apron. "Barb's here. We can handle things until Lila gets in. You have to get ready to see Dagwood."

She didn't have to tell me to leave twice. "Dwight . . . and I thought you didn't like him."

Marlena shrugged with a grin that told me she was up to no good. "You said this was date five. Your men don't make it much longer than that. The sooner Dwane is gone, the sooner you'll hook up with someone like Mr. Hottie."

With a sigh, I stripped my apron over my head and tossed it into a hamper. "His name is *Dwight* and things are different with him. He's got a job with State Farm. He's stable." I grabbed my purse out of a drawer in the back room and stared at her, raising my eyebrows and daring her to contradict me.

Marlena placed her hand on the doorjamb to the back door, barring my exit. "Oh, he's stable all right, but he's so full of stability that he'll suck the life out of ya."

My heart thudded against my chest at her statement. Going out with Dwight was *nothing* like having the life sucked out of me. I'd had the life sucked out of me on two occasions. The first was figurative and had happened when my mother was killed. I didn't care to dwell on that memory. The second had happened that afternoon and was quite literal. *Give me stability, thank you very much.*

I stood in front of Marlena's beefy arm and waited for her to move, giving her a look of impatience.

Marlena's voice lowered. "I care about you, Ellie. You're a sweet girl. You deserve better than the boring guys you date. You're young. You need a little excitement. Live a little."

"I live plenty, and I happen to like dependable guys."

"If you like them so much, than how come you go through them like Kleenex?" She dropped her arm and brushed past me before I could respond.

Scowling, I pushed the back door open and stormed out into the humid North Carolina heat. I was late for my second job, helping my stepmother Myra at the bed and breakfast she and my father owned. I considered stopping by my apartment and changing first but realized I didn't have time if I wanted to finish at the Dare Inn and get home in time to shower before my date. Dwight was supposed to pick me up just before seven.

The great thing about living in downtown Manteo was that everything was within walking distance. My parents' B&B was only four blocks from the restaurant where I worked, and my apartment was in the alley behind the restaurant. If a grocery store would open downtown, I'd hardly have to drive at all, especially since I rarely left Roanoke Island. Good thing too since I drove a rust-bucket piece of crap.

Although it was a short walk to the inn, it was long enough to work myself up into a nervous ball of anxiety. The encounter with the guy at the New Moon shook me up more than I'd been in years. I chalked it up to my overactive imagination, desperate for the bizarre occurrence to be anything but the curse. I was halfway to believing it was all in my head—but for the fact that he'd had a hard time breathing too. Never mind the electrical current and the scorch mark on my palm. I stared down at the darkening shapes on my hand. *I must have set my hand on wet paper or a soggy cardboard box. The ink bled onto my palm, that's all.* And the hallucination I'd had could be marked off as stress.

Even so, I would have felt better if Marlena or the older couple had had problems breathing . . .

But I wasn't ready to slap a curse label on it. My only hope was that my dad was having a lucid day and/or my stepmother Myra could help me find a reasonable explanation for it all.

I'd worked up a sweat by the time I walked in the back door of the inn. Myra was on the phone in the small office and gave me a soft smile. My job in the late afternoon was fairly simple: I set out the snacks for the guests and hung around to answer questions and play concierge. That, and I folded towels. I was late enough that Myra had already set out the fruit, cheese and crackers, and bottle of wine.

An older couple sat on a leather sofa in the living area, huddled over an open map.

"Hi." I walked into the common room, suddenly worried I might have some telltale stains from the restaurant on my clothes or face. *Too late to worry about that now.* "Need any help with directions?"

They looked up, and I recognized them from earlier that afternoon. They were the couple in the restaurant who left me alone with the guy. My stomach flipped with nerves.

The man smiled and patted his knee. "Weren't you our waitress this afternoon?"

I leaned my hip into the chair across from them. "Sure enough. My parents own Dare Inn so I help in the mornings and afternoons."

"I love your little town. Have you lived in Manteo long?" the woman asked.

"My whole life." And not a day had gone by since I was eight that I wished I didn't.

"There's so much history here," she continued. "It's so fascinating what happened to that town. Imagine. An entire colony completely disappeared. Everything."

I forced my smile to stay plastered on my face. You can't live in Manteo and not answer these questions half a dozen times a day during the summer months. And working in a service job made it an even more frequent conversation. Normally I didn't mind, but the afternoon's events had shaken me up. The fate of the Lost Colony of Roanoke had been pounded into my head since before I could string words into a coherent sentence. And not the version they told at the visitor center or reenacted at the play every summer. My family had its own version of crazy to hand down. If I were to believe my father—and I didn't—my ancestor had a firsthand account.

But I kept all of that to myself and shook my head in mock sympathy. "Tragic."

"To think that all those poor people were wiped out by Indians," she tsked.

"Actually, historians now think that the colonists split up and went to live with other Native American tribes. Which explains why the entire town disappeared. They took their belongings with them."

Her eyes narrowed and bore into mine. "Do you think that's what happened?"

If she had asked me earlier that morning, I would have wholeheartedly said yes. Now I wasn't so sure. And that worried me more than the afternoon's events. I shrugged and raised my eyebrows, giving her a mischievous look. "I guess we'll never know. That's what makes it so fascinating." And that's what kept Manteo thriving for four months out of the year.

"Has your family lived here long?"

"As long as we can remember." I sat down on the arm of the leather club chair and leaned forward, needing answers, but worried I wouldn't like them. "Say, today at the restaurant, before you left, did you have any trouble . . . breathing?"

The man sat up straighter, his eyes widening. "What do you mean by trouble? Was there some type of chemical leak?"

I jerked upright, suppressing a groan. "*What*? No!" Holding up my hands, I shook my head. "Nothing like that happened. I just wondered if perhaps you felt a little short of breath."

The older woman placed her hand over her heart, her chest rising and falling in short pants. "I didn't this afternoon, but now I am. What were we exposed to?"

I shook my head again. "No! You weren't exposed to anything! It was nothing. I had an asthma attack is all. It must have been the pollen." My smile was now cemented onto my face.

The woman's shoulders slumped in relief. "Well, why didn't you say so?"

Myra approached from behind and placed her hand on my shoulder. "How are you doing this evening, Mr. and Mrs. Crabtree? I see you've met my daughter, Ellie."

They gaped in surprise. Myra was second-generation Chinese, and you couldn't find anyone more Caucasian looking than me—fair complected, freckles on my nose, and long dark red hair. Some days Myra was ornery enough to let the guests puzzle it out. This must have been one of those days. "So where are you two planning to go for dinner?"

Mr. and Mrs. Crabtree were still trying to figure out our genetics.

"If you're looking for seafood, I highly recommend the Carter House on Highway 10, headed toward Nags Head. Their own employees often catch some of the seafood they serve."

"Is that so?" the man asked, squinting from me to Myra. It was obvious they wanted to ask about us, but politely refrained. "Sounds good."

Myra took a step backward toward the office. "If you'll excuse us, Ellie and I have something we need to attend to."

They waved us aside, and I cringed. Was I in trouble? Myra usually understood when I was late.

She led me to the small office and lowered her voice. "You and I both know you've never had an asthma attack in your life. What's going on?"

Leaning into the door frame, I screwed up my face and gave a half shrug. "It was nothing." I paused. "How's Daddy today?"

Her eyes narrowed in suspicion as she studied me. Then she shook her head and smiled. "He's better today, actually. He was asking about you."

I forced another smile. I'd done quite a bit of that in the last few hours. "It looks like things are under control here. How about I go fold towels and talk to Daddy?"

Myra knew I was up to something, but Daddy's good days were fewer and far between so it was hard for her to call me on it. "I left him in the screened-in porch. He was watching the neighbor's dogs."

"Thanks, Myra." I kissed her on the cheek and spun around.

"Ellie . . ."

I turned around, surprised at the worry in her voice.

"You know you can talk to me about anything, right?"

I smiled again, and this time it was genuine. "Of course, Myra. And I love you for that." I gave her another quick kiss and bolted out the back door before she could ask any more questions. Myra knew about the curse, but Daddy had the answers I needed.

I walked across the yard to the main house and grabbed two baskets of bath towels from the laundry room, carrying them through the living area to the porch off the front of the house. Daddy sat in a rocking chair, staring out toward the sound. You couldn't see it from here, but we were close enough that you could smell the salty air and feel the breeze.

"Hey, Daddy." I sat in the chair next to his, dropping the baskets in front of me with a loud thud.

He turned to face me, his gaze wavering before it cleared. A smile lifted his mouth. "Hey, Elliphant."

Tears burned my eyes. He hadn't called me that in weeks. He hadn't recognized me at all in days. "I miss you."

His eyebrows arched in surprise. "Did you go somewhere?"

I suppressed a groan, annoyed with my stupidity. Making comments like that only confused him. "No, Daddy. I've just been so busy I haven't had time to stop by and see you in a few days." Which was a lie. I'd seen him every day for the last six weeks.

He sat back in his chair and rocked. "Oh."

The soft rhythmic creak of his chair filled the space around us, and I leaned my head against the wood slats of the rocker, closing my eyes. Nostalgia washed over me, hot and sweet. Funny, the more you want things to stay the same, the more they change.

"How's the New Moon?"

My eyes flew open, and I sat up. Daddy was having a really lucid day. "Oh, you know. It's a job."

"I told you that you should have gone into archaeology like your mother." He winked. "Then you could play in the dirt for a living."

I nearly burst into tears. I used to spend hours playing in the dirt when I was a little girl, before my mother died, digging for the Lost Colony of Roanoke. I was sure that Momma and the rangers at the visitor center had it wrong. The colony was probably in my own backyard, even though Daddy used to tell me that I could dig to China and never find it. Daddy hadn't mentioned the memory in years.

"Daddy, I need to ask you about the curse."

His chair stopped, and his hands tightened on the edges of the curved arms.

"I've forgotten how the curse is broken. Can you remind me about that part?"

His rocking resumed, and he focused on the dogs playing in the yard. "I thought you gave up on that *nonsense* years ago."

His words pierced my heart. I *had* given up on the nonsense years ago, but the curse was his entire life, his legacy passed down to me. If I had only known how little time I'd have left with him, the real him and not the shell of him I saw every day, I wouldn't have been so callous about dismissing his stories as nonsense. I would have at least pretended.

"You felt it too," he whispered.

My heart jolted as my breath caught. "Felt what?" I whispered back, terrified of his answer.

"It opened. I thought I'd dreamed it." His face turned to me, fear in his eyes. "It happened."

The hair on the back of my neck stood on end. While Daddy never doubted the curse's existence, he'd never once claimed that it had broken. I pushed aside my terror and patted his hand. "Don't be silly, Daddy. That curse has held for well over four hundred years. Why would it break now?"

Confusion flickered in his eyes again. "The two Keepers would have had to have met."

Oh, shit on a brick. I had trouble catching my breath, but this time not from possible supernatural causes.

His eyes bore into mine, more lucid than I'd seen him in months. "Did you meet the other Keeper today?"

I snatched a towel out of the basket and started folding. "How in the world would I know? We don't even know that there still is another Keeper, let alone what he looks like." My mind backtracked to the few memories I had. "Besides, even if I had, how would that break the curse?" I fisted my hand to hide the mark.

"You would have to touch the other Keeper."

The towel in my hand shook.

"Did you touch the other Keeper?"

"How would I know?" But my defensive tone gave me away.

Excitement filled his eyes. "Who was it? A man or woman?"

"Daddy . . . we don't even know . . ."

"Ellie."

I took a deep breath and bit my tongue before I blurted out *this is crazy.* "Man." I turned my attention to the next towel.

"Old, young . . . Did he look Native American?"

I folded my hands on the towel on my lap, avoiding eye contact with Daddy. "Man, young. About my age. It's hard to say if he was Native American. He had dark hair and eyes, but you know the Lumbee Indians are so integrated with Caucasians and African-Americans that you can't always tell."

"Do you think he was Lumbee?"

I closed my eyes, nausea churning in my stomach. "I don't know. I *do* know that I'd never seen him before until he walked into the restaurant."

"What happened?"

I set the towel in the spare basket and began folding another. "Not much. He ordered a beer, I felt like I'd been slightly electrocuted, I nearly suffocated, then he left."

"So it's true."

This was all happening too fast, the consequences too high. I'd spent the last fifteen years convinced none of this was real. There was no way I could simply accept it as truth now. "No, it's not. There's got to be a logical explanation why I couldn't breathe." I sat up and held out my palm, then quickly closed it when I saw the red scorch mark and faint lines of the circle and square still there. "Maybe I developed a sudden allergy. Like maybe to peanuts or cashews. Claire only has to walk on a plane with peanuts and her throat gets tight."

Daddy's confidence wavered. Flashbacks of middle school hit me full force, when I told him I never wanted to talk about the curse again. Seeing his current disappointment made me feel like I was disappointing him all over again. But nothing good ever came from believing in the curse. The only thing the curse produced was four hundred years of endless waiting. The children of Egypt searched for forty years for the Promised Land. At least they got manna from heaven for their trouble. The ancestors of Ananias Dare got disappointment and heartache. I fully intended to stay as far away from the curse as possible.

Daddy sat back in his chair and rocked for several moments, both of us sinking into our own thoughts. It was like old times, when we wallowed in the murky limbo between Momma's death and Myra's entrance in our lives. When it was just Daddy and me, suffocating in our grief and our guilt.

"A storm's a brewing, Ellie."

Daddy was right. Clouds had begun to churn and darken in the short time since I'd walked over from the restaurant. "I'll make sure the trash cans are put away before I leave."

His hand covered mine and squeezed. "No, a *storm's* coming. I feel it in my bones."

A chill ran up my spine. "That's called arthritis, Daddy."

"Be ready, Elliphant. You're the Keeper now. You'll have until the beginning of the seventh day and not a moment longer."

That's what worried me.

～ CHAPTER THREE ～

Sometime between leaving Daddy and slathering my hair with conditioner, I'd convinced myself that I'd gotten myself worked up over nothing. From what little I remembered of the curse, nasty things were supposed to happen as soon as it was broken. Here it was over four hours since my encounter with *that man*, as I'd begun to refer to him, and the worst thing to happen was I couldn't find my new sandals to wear with my thrift store–find sundress. Honestly, that in itself was a tragedy.

But the misplacement of my sandals had everything to do with the fact my closet was a mess and nothing to do with evil spirits. What were evil spirits going to do with strappy sandals?

When Dwight knocked on my door promptly at 6:45, I answered barefoot and breathless. "Hi." I'd crawled out from underneath my bed and my just dried, long hair was a mess, negating my five minutes of styling.

Dwight stood on my porch wearing his work clothes—gray dress pants with a pale blue shirt and yellow tie. I loved me a man in a tie. "Ready?"

I opened the door wider to let him in. "I was just looking for my shoes. Give me a second."

"We don't want to be late." I heard a slight tone of worry in his voice. "All the good seats will be taken."

Good seats in relation to the Manteo Pioneer movie theater was a relative term. "I'll just take a second."

As I disappeared into my bedroom, I noticed Dwight glancing around my apartment. He'd only been inside once, and this time I made sure that it was picked up. Especially since I hoped to come back here later.

I grabbed another pair of sandals and stepped into them as I walked back into the living room. "See? All ready."

Dwight stood next to the door and eyed me up and down, taking in my pink, sleeveless dress. "The air conditioning tends to run cool at the theater here. Aren't you worried you'll get cold?"

I gave him a coy smile. "That's what I have you for."

Confusion flickered in his eyes. "I don't have a jacket to share with you."

I fought a groan as I picked up my purse. This man was dense. "That's okay. I'll take my chances." I followed him out and locked my door. As we descended the steps from my third-floor apartment, a weird tingling tickled my palm. I felt as though someone or *something* was watching me. I shook it off. All this curse nonsense was getting to me.

We walked to the theater, and I snagged Dwight's hand. The streets of Manteo were filled with tourists going to dinner and walking around the town and by the pier. The shops that lined Queen Elizabeth Boulevard, the main street downtown, stayed open late in the summer, snagging more sales of beach trinkets and Roanoke souvenirs. We passed Poor Richard's Sandwich Shop, a small restaurant and bar.

"Do you want to grab something at Poor Richard's? I didn't have a chance to eat."

He scrunched up his nose. "But we'll be late for the movie." In the few times I'd been out with Dwight, I'd learned he was a creature of habit who didn't like the rules changed midstream. He'd asked me out to the movie, not dinner. To throw in dinner was like derailing a train.

"We'll only miss the previews." I gave him a sweet smile. "Or we could skip the movie and just talk."

His eyes bugged as though I'd suggested we set his pants on fire. "But I really want to see this movie."

I forced a smile as we passed the restaurant and turned the corner at the old courthouse.

"Do you ever get tired of all the chaos?" Dwight asked as we stepped around a family who'd stopped to pick up their kid's fallen ice cream cone.

I shook my head. "No. It's so quiet the rest of the year that I like the reminder that there's a whole world out there outside of this little town."

"Why not go out there and see it yourself?"

Now didn't seem like a good time to bring up the fact that I found it physically difficult to get too far from Roanoke Island. "So what's playing tonight?" I knew it was an action movie, one that had been out several weeks. There was one small movie theater in town, and it only had one screen.

Dwight didn't notice that I'd avoided his question and told me that the special effects were supposed to be spectacular. He was excited that the theater had recently added digital so he wouldn't lose all the great CGI. I nodded and smiled, hoping this evening would end up with an entirely different kind of action.

The movie was loud and packed with explosions. The theater was freezing, and Dwight was too dense to catch any hints about putting an arm around my shoulders to keep me warm. To top it off, a kid sat behind me, kicking my seat the last half of the film. When we left the theater, I was cold, hungry, and cranky. I was cursed all right.

We walked through downtown on the way back to my apartment. The sky was still overcast and the clouds churned overhead as if they were angry. The wind had picked up, and I grabbed the bottom of my dress to keep it from blowing up. Not that Dwight would have noticed.

The crowds were thinning, but I loved the excitement of the people who wandered the streets during the summer months. Wondering where they'd come from. The places they'd seen. Since I could never get more than a couple hundred miles away from Roanoke Island without a crushing pressure on my chest—which Daddy always declared was a byproduct of the curse—I had to fulfill my desire to see the outside world with the Internet and cable TV. That and the stories of home the tourists shared with me from time to time.

When we reached the bottom of the wooden steps to my apartment, Dwight leaned over and gave me a peck on the lips. "Thank you for a wonderful evening, Ellie."

My eyes flew open. "Wait. Don't you want to come up?"

Dwight glanced at his watch. "Well . . . I have work in the morning."

It was barely nine o'clock. He sounded like an old geezer. I cocked my head and gave him a tiny smile. "Just for a little bit? Please?"

An inner battle waged on Dwight's face, and I wondered how he found the fortitude to deal with really difficult decisions. I stood on my tiptoes and wrapped my arms around his neck. "Just for a little while?" I kissed him long and slow, and I felt his arms encircle my waist before he pulled away.

"Ellie, not out in public. Anyone can see us here."

We were surrounded by buildings, and it was getting dark. Sighing, I let my arms drop and took a step back. "We were only kissing."

Dwight licked his lower lip. "I have a professional image to maintain."

He was an insurance adjuster from Michigan. A northerner. He was pretty much at the bottom of the Manteo professional image ladder, but my desire to get him in my apartment kept that fact from leaving the tip of my tongue.

I took his hand and tugged. "Then come upstairs."

He sighed before a shy smile lifted his mouth. "Okay, but just for a few minutes."

I stuffed down my excitement as I practically dragged him up the two flights of stairs. Unlocking the door, I caught movement on the porch out of the corner of my eye, in the shadows cast by the street lights.

Standing upright, I whirled around. "Did you see that?"

"What?"

"Something moved over there!" I pointed to the dark shadows behind my flowerpot.

Dwight danced in place, his feet skipping like he was jumping rope. "What was it? A rat?"

Irritation bubbled in my chest, and I put a hand on my hip. "No, it wasn't a rat. We don't have any rats here."

"Are you sure?"

I counted to three, reconsidering inviting him in. He wasn't very bright, and more than a little boring, and apparently not very courageous. But he had a steady, good-paying job and was a mostly attractive man. Sure, he wasn't anything like *that man* in the New Moon, but Dwight had his own quiet version of attractive. So his light brown hair was thinning and he had a slight paunch. There was more to a man than muscles, and dark, brooding eyes, and rough-looking three-day-old stubble. I hoped that buried deep inside all that mundaneness was a man who was capable of great love. Love like my parents shared. My daddy hadn't been an exciting man, and he'd loved my mother almost more than life itself.

In the end, there was no question. Right or wrong, I was desperate for some physical attention.

Once I closed the door, I kicked off my shoes, tossed my purse on the kitchen counter, and went to the refrigerator. "Would you like a glass of wine?" I sure needed one.

"Um . . . yeah." Dwight wandered around the living room, investigating my family photos.

I would have preferred a little more enthusiasm since I was going for a full-blown seduction here. Apparently, it was going to take more effort than I was used to. Far be it from me to back down from a challenge. I pulled a bottle out and set it on the counter, then found a corkscrew in the drawer.

Dwight picked up a picture frame. A nervous twitch made his hand shake. "Is this you when you were little?"

I craned my neck to see which photo he was looking at. "Yeah, that was taken when I was seven."

"Who's the woman?"

"My mother."

"She looks a lot like you."

I smiled, but it was forced. "So I've heard." We both shared dark red hair, fair skin that burned instead of tanned, and bluish-green eyes. And an aversion to believing in the curse.

I'd spent the last fifteen years standing by my assertion that four hundred years of tradition and folklore was a lie. For the first time since I was a kid, I was reconsidering.

Dwight set the frame down and moved to the other side of the counter, watching me open the wine. "So you've lived here your entire life."

"Yep." I jerked the cork out of the bottle, then poured wine into the glasses. "My family's always lived here. I've never left."

"What about when you went to college?"

I handed him a glass. "I didn't go."

His hand froze in midair. "You didn't go to college?"

I shrugged, trying to act nonchalant. "I could never figure out what I wanted to be when I grew up; no sense wasting money on all those expensive college hours." Not to mention I couldn't afford it, even if I could live with my phobia of being too far from Manteo.

"So have you figured out what you want to do with your life now?"

I walked around the counter, carrying my glass along with the bottle. "I'm only twenty-three. I've got time to figure it out." I sat down on the sofa and took a sip of wine. This really wasn't going well.

Dwight followed me, frowning as he sank into the cushions next to me. "In theory, by this time you should have some kind of inkling. Do you?"

I fought to keep from scowling. "If you're asking if I've found my purpose in life, the answer is no. But Myra says I'll figure it out when I'm ready." The truth was that my situation bothered me more than I liked to let on. It wasn't so much that I hadn't found my purpose, it was more that everything I tried felt so *wrong*. As though I were forcing my feet into shoes that were too small and tight.

"Myra? Your stepmother?"

"Yes."

"Forgive me for pointing out the obvious, but isn't she enabling you?"

I leaned back as my eyebrows rose. Leave it to Dwight to show some backbone when it came to insulting me. "Excuse me?"

"It's just that—"

"I live in my own apartment. I own my own car. I'm completely self-sufficient. How is she enabling me?"

Dwight set his glass on the coffee table. "But you work as a waitress. And that's only part of the year. Your parents must subsidize a portion of your income."

I wanted to laugh, but I was too irritated and insulted. He couldn't be further from the truth. "I support myself." I paused and took another sip of my wine. "The restaurant is open all year round. Tips may not be as good in the winter, but I still have a job."

He held up a hand and gave me an apologetic smile. "I'm sorry. I've obviously jumped to conclusions. I guess I just don't understand how you can be happy working as a waitress without any discernible life goals."

I took a gulp of my wine, trying to remember why I invited him up.

Dwight placed his hand on my arm and slid it up and down in an attempt to offer comfort, but the gesture felt stiff. "That didn't come out right."

I lowered my glass in surprise. That was the most physical affection he'd voluntarily shown me in the time I'd known him.

"I'm sorry. Really. I have this tendency to be judgmental sometimes."

You think? "Did you want to be an insurance adjuster since you were a kid?" My snarky question fell out before I could stop it, but Dwight seemed to miss the sarcasm.

"Yeah. My dad and his dad are in insurance. It's in my blood. Maybe inn keeping is in yours."

Hardly. It was more likely the curse was in my blood. I scrunched my eyes closed, muttering an obscenity under my breath. Damn that curse for sneaking back into my life. I'd shut the door on all of that nonsense years ago. There was a curse on Roanoke Island all right, but it turned out that the curse was my bad luck with men. "Tell me more about Michigan."

Dwight broke into tales about his family and growing up with snow in Grand Rapids while I consumed two glasses of wine. Since I'd skipped dinner, the wine was going straight to my head. Too bad Dwight had only drunk half of his.

I watched him as he talked. He really was an attractive man. If I squinted just right. But he was educated, even if he seemed a little slow in social situations. So maybe he wasn't perfect, but he had potential. I wanted the magical love my parents had had, but I was beginning to think I couldn't afford to hold out for perfect. Maybe their love was so rare that most mere mortals couldn't hope to find it.

I was partway into my third glass when I decided it was now or never. I set my wine on the table, then leaned over and grabbed Dwight's face. His eyes widened with surprise as my mouth touched his, and his body stiffened slightly. I worried he was about to shove me away, but as my lips and tongue coaxed his, he relaxed and put an arm around my back.

We kissed for several minutes, and I tried really hard not to grade his technique. Dwight might be an overachiever in the insurance world, but he could have spent a little less time studying actuary tables and more learning the art of French kissing. But the wine helped ignite my fire, and I reached for the knot of his tie, trying to loosen it.

His hand pushed mine aside, and he leaned his head back. "Let me do it. This tie was a gift from my mother, and I don't want to wrinkle it." He expertly unknotted his tie, folded it neatly, and laid it on the arm of the sofa.

My mouth dropped open in disbelief, and I was about to cut my losses when he turned back to me, pulled me against him, and took charge.

Maybe this could be salvaged yet.

I reached for the buttons of his shirt, wondering if they had been laid by golden geese. But he not only allowed me to unbutton his shirt, he let me pull it loose from his pants. Encouraged, I straddled his lap, hiking the skirt of my dress to my upper thighs. I slid my hands across his chest while he kissed me, but something was off, and it wasn't his scrawny upper frame or his tiny potbelly. I just couldn't figure out what it was. Perhaps there was a slight lack of enthusiasm on his part?

I sat back and lowered the straps of my sundress, dropping the top half to my waist.

Dwight studied my light-pink, lacy bra with interest. His hands skimmed my back, and his face lowered to my cleavage.

As he pushed down the cup of my bra, I leaned my head back and tried to remember what time I was supposed to be at the New Moon the next day. *No! Don't think about that right now.* But there was no denying that Dwight's lack of skills weren't limited to the neck up.

Maybe he just needed a little incentive. I unbuckled his belt and unbuttoned his pants while he turned his attention to my other breast. Slipping my hand into his pants, I searched for his erection.

And found nothing.

Well, that's not entirely right. I found *something*, but I had to search. A lot.

I sat up and cocked my head. "Um . . . I need to go to the bathroom for a second." I climbed off his lap and pulled up my bra, then I held up a finger. "I'll be back in a second." As I moved toward the bathroom, trying not to run, I snatched my cell phone off the counter and closed myself in the lavatory. Then I dialed my best friend, Claire.

She answered on the first ring. "So how did it go?"

I sat on the toilet and ran a hand over my hair. "Um . . . it's still going," I whispered.

"It's still going? Then what are you doing calling me?"

"Well . . . it's just that . . ."

"What?"

How could I put this? "I can't find his penis."

Claire paused for half a second. "How drunk are you?"

I hunched over my knees, trying to gauge my level of intoxication. "I've had a couple of drinks, but not enough to stop me from finding an important part of male anatomy. I mean, how hard can it be?"

"Obviously, not hard enough."

Giggles erupted, and I clapped a hand over my mouth. After a couple of seconds, I settled down. "This is serious, Claire."

Claire burst into laughter. "Are you sure he's not a tranny?"

"I thought trannies were guys dressing as girls, not the other way around." I took a deep breath to settle my giggles. "And no, he's got a part, just not an interested one." Great, I couldn't even get a boring guy excited about me. "What am I going to do?"

"What do you *want* to do?"

Covering my eyes with my hand, I sighed. "I don't know."

I heard Claire's exasperated exhale. "Ellie, why are you with this guy? Why are you doing this to yourself?"

Outraged, I sat up straight and hissed, "How was I supposed to know he couldn't get it up?"

"Anyone could have—no, that's too easy," Claire muttered. "That's not what I meant and you know it. Why are you wasting your time with this guy when you can barely stand him?"

"That's not true."

"*Please.*"

I had to concede that she might have a point. "I can't just send him away."

"Why not?"

"It will be too obvious."

"Well, then I suggest you stock up on Viagra."

I groaned. "You're no help."

"Yes, I am. You just don't like what I have to say."

"Ugh! I have to go."

"You might as well go since you won't be coming—"

I hung up on her before she could finish. And she was wrong. There was a reason I kept a vibrator in my bedside drawer.

When I returned to the living room, Dwight had removed his pants and shoes. He leaned back, wearing his white Fruit of the Looms and his unbuttoned shirt.

Maybe *I* needed to make more of an effort. Maybe he needed more foreplay. One part of me said to send him home and call it a night, but another part of me screamed *Ellie Lancaster is not a quitter. Well, maybe with piano, yoga, and knitting, but I'm not a quitter in this.*

I dropped my dress to the floor and sat on the sofa with renewed determination. This man was going to have sex with me whether he liked it or not. But as soon as Dwight leaned over to kiss me, I realized I couldn't go through with it. Call me a quitter, but I was done.

Rolling away, I stood, reaching for his pants and shoes. "You need to go."

His eyes widened. "What? Why?"

I glanced down to his crotch and then back to his face. "This just isn't going to work out."

He climbed to his feet, and I shoved his pants at him. He stepped into the pants and looked up at me. "Ellie, if you would just be reasonable."

I grabbed my dress off the floor. "Reasonable? If I were reasonable, I wouldn't have gone out with you after our second date, when you suggested that I should reconsider ordering dessert." I wiggled the dress to my waist, struggling to get the straps up my arms.

He shook his head in confusion. "But you had just mentioned you wanted to go on a diet! If you want dessert, you can get it—"

I opened the door and pushed him out while handing him is shoes. "You're damn right I can get dessert!"

I stood in the doorway, pulling the door shut behind me as I watched as Dwight clomped down the stairs, irritated that I'd put up with him through five dates. I really sucked at dating. Man after man after man had paraded through my life, each one worse than the last. My judgment was not to be trusted.

Maybe it was time to find my purpose in life. A purpose that didn't include men. Maybe I'd even try to move away. *No*, I could never move away from Daddy, and Myra needed me to help with the inn. But I could try to take a trip in the fall. I'd always wanted to see the Grand Canyon. I'd learn some breathing exercises to deal with my anxiety of getting too far from Roanoke Island.

Starting tomorrow morning, I was changing. No more flighty Ellie. I was going to be mature and responsible. I was going to figure out who I was. And I was giving up men. At least until I figured out me a little better.

As I turned to go back inside, I noticed someone in the shadows, six feet away. My hand froze on the doorknob.

The figure stepped out of the darkness, and my heart jolted.

It was *him*.

~ CHAPTER FOUR ~

"What are you doing here? Are you a stalker?"

A slow smile covered his face, and he moved toward a chair on the corner of my small porch. "If I were a stalker, would I really admit it?"

Good point. But stalker or not, finding him on my porch freaked me out. "Why are you here? How did you find me?"

He leaned back and crossed one leg over his thigh, tilting his head with a self-confidence he didn't have earlier that afternoon. "Ellie, you know why I'm here."

He knows my name. Wait. Of course, he did. He'd read my name tag. But that still didn't explain how he knew where I lived.

He grinned, waving toward my chest. "You might want to cover up." He shrugged with a smirk. "Or not. It's entirely up to you."

I glanced down to see my dress still partially down, exposing my bra. Jerking my dress up, I pressed my back into the door. "What are you doing here?"

He set his elbows on his thighs and leaned forward. "We have less than a week. We need to make a plan."

A plan for what? I nearly groaned when I realized what he meant. I shook my head. "I don't know what you're talking about."

His eyes widened slightly.

I couldn't deal with this right now. "You need to go." I turned my back to him and started to open the door, but he moved behind me, inches away, his mouth close to my ear. A small electrical charge ran up the length of my body, like when you put your hand in front of a TV screen.

This wasn't real. It couldn't be real.

"You *do* know what I'm talking about."

My breath came in short pants. Was he some crazy lunatic? He had to be. Why else would he be here? *Maybe I should scream.* "I'm warning you. Leave or I'm calling the police."

He backed up, and I whirled around to face him. His hands were up-raised in surrender. "I only want to talk, Ellie. Can we talk?"

My heart was a runaway freight train, and I could hardly catch my breath. "How did you know where I live?"

"It wasn't hard to find out."

"That didn't answer my question."

He shrugged and leaned his back against the post supporting the roof over my porch. "Does it matter? What matters is what started this afternoon."

"I don't know what you think happened this afternoon, but it's all in your head. I'm not interested in dating you. I have a boyfriend."

He looked over the railing. "That guy?" Turning back to me, he smirked as his eyes roamed my body, then rose to my face. "Well then I guess it's a good thing that's not what I'm interested in."

My mouth dropped at his insult. Why *wasn't* he interested? *What the hell is wrong with me?* "Then what are you *doing* here?"

His voice lowered. "I'm here about the curse, Ellie."

I turned around in a panic, my fingers fumbling at the door. "There is no curse."

"You're denying it exists?"

"Do you not understand English? That's exactly what I'm doing."

"You're a Curse Keeper, Ellie. You can deny it all you like, but that doesn't make it any less true. We opened something this afternoon, some-thing dark and ugly. It's up to us to deal with the aftermath."

I whirled around again, my body blazing with anger. "I didn't do this! *You* showed up at *my* restaurant! You grabbed my hand."

"I couldn't help grabbing your hand. It was like I couldn't control the urge. You felt it too, like you wanted to get away but you couldn't."

How did he know? I forced myself to calm down, especially when I saw the amusement in his eyes. "What kind of sick game is this? What are you up to?"

He stepped away from the railing and moved in front of me. He'd changed shirts since he'd been in the restaurant. This one was darker and tighter, hugging the muscles of his arms and chest. My body noticed and my body heat rose. But God help me, I was not going to fall for this arrogant son of a bitch.

"You feel that, don't you?"

I narrowed my eyes. "I don't know what you're talking about."

He grinned. "How do you explain this afternoon?"

"Asthma attack."

A sexy as hell look crossed his face. "And now?"

"I can breathe just fine right now."

His gaze dropped to my chest, then up to my eyes again. "Oh, really?"

The breathing trouble I suffered from now was nothing like that afternoon. I wasn't sure that fact made the current situation any better.

"I'm not talking about your lack of breath. I'm talking about what we feel standing next to each other."

I bet he wouldn't have any trouble getting an erection. Dear Lord in heaven, where had *that* come from? I lifted my chin and shot him a withering glare. "And here I thought you weren't interested."

A slow smile spread across his face. "I'm not. Trust me, Ellie. You'd know if I was." His statement sounded like a promise.

I swallowed.

"I'm talking about the electrical current between us. You can't deny it's there. It's part of the curse. It's part of the story that's been passed down. You have to know this."

I didn't. I didn't remember anything about the other Keeper except that he or she was a descendant of Manteo. "There is no curse."

Exasperation flooded his eyes. "Why are you denying it? This is what you were born to do. Four hundred years of waiting, and it comes down to you and me."

"That damn curse can wait another four hundred years because I don't want any part of it." I tried to turn around again, but he grabbed my arm and pushed me back against the door, his body pressing against mine. The current between us intensified, and it gave me smug pleasure to see his eyes dilate and widen in surprise. He felt it too. And it wasn't just an electrical current.

But the intention of his invasion of my personal space was far from amorous. His voice lowered. "You can't ignore this. Whether you like it or not, you're part of what's happening. The spirits have already been set loose— they'll flee at a slow trickle to start, but they're loose all the same. Have you felt them?"

I didn't answer. He really believed this.

"You have, haven't you? A feeling that you're being watched? Like something is lurking in the corner, in the dark?"

I refused to confirm that I had. "You're right. I *have* sensed something lurking in the darkness. You."

He tensed, his anger pouring off of him in hot waves. "We have a week to take care of the gate. Don't waste time denying it's real."

I splayed my hands on his chest and shoved him away, my own anger exploding. "You *do not* get to tell me what I can or cannot do. *I don't even fucking know you.* You show up outside my front door, lurking in the shadows. If I have anything to be worried about, it's *you.* There is no curse. It's all a bunch of made-up crap that caused my family nothing but trouble. It's probably someone's idea of a sick practical joke. Well, guess what? I'm not listening to another word of this. Now get the hell off my porch before I call the police."

He took a step back, shaking his head in disgust. "Manteo's line held onto our belief. We've taken our role seriously, waiting to fulfill our duty. Why am I not surprised the Dare line would be full of cowards and slackers?"

He was disparaging a four-hundred-plus-year-old man who may or may not have been my ancestor, and yet I felt insulted. I had been wrong. This night *could* get worse.

He stepped close to me and lowered his face to mine. If I didn't know any better, I would have guessed he was about to kiss me. But his body language said that was the furthest thing from his mind. "Humanity is at stake, and you call it a sick practical joke." Contempt filled his words. "The joke's going to be on you when all hell breaks loose. Hopefully, you'll be more willing to play your part then." He turned toward the steps.

"Who *are* you?"

He stopped and looked over his shoulder. "Collin. Collin Dailey. Manteo's Keeper."

I stayed in front of the door for several seconds, watching him disappear down the stairs. When anyone else used the staircase, I always heard the thuds of their footsteps, even in my apartment. But Collin's were silent.

That was a great stalker skill.

I fumbled with the doorknob and practically fell inside, slamming the door behind me. Collin Fucking Dailey was insane. That was the only reasonable and rational explanation.

So how does he know about the curse?

I grabbed the wine bottle and took a chug. How *did* he know? There was only one way he could: There really was a Manteo line of Curse Keepers. And if there was a Manteo line of Curse Keepers, that meant I was currently the Keeper in the Ananias Dare line.

Shit.

I grabbed my cell phone and called Claire.

"Well?" she asked when she answered. "Did you ever find it?"

"No," I waved, even if she couldn't see me. "I kicked him out."

"Good for you."

"That's not why I'm calling. Something else much bigger happened."

"Something bigger than Dwight?" She giggled. "It couldn't get much smaller."

"Ha, ha.. Very funny." I would have laughed too if Collin Dailey hadn't once again shaken up my world. Twice in one day. "Something happened this afternoon."

"What?"

"I think I met the other Keeper."

Claire went silent.

"Well? You don't have anything to say?"

She cleared her throat. "I thought you didn't believe in the curse."

"I don't. Well, I didn't . . . but I don't know how to explain what happened. Plus he knows about the curse. He knows I'm a Keeper."

"Wait, slow down and start from the beginning."

I told her what happened at the restaurant, and about how my dad was having a lucid day and told me that he felt the curse open. And that Collin showed up on my porch, announcing we had a week to shut the gate.

"Is that true? Do you only have a week?"

"I think it's until the beginning of the seventh day. I don't remember much else, Claire. You know I've forgotten most of that stuff."

"Maybe it would be better to start with what you *do* remember."

I took a long drink from the wine bottle, finishing it off. I sat it on the table, then ran my fingers through my unruly hair. "This is crazy. The Roanoke colony disappeared because they ran out of food and supplies and neighboring Native American tribes took them in. Not—not because a Croatan Indian and the son-in-law of the governor of Virginia created a curse."

"I'm coming over."

I sighed. "Claire, you don't have to do that."

"Are you kidding me? While *you* spent your entire life insisting the curse wasn't real, *I* spent my life hoping it was. I'll be there in ten minutes."

By the time Claire showed up, I'd changed into pajamas. She pelted me with questions before I had the door shut.

"So what's he like?"

"Who?"

She flopped on my sofa and crossed her legs. "Who do you think? The other Keeper."

I sat across from her and leaned back, putting my feet in her lap. "He's young."

"And?"

"And nothing. And he's not a Keeper. He's just a crazy person."

"Ellie, you have to admit that this might be real."

"You do realize that you are an unreliable sounding board? You lead a ghost tour every night and believe half the stories you tell." I sat up, crossing my legs. "Weren't you leading your tour when I called?"

She shrugged. "Yeah, but Drew took over."

Closing my eyes, I groaned. "Oh, Claire. I'm sorry."

"I'm not. This is big." She leaned forward. "We need to list everything you know about the curse. Maybe the two of us can piece it together." Hopping off the sofa, she rummaged through a drawer in my kitchen. She pulled out a notebook and pen, waved them in the air in triumph, then sat down.

I shook my head. "Why are we doing this? There is no curse."

"Fine. You're right." A smug grin pinched her mouth. "But if you don't believe in the curse, then you won't mind if I take what we know about it and use the information in my ghost tour. I'll tell them all about the pact between Manteo, the man our town is named after, and Ananias Dare, the father of Virginia Dare, the first English child born on American soil. Crap. The tourists eat this shit up."

Panicked, I grabbed her arm. "No! You can't do that! You know the curse is a secret! *You're* not even supposed to know. Terrible things happen when the Keepers share the secret." I didn't believe that was true, not fully, but it was a lot like the game of Bloody Mary. I didn't believe in that either, but you sure wouldn't catch me in front of my bathroom mirror reciting her name three times.

Claire's eyebrows shot up, and she jabbed a finger into my chest. "Aha! You *do* think there might be something to it; otherwise why would you care if anyone knew?"

She still hadn't made the connection, the terrible thing that had happened after I told her about the curse. Maybe it was too much for her to accept. Too devastating.

But her enthusiasm was contagious, although the enthusiasm mutated in me to a growing anxiety. I had to admit that I was starting to believe this might be real. "Claire, this is crazy."

Claire began her litany of facts, writing as she spoke. "The curse was laid over four hundred years ago by Manteo, the son of the werowance, the chief of the Croatan tribe, and Ananias Dare, son-in-law of the governor of the colony. They created a curse to bind the spirits of the hostile neighboring tribe." Claire stopped to take a breath.

"And it went horribly wrong," I added, with a groan. I couldn't believe I was doing this. "They bound Manteo's spirits instead. Along with the colony. The colonists and spirits were sent to the spirit world, but Manteo knew that the spirits were strong and would eventually break free. The colonists would likely return at the same time, but not alive. No human can go into the spirit realm and return to tell about it."

Lightning flashed in the window and a clap of thunder shook the windows. I jumped at the timing. I'd forgotten a storm was rolling in.

Claire grabbed a pillow and hugged it to her chest. "Go on."

"This is stupid. *That man* is crazy." Sexy as hell, but crazy as a loon. Even though I'd recently established I was no expert on men, I was pretty sure this was a bad combination.

"Then try to remember what you can and confront him with it to prove him wrong."

"You can't reason with a crazy person, Claire."

"What if he's right?"

"This isn't an episode of *The Twilight Zone*. He's crazy. "

"Will you please just *humor me*?" She leaned over her crossed legs, her gaze begging me to cooperate. "I've waited for this day since you told me about the curse in the third grade."

"And if Daddy ever knew I told you, he'd skin me alive." I tried to ignore the memory of what had happened to my mother only days after I told Claire. *What happened to Momma was a coincidence.*

Claire frowned. "He told Myra."

"Supposedly spouses are allowed."

"I'd marry you, but I'm already engaged to Drew. Besides, you hardly told me *anything*."

Maybe not, but it had been enough.

My hands shook. This was ridiculous. I'd spent several years thinking it was my fault that Momma died until I matured enough to realize the two events were unrelated. How could my mind jump back there so easily?

My mouth twisted into a grimace and I sighed. "If we're going to do this, let's get serious." I leaned back with my elbows propped on the sofa arm behind me. "The legend says that the curse would be broken someday, when the two Keepers met. I find it hard to believe that in over four hundred years, their paths never crossed."

"I have to admit that *is* strange. Your daddy says your family always lived close to or on Roanoke Island. But we both know that the Croatan's land was farther south, on Cape Hatteras. Maybe they stayed down in that area."

"Maybe." I dug through my memories, sifting out what might be useful. It was hard to believe that there was hardly anything left of all the stories Daddy told me. When I searched for anything more than the basic facts, I hit a giant brick wall.

"How do you close the gate?"

"Honestly, other than knowing there's some kind of ceremony, I have no idea." I couldn't remember anything about what the ceremony entailed. Or anything about the spirits, or how to protect myself. If, God forbid, this thing was real, something deep inside me told me I'd need to protect myself.

Claire shook her head. "Then you're in a world of shit. Aren't the spirits supposed to come back angry and vengeful?"

"Well, wouldn't you be if you had been locked up for over four hundred years?"

"Good point." We were silent for a minute before Claire flopped forward and grabbed my hand. "Seriously, this is all you can remember?"

"Do you not remember how all this curse business just vanished after Momma died? It was there, in my head, and then it wasn't." And whenever Daddy tried to teach me all over again, I'd shut him down. As a little girl who believed her mother died because of the curse—and because of me—I wanted nothing to do with it. I was grateful all of that nonsense died with my mother. Until now.

"Will you at least consider that this might be real?"

The evidence was beginning to stack up, but just because I'd found someone else who believed in the curse didn't make it real. Kids all over the world believed in Santa Claus and the Tooth Fairy and it didn't make *them* real. "Two things could convince me the curse is real. The first is if the Lost Colony shows up out of nowhere. The colony is supposed to return when the gate to the spirit world is cracked open. No colony, no open gate."

"And the second?"

"If I come face-to-face with a spirit."

∴ CHAPTER FIVE ∾

Claire stayed late and watched a movie with me to help me get my mind off everything. By the time she left, I was exhausted, but the storm and my worry kept me awake for hours. When it was time to get up to go help Myra at the Dare Inn, I would have given anything to hit the snooze button and sleep in until noon.

The humidity made my hair a thick mess of waves, so I pulled it back into a ponytail and opened the front door, only to release a startled scream. Clamping a hand over my mouth, I swallowed the bile rising in my throat. Seven dead birds littered my front porch.

The birds were laid out in a weird pattern. Six of them had their feet all turned toward the center of a radiating spoked circle, their heads pointing out. Five were blackbirds and one was a robin. A cardinal lay in the center of the circle. Was this some sick joke? How did they get there?

The first person who came to mind was Collin. This had to be his way of tricking or scaring me into helping him do God knew what. I may have been close to believing in the curse in the dark of night with Claire, Manteo's resident ghost chaser, but in the bright sunlight, I saw how ridiculous it was. I'd lost my breath because I'd freaked out. People had panic attacks. I was under enough stress lately that it would explain a panic attack even though I'd never had one before. As for the mark on my hand, Collin must put have put some kind of stamp on it when he grabbed me in the diner. He'd used permanent ink too, because no amount of scrubbing could get the mark off.

One thing was certain: whoever put the birds on my porch was sick and twisted. One more reason to be leery of Collin Dailey.

I had to figure out what to do with the dead birds. I couldn't just leave them there. I had half a mind to call the police, but how would I explain my suspicions about Collin without telling them about the curse? I couldn't. After my mother's death, I swore I'd never tell another living soul about it again. That wretched curse was dying with me. I was going to have to deal with this on my own.

I went back inside and got a broom and a paper bag. Carefully, I swept the birds into the sack, gagging the entire time. When I finished, I locked up my apartment, making sure the deadbolt was set, then dumped the paper bag into the Dumpster before walking to the bed and breakfast.

When I reached the street corner across the street, I took in the sight of my family's inn. It wasn't fancy like the Doe Inn down the street, but it had its own quaint charm. The bed and breakfast was made up of two buildings: the main house, which had multiple rooms on the first and second floors, and the residential house, which held a few other guest rooms in the back as well as the laundry. The exterior clapboard was painted a crisp white with black shutters. Both buildings sported new roofs that had been installed about a month ago.

I'd grown up in the residential house with Momma and Daddy, and then with Myra when Daddy eventually remarried. The Dare Inn had been part of the Lancaster family since the eighteen hundreds, but whenever I saw the place, it filled me with dread. I couldn't wait to move out after I graduated from high school. Nevertheless, I felt an obligation to help maintain it, even if that meant working for free and chipping in for repairs.

Dwight accused me of living off Daddy and Myra. He had no idea that I'd paid for that roof, as well as part of Daddy's respite care so Myra could work part time at the Fort Raleigh National Historic Site visitor center. If business at the Dare Inn didn't start to bring in more money, Myra would be forced to sell it and Daddy would lose the only home he'd ever known. With his Alzheimer's confusion, that might prove detrimental to his condition.

Myra stood on the back porch, cradling a cup of coffee. Her shoulder sagged into a post while she watched me walk up. "How did your date go last night?"

I was worried about her. She looked exhausted most days, and I was sure it was taxing to take care of the inn, and Daddy, as well as her job at the visitor center.

I moved past her with a fake growl. "Don't ask."

She pushed away and followed me in the back door. "That bad, huh?"

"Well, at least we got a partially paid roof out of it." I instantly regretted my statement as soon as it left my mouth. I'd met Dwight fighting the insurance company to reimburse us for part of the repairs after the hurricane.

Myra's face tightened with guilt. "Ellie, I'll pay you back every cent."

I gave her a smile. "Oh, Myra. You know I don't mind. I'm just investing in my future." We both knew that was a lie. Neither one of us expected me to inherit the inn. The bed and breakfast was on life support, and we were just trying to keep it going as long as possible. Which is why I worked there twice a day, every day, with no pay. I could get a job at the Tranquil House Inn if I wanted—and some days I really wanted to. I was tired of constantly being short on money.

Myra rested her hand on my arm. "You can always move back home, Ellie. You know you're always welcome here."

"Thanks, Myra. I know." At times I was really tempted, despite my uneasiness with the place. I felt guilty not being here and helping more, but I loved my little apartment. It may cost a fortune, but it looked out into the sound. Besides, I liked my independence too. I wasn't ready to give that up yet. But losing it all, the inn included, loomed in my future, closer than I liked.

I spent the next couple of hours changing bed linens, setting out clean towels, and starting the laundry. There were several commercial machines in the main house. We had a good routine worked out: I'd put everything into the washing machines and Myra or her friend Becky, who filled in while Myra worked, would transfer the loads to the dryers. By the time I showed up again, late afternoon if I had a lunch shift, they'd be ready for me. If I had a dinner shift, I'd hang around at the inn until the laundry was all done. It was a routine, a monotonous one, but to me, the definition of routine was boring.

When I arrived for my shift at the restaurant, Lila was filling salt and pepper shakers. She shot me a glare. "Thanks for getting me in trouble yesterday."

I didn't need any of her nonsense today. I'd already had enough nonsense in the last twenty-four hours to last me a lifetime. "I didn't get you in trouble. Marlena knew my shift was over and made me leave."

My answer didn't appease her. She was still grouchy when the doors opened and the early lunch crowd converged.

The dining room was packed by 11:30, and the sidewalk outside was crowded with tourists waiting for a table. I was carrying a tray of food from the kitchen when Bob, the manager of the Kitty Hawk Kites store across the street, burst in the door.

"They found it! Flip on the news! They found it!"

Everyone turned toward him and stared. Bob stood in the doorway, red faced and wild eyed, his thinning hair messy and out of place. I'm sure the tourists were worried this crazed man was about to attack. In fact, if I hadn't known Bob was usually a sedate, middle-aged man, I would have thought the same thing. That was what worried me.

Fear slithered up my spine, snaking out through every nerve in my body. "Found what?" someone shouted.

But I knew.

I knew.

"The Roanoke colony!"

My tray fell to the ground, plates breaking, food splattering everywhere. The customers around me shrieked and jumped out of the way, and I knew that I should clean it up, but I was too lightheaded and shaky. One thought ran through my head like a bulldozer, shoving every other conscious thought out of its path.

It's real. The curse is real.

"Ellie?" Lila's face came into view. "You don't look so good. Do you want to sit down?"

I nodded in my haze. Someone set a chair behind me and pushed me down.

"It's on the news! Someone turn on the TV!"

The television on the wall in the corner flipped on and someone changed the channel until a local station came on. A news reporter stood in front of a taped-off area. Trees filled the background, as well as a crowd. "... it's too early to know if this is actually *the* legendary site, but researchers are hopeful. What *is* known is that the village they have discovered is completely intact."

A male voiceover asked, "Mary, how is this possible? We've been told that archaeologists have already searched the spot where the village appeared. How could they miss it?"

The woman's hand held her earpiece to her, and she turned to look at the taped-off area behind her. "Witnesses tell me that late yesterday afternoon when the park closed, there was nothing but a field here. But when grounds-keepers came through this section around mid-morning, picking up fallen tree branches from the storm, they found the village. The current thought is perhaps the storm somehow uncovered the colony. If this turns out to be the actual Lost Colony, the experts are calling it the find of the century."

"Am I seeing structures behind you? They look like thatch huts."

"Phil, when I said intact, that's exactly what I meant. Fully erected houses, tools, even food—in edible condition according to one source. It's as though we've stepped back into 1587."

"How can we be sure this isn't an elaborate hoax?

The news reporter grimaced. "While that is a possibility, we've been told that multiple skeletal remains have been discovered, fully dressed in period clothing. Early reports suggest at least one hundred bodies have been discovered, including several children and a baby. If this is a hoax, it's a morbid one indeed."

"And they think this entire site was exposed by last night's storm? That seems pretty incredible."

"Part of the ground has been washed away, about two feet, and the village is now exposed. The storm is the only logical explanation anyone can come up with, though even then you must ignore the fact the huts would have stood taller than the ground before the dirt was washed away."

The cell phone in my pocket buzzed. The excited voices of the restaurant patrons filled my ears. I could only sit and stare at the TV.

"Somebody get Ellie a wet towel!" Lila shouted. "She looks like she's about to pass out."

It's real. Oh my god. It's real.

The bell on the door jingled, and Claire stopped in the doorway, searching the room. When she spotted me, she hurried over. "I just heard."

I looked up at her wide eyed and dismayed. "It's real."

She nodded, excitement radiating off of her.

My cell phone buzzed again, tickling my leg.

Lila pressed a wet paper towel to my forehead. "Why is this freaking you out so much? Business is going to *explode*."

I shook my head. "I don't know." My reaction was embarrassing any way you sliced it. I was a grown woman. I needed to get ahold of myself.

Marlena walked in from the back room and scanned the dining room. Customers were standing, the food I dropped was all over the floor. "What in God's name is going on here?"

People all began to talk at once. "Lost Colony . . . Roanoke . . . over one hundred bodies . . ."

Marlena's eyes landed on me. While she was always known for being in control, I was a close second. Finding me pale and sitting on a chair, covered in food, had to be an even bigger shock than the reappearing village.

"What happened to you?"

"I'm fine. It was just a surprise."

My cell phone buzzed again.

I stood and took a deep breath. So, I now had five days to close a gate to the spirit world.

But first I had a mess to clean up. "Lila, I'm going to clean this up. Why don't you try to get everyone back in their seats? Marlena, can you tell Fred that he needs to remake all the meals from table nine?"

"Ellie." Claire leaned her face into mine and whispered fiercely, "What are you doing?"

"I'm getting back to work."

"You have a curse to fix."

I grabbed Claire's arm and dragged her to the back room. "How am I supposed to do that, Claire? I don't have the slightest idea what happened, or how to fix it. What do you want me to do?"

Her gaze fixed over my shoulder, her eyes widening. She looked like she'd just spotted the Better than Sex chocolate cake Myra made for the customers at the inn. Her mouth dropped open and she lifted her hand and pointed. "There's your answer, right there."

I whipped my head around, and my stomach spasmed before falling to my feet.

Collin Dailey stood in the back entrance of the restaurant. The door was partially open, the sunlight casting a glow around him. He looked like an angel with his impossibly good looks and an aura of golden light. I felt my resolve weaken until he opened his mouth. Condescension dripped off his words. "Do you believe it now?"

My heart snapped closed like a Venus flytrap. Collin Dailey was an egotistical prick. But prick or no, unfortunately for me, I needed him.

He took my silence as agreement. "We need to go."

I looked into the dining room, then back at him. "Now? I'm not done with my shift yet."

His jaw dropped in disbelief. "You're seriously telling me that saving humanity from vengeful sprits can wait until you finish *your waitressing shift*?"

"Well . . ." When he put it that way, it seemed ridiculous. But I needed the money to pay my rent. I was going to be counting pennies as it was. Not to mention I couldn't leave Marlena with the chaos out front.

He took two steps toward me and grabbed my arm. "Are you really this self-centered?"

I jerked my arm out of his grasp, my anger making my head buzz. "Who the hell do you think you are?"

His voice lowered. "I am a Curse Keeper, a descendant of Manteo and worthy to carry the title, while you, on the other hand, are a spoiled, self-centered fool who thinks this is all a joke."

My eyes narrowed, and it was all I could do to keep myself from shoving him out the back door. "You don't know the first thing about me."

"You are shirking your responsibilities, and that's all I need to know."

I had to admit that it was hard to argue with that, but his attitude was infuriating. "Like it or not, you and I are stuck together until we figure out what we need to do." I took a deep breath. "Now tell me what we need to do."

All expression left his face. "You really don't know?"

"No."

"*Any of it?*"

"She knows a little," Claire said, still eyeing Collin with a hungry look. "She's not completely clueless."

I'd almost forgotten she was there.

He cocked an eyebrow, turning his attention to her. "And you are . . . ?"

"Claire."

He turned back to me. "You *told* someone?"

"How do you know she's not my sister?" From what I remembered, it wasn't against the rules to tell siblings about the curse, since it was a familial duty. The only problem was that Claire and I didn't look anything like sisters. But then Myra and I didn't look anything alike, and technically, she was my family.

He started to speak, then stopped, rubbing his forehead. "Okay, is she your sister?"

I could have lied, but I figured we were already on shaky ground. "No."

"Then why—"

"She's the only one who knows. She's *practically* my sister, so what's the difference? You say you want to fix this thing, but it looks like you want to spend all your time belittling me."

"It doesn't take much effort, trust me."

I gasped. "Get out."

His eyes widened. "What?"

I shoved his chest and he stumbled toward the back door. "I said get the hell out!"

"You can't do that!"

"Oh yeah? Watch me!"

I pushed the bar on the back door and the door flung open. Collin stumbled backward and through the opening. I slammed the door shut and made sure it was locked.

"What did you just do?" Claire asked in disbelief. "You need him."

My fury still burned in my chest. *Quick to anger, slow to cool,* Daddy always used to say about me. "No man's going to talk to me like that and get away with it, Keeper or not."

"So you're going to just leave the gate open and let the rest of the spirits spill out?"

"No, of course not." I shook my head. "Collin Dailey has been bred for this. He practically admitted as much last night. He'll come crawling back, trust me on that. He needs me just as much as I need him. The ceremony requires the presence of both Keepers. He can't do it without me. But if he wants my help, he's going to have to eat a little humble pie, because I won't tolerate him treating me like that again."

Still, I remembered Daddy's insistence that all hell would break loose, literally, when the gate opened, and that devastating consequences would occur if the gate wasn't closed. Not that I could remember a single one of the consequences specifically. But the fear and unease that oozed from Daddy stuck with me, even if the details didn't. Something terrifying was out there, and I let my temper send away the one person who could help me make it all go away.

Claire sucked in a deep breath and released it. "I sure hope you're right, Ellie."

I stared at the back door. I hoped I was right too.

⌁ Chapter Six ⌁

It was late afternoon before Collin returned and I'd begun to think that I might have pushed him too far. I was just about ready to start scrambling for a backup plan, not that I could come up with one. I was by the kitchen returning a tray when I heard the tinkle of the bell, and I knew he was there.

Marlena walked up next to me, eyeing Collin as he scanned the room. "Well, look who just showed up. Tall, dark, and handsome."

I had to admit that he did look sexy when he wasn't wearing a scowl, and he was strangely without one now. While I'd hoped he'd return, I didn't expect him to be so . . . happy about it. "He's probably here for me."

Her eyebrows rose in surprise.

What possessed me to admit that to her? Marlena was going to be majorly disappointed when she realized that Collin wasn't here for the reason she thought. Not that she'd ever know the real reason.

She ambled over to him, heading Lila off at the pass, not that Collin didn't give Lila an appreciative glance. But then who could blame him? While I had more of a girl-next-door look, Lila had long, thick dark hair, gorgeous dark eyes and skin, and a chest that drew attention from most bodies to walk in carrying a Y chromosome in their DNA strands.

"You want your table from yesterday?" Marlena asked, looking like a kid on Christmas. Marlena had been married for ten years and had three kids. She'd told me once that she had to get her romantic thrills living vicariously through me. Marlena wasn't about to let this guy get away.

"Actually, I was looking for Ellie. Is she still working?"

Marlena turned in my direction, her eyebrows rising. Her mouth stretched into a conspiratorial grin. I couldn't help but laugh.

"As a matter of fact she is, but she's got another twenty minutes before her shift ends. How about I seat you at a table in her section? I'll send her over to take your order."

She led him to a table for two by the windows overlooking the street filled with tourists. With the discovery of the colony, Manteo was about to be overrun with curiosity seekers. When I thought about all those people hanging around with scary spirits breaking free, a chill ran up my spine.

My phone buzzed in my pocket, and I pulled it out to check who was calling. Myra. She'd tried to call me while I watched the news reports that morning, and she hadn't answered when I'd called her back. I stepped into the back room, watching Collin from around the corner.

"I've only got a second," she said. "Did you hear the news?"

"Yeah, the town's going crazy about it."

I heard someone call Myra's name in the background. "How are you doing with all of this?" she asked. "Are you okay?"

I watched Colin leaning his forearms on the table, scanning the room. Part of me wanted to tell her about Collin and what had happened the day before, but she'd worry about me. Myra had enough to worry about. "Of course, I'm okay. Why wouldn't I be okay?"

"Well . . . the curse . . ." The person calling her name was more insistent. "I have to go, Ellie." I heard the hesitation in her voice.

"I'm fine. Go do what you need to do. If we're busy in town, I can only imagine how crazy it is there. We can talk later."

"If you need anything, you call me, okay?"

"Thanks, Myra."

I wondered if Daddy had heard the news or if he was coherent enough to understand. I wished I'd taken more advantage of his lucid day. I'd completely blown it.

After returning my cell phone to my pocket, I held out my right palm and gasped. While the pink of the burn mark was fading, the harsh lines of a square surrounding a circle seemed to be darkening. I didn't remember anything about what the mark was or what it meant from the stories. Why hadn't

I asked Daddy yesterday? Why had I been so stubborn in my disbelief? When I thought about how real this all was, my stomach flip-flopped from nerves. How was Ellie Lancaster, waitress and maid from Manteo, North Carolina, going to save the world?

Unfortunately, the answer was sitting at a table in the New Moon, staring right at me.

A slow smile spread across his face, and my stomach performed more acrobatics that had nothing to do with the curse, and everything to do with the hormones rushing through my body. I needed to get a grip and stop acting like a teenage girl with a crush. I needed to save the world, not find a boyfriend.

Although a boyfriend would be a nice side benefit.

As I walked toward him, I reminded myself that Collin was not boyfriend material. It didn't take a genius to see that Collin Dailey was a "love 'em and leave 'em" kind of guy. He was a guy used to getting his way with the charm he exuded now. It was easier to catch a fly with honey, and I was currently Collin's fly.

I stopped next to his table, trying to keep my face expressionless. If he was going to use his sexier-than-hell charm on me, I might as well make him sweat a bit. I put my hand on my hip and jutted it out while piercing him with my most withering gaze. Lesser men had tucked their tails and run, but Collin simply stared back, the corners of his mouth lifted in the barest hint of a smile. Damn him. "Can I get you something?"

His eyes narrowed seductively, and his voice lowered. "You know what I want."

Holy shit. If I'd thought he meant what he insinuated, I might have had a mini orgasm on the spot. But last night Collin had made sure I understood what he was interested in, and it had nothing to do with the parts of me under my clothes that begged for attention.

How in the hell was I going to survive five days with this guy? My only hope was to shut the spirit world gate as quickly as possible.

Despite my discomfort, I held my ground, my gaze unwavering. "Since I didn't take your order yesterday, I don't remember what you wanted. Perhaps you could refresh my memory."

He turned away with a grin and looked out the window. "You're not going to make this easy are you?"

I didn't answer.

When he turned back, his cocky grin was gone. In its place was a look of contrition. "It's obvious we've started out on the wrong foot." He waited for me to jump in and say something, but I continued my death gaze. "*And I admit that I'm mostly to blame.*"

"*Mostly?*" My tone was dry and sarcastic, but I'd answered, and my reply eased the tension in his shoulders.

He started to say something, then stopped. "Why don't we forget our awful first impressions and start over." He held out his right hand. "Collin Daily."

Was this some trick or did he really want to try to start fresh? Did it matter? We weren't going to prom. We were going to try to wrangle a gate to the spirit world closed. I looked down at his outstretched hand. He held it at an angle but I could see the outline of a mark on his palm. A reminder that the last time we'd touched had nearly suffocated me. What would happen this time? I crossed my arms. "Ellie Lancaster."

He looked taken aback that I hadn't accepted his hand. "You felt it too, when our hands touched yesterday? And the electrical current last night."

I was surprised he admitted to a reaction. Bad boys like him didn't like to share their feelings.

He smirked. "You don't know what that was, do you?"

I didn't answer. He knew I didn't, and the smug look on his face told me how aware of that fact he was.

He leaned closer and his voice lowered. "That's our power. The magic that runs through our blood."

"It's real," I whispered in awe, despite my plan to remain aloof. I didn't know about the electrical shock part, but Daddy had always talked about the power in our blood. This must have been what he meant.

"It's very real." Collin glanced around the half-full dining room. "I don't think we should talk about this here."

I nodded. "Give me a second."

I left him at the table and found Marlena watching with a grin. "Hey, Marlena. Do you mind if I take off a bit early?" I tilted my head toward Collin.

Excitement filled her eyes. "What happened to Dweeb?"

I shook my head with a grimace. "History."

She waved to the back. "Good. You need a real man like that fine specimen over there. Don't blow it."

I shot her an exasperated look. Why did she assume that I would blow it? But it didn't matter. It wasn't like this was the beginning of any kind of relationship. Collin and I would close the gate and then we were done.

Grabbing my purse from my drawer, I headed back to the dining room and found Collin waiting for me by the door. Lila stood next to him.

"How is it that I haven't seen you around?" she asked, playing with the ends of her ponytail. "You a tourist?"

Collin blessed her with his sexy smart-ass grin. "Nope."

"So where're you from?"

Collin opened the door. "I'm living in Wanchese."

"*Wanchese*? Are you a fisherman?"

I grabbed Collins arm and pulled him outside. "Bye, Lila."

When the door closed behind us, I dropped my hold. "I need to change before we do anything." I was still wearing the food I'd dropped hours ago.

"Good. We need to get your relic anyway."

Oh, shit. My chest tightened with anxiety. And here we'd been getting along. "My relic? Sure."

Collin followed me around the corner of the building into the alley behind the restaurant, then up the steps to my third-floor apartment. I usually didn't mind the stairs, and now I was downright thankful for them. They bought me more time before I was forced to tell Collin the truth about the Ananias Dare artifact.

When we reached my front door, I paused and narrowed my eyes. I'd almost forgotten.

Confusion spread across his face. "What?"

"I don't appreciate the calling card you left on my doorstep."

His eyes clouded in confusion, then alarm. "Did something happen last night?"

I shook my head. So maybe it wasn't Collin. "Someone left dead birds on my porch. I'm sure I pissed Dwight off, but he doesn't seem the vindictive type. At least not with dead animals."

Collin walked to the railing and looked over the edge. "How many birds were there?"

"Six birds in a circle with their feet pointed in. One robin and five black-birds. A cardinal in the center."

"Ellie . . ." He stopped, an incredulous expression covering his face. "The gate to the spirit world was just opened, and you think your nerdy ex-boy-friend put dead birds in a pattern on your porch?"

No, I didn't. But my mind wasn't willing to make that leap yet. I needed to take this slow. Unfortunately, I didn't think the spirits spilling out into the world gave a rat's ass how slow I needed to go. I pushed the door open but hesitated in the entrance. "I don't usually let strange men into my apartment."

"You let in the guy who ran out of your apartment last night. I wouldn't exactly call him normal."

Collin had a point. Still, he made me nervous. Right now all of the curse nonsense was contained to the outside world. Once I let Collin in, the curse would permeate every part of my life, including my personal space.

Collin noticed my hesitation. "If you'd rather I wait outside, fine. But I'm not sure what you're worried about. I have no interest at all in—"

I walked through the threshold and headed for my room. "I got it. No interest. No need to repeat yourself. Come in." I looked over my shoulder. "And for the record, I'm not interested in you either."

Collin followed me in and shut the door. As I shuffled through the pile of clothes on the chair in my room I tried to figure out how to tell him about my relic. There was no point to hiding the truth. He was going to be pissed, but it wasn't like he liked me anyway. We had a job to do, and we needed the artifact to do it.

When I walked out, pulling the hem of my T-shirt over the top of my skirt, I found Collin sitting at the kitchen counter, his expressionless gaze on me.

"About the relic . . ."

His eyes narrowed at my hesitant tone.

"I don't exactly have it."

His jaw tensed, but his tone was conversational. "And who exactly does?"

I took a deep breath. "A pawnshop."

I expected him to yell. I expected him to have a fit. I didn't expect him to stare at me as though I'd told him it was about to rain. Finally, he sat up a bit straighter. "And why is your artifact at the pawnshop?"

I walked around him into the kitchen and opened the refrigerator. Anything to keep from having to look at him. *How much should I admit?* The less the better. "I didn't have enough money to pay my rent a few months ago. So I pawned it."

When he didn't answer, I went against my instinct and turned to look at him. I didn't know him well enough to read his face. Was he angry but holding it in? Was his mind scrambling to figure out what to do?

"You pawned your artifact?"

I didn't see any point answering. I'd just told him that I had.

"How could you be so irresponsible? Do you really not take this seriously?"

I threw my hands into the air in exasperation. "No! Until this morning, no I didn't take it seriously. Who would?"

He stood, his hands clenched at his side. "*I* took it seriously. This was a sacred duty, Ellie. Passed down from generation to generation. It's our obligation. *Our right.* How can you treat it so casually? So *irreverently*? Do you realize what's at stake?"

My mouth opened, but I was at a loss for words. Every excuse I had had sounded so rational yesterday.

Collin shook his head, then stormed out the door, slamming it behind him while I watched, my mouth still gaping.

I sat on the stool Collin had just vacated and covered my face with my hands. Of course he was angry. Collin had bought the curse story hook, line, and sinker and had spent his life preparing to perform his duty. And then there was Ellie Lancaster, who not only refused to believe the curse but who pawned the very thing necessary to send the spirits back. He had every right to be angry and frustrated with me, so why was I so upset?

Because Collin only reinforced that I'd let my father down. The only thing my father had ever asked of me, the thing he'd tried so hard to prepare me for, and I'd thrown it all away. In my defense, any sane person would have questioned the story. Keepers had been waiting over four hundred years for this moment. Why would I think the curse would actually break while I was on duty, even if I believed it?

So why don't you feel any better?

Fifteen minutes later Collin stood at my front door, calmer but more distant than before he left. "If you pawned it a few months ago, they should still have it."

I nodded. I hoped so.

He looked into my eyes. "What's your relic? What are we looking for?"

My breath caught in surprise. "You don't know?"

"While I obviously know more than you, I don't know everything. So no, I don't know what your artifact is. But I do know we need it if we want to perform this ceremony. What is it?"

"A pewter cup." I couldn't believe Collin Dailey was admitting he didn't know everything. That meant I could admit I didn't know what his artifact was without looking like an idiot. "So what's yours?"

"That sounds like a bad pickup line."

I snorted. "If anyone would know about bad pickup lines, you would."

His eyebrows rose, and he gave me a sardonic smile. "You think I need pickup lines?"

Cocky Collin was back. I wasn't sure whether I preferred him to angry Collin or not. Damn my mouth. I knew for a fact this man didn't need pickup lines, but I sure wasn't going to admit that to him. "You didn't answer my question. What's your artifact?"

"A wooden bowl."

That made sense. I did know the relics were part of the ceremony. I only knew that because when Daddy had realized he was losing his memories several years ago, he handed me the cup and told me it was the Dare relic and was essential to the ceremony. I took it grudgingly, but refused to listen to any more nonsense. "So what do you want to do?"

"It's a little after four o'clock. Let's go to the pawnshop and see if it's still there."

"Together?"

"Of course together. I could send you alone but honestly, I think we need to stick together as much as possible until this thing is done."

"What? You don't trust me to get it?"

"I don't trust you to not get killed. Spirits are on the loose, and they don't want to return to where they came from. They know we plan to send them back and they'll do anything they can to keep that from happening."

My breath caught in my chest. "And the only thing that can send them back is us," I wheezed out. I hadn't considered that aspect. How would the spirits even know who we were? How did one defend oneself against an angry spirit? I wasn't about to ask the angry human in front of me.

He looked grim. "While I think you're an irresponsible slacker, unfortunately, I need you. So get whatever you need and let's go."

Was he suggesting we'd be gone for the next six days or only for the evening? "To the pawnshop?"

A disgusted look crossed his face. "No, the moon. Of course the pawnshop. Are you always this dense?"

"Are you always this rude?"

He shrugged.

I could have countered but what was the point? I left Collin at the door and grabbed my purse. I wished I had time to talk to Daddy. But that would only help if he was having a good day, and those were becoming rarer and rarer. Wishing was wasted effort, something I'd learned years ago, on a cold stormy night when I was eight years old. Instead of wishing, I was putting my life in the hands of the stranger in front of me.

Why did I worry that I'd live to regret it?

⌁ Chapter Seven ⌁

I climbed into Collin's beat-up pickup truck, wrinkling my nose as I shut the rickety door. The windows were down and the red vinyl seats were hot and tacky. I was putting my life into his hands with all the curse nonsense, and apparently that also meant I'd literally be putting my life in his hands with this rust bucket. "We can take my car. *Really.*"

The engine sputtered, and he turned to me and smirked. "Oh, ye of little faith."

Why did I think his words had a double meaning?

The truck jerked backward as I tried to fasten my seatbelt. "Can you wait?"

"No. We don't have time to waste." He pulled onto Sir Walter Raleigh Street and I cast a glance at the inn as we passed by. Myra's car wasn't parked next to the house, not that I expected her to be there. I hoped Daddy's home care nurse could stay longer. If I wasn't working at the New Moon, I usually filled in for Myra when she couldn't get home in time.

I turned my attention to the road. I didn't want to explain Daddy's situation to Collin. A wave of melancholy washed over me as I tried to remember Daddy as the vibrant man I knew from before my mother's death, but it was so long ago that the memory had become fuzzy. I definitely did my best to block out the year after her death. Mostly what I remembered of Daddy pre-Alzheimer's was after Myra came into our lives, filling our days with hope and love. I preferred not to think of Daddy as the broken shell he was now, and I didn't like others thinking about him that way either. The man with the vacant stare wasn't my Daddy.

"Well?" Collin asked.

I shook myself out of my stupor. "What?"

"So where are we going?" Collin asked.

"Kill Devil Hills."

His eyebrows rose as he turned to look at me. "Kill Devil Hills?"

I shrugged, staring out the windshield. "I didn't want anyone in town to know that I pawned it."

His mouth pursed, and his brow wrinkled in disapproval. I shouldn't care one way or the other what he thought, but to my annoyance, I did. Still, Collin Dailey didn't get to stand in judgment of me. He didn't know what I'd been through.

"So if my relic is a pewter cup and yours is a wooden bowl, what does that mean?"

Collin shifted in his seat and he gripped the steering wheel. "We use them in the ceremony."

I'd already gathered that part. "I don't know anything about the ceremony—"

"That's a surprise."

"So we get the relics, we perform the ceremony, and we shut the gate."

"Something like that."

"Care to elaborate?"

He shot me a nasty grin. "Not really."

I was going to see Daddy the minute I got back. I'd learn to perform the damn ceremony without Collin Fucking Dailey. Well, maybe I couldn't perform it without him, but if I knew more about the curse I wouldn't be so dependent on him for answers. I got the sense that he'd only dole out information on a need-to-know basis. "So, if we can't get my relic back, can we use something else?"

"We could try, but I doubt it would work."

My stomach twisted. "I really hope the cup is still there."

"Wait. How long was the contract for? Ninety days, right? So then you have an additional sixty to pay it off."

I glanced at my lap and twisted the hem of my T-shirt.

"Ellie?" Collin sounded desperate. "Tell me the contract was for ninety days."

I suddenly found the dirty gas station at the corner fascinating. "I could, but that would be a lie."

"How long was the contract for?" His voice was strained as his knuckles wrapped around the steering wheel turned white.

"Thirty days."

"And when exactly did you pawn it?"

I bit my lip. "Let's just say my time is up."

Collin pulled onto the highway and with the windows down, it became too loud to carry on a conversation without shouting, although I was pretty sure that Collin felt like yelling anyway.

Every time I left the island my chest tightened and today was no exception. The waves crashing in the sound calmed my rising anxiety, and I focused on their rhythm as Collin drove over the bridge linking Roanoke Island to the Outer Banks and then north through Nags Head and toward Kill Devil Hills.

June was high tourist season, and the traffic was brutal. We sat at a few stoplights in Nags Head, the heat near stifling in the unair-conditioned truck cab. Collin's face was expressionless. It was hard to tell if he was still irritated with me or if he was stewing in silence. Still, the silence drove me batty. I couldn't stand quiet, and the rumble of car engines around us didn't count.

I put my elbow on the edge of the open truck window and snatched it back inside when I made contact with the hot metal. Rubbing my tender skin, I turned to face him. "So where's your wooden bowl?"

He hesitated. "Somewhere safe."

"If it's *safe*, then I know it's not in this truck."

To my surprise, the corners of his mouth lifted into the barest hint of a smile.

"So where is it?"

His smile fell.

The truth dawned on me, and I sat up in excitement. "You're not telling me because you don't have it!" So much for Mr. Smugpants.

His eyebrows rose in disapproval. This look had become all too familiar in the short twenty-four hours or so I'd known him. "While it's not in my immediate possession, I do know where it is."

"And I know where mine is, yet you had a hissy fit over it."

He shook his head with a smirk. "No, you have no idea if your cup is at the pawnshop or not."

"So where's your magical bowl?"

He paused. "Safe."

"You said that already. Safe where?"

"The North Carolina Outer Banks Museum in Morehead City."

"A museum? What? Has your family loaned it to them?"

"Something like that. And it's safe behind glass in a display case. Who knows where yours is?"

His explanation sounded perfectly logical, but he wouldn't look at me. He was hiding something. He said, "Your pawnshop is in Kill Devil Hills?"

Way to change the topic, Collin. I'd let it go for now and pull this out later when I needed leverage. "It's not *my* pawnshop, and I already told you that the cup was there. The place is just off the highway. On the western side."

We drove the rest of the way in silence, and I was glad that we made it with an hour to spare before the shop closed at six. I took a deep breath and I opened the door to the store, praying that the cup would still be there.

"Hey, Ellie!" Oscar called from behind the counter.

Collin leaned toward me with a smirk. "Not *your* pawnshop, huh?"

I shot him a glare. "It's like *Cheers* here. Oscar knows everyone's name."

"You know *his* name?"

"Shut up." I left him at the door and approached the store owner, dread burrowing in my gut. "Hey, Oscar, how's it going?"

"Not too bad, Ellie. Business has been picking up after all that Hurricane Noreen mess."

I stopped across from the burly man who stood on the other side of the case. Oscar was probably in his late forties or early fifties and had a full head of graying brown hair that went past his shoulders. He sported a bushy beard that rivaled the frizzy mess of hair hanging down his back. Rumor had it that Oscar had been a surfer in his youth, and the deep crow's feet around his eyes helped substantiate the claim. Every time I came in he was wearing heavy metal band T-shirts and jeans, but despite his rough exterior, Oscar had a heart of gold.

"You got something new to pawn, Ellie?"

I cast a glance at Collin, who was poking around the store. Oscar kept an eye on him while talking to me.

"No, I was checking to see if you still had my cup."

Oscar's smile fell. "I held it as long as I could, Ellie."

My stomach balled into a knot. "You sold it."

He nodded.

Now what were we going to do? I didn't really have a plan to get the relic back if Oscar did still have it, but it didn't matter now. We were sunk.

Collin moved next to me in his quiet stealth. "How long ago?"

Oscar looked from Collin to me. "A friend of yours?"

"Kind of."

Oscar kept his attention on me. "I sold it last week to a collector. I'm sorry, Ellie. I held it back two weeks longer than I should have."

"That's okay, I know. Thanks." My breath stuck in my chest when I caught Collin's ugly glare.

Oscar noted it as well and tensed.

I turned my back slightly to Collin. "Any chance you can tell me who bought it?"

Oscar shook his head. "Sorry, Ellie. I can't tell you. Confidentiality laws."

I knew it couldn't be that easy, but had to ask anyway.

"Where's your restroom?" Collin asked in a gruff voice.

Crossing his arms, Oscar gave him a condescending stare. "The restrooms are for customers only."

"I'm a customer."

"Ellie's the customer here, not you. I don't see you buying anything, only giving me lip."

I shook my head with a groan. "Oscar, can you just let him go? Otherwise I'll be stuck with his bad attitude all the way back to Manteo."

Oscar tilted his head to the back. "I'm only doing this for Ellie. I don't like the way you're talking to her."

"Thank you. How kind of you," Collin muttered with a sarcastic tone before he headed toward the hall.

When he disappeared, Oscar's voice lowered. "You in some kind of trouble, Ellie?"

"What?" My eyes widened when I realized what he was asking. "Oh, no. Nothing like that. Collin's not my boyfriend or anything. We're just doing some . . . *business* together."

"You're a good girl, and I don't want to see you getting mixed up with the likes of someone controlling like him."

"Don't worry, Oscar. It's a family thing." Just not the kind of family thing he'd probably think.

"Is that why he's here looking for the cup with you?"

I nodded. "He's not happy I pawned it." Talk about an understatement.

Oscar knew that the cup was a family heirloom. He'd had possession of it five times in the last four years. He'd only given me fifty dollars the first time, but once he realized how much I wanted it back, he increased the amount he paid me each time. But every cent I'd made over the last four months had gone to essentials like food and rent. And the roof for the inn. The damn hurricane hadn't helped things. I may not have believed in the curse, but that didn't mean the cup didn't have sentimental value. Tears burned my eyes, and for the first time ever, I was thankful that Daddy probably wouldn't be mentally competent to understand that I'd lost it.

"I'm sorry, Ellie."

I offered him a teary smile. "It's okay. It's not your fault." I laughed. "It's not like I had the five hundred dollars plus interest anyway. I was just hoping you still had it."

"I wish you could catch a break, girl."

I sniffed, refusing to look where Collin had disappeared. "Me too, but what are you going to do? It's family." I tossed my hair and forced a smile. "Not to worry. I'll just find a rich husband to take all my money troubles away."

Collin emerged from the back and stared at me with a withering glare. I knew that he'd heard me. Did he really think I meant it? Who the hell cared what he thought? For all I knew, the world was about to end, and I really didn't want to be anywhere around Collin Dailey when it happened. Too bad we'd both be at ground zero. Together. Yippee.

"Marry me, Ellie Lancaster." Oscar winked. "Let me take you away from all of this."

Putting my hands on my hips, I gave him a saucy leer. "You know you don't have enough money for me, Oscar."

It was a running joke that started the first time I brought the cup in to pawn. When Oscar had only offered fifty dollars, I had protested, saying I needed more money. Oscar had teased that he couldn't give more for the cup, but he'd marry me instead. He was joking, and I knew it. He was old enough to be my father, and in some strange way had become like a father figure to me after I'd told him my financial tale of woe during my second pawn. Especially after I confessed Daddy's condition.

Collin moved toward the door, completely ignoring me. He was probably pissed we didn't know where the cup was. But that didn't give him the right to be rude.

"You sure you're all right with him, Ellie? I've seen his kind before and I don't like him. He'll use you and throw you away."

"I'm not a real fan, either. But unfortunately I'm stuck with him for a few days."

"Family or not, if he gives you any trouble, call me. I mean it."

The serious look in his eyes told me that he did. "Thanks, Oscar." I leaned over the counter and grabbed his arm, pulling him toward me so I could kiss his cheek. "You're the best." I dropped my hold and walked to the front door.

"My offer still stands, girl."

I smiled playfully. "Your marriage proposal or taking care of cranky men?"

"Both."

Laughing, I blew him a kiss. "Better be careful. One day I might accept."

Collin leaned against the hood of the truck with crossed arms, watching me with a condescending glare. Great, more judgment from the high and mighty Collin Dailey.

"Look, I know we don't know where the cup is—"

He lifted an eyebrow. "Who says we don't know where it is?"

My feet froze as my eyes narrowed. I knew that he'd heard Oscar. "The cup was sold, and we don't know who bought it."

He uncrossed his arms and pulled a small square of paper from his pocket, waving it before tucking it back inside. "Get in the truck. We're headed to Rodanthe."

I gaped in disbelief. "Is that what I think it is? How did you get it?"

He shook his head and headed to the driver's door. "Oh ye of little faith."

I really wished he'd stop saying that.

⌁ Chapter Eight ⌁

"How did you get that address?" I asked before I'd shut my door.

He gave me a lopsided grin. "Some things are better left unknown."

But I knew that Collin had to have slipped into the back and gotten the name and address while I was talking to Oscar. I felt sleazy and slimy even if I hadn't done anything wrong. If Oscar ever found out, he might think I'd been part of Collin's scheme. And while I didn't care what the jackass next to me thought of me, I *did* care what Oscar thought. Nevertheless, there was nothing I could do about it now, and we really did need to find the cup.

This was what really paved the way to hell: bad deeds reasoned away as good intentions.

No, the spirits being unleashed upon the world were what paved the road to hell, and it was up to Collin and me to make sure that didn't happen. And that included getting the cup.

"So it's in Rodanthe."

"That's who he sold it to, a Mrs. Evelyn Abernathy in Rodanthe, North Carolina."

"Since Rodanthe's on the beach, it's going to take forever to get there with the tourist traffic."

He shrugged. "At least we have a lead."

We drove for ten minutes of agonizing silence. I knew that Rodanthe had to be over an hour drive with the traffic. I was never going to be able to stand the quiet. "Does your radio work?"

His eyes widened. "What?"

71

"The radio." I pointed to the dashboard. "Does it work?"

"Well, yeah . . ."

I leaned over and switched it on, turning the knob when static burst through the speakers. I tuned in to a Top 40 station.

A frown pinched his mouth. "I don't really want to listen to that."

Still hunched forward in front of the radio, I looked up into his face with an expression of mock innocence. "Does that mean you'd rather chat? Want to tell me what you know about the curse?"

His face scrunched with a grimace. "By all means, listen to the radio."

I sat back and grinned. "Thanks, I will." Then I began to sing along with the song. I laughed at Collin's pained look. "Perhaps you'd rather listen to country?" I shouted over the wind and the music.

"I prefer the silence," he shouted back.

I shrugged with a grin, singing the rest of the way to Rodanthe, as loudly as possible and with as much enthusiasm as I could muster. Collin appeared irritated by the curious looks of passengers in the cars passing by, but I didn't care. Life was too short to go out acting all stuffy and self-important. I'd rather go out singing, even if I was slightly off-key.

When we drove through Pea Island National Wildlife Refuge, my stomach twinged with butterflies. We were close to Rodanthe, and we had a name and an address but no plan on how to go about retrieving the cup. I turned down the radio and looked at Collin. "So I take it you have some kind of plan?"

"What?" His eyes widened in mock surprise. "I think you said something, but I'm deaf from being trapped in this truck with loud music and bad singing."

"I'm not that bad."

"Tell that to those dead birds on the side of the road. They heard your singing and dove out of the sky, head first into the pavement to escape the torture."

I looked behind us at the multiple seagull bodies lining the road. I hadn't noticed them before. "Very funny. Why are they really dead?" When I thought about the dead birds on my porch, the hair on my arms prickled.

"Honestly?"

"Of course, honestly. I wouldn't have asked otherwise."

His mouth twisted in uncertainty. "The impression you give me is that you want to know as little as possible. Otherwise why would you hardly know anything about the curse?"

I started to protest but stopped. I could see how he'd come to that conclusion. And if I were honest with myself, there was a bit of truth to his statement. "You haven't made it easy for me." I held up a hand when he started to protest. "It's not a condemnation, just a statement of how I felt. I'm on the defensive with you."

He was silent for a moment before he shifted his weight. "We haven't exactly gotten off to a great start." He grinned. "Maybe we should start again."

"You said that this afternoon. Right before you tried to prove your superiority over me."

Amusement filled his eyes. "It's not difficult to demonstrate my superiority over you."

"And this is your way of starting over?"

"Okay, let's try again."

"Or we just call it hopeless and tolerate each other until this thing is done."

He smirked. "That works too."

Why did I get the impression that was his intention all along? "You still need to explain the feeling I got from touching you yesterday."

His amusement turned to a seductive look. "I don't usually have to explain my effect on women."

I rolled my eyes. "Oh, Lordy. Please. Spare me the horrific details." I shifted in the seat so I could get a better look at him, pulling my skirt down to cover my thigh. "You said it's from the power in our blood."

His grin turned wicked.

I put up a hand. "*Please.* I really don't want to hear anything pornographic, so let's stick to the *Curse Keeper* power in our blood. I take it we need this power to close the gate?"

The teasing look on his face turned to a scowl. "What the hell *do* you know? Anything?"

I opened my mouth to answer with a snappy retort but caught myself. As much as the man sitting next to me irritated the shit out of me, I needed him. He had all the answers, and I had none. Considering his position, his condescension was justifiable. I only had to endure him until we closed the gate, and then I never had to see him again. I paused. *I never have to see him again, right?* Crap. I couldn't begin to consider what my responsibilities might be after we closed the gate. Now didn't seem like a good time to ask. I was sure Collin was eager to get rid of me too.

Traffic slowed to a crawl, and Collin glanced at me before returning his attention to the road. "We need our combined power to shut the gate and/or contain the gods of creation and the four wind gods. We'll be able to contain the lesser spirits on our own. Or at least I hope."

"Oh." This was real. Spirits were emerging from their realm, roaming the earth, and I was really part of containing them. I gulped.

He sighed and shook his head. "We need to work on getting the cup back."

I took a few seconds to calm down. "So why do you think those dead birds might have something to do with all of this?"

"I don't know for sure, but the storm last night was probably caused by one of the wind gods. He's probably who unearthed the Lost Colony."

"So what does that have to do with the dead birds?"

"I suspect the wind god sucked the life out of them."

I grabbed the dashboard. "Wait. What do you mean *sucked the life out of them?*"

"Ellie, these spirits have been locked up a long time. Not much is known about them, but we do know that they were meant to straddle the earthly and spiritual worlds. They should never have been locked up in one realm or the other. Perhaps they're weak from being gone so long and need the life force of the animals to renew their energy."

"What's to keep them from sucking the life out of humans?"

"Honestly?" He paused, and I held my breath, waiting for his answer. "Nothing. Again, this is speculation. Lots of information has been passed down the Manteo line, although we've known all along it wasn't gospel. But we suspected the spirits would reenter the world in weakened states and need to reenergize."

"And they reenergize by killing things?"

"Energy is never created, Ellie. It flows from one object to another. It's a simple law of physics. For an object or entity to acquire energy, it has to come from somewhere."

This suddenly became very real, very fast. "So we have to keep the spirits from killing people?"

"We have some time. They'll start with weaker creatures, creatures they can control, and work their way up."

I swallowed, letting his words settle in my head. I was *way* out of my element here.

"My grandmother believed that's the real purpose of the week the Keepers have to renew the curse. That it would take the gods a week to recover their full potential, but once they reach their full potential, nothing could close the gate."

"So you're telling me that the sooner we send these things back, the less havoc they'll cause?"

He shrugged. "Pretty much."

"And the dead birds on my porch? They were in a pattern."

He sat up, twisting his mouth. "I think it was a message to you."

"What kind of message?"

"I think it's a countdown. Six birds—six days. The robin signifies today and the blackbirds are the five remaining days. The cardinal . . ." His voice trailed off.

I didn't want to think too hard on what a red bird signified. My mouth turned dry and I swallowed. "So one of the gods left the birds?"

"One of the gods or maybe a spirit, but it was definitely a message."

"Did you get one?"

"No." His mouth puckered, and he actually looked unhappy about it.

We rode in silence the rest of the ten-minute drive. I didn't feel like chatting, and Collin didn't seem inclined to share any more information. Not that I could have handled any more information. I was overwhelmed with the little he'd shared. I needed to focus on retrieving the cup. Then I could think about confronting life-sucking spirits. I tried not to think about what would happen if we didn't recover my artifact.

When we reached Rodanthe, Collin turned down a side road, toward the ocean. On the Outer Banks, you didn't have to drive very far on either side of the highway before you reached the ocean or the sound. But it soon became apparent that Mrs. Evelyn Abernathy had money. Her two-story house sat right on the beach, and if the structure had been damaged from the storm months earlier, it had already been repaired.

Collin parked his truck across the narrow lane and leaned over his steering wheel, watching the house.

"Got a plan?" I asked. "Because I don't have enough money to buy it back. How much did she pay anyway?"

"Eight hundred dollars."

Eight hundred dollars. I thought Oscar was being kind when he gave me five hundred. "Do you have eight hundred dollars?"

He gave me an amused look. "What do you think?"

I wasn't sure why he looked so happy. We were screwed. I bet she wouldn't take a hot check, not that I could write one. I'd run out of checks months ago.

Collin pointed toward the house. "Look, there's no car in the carport. I bet she's not home."

"So we wait?"

"No, I'll go up and check it out. Stay here." He opened the door.

Something about the way Collin answered set me on edge. "I'm coming with you."

He stopped and pinned me with his dark gaze. "It would probably be better if you wait in the truck."

We had a momentary standoff before I lifted my chin. "It's my cup. I should go with you."

Turning his back to me, he mumbled, "Suit yourself."

I followed him up the steps to the back door. When we reached the deck, I stared at the ocean, taking in the sea breeze and whooshing sound. Daddy used to say that we were born of the sea. Despite living next to the ocean my entire life, I'd hardly been on it, yet every time I was next to it like this, I felt *something*, a sense of belonging and rightness. But whatever the feeling was, it was even stronger today, and the mark on my palm tingled, especially the closer I stood next to Collin. Could my connection to the sea come from the curse?

Collin knocked on the back door and stuffed his hands in his back pockets as he glanced around the beach. While my gaze was focused on taking in the scenic view, I could tell his was methodical. What was he up to?

We waited for several seconds before Collin knocked again.

"She's probably not home," I said, stating the obvious.

He continued his scan of the area. "Looks like it." He then peered through the large glass windows overlooking the sea.

Against my better judgment, I glanced too. I'd never been inside a beach house, though it was my dream to live in one. My financial path made that dream nearly impossible and despite all my teasing with Oscar about marrying for money and my wasted efforts with boring men, I knew I'd never settle for anything less than what my parents had. My mother and Daddy, not Myra. Before Daddy got sick, he and Myra had had a comfortable relationship, which as an adult I realized was exactly what Daddy needed after Momma's death. But Momma and Daddy had had fireworks. Even as a little girl, I'd known their relationship was different than my friends' parents. What my parents had was special.

But I didn't see any men with money waiting to set me ablaze, so when the opportunity presented itself for me to get a look inside the house, I couldn't resist the temptation.

The inside was neat and tidy, the walls lined with white wood paneling. Pale blue and white furniture filled the living room. The kitchen in the back had white cabinets and pale gray marble counters. Bookshelves flanked one wall of the living space, stuffed with books and knickknacks. One in particular caught my eye, and I sucked in my breath.

Collin jerked his head in my direction. "What is it?" But one look at my face told him everything. "You see it? Where?"

I pointed toward the shelf, second from the top on the right side. The ugly pewter cup sat on the pristine white shelves looking old and out of place.

He lowered his voice. "Ellie, why don't you go back to the truck."

The hair on the back of my neck stood on end. "Why?"

"Will you just do as I ask?"

"No."

"*Ellie.*"

"No. What are you going to do?"

He closed his eyes and ran a hand over his forehead. "You really don't want to know."

I leaned toward him, my eyes wide. "You're going to steal it!"

"Shh!" He was next to me in half a second, his hand on my arm. He stepped in close, pressing me back against the door. I was acutely aware of his chest against mine. My body tingled with expectation. Both physically and supernaturally.

Collin felt it too, his eyes widening, his pupils dilating. His chest expanded as he took a deep breath. He seemed to recover his senses after several seconds but stayed tight against me, his hand still wrapped around my arm. "We need the cup, Ellie. You admitted that you don't have enough money to pay the woman, and I know that I don't."

I knew we were desperate, but I couldn't resort to this. "No, Collin. We're not going to steal it. I'm not stooping to that level."

"Be reasonable, Ellie. You know this is the only way." He leaned close into my ear and his hand reached for my face.

My heart thudded against my rib cage. "Stop it, Collin."

His hand dropped, but he remained inside my personal space. He grinned, but it was fake. "I'm giving you a piece of advice, Ellie, although I'm not sure why, so listen close: I'm not to be trusted. I know what I want and I'll do anything to get it. Understand?"

I took a deep breath. "I *know* you're not to be trusted. I've known since the moment you walked into my restaurant, but like it or not, I'm stuck with your condescending, know-it-all ass. So let me give *you* a piece of advice: If you *ever* touch me again, I'll coldcock you. *Understand?*"

A real grin spread across his face and he lifted his hands in surrender as he took two steps backward.

"We are not stealing the cup, not until we've tried talking to her first. Give me tonight to come up with the money, and we'll come back tomorrow to pay her. And if that doesn't work, then we'll consider other alternatives."

He shook his head. "That won't work. If the cup is stolen after we approach her, she'll know it was us."

"I don't care. We'll try it my way first or we won't do it at all."

He took a step closer, but kept a foot between us. "You don't mean that, Ellie. You won't turn your back on all of this now that you know the curse is real, and I'm counting on that. Remember those dead birds on the side of the road and on your porch? Guess who's their ultimate meal of choice? They crave power and energy, and who has more power than anyone else on earth? The Keepers of the curse that sent them away. When they think they're strong enough, they'll come looking for *you*, Ellie Lancaster."

My breath came in short pants. "Is that meant to scare me?" If it was, he was doing a really good job.

"You *should* be scared. And this has only just begun." He laughed and looked toward the ocean. "Fine. I'll give you your one night, and we'll come back tomorrow, but if it doesn't work, we do things my way from here on out. Agreed?"

Did I have a choice? If I were cornered by a spirit and had to decide between stealing the cup or dying, I'd steal the cup without hesitation. But I wasn't cornered by an evil spirit. At least not yet. "Agreed."

He slunk down the stairs in his quiet way. I wondered if he were a ninja. The descendent of a Croatan Indian chief, a ninja. If I weren't so freaked out, I would have laughed.

Once I knew he was at the bottom of the steps, I leaned over the deck railing to catch my breath. If Collin and I were supposed to be working together, why did he consider me the enemy?

⌁ Chapter Nine ⌁

After I got my wits about me, I found Collin waiting in the truck. He didn't say a word, merely started the engine and drove back to Manteo. An accident blocked the highway for a while, making the drive home uncomfortably long. Whenever I tried to ask Collin for more details about the curse, he refused to tell me anything, saying, "It was your responsibility to learn this already. So for now, I'll tell you what you need to know when I think you need to know it."

I couldn't help wondering if Collin's decision to keep the information from me was less about proving his superiority and more about ensuring I'd be as uninformed as possible so I'd be at his mercy. But then again, weren't we working on the same side?

We passed the dead birds on the side of the highway, and I couldn't help thinking that could be me in a few days.

But I'm a Curse Keeper.

I was destined to be one of two people who would fight the spirits. I just needed to learn how.

When Collin pulled his truck into the parking lot in front of my apartment, the sun had begun to set. I got out and started up the stairs without a word, surprised when Collin followed behind me.

"That isn't necessary," I said over my shoulder. "I'm perfectly capable of going upstairs on my own."

"It's getting dark, Ellie. Don't you feel the spirits lurking in the shadows?"

A retort would have been so easy, if I hadn't felt the presence of something just out of reach. If I was still having trouble believing all of this was real, the moving shadow in the corner of my porch would have convinced me.

I unlocked my door with a shaky hand.

Collin stood next to me, but keeping his distance. "Ellie, listen to me. When you go inside, don't come out until the sun comes up."

The blood rushed from my head to my feet. I looked up into his anxious face. "Why?"

His gaze locked onto mine. "You know why."

I turned toward him, the keys still in my hand. "What's out there, Collin?"

"You'll be safe tonight. If you stay inside."

"You didn't answer my question."

His voice lowered. "You know what's out there."

But I didn't. Not really. I knew there were creator gods, four wind gods, one of which probably killed a bunch of birds, and other even lesser spirits, but it wasn't enough. Not nearly enough to help me protect myself.

"I'll be back tomorrow morning. Now go inside and close the door."

"But—"

He leaned an arm against the wall. "I realize you don't trust me and I don't blame you. I haven't really given you reason to. But trust this: I need you, and I need you alive. If I didn't think you'd be safe tonight, I'd stay with you. But I don't believe the spirits are strong enough to do anything to you. Not yet. In a few days, they'll be strong enough to roam during the day as well, but you're okay tonight. Now I need to go take care of some things, and I'll be back tomorrow morning. Then we'll get your cup, one way or the other."

I nodded, a lump of fear in my throat.

"Now go inside. And don't open the door for anyone until the sun comes up."

Paralyzed with fear, I did what he said, locking the deadbolt with fumbling fingers after I went inside. Like a deadbolt would keep spirits outside. I froze. If deadbolts didn't keep them out, why would a door?

I reached for the doorknob, preparing to go after Collin, but his warning echoed in my ears.

Great. I was screwed.

Not only could I not run after Collin, I couldn't go talk to Daddy. And I couldn't look for ways to raise a thousand dollars, which I suspected was what it would take to buy the cup back. Or more.

Maybe that was Collin's real motivation for keeping me in my apartment all night. To keep me uninformed and penniless. But Collin didn't know that Daddy had Alzheimer's. And I still had a phone and the Internet. Unless he cut my lines. I shook my head. Now I was bordering on paranoia.

Right, because believing that evil spirits are out to get me isn't paranoid.

What the hell had happened to my life?

The real question was why didn't Collin teach me to defend myself against any malevolent spirits that might come my way? Why just tell me to stay hidden? Paranoia or not, I didn't trust him. Which brought up another point. In Rodanthe, Collin had told me not to trust him, then a few hours later on my front porch he told me that I *should* trust him. So which was it?

I was siding with not trusting him. So did that mean I could go out or not?

I needed to talk to Daddy, but given his condition, that rarely went well over the phone. If nothing else, I could talk to Myra and see if she knew anything about the colony site.

I snuggled into my overstuffed sofa and called Myra. She answered her cell phone on the first ring. "Ellie, are you okay? I've been calling you for hours, and you never showed up to the inn this afternoon."

I glanced at my phone and realized I hadn't turned it off vibrate after I left the restaurant. And my phone had been in my purse. And for some reason, it had completely slipped my mind that I needed to work at the inn. "Sorry, Myra. I was in Rodanthe." Although I rarely left Roanoke Island, Rodanthe was still within my comfort zone. Still, it was unusual behavior for me, and Myra would know it.

After a second pause, she asked, "Do I want to know why you went to Rodanthe?"

And tell Myra that I'd hawked Daddy's precious cup? "You probably don't. Tell me about your day."

She sighed. "Which part? The crazy day dealing with the press and curious onlookers or your dad when I got home?"

I sat up straight, leaning over my knees. "What's wrong with Daddy?"

"Nothing, Ellie. I didn't mean to scare you. He was just agitated when I got home."

"So he's having a bad day?"

"Had. It was so bad I gave him a sedative and put him to bed early."

"Why was he so worked up?"

"The curse."

I took two deep breaths before I could continue. "What did he say?"

"Oh you know, the usual, but somehow he knew the colony had been found, even though I specifically told his home-care worker to keep it from him. He kept mumbling that the curse had been broken."

My blood rushed in my ears. "Anything else?"

Myra hesitated. "Why the sudden interest? You usually don't want to hear anything about the curse."

I shrugged before I realized she couldn't see me. "Oh, I don't know. The Lost Colony discovery is making me feel guilty that I didn't indulge Daddy more with the curse stuff."

"Well, I for one am glad you didn't. I can't help but wonder if all this curse belief drove your father mad."

We both knew it wasn't true. Alzheimer's didn't work that way, but it was always nice to have *something* to blame. The curse was a convenient and ever-present scapegoat.

"So why do they think the colony just appeared out of thin air?"

"It's amazing you put it that way. I heard several archaeologists use that exact phrase today. They said they had examined that site a couple of years ago. They performed ultrasounds of the site and found nothing. And now it's all just *there*. It's unbelievable."

I couldn't help thinking about my mother. She would have loved this. She'd devoted her life to finding the colony to prove my father's belief in the curse wrong. I still found it surprising that two people with such different beliefs could have been so crazy in love. "What do they think happened? Why is it suddenly there?"

"The storm? It's as good a guess as any, but they would expect the huts and artifacts to be covered with dirt and mud. It's as though the village had always been there, undisturbed for over four hundred years. They've never seen anything like it. For all they know it's an elaborate hoax, but the logistics of setting up something like this, especially in about twelve hours, is incomprehensible."

"Huh."

"So why were you in Rodanthe?"

I knew she wouldn't drop it. I could either tell her the truth or a partial version. I chose partial. "I was there with a guy."

She paused. "Dwight?" The tone of disappointment in her voice told me she knew it wasn't him. She probably figured I'd just moved on to the next of many men.

"No." After a few seconds of silence I answered. "Collin."

"Collin who?"

"Collin Dailey. I met him at the restaurant." What on earth possessed me to tell her that I went to Rodanthe?

"When did you meet Collin?"

"For heaven's sake, Myra. I'm twenty-three years old."

She sighed. "I know. I know. It's just that I worry about you."

"And I love you so much for caring. Don't worry about Collin. We're just friends."

"You went to Rodanthe with a guy who's just a friend? A guy you just met?"

"*Myra.*"

"Okay. Okay. I'm butting out."

"Sorry that I didn't come do my job today. I hope that's not why Daddy was upset. He's used to seeing me every day. I have to work tomorrow night so I'll make sure to see him in the morning."

"Ellie, I'm not mad about you not showing up this afternoon. Heaven knows you do more than your share around here. Just call me next time so I don't worry about you, okay?"

I closed my eyes. I was so lucky to have Myra in my life. If it weren't for her, I'd practically be an orphan. "I love you, Myra."

"I love you too, sweetie. Now get some sleep."

"You too."

I hung up the phone, worried about Daddy, but more worried about where I was going to come up with the money to buy back the cup. I spun my head around, searching the room. Anything of worth had already been pawned, and I wasn't asking anyone for a loan. I would have pawned my car, but I doubted I'd get five hundred dollars for it, let alone eight hundred or more. And then how would I get around?

I pushed the worry to the back of my mind. Maybe I'd come up with a solution if I thought about something else. I changed into pajamas and heated up a can of soup before snuggling up with an afghan and my laptop on the sofa.

I searched the Internet for anything I could find about the curse or Croatan spirits. There was nothing about the curse—no surprise—but almost as little about Croatan spirits. That meant I was dependent on Daddy and Collin for answers. I sure hoped Daddy would be having a good day the next morning.

Giving up, I put all the dirty dishes I'd acquired the last few days into the dishwasher and turned it on. Who said I wasn't responsible? Possibly the monster pile of laundry in my closet, but I decided it was best to take baby steps to responsibility. No sense rushing headlong into things.

As I moved toward my bedroom, looking forward to my comfy bed, I heard a moan outside my front door. I froze, my feet stuck to the floor, the mark on my hand tingling. I shook my head. This was stupid. It had to be the wind, which had picked up since the sun had set.

Only I heard the sound again, and it definitely sounded like a moan. I moved to the peephole and didn't see anything. Just when I decided it was my imagination, the moan grew louder, sounding like someone in pain.

"Who's out there?" I shouted through the door.

No answer.

My heartbeat raced out of control. *Don't be ridiculous. Collin is making you paranoid.* I took a deep breath. "Who is it?"

No answer. Then the moan returned, louder than before.

"This isn't funny, Claire! Stop it right now!"

"Curse Keeper." A low groan floated through the door.

Could it be a spirit? The tingle in my hand had turned to a burn. I unbolted the door and opened it a crack.

A silver, shimmery orb floated in front of me, several feet off the ground. The door flew open out of my hands, the sudden force sending me stumbling backward.

I regained my balance and tried to shut the door, but it wouldn't budge. I half hid behind the door as my heart leapt into my throat.

The orb shimmered brighter. "I am Aposo and I bring you a message from Ahone. He warns that the gods are upset with you."

Who was Ahone? "Why are they upset with me? I didn't do anything. I wasn't the one who locked them up for four hundred years."

"But you are the daughter of the sea and you plan to close the gate."

"Look, it's not personal." The daughter of the sea? What was that? There was so much I didn't know.

"The world is out of balance. The spirits are weak. The Manitou cries out at the injustice. You *must* reseal the gate."

My jaw dropped. "*What?*"

"Ahone fears for his creation. He sacrificed to save his children before, and he will sacrifice again, but this time at great cost. You must do everything in your power to reseal the gate, but be warned: Okeus will do everything within his power to stop you."

Shit, who was Okeus?

"Your door is marked and will protect you, but you must learn to create the markings yourself. You must learn to protect yourself when you leave your hallowed space."

My door was marked? I cast a quick look at it, afraid to take my eyes off the spirit. The door was covered with primitive symbols, drawn in something like charcoal, all the way around the perimeter. Did Collin put those there?

"Okeus will send his own spirit with a message: Join with Okeus or die. But Ahone warns you that to join with Okeus *is* death, not just in the earthly and the spiritual realms. Ahone wishes for his beloved children to have eternal life."

"Will he protect me?"

"He cannot interfere except to seal the gate."

I took several deep breaths. I needed to keep it together and not lose my head. "What am I supposed to do?"

"Close and reseal the gate."

Tears of frustration burned my eyes. "But I don't remember how to close the gate!"

"The gate must be sealed before the beginning of the seventh day."

"You're not listening to me! I don't know how to close the gate!"

The orb began to fade. "You have until the beginning of the seventh day." And then it was gone.

The magical hold on the door was gone and I staggered, moving quickly to shut it. So I could expect a visit from Okeus's messenger? In my research, I hadn't come across either name. I locked the deadbolt, grabbed my laptop, and climbed into bed, making sure the bedroom window was locked first, even though it was three stories off the ground. Obviously, spirits didn't have any trouble floating.

Since Okeus seemed like my biggest concern, I searched for him first. It took a couple of attempts before I spelled Okeus—pronounced *Okee*—correctly to get a hit. On the few sites I found with information, words like *malevolent* and *warlike* and my personal favorite, *wrathful*, littered the page. Ahone—the pronunciation was guessed to be *Ah-hone*—was always mentioned hand in hand with Okeus and was described as the creator god. Ahone was considered benevolent and peace loving. Some historians thought he might also be the Great Hare, who created man and sent him to the four corners of the earth.

Along with Ahone were the four wind gods, who ate the Great Hare's giant deer. I wasn't sure if that was a good thing or bad, but since Ahone's messenger insisted Ahone wanted me to shut the gate, I was guessing bad.

How the hell was I supposed to protect myself from a wrathful god and four wind gods? The websites said the Native Americans offered sacrifices to appease Okeus, but I sure wasn't doing that. If I was forced to choose sides, I was obviously running to the side of the peace-loving god. And hopefully hiding behind him.

I was just on the edge of sleep when I heard pounding on my bedroom window. My hand burned. I jerked upright with a start. There were only a couple of things that could be outside my bedroom window and none of them were good. While I had symbols outside my door, I suspected there were none outside my bedroom window. Opening that window was the last thing I planned to do.

Apparently, something else had another idea.

The glass shattered, blowing into the room while my gauzy curtains flapped like crazy. A voice called out, "Daughter of the sea, present yourself."

"No fucking way!" I shouted, jumping off the bed and hiding beside the mattress. I really needed to find out about this daughter of the sea title.

"Okeus has a message for you."

I peered over the side of the bed. A dark, hazy image hovered outside my window. "I can hear you just fine from here."

"Okeus offers you riches beyond measure if you pledge yourself to him."

I always wondered how tempted I'd be by something like this, but in this case, it was an easy decision. "I have a message for Okeus—no thank you."

"Stupid human. To defy Okeus is death."

"Well I heard that siding with Okeus is eternal death. So no thank you."

"Ahone." The name was uttered as a curse word. "You are foolish to listen to a god so weak he does nothing but hide in the heavens. Okeus is strong and rewards those who are loyal to his cause. Ahone will give you nothing."

"I'll take my chances."

The spirit pushed through the opening in the window into the room and shot in front of me, releasing a high-pitched scream resembling the cry of a dinosaur from *Jurassic Park*. "You have until the eve of the seventh day to decide, and if you do not choose Okeus, he will demand retribution. I will visit you again to seek your decision."

And then the spirit was gone.

I huddled next to my bed for several minutes, shaking so hard I couldn't even stand if I wanted to.

The wind howled outside and the curtains flapped against the wall. While the markings on the door had worked, the window was obviously unprotected. I either needed to learn the symbols or get Collin to mark the windows. The latter was an alternative of last resort.

One thing was for sure—I wasn't sleeping in my bedroom. I grabbed my pillow and laptop and headed into the living room, moving my big chair in front of my bedroom door. I had little faith it would hold out a spirit, but it was better than nothing.

After I got settled on the sofa, it took me a long time before I could go to sleep. My palm itched and my dreams were filled with animals, all crying out, "Daughter of the sea, witness to creation, help us."

❧ CHAPTER TEN ❧

I was awake before the sun came up, and I really needed to pee. But I had to go through my room to get to the bathroom, and there was no way I was going into my room until the sun made an appearance. After I finally unbarricaded the door and took care of my bathroom business, I inspected the damage to my room. The lower windowpane had completely shattered, scattering glass everywhere. When I saw the dead hawk at the foot of my bed, I shrieked and jumped backward. I needed to get control of myself, clean up the mess, and get to the inn.

My downstairs neighbor didn't appreciate the vacuum cleaner running at six in the morning. The thumping on the floor clued me in. After covering the window with plastic from a dry-cleaner bag, I scooped the bird into another bag and opened the front door to put it on my porch. The dead birds in a circle outside my door shouldn't have surprised me, but I was preoccupied with my current situation. Today's warning had four blackbirds, two robins, and a cardinal in the center. Four days left.

After I swept up the birds, I stopped to examine the symbols on the door. They were incredibly primitive and looked like they'd been drawn in charcoal or chalk. Wavy lines and circles surrounded the perimeter. I needed to write them down so I could draw them on my window.

I took a shower and towel dried my hair before French braiding it and getting dressed, throwing on a flouncy blue skirt with tiny white flowers and a white sleeveless buttoned blouse. I loved that skirt and it always put me in a better mood when I had a bad day. I hoped it worked today because I needed all the help I could get.

I decided to go to the Dare Inn. It was too early to tidy up the lodgers' rooms, but I could fold the towels from the afternoon before and help Myra with breakfast. Just before I headed out the door, I grabbed my backpack. Daddy's house was full of antiques, and I was sure I could find something there to sell. Myra and I had never discussed selling them to help keep the inn afloat. Perhaps because dismantling the contents was too similar to the way Daddy's mind was deconstructing. We needed something to stay the same.

Regret and guilt stuck my feet to the floor. I couldn't believe I was considering stealing from my parents, but if Daddy were coherent, I knew he'd give me whatever I needed to reseal the gate. Not that I'd ever admit to pawning the cup.

Myra was in the kitchen in the residential house, pulling a breakfast casserole out of the oven when I walked in. "What are you doing here already?" She glanced at me and her forehead wrinkled with worry. "And you obviously didn't sleep well. You look exhausted, Ellie."

I grabbed a blueberry muffin from a basket and peeled off the wrapper. "What gave me away? The fact I'm a couple hours early or the dark circles under my eyes?" I took a bite and gave her a tight grin.

She moved toward me and put a hand on my arm. "What's going on, Ellie? Is it this curse stuff?"

I loved Myra. She might not have given birth to me, but she'd mothered me longer than my own mother had. Myra and Momma shared something else in common besides their love for Daddy and me: their outright disapproval of the curse. Poor Myra hadn't found out about the curse until she and Daddy were married at least a year, when she'd stumbled upon Daddy and me arguing about my refusal to relearn the curse facts. She'd taken my side and slept in the spare bedroom for a week. I never heard her and Daddy talk about it again until he started showing signs of Alzheimer's.

Telling Myra what was going on wouldn't do any good. She'd think I'd lost my mind like Daddy, especially after my own belligerence over the curse all these years. And for all I knew, telling her would put her in danger as well.

I kissed her cheek and moved around her toward the laundry room. "I'm fine. Stop worrying so much."

"Ellie?"

I stopped in the doorway and turned toward her, hiding the fear blooming in my chest.

"I know the inn has been hard for you. You work here every day and then you put money into it—"

"Myra, stop."

"You don't have to do it. We'll probably lose this place anyway."

I'd known that for a while, and since Myra handled all the books, she had to know it too, but this was the first time she'd admitted it.

"I know."

"You know?" Tears filled her eyes. "And you do it anyway?"

My chin trembled. "Myra, I love you and I love Daddy. I'll do anything for either of you. This included." I spun around to get the towels.

"I'm considering selling."

Sighing, I leaned into the door frame, but kept my back to her. I couldn't face her. Face the proof that I'd failed her and Daddy. The inn had been owned by our family for over a hundred and fifty years, and it was up to me to make sure it stayed that way. But I couldn't figure out how to do it, no matter how hard I tried. "Don't do that, Myra. Just hang on a bit longer."

"It's not fair to you. I see you and how exhausted . . ." Her voice broke. "You're young. You should have fun instead of—"

I rushed to her and pulled her into an embrace. "Stop, Myra. This is my home too, even if I don't live here. Too much is happening right now to make a decision this big. Don't think about selling yet. All these tourists will bring more business. Things might turn around. Just wait and see how everything turns out." If the curse wasn't fixed, I'd pack Daddy and Myra into my own car and get them the hell out of here if I had to. We wouldn't be anywhere around Roanoke, in the line of fire.

Something in my tone caught her attention. She pulled back and looked into my eyes. "What do you mean wait and see how everything turns out?"

I resisted the urge to sigh. I was tired and not thinking straight. I needed to watch what I said. I forced a grin. "Wait and see if I win the lottery."

"You don't buy lottery tickets."

"Not yet I don't." I headed back to the laundry room. "But I'm feeling lucky today." I hoped to God that was true.

She was gone when I came out with the towels. I perched the basket on my hip and headed for the front porch. It was almost seven thirty, and the bed and breakfast guests would be coming down to eat before they left for the day or checked out.

I found Daddy on the porch, rocking in his chair. He wasn't usually there in the morning. Myra often had him sit in the office with her, watching TV, but she must have known I'd want to see him.

I loved her all the more for it.

"Hey, Daddy." I sat in the rocker next to him and plopped the basket on the floor.

His gazed lifted, confusion flickering in his eyes.

My vision blurred with tears, and I turned my attention to the towels and swallowed the burning lump in my throat. He wasn't my daddy today. When I could talk, I forced a cheerful voice. "It's a beautiful morning, isn't it?"

"The curse is broken."

My hands stopped midair, holding a partially folded towel. I set it in my lap and looked into his face. "Yes."

His jaw quivered. "I have to save Ellie. I have to keep her safe from the evil spirits with the words of protection. I have to find the other Keeper." He started to get out of his chair, his voice rising in fear.

Words of protection? Were there words to help me protect myself? I got up and eased him back in the chair. "Daddy, it's okay. You're not the Keeper anymore."

He shook his head and arms violently, trying to throw off my hands. "Who are you? Where's my baby? I have to save my baby!"

I was used to his regressions, when he thought I was a child again. But that didn't buffer the pain and disappointment that pierced my heart with each occurrence. This time was too much. Collin, the spirits last night, the realization that I'd lost the one thing I needed to make this all stop, but most of all knowing that I'd truly failed my father both with the curse and the inn, all piled onto the fact that Daddy was near hysterical and there was nothing I could do about it. Tears flooded my cheeks.

I sucked in a breath. "John, it's okay." Part of me died every time I had to call him by his given name, but calling him Daddy when he was like this only made him more agitated. "Ellie's safe."

This calmed him a bit, and he searched my face. "Is she with Amanda?"

I couldn't contain my sob. He thought Momma was still alive. "Yes."

He shook his head, his eyes wild. "No! You're lying! Amanda's dead! Get away from me! You're an evil spirit!" He began to mumble something in a language I didn't understand.

He was using the words of protection.

I listened closely, forcing myself to calm down so I could get the words, but he was too upset and the words too unfamiliar to grasp.

Myra appeared in the doorway, concern on her face when she took in the sight of my father and my tear-streaked face. "It's the curse, isn't it?"

I nodded, a fresh batch of tears falling.

She gently pushed me to the side and squatted in front of Daddy. "John, it's okay. Ellie's safe. I've hidden her from the spirits using the protection symbols you showed me. She's safe."

He relaxed in his chair, but tensed when he realized I was still there. "A spirit is here."

"No, John. That's my friend, Elinor. She's helping me with the inn today."

I couldn't take any more. I grabbed the basket and went back into the house, collapsing onto the sofa, bawling into the overstuffed cushions.

Several minutes later, Myra's soft voice was in my ear. "Ellie, I'm so sorry." She sat next to me, caressing the back of my head. "I know how hard it is when you see him like that."

I sucked in a deep breath, trying to calm down, and wiped my cheeks. "It's okay. I'm fine."

"You're not. Go home. Take the day off. We'll manage fine without you here."

I wished I could take the day completely off. Go lay out at the beach like Claire and I used to do before life got in the way and threw responsibility at us. But I had Curse Keeper work to do today. I had to save the world, as absurd as it seemed. "What did you mean when you told Daddy that you'd hidden me away with symbols?"

Her mouth lifted into a grim smile. "I told you that he was upset yesterday. He thought you were a little girl and said he couldn't find you so I told him that I'd hidden you somewhere the spirits couldn't reach you. But he said it wasn't enough, and he wrote down several symbols that he said I needed to put outside your door."

I couldn't believe what I was hearing and sat up straighter. "Do you still have the paper?"

"Well, yeah, but . . ."

"Could I have it?"

Her eyes narrowed in suspicion. "Why?"

Obviously, I couldn't tell her the truth. "If Daddy gets upset again, maybe I could write one or two down to convince him that I'm not an evil spirit."

Myra considered what I said for a moment before nodding. "That might actually be a good idea." She got up and opened a drawer in the small antique desk in the corner. After she pulled out a folded piece of paper, she handed it to me. "Here. Just be careful with it. I don't want to encourage his delusions."

I took the paper and clutched it in my hand. "I'll be careful."

"You go home. If you stay . . . your dad . . ."

I stood and wiped my face again, fighting back more tears. I couldn't bear the thought that my presence upset him. "I know."

"He loves you, Ellie. Deep inside, in the part of him that's trapped, he loves you. That's why he's so frantic to save the little girl you."

I nodded, not trusting myself to speak, and headed for the door. As I passed the dining room, a pair of antique silver candlesticks on the buffet in front of the window caught my eye. How much were they worth? Probably a lot. They'd been in our family for years, most likely centuries. I closed my eyes and shook my head. What was I thinking?

Did I really have a choice?

With a grieving heart, I stuffed the two pieces into my bag and headed out the door. Myra was bound to notice them missing. What would I tell her? I wanted to cry all over again, but crying only made me weak, and I had to be strong. Evil lurked around me and somehow I knew it would feed off my weakness. I had to be strong, and I had to pretend to be brave even if I didn't feel brave.

Collin's truck was parked outside my apartment building when I got home. I peered in the rolled-down windows; he wasn't in the cab. I wasn't surprised to see him sitting in the chair on my front porch, but I *was* surprised to see him with two cups of coffee from the coffee shop on the other side of the alley. He stood and handed me one. "I took you for a skinny caramel macchiato girl."

"How did you know that?" I unlocked the door, then took the cup from him, narrowing my eyes with suspicion. Why was he being so nice?

"You can tell a lot about a person from the coffee they drink. Caramel means you aren't serious about your coffee drinking. The macchiato part makes you feel sophisticated. And the nonfat goes without saying."

Was he insinuating that I was fat? "There's no way you could possibly know what I drink."

He grinned, a real grin, not the smartass one he mostly used. "I asked Tiffany at the coffee shop across the alley what you usually get."

"*And she told you*? You could have been a stalker!" I opened the door and went inside, but Collin stayed on the porch.

He shrugged. "I have a way with women."

Talk about an understatement.

He pointed to the symbols on the ground and all around my door. "Did they work?"

"The door worked just fine."

He waved toward my bedroom. "What happened to your window?"

"A bird flew into it."

His eyes widened in surprise. "A bird? Anything else?"

Something about the way he asked made me uneasy. Like he'd expected me to have trouble last night. I cocked an eyebrow. "Did anything happen to *you* last night?"

He remained expressionless. "Nope. I had an uneventful evening eating a frozen pizza and watching mindless TV."

He was lying to me. I wasn't sure how I knew it, but I did. Perhaps it was the Keeper link, but no matter how I knew, the fact that he was lying set me on edge. His warning when we were in Rodanthe, that he'd do anything to get what he wanted, remained fresh in my memory.

"What happened after the bird flew in the window?"

I should have told him, but some instinct told me to keep it to myself. And at the moment, instinct was all I had to go on. "Did you expect something to happen?"

He took a deep breath and glanced around the doorway. "Did you stay here last night?"

Now I was really suspicious. "Why do you ask?"

"It's pretty early, and you've already been out and are now getting home. Before eight o'clock."

I took a sip of my coffee. "I just got home from my second job."

"You have two jobs, but you still had to pawn your relic? How many pairs of shoes do you own?"

Let Collin Dailey think whatever he liked as long as he didn't know about Daddy. "Are we going to Rodanthe or not?"

"Did you get some money?"

"How was I supposed to get money when I was locked in my apartment all night?"

"So you didn't?"

"Not exactly." I didn't want him to know I'd just gotten the candlesticks or he'd ask me where they came from. I wasn't sure why I felt a desperate fear that he'd discover Daddy, but it was more instinct. I'd been basing a lot of decisions off of instinct over the last twenty-four-plus hours. I didn't see any reason to change now.

"What does 'not exactly' mean?" He still stood on my porch. Why hadn't he come in?

I carried my backpack into my bedroom, leaving the door open. "It means I realized I had something else to take to the pawnshop."

I found another bag in my closet and transferred the candlesticks. Just as I was getting ready to head back into the living room I remembered the paper in the pocket of my skirt. I pulled it out and unfolded the note. Several Native American symbols covered the page, written in shaky handwriting. I studied them closely, trying to commit them to memory so I could compare them to what Collin had written outside my door. I stuffed the paper in my purse and left my bedroom. Collin was still outside the door.

"What do you have to pawn?" he asked as soon as he saw me.

"Silver candlesticks." I handed him the bag, pretending like they didn't matter. I had to forget the stupid things, because I'd never see them again. If I was lucky enough to get a thousand dollars for them, I'd never have the money to buy them back.

Collin opened the bag and pulled one out. He released a low whistle. "You're telling me that you sold your little pewter cup before you departed with these?" Disbelief dripped from his words.

"Correction: I didn't *sell* my cup. I *pawned* it. I meant to buy it back just like all the other times."

"*All the other times?*"

I stepped out of my apartment, setting my coffee on the railing of the porch so I could lock up again. I paused to take in the marks around my door. I immediately recognized at least three of them from the paper. "What are these things?"

"Protection symbols."

"They keep out the evil spirits?"

"Not just the evil ones. The good ones too."

I shot him a questioning look. "Good ones?"

"Not all spirits are evil. There are good ones, just like people. And sometimes people—and spirits—are a mixture of both."

While Ahone's messenger had appeared unthreatening, Okeus's certainly didn't. I decided if I encountered any more spirits before closing the gate, I was assuming the worst about them.

I held out my palm and showed him my mark. "And this?"

"The Curse Keeper symbol. The circle represents the spirit world. The square represents our world. They are neither inside nor outside one another, but coexist."

"You have one too? What does yours look like?"

He held out his hand, palm up. I grabbed it and pulled it closer. It looked identical to mine.

"If you wanted to hold my hand, you only had to ask."

I rolled my eyes. "As if." I placed my open palm next to his. "They're the same."

"Of course. It's the mark of the Curse Keeper. Since we're both Keepers . . ." His voice trailed off.

I looked up into his face and winked. "And here I thought your mark would be better since you're so superior to me."

To my surprise, Collin laughed. "Obviously, I didn't have a say in the matter."

"My mark appeared when you grabbed my hand in the restaurant." My eyes widened and I whispered. "You knew. You did this."

Disbelief and worry replaced his amusement. "No. When I came to the restaurant I didn't know, but when I couldn't breathe, I began to suspect. It was just like my grandmother always told me it would happen. And when you were so close, it was as though I couldn't stop myself from grabbing your hand. As though you were a magnet, drawing my hand to yours. I told you already. I couldn't have stopped it if I wanted to."

"But that's what broke the curse."

A softness I'd never seen before filled his eyes. "I'm sorry."

I leaned my back into the door. "What's done is done."

He watched me, waiting.

"My mark tingles or burns when something is near."

His eyes hardened. "When were you near a spirit?"

Oh shit. I needed more sleep. I sucked at keeping secrets when I was tired. "Yesterday at the house in Rodanthe. When you touched me, it tingled then. But even before that. When I looked into the ocean while I was standing next to you. I felt it then."

Collin's shoulders relaxed. "When I said we were like magnets, I meant it. The power in our blood is strong, but it's stronger when the two of us are together, and even more so when our marks touch. We're naturally drawn to each other." He moved closer and lowered his voice with a wink. "Thank God you're not an eighty-two-year-old woman."

"What if I were an eighty-two-year-old man?"

"Even worse."

"So . . ." I found it difficult to think with him so close. "You're saying that what I feel right now is because of the curse, the power or magic in our blood?"

"It depends. What are you feeling right now?" He turned his hooded eyes on me, giving me a come-hither stare.

I swallowed. "An electrical charge. Why? What are you feeling?"

A sly grin spread across his face. "An electrical charge."

I couldn't get caught in Collin's seductive trap. I knew he had a way with women and maybe he thought I'd be more cooperative if he put me under his sexy spell. Or maybe he didn't have a goal. Maybe he couldn't help himself. "Then I guess we'll come in handy if there's a power outage." I gave his chest a small shove. "Let's go."

Collin laughed while I tromped down the stairs. "It's going to be an interesting day."

↶ Chapter Eleven ↷

Our truce ended less than a minute later when I told Collin I wanted to sell my candlesticks to Oscar.

"I am not driving back to Kill Devil Hills," Collin growled, standing in front of his truck.

"I'm not selling them to someone else. I trust Oscar. So if you don't want to waste your gas, I'll drive my own car!"

He dangled the bag in the air over his head, wearing an evil smile. "Seeing how I have the bag, I get to decide where we go."

I reached for it, but Collin held the pack higher, out of my reach.

"Really?" I asked. "What? Are you a twelve-year-old boy now?"

He laughed. "I think all men are really twelve-year-old boys deep down inside."

"I'm serious, Collin. They're mine. Give them back."

He watched me for a moment, then handed me the bag, but he didn't release his grasp. "Ellie, do you plan to pawn these or sell them?"

I wasn't sure why he cared, but his face had softened again. It was as though his façade had dropped, and he let me see the real him for a moment.

God, I'm a pushover. "Sell them." I looked away. "I'll never be able to buy them back."

Collin's voice lowered with a tenderness I didn't expect. "You can pawn them for ninety days, Ellie. Then you get sixty more to pay them off. That's five months."

I looked into his face, shaking my head. "Can you imagine the interest? Oscar charges twenty-two percent. I'll never come up with the money to pay it off." I shoved them back at him, ordering the tears in my eyes to dry up as I walked around to the truck's passenger door.

Collin slid in the truck and set the bag on the seat between us. "You don't have to do this."

"I don't have anything else."

He didn't start the truck, instead staring out the windshield. "No. There's another way. *I* can get the cup. Why don't you stay here and wait for me? I'll be back in a few hours."

I shook my head. I couldn't believe he was being so nice. If you could call offering to steal from some unsuspecting woman nice. Strangely enough, with Collin, it was. "No, it's my cup, and you're right. I shouldn't have pawned it. I need to accept responsibility and fix this myself."

He nodded, then started the truck.

We drove in silence until we hit the bridge. Collin slowed down and cast a worried look at me, but the blood had already rushed to my feet, leaving me lightheaded.

Dead birds covered the pavement. Hundreds of them.

Yesterday we'd seen seagulls but today there were multiple species. Doves, pigeons, gulls, wrens, owls, ducks, and several hawks.

The combination of seeing the birds and leaving the island tightened my chest, and I gasped for air.

"Ellie?"

"They're getting stronger, Collin."

"It's okay."

"*No it's not!* They're getting stronger, and Okeus is going to come after me." I grabbed the dashboard and the door. "How am I supposed to protect myself?" I sounded hysterical. I *was* hysterical. This was proof that I was as good as dead. It was only a matter of time. Days. Especially after last night.

Collin pulled over to the side of the road, the sickening thuds of tires rolling over bird carcasses making me want to vomit.

"Why do you think Okeus is after you?"

Shit. Shit. Shit.

"What aren't you telling me, Ellie?"

Collin knew more than I did, which is why, logically, I knew I should tell him what happened last night with both messengers. He might be able to protect me. But it burned in my gut that I was dependent on him for protection. Besides, Collin was hiding things from me. He'd told me himself that he couldn't be trusted. For now, I'd keep the information to myself and see if I could re-create the symbols around my window. And if Collin proved himself trustworthy before then, I'd tell him. "*You* told me that they would come after me. On Evelyn Abernathy's porch."

He tilted his head, distrust in his eyes. "How do you know about Okeus?"

"A simple Internet search."

"Simple?"

I turned to look out into the sound. "Okay, not so simple. It took some digging."

"Why did you decide on Okeus? Why not Ahone or a windengo or the Great Spirit?"

"Because Okeus is evil."

Collin sighed. "Okeus isn't pure evil, Ellie, just as Ahone isn't pure good. I told you, just like people, they're a mixture of both."

"But the Internet—"

"Ellie, so much about the Croatan beliefs and rituals was lost that most people have no idea what they are talking about. Sure Okeus can be wrathful, but he can also be good to his people. He'd come in handy in a time of war."

"That's good, if you're on *his* side."

"It's no different than warring countries invoking God to help them."

Collin seemed to be defending Okeus too much to suit me. More reason not to tell him about Okeus's warning. Had Okeus made Collin the same offer? Had Collin accepted? "You said that the symbols of protection kept me safe last night. What kept *you* safe? You left my apartment when it was getting dark. Did you come across any spirits?"

His face hardened. "No."

"Nothing? Weren't you worried?"

He turned away. "No."

"What? The spirits won't mess with Big Bad Collin?"

His jaw tightened. "I know how to protect myself."

"So teach *me*."

He inhaled and pushed out his breath in frustration. "Fine. If we get the cup back *your way*, then I'll teach you how to protect yourself."

I cocked my head in disbelief. "If we get the cup back my way? Why wouldn't you just teach me? It's like you *want* me to get killed."

He shook his head and turned toward me. "You don't know anything, Ellie."

"*So teach me*."

"You should already know this. It's not my job to teach you. Which parent was the Keeper before you? Why don't you ask him or her to fill you in?"

My breath caught in my chest. "I can't."

"Why not?"

I didn't want to tell him about Daddy. "My momma's gone." I purposely left my family's Keeper line vague. The less Collin knew about my family, the better.

That gave him pause. Finally, he said, "I'm sorry."

I shrugged. "She left years ago. I'm over it." Mostly.

Shifting the truck into drive, he shot me a glance before turning his attention to the road. "It's nine in the morning. We have eleven more hours of daylight. Let's focus on getting the cup; then we'll deal with the rest."

I needed the cup whether he helped me or not. I knew there were words of protection, thanks to Daddy's mumbling. If Daddy knew them, Collin was sure to know them too. That meant I had eleven more hours to get him to spill. I might have to resort to my own bag of tricks. "Okay."

"We need to sell your candlesticks first." No-nonsense Collin was back. It was probably better this way. At least I knew where I really stood with him. When he was nice, I felt like I was part of a con job.

"Yeah."

"I know a guy who will give you top dollar for them, but only if you sell. Are you sure you want to sell them? Five months—"

"Sell."

He turned south on Highway 12. We rode in silence all the way to Rodanthe. I gaped as he drove through the town.

"Wait." I turned around to watch the town disappearing behind us. "Where are we going? Where's your guy?"

"Cape Hatteras."

"Cape Hatteras? But Cape Hatteras is farther than Kill Devil Hills."

"I know a guy in Buxton."

"And I know a guy in Kill Devil Hills. Oscar."

Collin's face remained expressionless. "I don't like your guy."

"I don't care if you don't like him. They're *my* candlesticks!"

He turned toward me, lifting his eyebrows. "Are they?" His gaze returned to the road.

The realization hit me like a Mack truck: He was protecting me. He thought I'd stolen the candlesticks, and he assumed Oscar would turn me in if he found out. Just when I thought I'd figured him out.

Damn him.

Collin drove into Buxton and pulled up in front of a thrift store. The building was completely run down, with several massive metal buildings behind it, all surrounded by a dilapidated wooden fence.

"Really? You're going to get a good price *here*?"

Collin opened his door. "Trust me." He got out and looked through the open window. "Stay here."

The hell with that.

I followed him to the front door.

His mouth puckered into a frown of disapproval. "I told you to wait. I mean it, Ellie."

I put a hand on my hip. "Yesterday, you told me not to trust you. This is me not trusting you."

He shook his head and a cocky grin spread across his face. "Me and my big mouth."

We entered the store, and I nearly gagged from the smell of decay. I leaned close to him, whispering, "You can't be serious."

The oldest, most broken-down crap I'd ever seen filled the store. And if the inventory didn't make me doubtful, the ambiance did. Concrete walls and floor, dim lighting. It looked like a scene from some horror movie.

Collin shot me a look of warning and then walked toward the back room, lowering his voice. "Let me do all the talking."

I pinched my lips together in an exaggerated manner and made a face at him.

He snorted. "Mature, really mature."

A teenage girl sporting a goth look stood behind a counter but didn't say anything as we slipped behind a curtain hanging over a doorway. Collin must have been here before because he seemed to know where he was going, heading for a room in the far back corner. He maneuvered through a maze of odds and ends in the storage room, then opened a closed door without knocking.

This room was better lit, but not by much. Tables lined the walls, covered with multiple electronic parts and pieces. An obese man who appeared to be in his forties sat at one of the tables, turning a tiny screwdriver inside the torn-apart computer in front of him.

The guy looked up, saw Collin, then turned his gaze to me, staring at my face, then sliding down to my legs and lingering there. I was used to guys checking out my legs, especially since I wore a lot of skirts, but this guy creeped me out.

"What can I do for you, Dailey?" he asked, but kept his gaze on me.

"I've got something to sell, Marino."

Marino turned back to his computer. "I'm not sure you have anything I'm interested in. Not after our last deal."

Collin pulled a candlestick from the bag and set it on the table next to the computer.

Marino lifted an eyebrow. "Where'd you get it?"

"A guy down in—"

Shaking his head in annoyance, Marino waved to the door. "Never mind. Get out."

I took a step toward him. "They're mine."

Collin cursed under his breath.

Marino spun his office chair around to face me, crossing his arms over his gut. His eyes widened in amusement. "Yours?"

"Why do you think I'm here with Dailey? He's helping me."

Marino's belly laugh filled the room. "Helping you? Sweetheart, Collin Dailey doesn't help anyone unless it helps *him*."

I tilted my head and gave him a saucy look. "I'm not stupid. I figured that out less than five minutes after I met him." Fear set my nerve endings on edge, but my hand didn't tingle. I suspected this guy might be dangerous, but he was a human threat, not supernatural.

Marino laughed again. "I like you. You've got spunk. *You* I'll work with." He picked up the ornately detailed silver piece and spun it in his hand, examining every square inch. "How many you got?"

"Two."

"And how much do you want for the pair?"

Collin tensed next to me. He really didn't think I knew what I was doing.

"Twenty-five hundred."

Marino looked up. "Twenty-five hundred? Are you insane?"

"I'm hanging out with Collin." I waved toward him. "What do you think?"

Marino laughed again, bracing his hands on his legs. "Now I *really* like you. I'll give you one thousand."

"Two thousand and not a penny less. If you don't want them, I have a guy in Kill Devil Hills who does."

Marino leaned back in his chair and rested his hand on the table, studying me. I really didn't like the way his eyes lingered. "Mikey? He won't pay you more than eight hundred."

I lifted a shoulder in a half shrug and gave him the barest hint of a smile. "I'll take my chances." I moved toward the table with an outstretched arm.

"Eighteen hundred. Final offer."

I paused for a second. "Deal."

Marino heaved out of his chair, huffing as he moved toward a safe in the corner that I hadn't noticed earlier. He opened it, counted a small stack of hundred dollar bills, then handed them to me.

I moved to take the cash, but he held the bundle tight. Marino narrowed his eyes at Collin. "You can leave."

Collin tensed. "Sorry, I'm not going anywhere without the lady."

"*Lady*?" Marino chuckled, eyeing me again. "I'll give you that considering your usual acquaintances. It makes me all the more intrigued. Give us twenty minutes."

Twenty minutes? I didn't even want to consider what Marino wanted to do for twenty minutes. My skin crawled being this close to him.

Collin grabbed the candlestick. "Ellie, let's go."

I needed the money. How else would I get the cup back? "Mr. Marino, I think there's been some kind of misunderstanding here."

"The only misunderstanding is Collin's refusal to do as I say."

I released my hold on the cash. "Collin has nothing to do with any of this. These are my candlesticks, and it's my transaction. Either you buy them or you don't, but that's the only *exchange* going on today."

He sighed and his forehead wrinkled as he considered my words. "Five minutes."

I hesitated.

"Ellie," Collin growled.

I lifted my chin. "Two." What could happen in two minutes?

"*Ellie!*"

Marino smiled. "Deal. If you like, I'll give you the cash now."

I snatched the money from his hand before I changed my mind. Marino laughed as I spun around and handed it to Collin while jerking the candlestick out of his tight hold.

Anger radiated off of him. "What the hell are you doing—have you lost your mind?" he hissed as he leaned close. "Marino is not a guy you can fuck with."

The gravity of what I had just agreed to hit me full force, but we needed the cash. "I have no intention of fucking him," I whispered. "Look, I'm not as innocent as you seem to think. I can handle this." I forced a confidence I didn't feel into my words.

Collin gritted his teeth and turned to Marino, the veins on his neck bulging. "I'm waiting for her outside this door, and if I get the slightest inclination she doesn't want to be here, I'm coming in to get her."

Marino laughed and waved his hand to the door. "The time starts as soon as you leave."

Collin stood with his hand on the doorknob, searching my face.

Go I mouthed, my back still to Marino.

Collin stormed out and slammed the door shut behind him, and the force caused a faded picture with dogs playing poker to shake against the wall.

I spun around, my heart hammering a staccato of fear. "My two minutes starts now."

"No need to worry, Ellie. I only want to talk. I'm curious."

Talking was good. I could do talking. "About what?"

"What is Collin Dailey's interest in you?"

"It's a family thing."

"You're related then? You're not together?"

"Not exactly."

"Not exactly to which question?"

"Both."

He grinned and moved closer. "You're telling me that you're not fucking Dailey?"

I flinched. "That's a rude way to put it."

"Ellie, Collin only fucks women. He never gets into a relationship with them, and he sure as hell never loves them. So why is he so protective of you?"

None of what Marino said surprised me, but his bluntness caught me off guard. "I told you. It's a family thing. He feels obligated."

Marino shook his head. "The only person Collin Dailey feels obligated to is Collin Dailey. If he's not fucking you, and he's keeping you with him, then you must have something he considers valuable."

While that was true, I was sure Marino would never guess what Collin really wanted, and I wasn't going to be the one to tell him.

"One minute," Collin shouted through the door.

Marino turned his head to the side, narrowing his eyes. "Fascinating." Excitement filled his eyes.

My breath hung in my throat. "What?"

"The man outside that door is not behaving like the man I know. Why?"

"I have no idea. He's only helping me sell my candlesticks."

He laughed. "You're a liar. A good one, but Collin gives you away. If he wants you so badly, that makes you incredibly desirable." He reached his hand to my cheek and slid it down to my throat.

I took a step backward. "You think he loves me?"

He laughed again. "Hell no. I told you Collin doesn't love women. He's only capable of loving himself, but you have something that he'll risk his own life for, and that, my darling, is intriguing. I want to know what it is."

"I don't know what you're talking about."

Dropping his hand, he studied me again. "I think you do. This is about the Ricardo deal, isn't it?"

My eyes widened in surprise. What was he talking about?

Marino's grin spread across his face. "I knew it."

The door burst open and Collin filled the doorway. "Time's up. Let's go, Ellie."

I turned around, and Marino moved next to me, blocking my path with his arm. "I want her. I'll pay you for her."

"*Excuse me*?" I said.

Collin's face paled. "She's not for sale."

"Five thousand."

"I said she's not for sale."

"You can't do that!" I shouted, indignant. "You can't sell people!" But I knew that it could be done. Human trafficking was all too real. Who the hell was Collin mixed up with?

Both men ignored me, caught in their own standoff.

Marino plastered a smile on his face and held out his hands. "I'll forgive your debt on that rat trap you call a boat."

Collin's expression weakened.

Marino grinned. "And I'll throw in ten thousand."

Collin paused. "What about my map?"

My eyes bulged in disbelief. "What the *hell* are you doing, Collin?"

Marino waved a hand. "Fine, you can have the map too."

I'm going to vomit. Nausea swept over me, and I couldn't move. Collin was considering Marino's offer. He was going to sell me.

"Why do you want her so much?" Collin asked.

"Because *you* do."

Collin looked at the wall, his face expressionless. "She gave you her two minutes. We had a deal and we've met our end. You're a son of a bitch, Marino, but at least you're known for being a man of your word. Are you going to change that now? *Over her?*" He said the last words with contempt. "I can assure you that she's not worth it. She's one of the worst fucks I've ever had, and you and I both know I've had more than I can count."

Marino turned to me, lowering his voice. "Every word of protest only makes me want her more." He lifted the back of his hand to my cheek and I smacked it away. He chuckled. "But you're right. I am a man of my word."

Collin kept his gaze on Marino, his chin lifted. "Ellie, let's go."

I stepped toward him, lightheaded and shaky, but I forced myself to keep it together and clenched my hands into fists at my sides.

Marino sat in his chair, grunting as he landed. "This isn't over, Collin. We'll visit this again."

"And she'll be history by then."

"Then bring her to me when you're done, and perhaps we'll forget all of this ugliness."

I moved into the storage room, and Collin fell in step behind me, leaning into my ear. "Keep going and don't stop until you get out the front door. Here." He put a set of keys in my hand. "You need to go."

Whipping my head around, my mouth dropped open. "Where are *you* going?"

"I've got something to take care of."

I stopped, but Collin stood behind me and pushed me to the door. "What? The map you were going to sell me for?"

"We don't have time for this, Ellie. Will you just do what I ask?"

"No."

Collin opened the door to the parking lot and dragged me outside. "*For God's sake, Ellie.*"

I jerked out of his grasp. "One of the worst fucks you've ever had? *Are you kidding me?*" I knew standing there yelling at him was stupid. Dangerous even. I needed to get the hell out of there. But anger gave me power and fear made me helpless, so I was hanging onto my anger.

His face reddened. "Get in the truck."

"No."

The veins on his neck and temple throbbed. Collin looked like he was about to have a stroke. "*I swear to God, Ellie*, I will tie you up and gag you if you don't get in the truck *right now*."

He was serious. He would really do it.

When he saw the hesitation on my face, he pushed me toward the driver's door.

I shouted in frustration and pounded my hand on the door panel.

He shoved me inside, climbed in next to me, then wrenched the keys from my grip and drove a block away, pulling into the parking lot of a car wash. "Drive two blocks south, then three blocks east to the Buxton Police Department. Park out front and wait for me. You'll be safe. Marino wouldn't dare touch you there."

"We need to discuss the fact that you considered selling me."

He stopped again and cocked his head. "You seriously can't think I considered selling you to Marino."

I glared. "It sure looked like it to me when you were bargaining with him."

"Are you really that stupid? I need you. As much as it pains me to admit."

"Then I'm not leaving. I'm going with you, Collin."

"The hell you are."

I was more scared than I'd ever been in my life, even more so than last night, and the last thing I wanted to do was go anywhere near that horrible man's business. But I also knew I couldn't be alone. I was sticking with Collin whether he liked it or not. "If you don't take me with you, I'll just follow you."

He pounded his fist into the steering wheel. "Son of a bitch. You are the biggest pain in the ass I've ever met."

"I've made two of your top lists. Yay, me. I'm going."

"I'm not saving your ass next time."

"Yeah, I love you too. Let's go."

ᔔ CHAPTER TWELVE ᔕ

Collin left the truck parked in the car wash parking lot. We hiked across a field toward a warehouse, the weeds scratching my legs. Wearing my lucky skirt meant I wasn't dressed for this, but at least I'd worn my Vans instead of sandals. "What is this map anyway?"

"You don't need to worry about it."

"Is it curse related?"

"Yes."

"Then I get to worry about it. What is it?"

He cursed under his breath. "A map that shows important locations. The portal to the spirit world. The sites where there were temples erected to the gods. The gods might be hiding there while they get stronger."

"You don't think I need to know about that?" I sighed in exasperation. "And you got pissed at me for pawning my cup."

His body tensed, and his fists balled at his side. "The key difference is that I didn't pawn the map. Marino stole it from my brother."

"You have a brother? Younger?"

He stopped and looked down at me in exasperation. "Would I be the Curse Keeper if he were older?" Closing his eyes, he shook his head. "*Please* tell me that you know the answer to that."

I plastered on a fake smile and recited, "The oldest child becomes the Keeper once they turn eighteen." I glared at him. "I learned that when I was four years old."

"Is that *all* you learned?"

"No." I didn't want to discuss my Keeper knowledge, or lack of it, at the moment. "If you weren't going to sell me, why did you pretend to go along with Marino and bargain with him?"

He groaned and resumed his trek across the field. "Ellie, I only played along because I wanted to know if he still had my map. How many times have I told you that I need you? You're no good to me if you're stuck with Marino or dead."

"That has got to be the sweetest thing anyone has ever said to me." Sarcasm dripped from my words.

"Besides, we never would have been in that position if you'd done what I said and kept your mouth shut."

"Marino wasn't going to deal with you."

"He would have come around." But his tone told me he knew it was a lie.

"Why haven't you gotten the map before now?"

"I thought he'd sold it. I never expected him to admit that he had it. My hope was that he'd tell me who he'd sold it to."

"Why would Marino want to buy me?" The possible answer to my question made me queasy.

"Not what you think. I was stupid to bring you here and even more stupid to show my hand to Marino. He knows I don't give a fuck about women so for me to show the slightest bit of interest in you set alarms off in his head. I'm sure he thinks you have some key information that makes you so valuable to me that I don't want you out of my sight. He assumes that means money, and lots of it. Marino sees big fat dollar signs, and he thinks you hold the key to getting it."

Collin's answer appeased me. Sort of. "So is that what you do? Steal things and sell them to Marino?"

Collin grinned with a shrug.

"If he thinks you're going to use me to steal something and then turn around and sell it to him, then why would he want me? Why not just wait for you to bring it to him?"

"To cut out the middleman, Ellie. Any time you can eliminate the middleman, you do it."

I didn't like the way he used the word *eliminate*. "He asked if I knew about the Ricardo deal."

"*Fuck.* It was those goddamn candlesticks." Collin sucked in several deep breaths and shook his head. "There's nothing to be done about it now."

We stopped at a six-foot privacy fence and squatted next to it, Collin peeking through a crack between the boards.

"Is this a good idea?" I asked, pressing my face to the cedar plank. The wood was so old and rough I'd be lucky to not get splinters.

"Theft is always a *bad idea*, Ellie," Collin said with a mocking tone.

"I meant stealing the map right after you confronted Marino, in broad daylight."

"No. If he expects me to try to get it, it would be tonight. Not during the day. No one would be that crazy." He turned to me and smiled a mischievous grin. He thought this was fun. Collin Dailey was one of those freaky, thrill-seeking idiots. He noticed the expression on my face and raised his eyebrows playfully. "Not too late to back out. You can wait right here for me."

I was tempted. Marino scared the shit out of me, and I didn't want to go anywhere near him or anything that belonged to him. But I didn't trust Collin. He kept things from me—like the map—and I needed information so I wouldn't be so dependent on him. If he found the map, who was to say he wouldn't hide it and tell me he hadn't? Like it or not, I was stuck with him. "You can't get rid of me that easily."

His smile broadened, and I swore that there was something in his eyes that looked like a challenge. I hoped I was imagining things.

He pulled his backpack off his shoulder and set it on the ground between us, removing a pair of gloves. "Don't touch anything. Marino won't call the police, but he might look for our prints." He looked up. "You don't have a criminal record do you?"

My head jerked back. "No!"

He turned his attention to his pack. "Then you're probably safe. No prints on file to match you to."

I didn't want to ask about Collin's criminal record. The bolt cutters he pulled out of the backpack he kept stored in his truck answered that question.

"Anything else I should know?"

"Stick close to me. Keep quiet. If we see anyone, let me do the talking."

"Okay."

His mouth pinched with irritation. "You said that last time and look where that got us."

"It got us eighteen hundred dollars, and the whereabouts to your map. You're welcome."

Collin shook his head. "I don't think we'll have any trouble, but if we do, run back to the truck and let me deal with it." He stared into my eyes, a serious expression on his face. "Promise me that you'll listen to me this time."

"You expect me to just leave you?"

"I can get out easier if I'm on my own and I don't have to worry about you."

I grinned. "Awww . . . You're worried about me."

"Although I'm beginning to rethink this belief, for now, dragging you around alive is easier than carting you around dead. If you want to call that worrying about you, then yes, I am." He cocked his head and lifted an eyebrow. "If it makes you feel any better, if I didn't need you, I'd leave you behind without a second thought."

Good to know.

He slung the bag over his shoulder, stuffed his hands into the gloves, and grabbed the bolt cutters. "Let's get this over with."

We skirted the fence until Collin found two loose boards. He lifted them so I could climb through, then he followed behind me. We stood at the back of a mini-junkyard. Old cars, motorcycles, even bikes littered the ground. A large metal building stood in front of us.

Collin pointed to the rusted storage unit. The hundred-foot-long or so structure took up most of the fenced-off area. "I think it's in there."

I trailed behind as he hung close to the building, making his way to the front. Stopping at the corner, he scanned the lot, the muscles on his neck and arms tightening. After a couple of seconds, he held a finger up to his mouth, then pointed around the corner.

I nodded, swallowing the lump of fear in my throat. This was real. We were breaking into this building. While part of me was terrified, a hidden part of me was more alive than I'd ever felt. Well, almost as alive as I felt when I'd been close to Collin that morning. I decided to attribute that occurrence to a phenomenon out of my control. The Curse Keeper blood had caused my reaction, and I'd do best to remember that not only was my reaction not real, but that Collin would screw me and forget about me the minute our job was done. Marino had confirmed that less than a half an hour before.

But this adrenaline rush surging through my own blood had nothing to do with the Curse Keeper magic. Collin may have been one of those thrill-seeking idiots, but it turned out that Elinor Dare Lancaster was too. No one was more surprised than me.

Collin slipped around the corner and motioned for me to wait. The storage shed was locked with a chain and a padlock. All it took were two snips of the bolt cutters before the chain dropped to the ground with a thud. He pushed the sliding door open, looked inside, then motioned for me to come. When I reached him, he pushed me inside, then closed the door behind us, plunging us into darkness.

After my encounter with the spirits last night, darkness wasn't something I welcomed. But I reminded myself that it was bright daylight outside, even if there was hardly any light in here. I ran my thumb along the raised outline of the symbol on my palm, taking comfort that it didn't tingle. At the moment, the real threat was the man in a room several hundred feet away.

Collin flipped on a flashlight, jerking me out of my thoughts. He knew exactly where to go, heading to a row of filing cabinets in the back corner. I trailed along, my eyes adjusting so that I could make out rows of metal shelves on the other side.

Collin handed me the flashlight and whispered, "You might as well make yourself useful. Hold this and shine it in the bag, then where I point."

I took the flashlight and nodded.

He opened a small tool kit and removed several small tools. "Here." He pointed to the lock on the first cabinet. It only took a few jiggles before the lock popped. Collin opened the drawer and started thumbing through files before moving to the next drawer.

"What's it look like?" I whispered.

"A map."

"No shit. Big? Small? Old? Is it original?"

He grimaced. "No, it's not original. The original would have been on an animal skin and probably would have decomposed by now." His condescending tone was beginning to bug the crap out of me.

"So it's new?"

"Not exactly."

I put my hand over his, glaring up into his face. "Then what exactly is it?"

He flipped his hand around and grabbed mine, pressing our palms together. Collin might have been wearing a glove, but that didn't stop the mark on my hand from blazing with power.

The spirits might be getting stronger, but Collin and I were getting stronger too.

He froze, his irritation draining away.

An electrical current danced across my skin. I felt alive. Powerful. Hyperaware of everything around me. There was a cricket in the corner, and spiders crawling behind the cabinets we stood in front of. A bird perched in a tree in the corner of the lot, watching a worm that wriggled across the surface.

I lowered the flashlight, the pool of light shining on my feet.

"You feel it too?" Collin asked, all pretense gone.

I nodded.

"We feel the Manitou." Awe filled his voice.

"What's the Manitou?"

"The life force that flows through every living thing."

It was simultaneously overwhelming and comforting. The sense that there was more than just me or Collin, that there was so much more out there. And we could feel it. Experience it. Being a Keeper meant I had a responsibility, but for the first time I realized I also had a gift.

The current between us drew me closer and I found myself pressed against his chest. I closed my eyes and heard the blood rushing through his veins and the rapid beat of his heart. I reached outside of the two of us and felt a group of flies hovering over a dead mouse in a corner. A cat slinking through the grass. A dog lapping water from a bowl.

My hand burned and my eyes flew open in surprise. I started to jerk away from Collin, but his fingers looped over my hand, keeping our palms together.

"My mark is burning."

Collin's eyes widened. "There's something here."

"Marino?" But before Collin shook his head, I knew it was something worse. I felt it. Something dark and oppressive. It didn't have a physical form, but its presence occupied a space on the other side of the warehouse. Fear mingled with the electrical current flowing throughout my body.

Then the current was gone—Collin had pulled his hand from mine.

"*Shit.*" He shut the drawer and eased open the one below it. "Hold up the light."

I'd forgotten the flashlight in my hand. "You can't be serious. *You're still looking?*"

His eyes were wild. "We need the map."

I could hardly catch my breath. "What's out there, Collin?" I couldn't feel its force anymore, but I knew it was lurking. The mark on my hand was on fire.

"I don't know, but from the strength, I'd say it's a god." He kept his attention on the files, shutting the drawer and moving to the next one.

"There's a vengeful god in this building with us, *yet we're still here*? I'm not staying here waiting for something mean and nasty to get me." I turned around to leave. I only had to make it to the sunlight, and then I'd be safe. I hoped.

Collin grabbed my wrist and pulled me back. "You do *not* want to leave me right now. It *will* get you, Ellie. You need to stick with me, and we'll get out of this together."

My hand shook and the flashlight beam skittered across the ground. "You're going to get us both killed."

His mouth lifted into a sarcastic grin. "Not today." He used his tools on the next cabinet, popping the lock and moving to the top drawer.

The hair on the back of my neck stood on end. Whatever was out there was closer. "Collin!"

"Another second . . ." He pulled an old piece of parchment out of a file and spread it open. "Got it!"

Something cold and heavy tickled my neck. The weight of it buckled my knees. The mark on my palm itched and burned.

An icy dagger dug into my shoulder blade. I screamed.

Collin spun his head toward me, shock and horror on his face.

Whatever had me jerked me backward, and I fell, sliding across the warehouse floor. "Collin!" The flashlight dropped to the floor with a loud clank, rolling toward the wall.

I couldn't see what was pulling me, but I slapped a hand to the spot on my shoulder and felt nothing. *Nothing* was there, yet I felt its grip sink even deeper into my shoulder blade. How the hell did I fight *nothing*? I skittered toward the storage shelves and frantically reached for a metal support beam, looping my fingers around the steel. The spirit continued to pull, the pain in my shoulder unbearable. I swallowed a sob as my legs flew in the air, parallel to the floor. I hung four feet over the ground.

"*Collin!*"

The room had plunged into darkness and I couldn't see him anywhere. And he sure wasn't answering.

The spirit stopped pulling, but kept me hovering over the ground. A cold current of air wound up my bare leg. I kicked and thrashed, but it continued coiling around my calf, up to my thigh. Everywhere it touched, the body heat flowed out of me.

This thing was going to suck the life out of me.

"*Collin!*"

I couldn't die like this, in some dank, nasty warehouse in Buxton. If Marino found my body, he'd probably toss me into the ocean, and Myra would never know what happened to me. Why hadn't Collin taught me the words of protection? *Goddamn him.* And now he'd deserted me just like he promised he would. Maybe he decided I was more useful to him dead after all.

The coil wrapped around my other leg and both limbs went numb.

No! I refused to just give in. I wasn't going out without a fight. Somewhere in my head were the words I needed, hiding behind the mental wall I'd built to block them out. Why couldn't I break through?

I latched onto one word, a word I'd heard Daddy mumble that morning. "*Umpe.*"

The spirit paused for a second before continuing its quest. I began to shiver from the cold seeping in my body.

There were more words. What else had Daddy said? Another word appeared in my head, connected to the first. "*Mowcottowosh umpe.*"

The coiling current of air, now circled around my waist, stopped. Somehow I knew once it hit my chest I'd be dead. I took advantage of the pause to shake my legs. The god's grasp loosened.

The doors to the building flung open, spilling sunlight into the space. The bands around my stomach retracted, but clung to my legs. The dagger in the back of my shoulder was still in place and began to burrow deeper. Fuzziness flooded my head and I fought against it. If I passed out, I was a dead woman.

Collin stood in front of me, holding up his glowing palm and reciting words in the ancient language Daddy had uttered that morning, words I didn't understand.

The god's hold loosened, and I fell, the cement floor knocking the wind out of me. The pain in my right shoulder blade was excruciating.

"Ellie, we have to go." Collin reached his hand toward me, impatience in his voice.

"I'd love to get up," I mumbled, gasping for breath as I crawled toward him, "but the stab wound in my back is making it difficult."

"*What stab wound?*"

Men's voices shouted outside. We'd made enough noise that we were sure to have caught Marino's attention in the building next door.

I climbed to my feet, and Collin grabbed my left arm, throwing it over his shoulder.

"Can you walk?"

I nodded. Now that I was up and the coils were gone, some of the feeling had returned to my legs. I was weak, but the pain in my back was intense, sending waves through my head and threatening to steal my consciousness.

"There's a back panel we can crawl through. It should buy us some time with Marino."

I didn't answer, instead focusing on moving in the direction Collin dragged me. We maneuvered behind the shelves to the back corner. Collin dropped his hold, and I collapsed to my knees.

Collin squatted and went to work on a square in the wall, close to the floor. He slid the panel door to the side, peered out the hole, then looked over at me. "You crawl through first, and I'll be right behind you."

I lowered to my stomach and suppressed a grunt, considering stealth seemed to be top priority, but it wasn't easy. Every part of me ached from dropping to the floor when the spirit released its hold. I belly crawled to the hole and started through the space, but it must not have been fast enough to suit Collin. I felt his hand on my ass, pushing me through. When we were both out, he reached in to slide the panel back in place, then grabbed my arm and dragged me to the fence.

Collin lowered me to the ground and studied my face, looking worried. "Can you walk to the truck?"

I nodded, not trusting myself to talk. I'd crawl to the truck if I had to. There was no way I was sticking behind to let Marino get me.

Collin lifted the boards to the fence and pushed me between the slats. I fell to the ground face-first, but before I had time to roll to my side, Collin had me up and moving. The injury in my shoulder blade was icy cold and now spreading down my back. It took every ounce of energy to keep from fainting. I'd never been a swooning kind of girl, and I refused to give in to it now. Especially around Collin. I'd never hear the end of it if I passed out.

Halfway across the field, my legs gave out, but before I hit the ground, Collin bent down and threw me over his shoulder. As he took off, he braced one of his hands on my upper thigh, beneath my skirt. Lucky for him I was in too much pain to protest.

When he reached the truck, he opened the door and dumped me inside, none too gently. I landed on my side and stayed there while Collin climbed in and tore out of the parking lot, my thoughts slowly fading away.

ᴄ CHAPTER THIRTEEN ᴄ

I drifted in and out of consciousness until I realized Collin had stopped the truck. Two things struck me: I was shivering so violently that I'd bitten the inside of my cheek, and Collin was unbuttoning my shirt.

I slapped at his hand, but my uncoordinated move missed. "What are you doing?"

"Ellie, I have to see."

He had perched me upright with my back in the corner between the seat and the passenger door. I glanced out the windshield and noticed we were surrounded by trees. And nothing else. Why had he taken me into the woods? Panic raced through my body, and I tried to push him away.

My feeble efforts didn't stop his progress. He was obviously used to undressing women, because he had my shirt unbuttoned and tugged off in only a few seconds. Just as I was about to scream, he turned me at the waist and pushed my chest against the door, moving my braid out of the way to look at my back.

"Fuck!" he growled. He opened the glove compartment and threw things around.

"What?" I gasped, trying to catch my breath. "What are you looking for?"

"A pen. A marker. Anything to write with." He grabbed my purse and rifled through it, pulling out an ink pen, then he took hold of my shoulder.

I felt the pressure of the ballpoint on my skin and cried out in pain.

The pen started to move and after a few strokes, my back was on fire, countering the cold. I gripped the frame of the open window, refusing to cry out again. "What are you doing?" I managed.

"Saving your life."

After he finished, the burning sensation continued, but it was easier to breathe. I rested my forehead against the door while the pain subsided. "What happened?"

"In the warehouse or just now?"

"Both."

"You were attacked by a spirit, probably a god."

"I figured that part out already. Was it Okeus?"

There was a pause before he said in a tight voice, "No. I don't think so." He paused. "For one thing, he didn't announce his presence. He's supposed to be arrogant enough that he wants those he appears to to know that it's him. And second, I don't believe Okeus would leave a mark on your back like this thing just did."

"A mark on my back? What the hell are you talking about, Collin?"

"Tell me exactly what happened after it got you."

I turned around, closing my eyes for a second to stop the spinning in my head. "Not until you tell me where you were. Why didn't you help me? Where were you?"

"I was there. I saved you."

"Not right away. Not until the thing almost killed me. *Where were you?*"

He closed his glove compartment. "Tidying up."

"What does that mean?"

"I didn't want to leave any signs that we were there."

"Because the commotion we caused didn't clue them in?"

"We could have been anyone for all Marino knows. If I'd left evidence that it was us, he'd send someone after us."

"Someone scarier than the thing that stabbed me and then wrapped coils around my legs and up my body, zapping the heat from my body?"

"Is that what it did?"

"No, I just made that up. Of course that's what it did. Which god was it?"

"I suspect a wind god. Possibly Wapi, the god of the north. He left his mark on your back. What you felt, him sucking the heat from you—he was consuming your Manitou, like the birds we saw. He left his mark in order to find you later and finish the job."

My heart tried to fling itself from my chest. Now I had two evil gods intent on finishing me off. "What did you write on my back?"

"A symbol to counteract his."

I began to shake again, but this time from fear and not cold. "What's to stop him from finding me and doing it again?"

"The symbol I put on you will protect you from *him* stealing your Manitou. He can still kill you, but not by taking your Manitou. But if any of the other gods takes your Manitou, you'll be condemned to Popogusso."

"I take it Popogusso is someplace I don't want to go?"

"Not unless you have a desire to spend eternity in hell."

I broke out into to a cold sweat. Having the life sucked out of me was worse than I thought. "Duly noted."

"I figured it would take another day or two before they would be strong enough to attack us. Obviously, I was wrong." He sounded a bit pained to admit it.

"Will you teach me to protect myself now?"

He studied me for a moment. "I have something better that I was waiting to bring up. Since you have so blatantly disregarded everything to do with the curse in the past, I figured you'd fight this as well. I was waiting for you to be more accepting of your circumstances."

I cocked my head. I wasn't sure I liked the sound of this. "What is it?"

Collin grabbed the bottom of his T-shirt and began to pull it over his head.

"What are you doing?"

He didn't answer, instead tossing his shirt to the floor.

I scooted back in the seat. "I am not having sex with you."

A cocky grin spread over his face. "That's not why I took off my shirt. Nice to know that was your first thought though."

A blush rose to my cheeks. "Then why did you . . . ?" But I'd figured it out before I finished the sentence. An elaborate Native American symbol was tattooed on his chest, over his heart. A circle intersected with two squares, the eight points similar to the points of a compass. Smaller symbols surrounded the outer area and the center of the circle had a vertical zigzag mark. My mouth dropped open and my eyes rose to his. "You don't expect—"

"No, I don't expect you to get a permanent tattoo, but I've been thinking about it. We can give you a henna mark. It will last for at least a week, long enough to protect you until after the ceremony."

I could live with a henna tattoo, but then I remembered my palm. I held out my outstretched hand. "What about this? Is it permanent?"

He took my hand and traced the outline of the circle, sending shivers up my back. "I'm not sure. I think it probably is."

I sighed. There was nothing I could do about that. I'd wear it the rest of my life as long as it saved my hide and did its job, whatever the job was. "Does the henna tattoo have to be on my chest? It might show through my uniform at work."

He grinned again, still tracing my mark. "No, it can be anywhere on your body, although you wouldn't have to worry with the uniform shirt I saw. Are you a stripper at your second job?"

I shot him a glare.

"The Curse Keepers in the Manteo line have always had the symbol tattooed on our chests on our eighteenth birthday. The day we accept our role."

His words sunk deep in my heart, and I was ashamed at the way I'd ignored my part in this. And now I was paying the price. "What does the symbol mean?"

"I'll explain it to you when I tattoo you."

"*You're* going to do it?"

"I put the mark on your back just now. Besides, I know the symbol and the ceremony."

There was a ceremony? I should have suspected. Native American history was steeped in ceremonies and stories.

I realized that Collin was still holding my hand. And that he was shirtless. And so was I. I tried to pull my hand free, but his fingers dug in as he grinned.

"I can read you like a book, Ellie. You wear your emotions on your face. You'd make a terrible con. I bet you suck at poker."

"Good thing I have no intention of becoming a con." No sense telling him I'd never played poker.

"What do you want to do with your life?" He still wore his grin, but his tone turned serious. "Do you plan on being a waitress the rest of your life? Are you waiting for some rich tourist to show up and sweep you off your feet so you can get your house with a three-car garage and granite counters?"

He had no right to judge me, but he'd heard me tell Oscar pretty much the same thing the day before so I guess I couldn't blame him. I could have defended myself, but instead decided to turn it around on him. "What do *you* want to become? You want to be a thief for the rest of your life?"

The look in his eyes turned wicked.

"You told Lila you lived in Wanchese, and Marino said you had a boat. Are you a fisherman?" Wanchese was the other town on Roanoke Island, the commercial fishing port and where a lot of fishermen lived.

He winked. "Guilty as charged."

"Somehow being a criminal and a commercial fisherman seem contradictory."

"Don't be so sure about that."

"You used to live in Buxton."

"Good job, Detective Lancaster," he teased. "What else have you deduced about me?"

"You have a younger brother."

"That doesn't count. I told you that one."

"You are loyal to your family and traditions."

Surprisingly, the smile fell from his face. "Yes, Ellie I am. To a fault. Don't forget it."

I wasn't sure what that meant and I was afraid to ask, not that I thought he'd tell me anyway. "What does *mowcottowosh umpe* mean?"

His grip tightened. "Where did you hear that?"

I sure wasn't going to tell him that my father had recited it to me in an attempt to drive me away, thinking I was an evil spirit. "I must have heard you say it when you got rid of the god."

"I never said those words."

"Do you know what they mean?"

He turned his head to look out the windshield.

"You do know. Tell me. Why would I know them if you didn't say them?"

"The Manteo Keepers have known things your side doesn't. Information beyond what you should have learned as the Dare Keeper. Manteo performed the ceremony that created the curse, an act he regretted to the day he died. He spent the rest of his life trying to prepare our line for the day the curse broke."

"So why would I know words you didn't use?"

"Those words come from the protection spell for the Dare line. *Mowcottowosh umpe* means 'black water.'"

"Why would black water stop a god?"

"It didn't stop a god. I never said those words."

"Maybe you didn't, but I did. And maybe it didn't stop the god entirely, but it made him pause."

Collin didn't answer, instead staring at the mark on my palm.

"If the god put his mark on me so it could come back to suck my Manitou later, I guess that means it's not dead."

"Gods and spirits don't die. They can only be subdued temporarily or sent back to the spirit world."

"So what did you do to it?"

"I used the power of my Curse Keeper mark along with the words of protection to send him away."

"Why not send him back to the spirit world?"

"Two reasons. One, while I think you and I can take care of lesser spirits on our own, we have to combine our power to send gods and demons back. Like in the warehouse when our palms touched. And two, anything we send back right now won't stay there. The gate to the spirit world is open and it would only return. They will only stay locked away if the gate is closed."

"Will you teach me the words of protection?"

"No."

I started to pull away, but his hand tightened around my wrist.

"I can't teach them to you because you have your own. Our line didn't pass yours down because they assumed you would take your role seriously. Obviously, they were wrong." In spite of his words, his voice was soft and nonaccusatory.

I watched his face. Collin was still hiding things from me, but at least he was finally sharing information. "We're stronger together now. Will our power increase?"

"Probably."

"What do we do with it?"

He looked up and smiled, but it didn't reach his eyes. "So curious now. Where was this curiosity when you were growing up? When you should have learned all of this?"

I had no intention of sharing my ugly past with Collin Dailey, especially when he refused to share his. Some things were better left buried. "What time is it?"

He looked confused. "What?"

"I have to be at work at four. What time is it?"

"A little before noon."

"That early?" It had been an eventful day. I tugged on my hand. "Can I put my shirt on now?"

He dropped his hold. "I never stopped you from putting it back on before."

We both knew that was a lie, but I figured arguing the point would only dig me deeper. We seemed to be working together now so why stir things up again? Besides, I'd sat next to him for several minutes topless except for my white bra, and it seemed to have no effect on him. That was a good thing, so why did it bother me?

Maybe because staring at his bare chest did strange things to my stomach and other lower parts.

Collin grabbed his shirt off the floor as I picked up my blouse off the seat. As he bent over, I noticed more symbols tattooed on his back and his arms. What did they mean? Did I only need just one?

"We can get something to eat on the way back to Rodanthe. Hopefully, Mrs. Evelyn Abernathy will be home, and we can retrieve your cup."

"And get me to work on time, right?" I'd left fifteen minutes early the day before. I needed all the hours I could get.

"There are more important things to worry about than your waitress job." Cranky Collin was back. Yay.

"I have bills to pay, Collin."

"And so do I, Ellie, but look where my priorities lie."

Ah, another dig. And we'd been getting along so well. "We have at least two hours to work on getting the cup back, so calm down."

He tugged his shirt over his head and started the truck. "I'll calm down when this whole mess is over."

"That makes two of us."

We drove out of the woods and back into Buxton. I looked at him in surprise. "Is this a good idea? Shouldn't we get out of here?"

"We should, but since you can't protect yourself from evil spirits, I have to get some supplies so I can mark you."

I needed the mark whether I knew the words of protection or not, but I decided to be the bigger person and not point that fact out.

Collin pulled off the highway at a rundown strip mall, stopping in front of the Curl Up and Dye hair salon.

"Do you need a haircut or are you trying to tell me something?"

He made a face. "Very funny. I have to get something here."

"Is this another front for more shady activities?"

His eyebrows rose as he turned to me. "I just admitted to partaking in nefarious activities earlier so this should come as no surprise. Does that mean you're going to stay in the truck this time?"

"No."

He shook his head with a grimace. "You are the *biggest* pain in the ass."

"You said that already. Let's go." I had the door open and was climbing out.

As we made our way to the front door, Collin leaned toward me. "I suppose asking you to keep quiet and let me do all the talking is wasted breath?"

"Probably." I opened the front door and waved him in. "After you, sir."

He chuckled, although it looked as though it pained him to do so.

When we entered the salon—and I use the word loosely—the eyes of six women fixated on Collin. Their jaws dropped and I could swear one of the customers actually drooled. Then they turned to me and glared. Part of me wanted to tell them that they were hugely mistaken. The last man on earth

I'd be with was Collin Dailey, but Collin would have loved that a little too much. No sense feeding that man's ego any more than it already had been.

One of the beauticians sauntered toward him, her hips swinging so much it was a wonder they didn't cause an earthquake. Collin gave her an appreciative leer.

She stopped in front of him, giving him a seductive pout. "What can I do for you, sugar?"

Collin glanced down at her wedding ring, then back up to her. "Seeing how you're already married, I suppose I'll have to settle for second best now."

The woman touched her mouth and actually looked like she was about to blush. *Please.* I couldn't believe women fell for this bullshit.

"Any chance Rosalina is here?"

The woman grinned. "Rosalina, huh? Yeah, she's in the back on break." She looked over her shoulder and yelled, "*Rosalina!*"

A Hispanic woman poked her head out from the back room. "Yeah?"

"A gorgeous man is here asking for you."

A woman who looked to be in her early twenties walked out and smiled. "Collin." She glided toward him with a grace no one else in this salon possessed—in fact few women alive possessed that kind of grace. She was beautiful, and not the made-up beauty most of the women here were trying to achieve. Her thick, long, black hair was pulled back into a braid, but it looked loose and messy in a fashion model kind of way. Her face was practically makeup free, but her thick dark lashes made it apparent she didn't need mascara. She was beautiful, and she was the perfect counterpart to Collin's good looks. Brad and Angelina had nothing on these two.

When she reached him, she put her hands on his arm and stood on tiptoes to kiss his cheek. "Where've you been the last month?"

"Around."

That was an interesting piece of information. I had a feeling Collin was new to Wanchese. Had he moved there a month ago? Why? I took a step closer to them. "Aren't you going to introduce us, Collin?" I'd planned to actually sit back and observe this outing, but this opportunity was too good to pass up.

Collin's shoulders tightened. "Rosalina, this is Ellie. Ellie, Rosalina."

That was a disappointment. I wanted more information. "Nice to meet you, Rosalina. How do you two know each other?"

Rosalina looked from Collin to me, then back again. She didn't look amused. Was she jealous? *Of me?* "Family friends. And you?"

"I guess you could say the same."

"So then you two aren't together?"

Collin laughed. "Rosalina, you know me better than that."

What the hell did that mean? That I wasn't good enough to get laid by the demigod Collin Fucking Dailey? Again, why did I care?

I rolled my eyes and scoffed. "As if. I have no interest in him."

The woman looked surprised, as did the other women in the salon, all of whom were listening to our conversation. An old woman looked over her shoulder at the woman cutting her hair. "Is she one of those *lesbians*? You know they're quite popular now."

I started to set her straight, but what did I care what these women thought? Instead, Collin patted my head like I was a puppy. "Yes, she is. She's into alternative lifestyles, which is why I need to talk to you, Rosalina."

I didn't like the sound of where this was going.

He moved to a corner with her, and he whispered something. She nodded and whispered to him, then disappeared in the back room. His eyes found mine. "Ellie, why don't you wait in the truck?"

He was up to something, and I'd bet my ass it was something no good. "I think I'll stick around."

A few minutes later, Rosalina returned with a brown paper bag. They whispered again and Collin handed her some cash. She glanced down at it, then kissed him on the cheek again. But the way her hands clung to his arm and her lips lingered on his cheek told me she wanted more. Did Collin not want her or was she smart enough to not act on her desire, steering clear of Collin the man-whore?

Collin spun around and grabbed my arm, maneuvering me toward the door.

"What was that about?" I asked when we reached the sidewalk.

He grinned. "Jealous?"

My forehead wrinkled in confusion. "Jealous? Jealous over *what*?" I climbed into the truck and waited for him to get in on the other side. "I want to know what's in the paper bag."

"You really have to ask?" He started the truck and was about to back up when Rosalina burst out the door, a white paper in her hand.

She moved to the driver's side door and handed Collin an envelope through the window. "Conner said to give this to you when I saw you."

Collin's hand tightened on the steering wheel. "Conner knew I'd come see you?" This obviously sounded like bad news to Collin.

"Yeah, about a week after you left, he brought it to me and told me to have everything ready."

I leaned over the brown bag that sat between us, nudging the top open with my finger. All I could make out was a box, a folded piece of paper, and a few cuticle sticks.

Collin jerked the envelope from Rosalina's hand. His jaw clenched. "Connor needs to stay the fuck out of it."

She held her hands up as she backed up to the curb. "Don't shoot the messenger."

Collin ignored her and backed out of the space.

I watched Rosalina standing on the curb, a sad look on her face. "Who's Conner?"

If looks really could kill, the one Collin gave me then would have made it look like I'd been attacked by a serial killer. "None of your fucking business."

So our truce was over. Again.

ᵔ CHAPTER FOURTEEN ᵕ

Collin stopped at a convenience store and pulled up to a gas pump. "I'm going to go pay for gas. I suggest you head to the bathroom and then get something to eat."

"What am I, six years old? I think I can figure out my own bodily functions."

He actually grinned.

I grabbed my purse, and he followed me into the store, standing so close I could feel the heat steaming off his body.

"What are you, my bodyguard?"

"When you're in Buxton, yes."

Marino. For once I kept my sarcastic comments to myself.

He followed me to the women's restroom, looking like an attentive boyfriend. Several women in the store cast looks of longing and jealousy in our direction. If they only knew.

"I'm going to get us something to eat and pay for the gas. I can keep an eye on the restroom door most of the time, but if you have any trouble, scream."

I nodded and swallowed.

"Where's your phone?"

"What?" But it didn't take a genius to know we might need to call each other. I dug it out of my purse and handed it to him.

He punched his number in. After answering his phone, he handed mine back to me. Then he opened the bathroom door and pushed me in. "If you don't see me when you open the door, stay inside until you do."

I closed the door behind me and locked it, thinking about how flimsy those little locks on doorknobs actually were. Marino only had to slam the door with his massive body and it would come crumbling down. But then, people like Marino never did the dirty work. They got someone else to do it for them.

After I finished my business, I washed my hands and looked at myself in the mirror. I could see why Rosalina had looked at me in surprise if she thought that Collin and I were together. While she was supermodel perfect, I was average height, average weight. Pretty, but with an average face. My dark red hair was unruly most of the summer, and my skin was so pale it literally glowed under black light.

Why was I comparing myself to Rosalina?

I had no delusions that Collin was interested in me, and even if he was, if I were smart, I'd steer clear of getting involved with him. But then there was the history of my failure with men. Did I expect too much, hoping for the kind of relationship Daddy had with Momma? Should I learn to settle?

I shook my head with a sigh. Now was not the time to reason out my love life. Or lack thereof.

There were dirt smudges on my white shirt. I grabbed a wet paper towel and scrubbed it clean the best I could. We still had to see Evelyn Abernathy, and I didn't want to look like a homeless beggar.

When I opened the door, Collin stood in front of the refrigerated case, but he was with two men and none of them looked happy.

". . . wouldn't know anything about that. I've been at the Curl Up and Dye all morning," Collin said. "If you don't believe me, stop by and check it out for yourself. The ladies loved having me there."

One of the guys, a muscled guy who stood taller than Collin, crossed his arms. "I'm sure they did."

"Anything else I can do for you boys?" Collin asked.

"Where's the girl?" the other guy asked.

Collin leaned his shoulder into the glass. "I left her at the Curl Up and Dye. Why do you ask?"

"Marino's not done with her."

"Unfortunately for Marino, I'm not done with her either."

"Should we remind you what happened the last time you pissed off Marino?"

Collin rubbed his jaw. "That's not necessary."

"He's giving you two days."

Collin gave them a half-shrug and a smirk. "I'll keep that in mind."

The men walked away and I heard the tinkle of the entrance door. Collin turned to look down the hallway. When he saw me, he held up a finger and pointed to the bathroom. I went back inside and locked the door.

Marino was serious. I felt a little safer knowing that Collin needed me until we repaired the curse, but I had no delusions that he'd protect me when this was done. What would I do then?

My cell phone rang in my purse and I jumped, startled out of my thoughts. When I dug it out, I saw an unfamiliar number. Oh, God. Had Marino found out who I was? All he knew was my first name. What if he'd found out my last name and got my number?

"Hello?" I answered with a shaky voice.

"Meet me at the back exit in five minutes. I'll call you when I'm ready." Collin hung up and didn't wait for me to answer.

Less than five minutes later, Collin called again. "I'm pulling around back. Come out, get in, and stay low." Then he hung up again.

Taking a deep breath, I exited the bathroom, my stomach a jittery ball of nerves.

A middle-aged woman braced her butt against the hallway wall. She threw up her hands in exasperation. "Took you long enough!"

"Sorry." I turned my attention to the store, and when I didn't see Marino's men, I headed down the hallway to the exit. Collin's truck was rounding the back corner of the convenience store. I waited until he pulled up next to the door before I ran to the passenger door and climbed in. I yanked the door shut, but Collin was pushing my head down.

"They're watching me, and they're going to wonder why I drove back here. I'm pulling over to the air pump and putting some air in my tire. Stay down."

He didn't have to tell me twice.

He stopped the truck and hopped out. I crouched on the floor of the truck, thankful for the first time that Collin drove an old clunker from when they made vehicles big and their interiors bigger.

I heard the sound of the air pump and then a minute later, the driver door opened. I lifted my head in alarm, relieved to see Collin slide in the seat and shift the truck into drive.

After several minutes, I asked, "Can I get up now?"

"Yes. I haven't seen any sign of them for a few miles."

I climbed up on the seat, smoothing my skirt over my legs.

Collin cast a glance in my direction and grinned. "No sense doing that. I already had a look up your skirt earlier."

Resting my elbow on the open window ledge, I leaned my head on my hand. "I hope you enjoyed the view." But my words lacked the sarcastic punch required to make it effective.

Collin didn't seem to notice. "I've seen better."

My day had sucked and it wasn't even one o'clock. So much for my lucky skirt. My close call with Marino's men had put me at the edge, but Collin's statement was the final straw. It was stupid and immature and irrational, but tears filled my eyes, and I tried to swallow the burning lump in my throat.

Collin turned toward me, horror on his face when he realized I was close to tears. Not the *what can I do to help her* kind of horror or even the *I've gone too far and hurt her feelings* horror either. It was the flat-out disgust of a man caught in a truck with a crying woman.

"Leave me the fuck alone!" I shouted. I wanted to jump out of the moving truck and die from embarrassment and massive internal injuries.

His hand tightened on the steering wheel. "I didn't mean what I said about your ass. You have a very nice ass." It was halfhearted and he obviously said it to get me to stop crying.

"Shut up, Collin!"

His hand flopped over, palm open as he tried to make his point. His mark was in plain view. "I'd say you rank at least in the top fifty percent, maybe even top twenty."

I gritted my teeth. "*Shut. Up.* I'm not crying over your immature comment about my ass, so get over yourself."

He looked stunned.

"I don't give a flying fuck what you think of my ass, and you better get that through your head right now!" I shouted, and it felt good. It was like letting the valve off a pressure cooker that had been building all day.

Collin looked confused. "Okay . . ."

"I was almost killed by an angry wind god, and Jabba the Hutt wants to buy me. I think that grants me a few seconds of tears."

He paused, then slowly nodded. "Yeah, I guess you're right."

"And when I came to in the woods, you were stripping my shirt off without explanation—"

"You were unconscious!"

"—you just started drawing on my back with a fucking ink pen—"

"I was saving your life!"

"And you told Marino he can have me when you're done with me. What the fuck? I am not someone's possession!"

"Again, trying to save your life."

"And I'm a lousy fuck? What the fuck was that?"

Collin grinned.

"What the fuck are you smiling about?"

He smirked. "Before a minute ago, I probably heard you say fuck less than a handful of times. In the past thirty seconds, I've lost count."

"How often I say fuck is none of your fucking business."

He lifted a shoulder with a sheepish grin. "True. I'm a fan of the word myself." He smirked. "In more ways than one."

I punched him in the arm. "You do not get to laugh at me when I'm pissed at you."

He smiled. "I can't help it. You're kind of cute like this."

Cute was the last word I expected Collin Dailey to use, especially regarding me.

He held up his hands in surrender. "Go ahead and cry if you want to. I'm not stopping you."

"Shut up!" I yelled and hit his arm again.

He reached over his chest and covered my hand with his left one, probably to avoid our marks touching. "You've got quite the temper." He looked over with something in his eyes I hadn't seen before. Appreciation? Respect?

I snatched my hand from his and turned my back to him.

"So are you going to cry or not? I've got to warn you that I don't have any tissues."

"I don't feel like crying anymore." It was true. My anger had dried up my tears.

"For the record, I officially retract my first comment about your ass. However, to make a final judgment, I'd really need to see it again." His hand lifted the edge of my skirt.

I slapped his hand. "Not a chance."

His hand covered mine again. "I'm sorry."

My jaw dropped, and I turned around to face him. I never, ever expected to hear Collin Dailey apologize for anything. Ever.

"You've been through a lot this morning and you've handled it so well, I never questioned how you were *really* handling it." He shrugged. "I've had my fair share of incidents and this morning set me on edge. I can't imagine what it's done to little Ellie Lancaster of Roanoke Island, whose life goal is to be a waitress and get married."

I could have taken offense at his statement, but it was obvious he meant no malice. This was Collin's way of apologizing. I was flabbergasted. "Thanks."

His face turned serious. "It's going to get worse before it gets better."

I nodded. I'd figured that out already.

He swallowed, clearly uncomfortable. This was probably as honest as Collin got with someone. "Look, I'll help you the best I can with this, but I'm not really . . . that kind of guy."

"I know. I don't expect you to be."

His eyebrows rose in surprise.

"I'm not blind, Collin. I know who you are, or rather what you are. I don't expect anything from you other than information, and to do your part in the ceremony. You don't owe me anything, and it's not your fault if I've forgotten everything about being the Dare Keeper."

He seemed to accept my answer. "So how about we start again?"

"And how many times would that be that we started again?"

"Does it matter?"

I shook my head. Collin was making an effort. Who was I to argue? "How did you get involved with Marino anyway?"

Collin shifted in his seat, looking out the windshield. "It's a long and sordid tale all revolving around a boat."

"*Your* boat?"

"Yep. The *Lucky Star*. It was my father's. My family have been commercial fishermen for generations. The Croatan were fishermen. We like to follow tradition."

"Is your brother a fisherman too?"

His face hardened. "No, he turned his back on his family and our tradition."

"You mean he doesn't believe in the curse?"

He sighed. "No."

I supposed if his brother was younger, it didn't matter if he believed or not. Collin was the Keeper. But I could see how it must have hurt Collin. Just like I'd hurt my father.

"You went to Marino for money?"

"My father knew Marino. My father up and left one day, fifteen years ago. We never saw him again. There were bills and I was a kid, barely ten, but I was the man of the family. I felt a responsibility to take care of my mother and my little brother. On weekends I worked on a boat with my uncle, and he'd pay me."

"You were a kid, Collin. It wasn't your responsibility."

He shook his head and glanced at me. "You don't understand, Ellie. It's the way of our family. I dropped out of high school my junior year and started fishing on my father's boat. But it was old and hadn't been used for several years. I needed money to fix it. Money I didn't have. My dad used to deal with Marino. A couple of months after my dad disappeared, Marino stopped by and told me if there was anything my family needed to come seek his help. So I did."

I knew about that kind of responsibility and that kind of desperation. Collin and I were more alike than I realized.

"It started as small jobs for him and then I branched out on my own. He'd buy whatever I had. Before I realized it I was too deep to get out. When you get caught up in Marino's web, there's really no getting out of it. Not permanently. I've tried before, and it doesn't work."

"So why don't you sell the boat and start over with something else?"

A hardness covered his face. "Some of us want more than husbands and fancy houses."

"And who the hell says that's what *I* want, Collin? You hear one thing out of context and think the worst of me."

"So what do you want?"

I released a loud sigh. "Honestly, I have no idea. I've spent twenty-three years feeling like I didn't fit in anywhere. Like I couldn't find my place in the world. Something was always missing. Maybe this was it."

Collin was silent for a moment. "I know what you mean."

"So what happens when it's over? When we close the gate? Do we just go back to our lives before?"

Collin shifted uncomfortably. "I don't know."

He was lying. For a man who usually snowed women, he sucked at lying to me.

"So we get my cup, then what?"

"Hopefully, we get your cup this afternoon, then we'll go mark you with the symbol."

"After I get off work."

"Ellie," he grumbled.

"Look, you have Marino for money. I have my job at the New Moon. And while you think I'm using my money to buy new shoes, I'm really helping keep my father's bed and breakfast afloat. So you're not the only one fighting to find money for family obligations."

He looked surprised. "I had no idea."

"I know. And now you do. I don't tell many people. I'm not sure why I told you."

He turned to me. "I don't tell anyone my story either. So I guess we're even."

We were far from even, but I'd save that until later.

⌐ CHAPTER FIFTEEN ⌐

After encountering Marino's men at the convenience store, Collin had been in such a hurry he hadn't gotten food. The last thing I'd eaten was the muffin at Myra's around seven that morning. Collin must have realized the last thing he'd seen me consume was the coffee he brought me. After my earlier emotional outburst, he was probably worried I'd freak out again. He stopped in Avon and picked up sandwiches and bottles of water. I had to admit that I felt better after I ate something. I even felt hopeful. Collin and I had reached a new level in our partnership and for the first time, I let myself think that I was capable of helping Collin close the gate.

It was after two o'clock when we reached Rodanthe. Collin parked in front of Mrs. Abernathy's house. A car was parked in the carport.

Collin turned off the engine and pointed to the car. "Okay, Ellie. Lesson one in the art of casing a place. Figure out as much as you can about your mark."

"You mean victim."

He shrugged. "Semantics." He turned to me. "Tell me what you know about Mrs. Evelyn Abernathy."

"She lives in a beach house."

He pursed his lips and gave a slight nod. "I was hoping for more than that. What does the fact that she lives in a beach house tell you?"

"That she has money."

"Good, but not necessarily. It might have been a family property that she's hanging onto by her fingernails. I suspect that's not the case here. Why?"

I remembered looking inside the house the night before. "The inside. The kitchen looked new and the furniture was nice."

"Good. What else?"

I studied the house again. "Her car. It looks expensive."

"It is. It's a Lexus. And not just a Lexus, an ES."

"Is that supposed to mean something?"

He shook his head in mock disgust. "Any self-respecting gold digger would know her Lexus models."

"I'll add that to my to-do list."

"Good girl. Nothing but the best luxury car for you." He tapped my nose.

I batted his hand away. "So why do we care about this?"

"She has money, and she bought the cup in a pawnshop. She's a collector, and she knows her stuff. She knows the real steals aren't in the antique malls but the grungy places. She's not afraid to get her hands dirty to find just the right piece. But I don't think she has an emotional attachment to it."

"How would you know that?"

"The way she displayed her books and knickknacks. It was all very put together and organized. The displays of a collector with an emotional attachment have a more 'lived with' look. The collectors read the books. They use the bowls. They handle the pewter cups." He looked at me. "But the serious collector displays for maximum exposure. They want people to see the fruit of their search. It's a game, and part of the game is displaying the trophy. We're lucky. She'll be more likely to sell it since she doesn't have an emotional attachment, but that means money matters to her. It will cost more."

My eyes widened in disbelief. "Where did you learn that?"

"Casing the Joint 101 at the school for Mischief and Shenaniganry, of course. I think I passed you in the hall on the way to Entrapping the Eligible Billionaire Bachelor."

I couldn't help grinning. "Very funny. So what do we do with all of this?"

"We use it to get what we want. We use everything at our disposal to get what we want. Always."

That came as no surprise. I'd learned that the day before, but I was surprised he admitted it.

"Let me do all the talking."

"It's my cup, Collin."

He turned to me in exasperation. "I have more experience with this, Ellie."

There was no arguing with that, but my gut reaction was that it would be best to go with the emotional ploy. Nevertheless I was glad we had money. "Are you going to pay for it? You still have the eighteen hundred dollars."

"More like sixteen hundred dollars."

"*What*?"

"I had to get gas. And then food."

"Gas and food don't cost two hundred dollars, Collin. Where did the rest go?"

"I had to pay for the supplies for your henna tattoo."

I remembered him handing a bill to Rosalina, and my anger exploded. "You paid one hundred dollars for henna supplies? There's no way on God's green earth they cost that much."

He shrugged. "I gave Rosalina a tip."

"You paid her one hundred dollars. With *my* money?"

"Consider it a finder's fee."

"It's *my* money, Collin." Knowing he paid one of his many women with *my* money pissed me off more than I cared to admit. "Give it to me."

"Give you what?"

"*My* money. Hand it over *now*. I only gave it to you before because I didn't feel like holding that much cash when Marino felt me up."

Collin's gaze turned murderous. "Marino felt you up?"

I gave him a dirty look. "I'll never kiss and tell. Now give me my money."

"*You kissed him*?"

"Will you just give me my damned money already!"

He reached into the glove compartment, pulled out a wad of bills, and handed it to me. I counted the stack. "Nice try. There's only twelve hundred here. I want the rest."

"I took you to Marino. That has to count for something."

"Yeah, it means I owe you a swift kick in the nuts. I wanted to go to Oscar. I can guarantee you that I wouldn't be in this trouble if I'd gone to him."

Collin didn't protest, instead pulling out his wallet, then taking out three hundred dollars and handing it to me.

I continued to hold out my hand. "The rest?"

"What the hell, Ellie? Are you going to nickel and dime me over this?"

"Yes."

He handed me another bill. "There."

I suspected there was more but decided to let it go for now. I stuffed the money into my purse and hopped out of the truck, walking toward Mrs. Abernathy's house.

Collin ran after me, moving in front of me and blocking my path. "What the hell do you think you're doing?"

"Getting my cup, now get out of my way."

His eyes widened in fear. "What's your plan?"

"Do you really think coming up with a plan to con this woman out of her cup should be discussed out here in the open?

"No, it shouldn't. Let's go back to the truck." He grabbed my bicep and started to drag me to the curb.

He was never going to cave, and I wasn't willing to make a scene.

"Let go. I have to tie my shoe or I'm going to trip."

Grumbling, he released his hold. I bent down and pretended to mess with my shoestring, then bolted for the door. The look of surprise on Collin's face when I looked over my shoulder was priceless. But it only took him a half second to catch up to me on the back deck. Just as I knocked on the door.

"Ellie, let me handle this," he growled through gritted teeth.

"Kiss my ass, Collin," I muttered back.

"You fuck this up, and I'll do more than that to your ass."

Why did that send a shiver up my back? *Focus, Ellie.*

An older woman made her way to the door and my stomach began to flip-flop. Damn. In my determination to beat Collin to the door, I hadn't come up with a plan yet.

She wore capri pants and a blouse that looked freshly pressed. Her white-gray hair was cut short and she wore makeup, but in a fresh sort of way. She opened the door and gave me an inquisitive perusal. I knew I looked like a hot mess. My shirt was still stained despite my effort to clean it in the restroom in Buxton and my legs were covered in scratches. Collin had said she was a serious collector, and I had no doubt about that, but the softness in her eyes when she took in the sight of me made me rethink our tactic.

Her eyes shifted from me to Collin and back again as she held onto the door. "Can I help you?"

"I hope so." I paused. "Mrs. Abernathy?"

She nodded, but looked nervous.

"I'm so sorry to bother you and I know I really shouldn't be here but . . ." My voice broke.

Wariness filled her eyes and she took a step back.

"You bought a pewter cup at the pawnshop in Kill Devil Hills. My boyfriend left me and he stole a bunch of my things and pawned them. I didn't know until it was too late. I went to get my cup and I found out it had been sold." This time I forced my voice to break. "I'm so sorry to show up at your door, and I'm not supposed to know who bought it, but I accidently found out who you were and I just had to see if there was any chance of getting it back."

She looked up at Collin. At least she hadn't sent me packing. She looked him over and narrowed her eyes. "Your boyfriend pawned it?"

I glanced over at Collin and looped my arm around his, leaning into him. "Oh, no! Enrique's not my boyfriend," I laughed. "Enrique's gay." I hugged his arm. "I don't know what I'd do without him after Tony left and destroyed everything."

The woman frowned.

She wasn't going to talk to me. Maybe I should have done this Collin's way. What would we do if we couldn't get it back? I was tired and scared and started to cry, real tears. "Please, I know I have no right to be here. The cup doesn't look like much, but it was my mother's." My voice broke again, and I wiped a tear from my face. "It's one of the few things I have left of hers."

The tension eased from her body and she took a step back. "Come in, both of you come in."

We followed her into the living room. I still clung to Collin's arm, and I looked up, giving him an evil grin. The glare he gave me said I'd pay for this later. Mrs. Abernathy motioned to the sofa, and I pulled Collin down next to me.

"Why don't you start from the beginning?" she said as she sat in an overstuffed chair next to us.

I leaned my head into Collin's shoulder and gave her a sad smile. "My ex-boyfriend Tony just swept me off my feet and before I knew it, he moved in with me. But it didn't take long before he started staying out late, and things started going missing. Just little things at first, things I thought I'd misplaced, but Enrique here told me 'Girl, he's stealing your stuff.' Didn't you, Enrique?"

Collin's arm tensed, but he gave me a goofy grin, tilting his head. "I warned you." He looked up at Mrs. Abernathy and raised his eyebrows in an exaggerated lift. "She's stub-born. This girl won't listen to a *word* I say." His hand squeezed my arm in a painful grip.

I had to stop myself from giggling. Collin was playing his role, digs at me and all.

I took a deep breath to focus. "Tony was just so . . ."

"Nerdy?" Collin supplied.

"No."

"Lacking in the bedroom?"

"*No.*"

Collin's eyes widened and he leaned toward the woman across from us. "Marianne was always complaining about how disappointing he was, and I was like, 'You need to find you a real man.'" He tilted his head to the side, his eyes widening. "Like that Collin fellow that comes into the Short Stop I work at. That boy is *fine.*"

I gritted my teeth. "Enrique, you and I both know that Collin fellow is worse than Tony. Out of the fryin' pan into the roaring bonfire with that boy."

Collin tilted his head toward me and nodded with a smug smile. "But I'm sure he's much better than Tony in the bedroom."

I pinched my lips together, my eyebrows rising. "That's not what I heard, but then, poor Mrs. Abernathy doesn't want to hear about *your* fantasy man." I patted his leg and turned to her. "I'm sorry about that. Enrique is just a little protective of me."

He patted my knee. "Especially since the accident." He nodded with a knowing look.

Her eyes widened. "What accident?"

Collin tilted his head toward me. "Sweetie, go on ahead and tell her about the accident."

I was going to murder him the minute we got out of this house. "Enrique, love. That's not why we're here. We're here to see about my cup."

He waved a hand in the air. "Don't you let her fool you. The accident is part of it."

"*Enrique.*"

"What accident?" Mrs. Abernathy asked.

"Well . . ." I stammered. "Enrique is making too much of it really. I was in a car accident. But it was just a fender bender." I waved my hand. "No big deal."

"Um, um, um. That's not it, precious. You don't have to hide it anymore." Collin leaned forward. "Don't you let her fool you." He turned to me and patted my cheek. "You are *so* brave. It's okay, you can trust this kind woman." Collin turned back to her again. "I keep telling her that she has to let people in. She has to learn to *trust* again. You know?"

"Enrique, you're getting much too personal with poor Mrs. Abernathy. Perhaps you should wait in the car."

She shook her head. "Oh no. He's such a good friend. You're so lucky to have him."

Collin gave me a smug smile. "Hear that? I keep telling you that all the time."

My fingernails dug into his arm. "And you know how much I appreciate it."

Collin shook his head. "That boy stole her things and sold 'em for drug money. Can you imagine? Family heirlooms."

I reached out and put my hand on Mrs. Abernathy's knee. "I can live without most of it. They're just things, you know? But one in particular is precious to me. It belonged to my mother. It was the one thing I have left since she died when I was a little girl." Real tears came to my eyes. "It's an antique pewter cup and I know that you bought it. I have money to pay you for it. I'll even pay you more than you bought it for. I'm begging you to please understand and help me get the last piece of my mother back."

"Is that the accident Enrique mentioned?"

"Yes," I said, cutting off Collin. "My mother was killed when I was little, in a horrible accident, and my life hasn't been the same since then." To my horror, my voice broke as I held back a sob. Her death had affected everything in my life. The curse included. I'd vowed that I was done with the curse after she died. *Because* she died. My mother's death left a gaping hole in my heart that was never filled, no matter what I did to fix it.

"I'm so sorry," she said quietly.

"The cup has been in our family for years, and honestly, Tony pawned and sold some much more valuable things. I don't care about any of them. I realize the cup doesn't look like much, but it was the most priceless thing I owned. If you could consider—" My chin trembled and I wiped a tear from my face. "If you would just think about selling it back to me, I'd be forever grateful."

She stood and leaned over to give me a hug. "You poor thing. Of course I'll sell it back to you."

"Thank you."

The cup was still on the shelf we saw it on the night before. She pulled it down and handed it to me. "Here you go, dear."

I hugged it to my chest, grateful I'd actually gotten it back. "How much do I owe you?"

"Five hundred dollars."

"Only five hundred dollars?" I asked in surprise. I knew she paid more than that. "You don't want more? Are you sure?"

Collin squeezed my arm. "Of course she's sure, *sweetie*. Don't be questioning Mrs. Abernathy."

Mrs. Abernathy nodded, "Yes, I'm sure. Five hundred."

Holding the cup in one hand, I dug five one hundred dollar bills out of my purse. I stood and handed her the money, then hugged her tight. "Thank you." My tears made my voice crack. The guilt of this woman losing money to help me was about to do me in. I lied to her and took advantage of her kindheartedness. I tried to comfort myself with the knowledge that I might actually be saving her life.

Mrs. Abernathy took a step back and patted my face. "You take good care of that cup now."

I nodded.

"And be careful about who you give your heart to. Too bad Enrique isn't . . . your type."

Collin twisted his face into an exaggerated smirk. "Don't you know it."

"You're so lucky to have a friend like Enrique." She patted Collin's arm. "And maybe you should give that Collin a chance. You just never know."

"See?" Collin said. "Even Mrs. Abernathy thinks you should give that fine man a chance."

I pushed him toward the door. "Thank you again, Mrs. Abernathy."

"God bless you, dear," she said standing in the doorway, watching us head to the steps. "You take good care of her, Enrique."

"Don't you worry your pretty little head about that. I'll take care of her all right."

He pushed the small of my back, practically shoving me down the stairs and toward the truck. I was too busy clinging to the pewter cup to care. We had my relic. Now we only needed Collin's and we were set.

We got in the truck, and Collin turned to me with a glare. "Your gay friend?"

"I'm lousy in bed?"

He waved his hand from his face to his abdomen. "What about this suggests that you can call me gay?"

"Do you really want to ask that? Besides, it worked. When will you learn to trust me?"

His mouth tightened. "When will you start doing what I ask?"

"Probably never."

"Well, there you go." His grimace made his mouth pucker.

He left the neighborhood and pulled onto the highway, his irritation ebbing after a few miles. "Did you have that planned when you knocked on her door?" I heard appreciation in his voice.

I curled my feet underneath me. "No. I worked it out as I went along."

He laughed. "Are you sure you didn't take Con Artist 101? You're a natural."

"I was too busy in my Entrap Your Man With Hot Sex lab." What possessed me to say that? The adrenaline rush for what we just got away with was making me reckless.

"They have a lab for that?"

His eyebrows rose and he looked me up and down, a different look in his eye than I was used to seeing. What was it? Respect? Lust? My brain wasn't sure I liked his change in attitude toward me, but my traitorous body did, tingling in unmentionable places. I shrugged. "Gotta make sure I can ensnare my rich husband, right? Obviously, I need help with the exterior package since my ass doesn't meet the Collin Dailey QA standards." Good God. What the hell was I doing? It was as though I was drunk. I was drunk on thievery.

A grin spread across his face, but both hands gripped the steering wheel so tight that his knuckles turned white, as though if he let go, his hands might do something he'd regret.

Now that was a laugh and a sure sign that my imagination had jumped into overdrive. I doubted there was much in Collin's life he regretted.

"Good story about your mom. That sealed the deal. And the tears. Perfect." He shook his head. "I never thought you had it in you, Ellie Lancaster."

I looked out the window, my euphoria evaporating.

Collin must have sensed my mood change. "That was a story, wasn't it?"

My throat burned, and I blinked to keep the tears in my eyes from falling. *I will not cry. I will not cry.* I took a deep breath and exhaled. "No. My mother died when I was little."

He paused. "Was the cup hers?"

"No. My father was the Keeper before me." We sat in silence for several seconds. I looked out the windshield, refusing to look at Collin. "My father told me the Curse Keeper stories before I could talk. Daddy took his role very seriously, and my preparation to take over when I was eighteen, even more so. He worked at the Fort Raleigh National Historic Site visitor center, the home of the Lost Colony, always watching. Always waiting. My mother, on the other hand, did *not* believe." I bit my lip. "She was an archaeologist at the site and thought the curse was nonsense. She always told me to remember that they were just stories. But she loved my father more than the air she breathed, and he loved her just as much, so she indulged us our *fairy tales* as she called them. But I could tell she hated every minute of it."

I took a deep breath and rested my elbow on the window, my head in my hand. I turned to Collin. "We were perfect. The perfect family until everything changed."

Collin swallowed, looking uncomfortable. "What happened?"

"One cold and stormy winter night when I was eight years old, a man broke into our house." I released a dry laugh. "It sounds so freaking cliché doesn't it?"

Collin didn't answer, his gaze on the road.

I should stop. It was obvious from the horrified look on Collin's face that he didn't want to know the intimate, ugly details of my life, but I'd suppressed it for so long, once I opened the door, it was all rushing out. Besides, he deserved an explanation. "Daddy wasn't home. He was at a meeting or something. Momma had just gotten me ready for bed. I remember I was wearing my favorite nightgown. It was long and white and very lacy. I always felt like a princess when I wore it. I was picking out a book to read with Momma when I heard a noise downstairs. I think it was the sound of breaking glass. I'm not really sure." I shook my head, as though I could lodge the memories back in place. "I haven't thought of this in so long."

"Ellie, you don't have to tell me this."

But I did. I needed him to know. "I grabbed my stuffed bunny and stood at the top of the stairs. I heard a man shouting, 'Where is she?' My mother was screaming, screaming my name. I was so scared. I didn't know what to do. I wanted to help Momma, but I couldn't make myself go downstairs. I sat on the top step, clutching my bunny." I took another breath to steady my shaking voice. "I don't remember much else, bits and pieces that make no sense. A man, but a hood covered his face. And blood. So much blood. I was covered in it and so was my bunny."

"Ellie." Collin's voice broke.

"It was my fault. It was my fault she died."

Collin pulled the truck to the side of the road. He shoved the gearshift into park and turned toward me, pain in his eyes. "It wasn't your fault, Ellie. How could it be your fault?"

"I told Claire. Only days before. Daddy always told me terrible things would happen if we shared the secret."

"Ellie, you don't know that's why she died. It was some sick, horrible person. *That* wasn't your fault."

"No, Collin. He was looking for me. The man was looking for *me*. He knew my name."

Collin's face paled.

"If I'd gone downstairs. If I'd just gone down there, he wouldn't have killed my mother."

He looked like he was going to throw up when he grabbed both of my arms. "No, Ellie. He might have killed you too."

My chin trembled, and I choked back a sob. "But then my mother might be alive."

Collin's chest heaved as emotions flickered in his eyes. Fear. Worry. Indecision. Finally, he shook his head. "No, Ellie. There was nothing you could have done."

"I was a coward." There it was. The burden I'd carried for years. That my cowardice killed my mother, along with my disobedience. I'd never confessed it to anyone. Not even Claire, yet I was telling Collin. Why?

"If that man killed your mother, a grown woman, how could an eight-year-old girl stop him? You are far from being a coward. Look at this morning. You stood up to Marino. Most grown men won't do that."

I closed my eyes. "I didn't tell you this for pity. I told you to explain." I opened my eyes and found him watching me with a guarded expression. "When my mother died that night, all my knowledge of the curse disappeared except for the most basic information. I don't remember anything about the spirits or gods. Or the words of protection. Or anything about the ceremony. Daddy tried to teach me again, but I was sure the curse killed my mother as punishment for me telling Claire. I decided if the curse could kill my mother for something *I* did, it was evil and I didn't want anything to do with it. If nothing else, I figured I owed it to my mother for giving her life for mine. She didn't want me to believe the curse so I wouldn't. "

Collin dropped his hold on my arms and turned to look out the windshield.

"I'd ask my dad to tell me now, and I have since you showed up, but he has Alzheimer's. He has more bad days than good and I haven't gotten anything." I shook my head in self-disgust. "I had a chance to learn it all again, and I threw it away. But I regret it now. I've regretted it since the moment you walked into the New Moon."

Collin sighed. "It's okay. We'll figure this out together." But he refused to look at me.

Collin would have never given up on his Curse Keeper responsibilities. He had a symbol tattooed over his heart, knowing there was little possibility that he'd need it. How did I make up for that kind of dedication?

He turned back to the steering wheel and turned on his blinker. "We need to get you back to Manteo so you won't be late for work."

"But you didn't want me to go to work. You said I needed to get my priorities straight."

He shrugged, keeping his eyes on the road. "I don't want to do anything else curse related until I mark you with the henna tattoo, and I want to wait until after dark to mark you. So you might as well get some hours in at the restaurant while you wait for sunset."

"Thanks."

We drove the rest of the way in silence, Collin doing his best to ignore me. When he parked outside my apartment, I got out of the truck and started for the stairs.

"Ellie."

I looked over my shoulder at him.

His mouth opened, but he hesitated, then smiled softly. "I'll see you later tonight."

And then he was gone.

◂ CHAPTER SIXTEEN ▸

Tourists had flooded Manteo, even more so than usual, and the New Moon was packed. I was busy nonstop with people waiting thirty minutes or longer for a table. I had the outdoor patio section, which I liked from time to time. Sure it was hot, but it fed my people-watching obsession. And working the patio meant I could keep an eye on things, not that I'd know what to do if a spirit showed up. It was hard to believe that only a few days ago I was looking for adventure. *Be careful what you wish for, Ellie.*

Claire's ghost tour started and ended a block away. She waved to me when her group—the largest I'd ever seen—passed by so I wasn't surprised she dropped in half an hour later. The sun had begun to set, and I was getting nervous. What if a spirit attacked with all of these people around? The responsible part of me wondered if I should take off from work, but now was very bad timing. The New Moon had never been busier and Marlena needed me. Not to mention I really needed the money.

Claire leaned against the exterior wall and gave me a mischievous look. "Well?"

"Well, what?" I asked, picking plates off a table since our busboy had called in sick.

"Did Collin Dailey ever show his face again?"

I looked at her dumbfounded for a moment, my brain scrambling to catch up. The last time I'd seen or talked to her was when Collin had walked out of the back of the restaurant the day before. That seemed like a week ago. I shook my head with a snort.

"Is that a yes? What did he say?"

"You have *no* idea."

"So tell me!"

I held my palm out to her. "Try this for starters. It's so much more than just a mark on my hand."

Her eyes grew as large as quarters. "So what is it?"

"It's how we send the spirits and gods back. Collin has one too."

"That is so romantic."

I laughed and carried the plates to a plastic tub. "There isn't a single romantic bone in Collin Dailey's body. Trust me."

She moved next to me. "Ellie, that man is hot. You have to fight evil spirits together. You share a mark on your hands and possess supernatural powers. What's not romantic?"

"Trust me. Collin isn't anything like that. He's . . ." I paused. I couldn't bring myself to tell her about Marino or Mrs. Abernathy in Rodanthe. "His moral compass is questionable."

"Moral compass?" This gave her a second pause. "That's only important if you want a relationship with him. Just sleep with him."

My mouth dropped open. "Will you listen to yourself? No, I will not just sleep with him. I won't be one of many women Collin Dailey screws and then throws to the side so he can screw another one."

Her eyes lit up. "You like him!"

"No! Maybe. I don't know." I crossed my arms.

"At least admit that he's hot."

I rolled my eyes. "Okay, he's hot. Even a blind woman could see that. But it doesn't matter if I like him or not. He's not interested in *that* with me, and he's made his indifference perfectly clear. Multiple times."

She scrunched her nose. "*Really?*"

"Really. I don't make the Collin Dailey cut." And damn if that didn't sting my pride. "Look, it doesn't matter. We're together because we have a job to do. Close the gate to the spirit world and save our world. End of story."

Claire pouted. "You're no fun."

"You knew that years ago."

She laughed. "It's not for my lack of trying to corrupt you."

"Maybe I can corrupt her instead." Collin stepped out of the shadows dressed in dark jeans and a black T-shirt and looking even sexier than usual. His voice was low and seductive, like hot oil sliding down my back, making my knees weak. His statement was more than flirtation.

How much had he heard?

He stopped in front of Claire, whose mouth now gaped. "I'm Collin. I don't think we've been officially introduced. Yesterday in the storeroom doesn't count."

"Claire," she mumbled.

"What are you doing here, Collin?" I forced irritation in my voice. I couldn't bring myself to admit that I was glad he was here.

My tone didn't faze him as he continued on his seduction track. "I can't let you wander around in the dark alone, now can I? And we have a date."

Our date was my henna tattoo application, but Claire didn't know that. She beamed with excitement.

Before I realized what was happening, Collin pulled me to his chest. I had to put my hands on his shoulders to keep from stumbling. He wrapped an arm around my back, his hold tight enough that I couldn't get loose without a fight. I searched his face, trying to find signs of head trauma. Because brain injury was the only explanation I could come up with for his behavior.

A sexy grin spread slowly across his face, as though he had a secret. "I've been thinking about you all day. I can't wait to get another look at your ass."

Irritation rippled through my body. He was playing me in front of Claire. This was payback for casting him in the role of my flaming gay friend Enrique. I wasn't about to admit defeat.

I lowered my eyelids and looked up through my lashes, putting some heat in my voice. "I've been thinking about you too." I lifted my hand to his cheek, my fingertips trailing over the stumble of his five o'clock shadow. "And I can't *wait* for you to see my ass."

Surprise flickered in his eyes, and then he grinned. The player was getting played and he knew it. The question was how far were we going to take this before one of us called uncle?

His other hand found my waist and skimmed up my back, pulling me even closer. "I'm going to undress you slowly so I can take in every inch of your perfect body."

Holy shit, he played dirty. I reminded myself this was a game, but my body refused to listen.

Claire continued to watch us, practically melting into a pile of goo. Collin was obviously quite pleased with himself.

I ran my fingertip over his lower lip and looked into his eyes, smiling seductively. "You have no idea *how much* I want that." I slid my hand to his neck and stood on my tiptoes, my mouth so close to his, I felt his breath on my cheek. "But won't your boyfriend get jealous?"

He laughed, still holding onto me.

I'd won. "Good try, Collin. You're a terrible con. Stick to the thievery."

"Maybe you're just immune to my charm. Like a mutant."

I was most definitely *not* immune to his charm, but the mutant issue was still up for debate.

He dropped his hold and stepped back. The hot night air pushed between us, but my body felt cold and lonely without him pressed against me. With all the men I had dated, I had never once felt a fraction of what I felt in Collin's arms. And *that* was dangerous.

Claire shook her head in confusion. "What just happened here?"

I gave her a face. "Collin was paying me back for something I did to him this afternoon." I had no doubt he had heard more of my conversation with Claire than I would have liked. "He has zero interest in me."

Collin smirked until Claire turned to him with her steely gaze. "You're shitting me, right? You claim to have no interest in her? At all?"

His eyebrows lifted in surprise and he stammered. "I . . . ." There was no right way to answer her questions, but it was fun to watch him sweat.

"I saw the chemistry between you two, and I'm pretty damn sure I need a cigarette now. Or two. I definitely need to go home and get laid."

"*Claire!*"

"You two keep lying to yourselves, but what a waste." She turned toward the sidewalk. "Call me later."

As she walked away, I turned my wrath on Collin. "Not funny, Collin."

His gaze found mine, his face completely serious. "Who said I had no interest in you?"

I couldn't deal with his games right now. "My shift ends in fifteen minutes. You can either wait for me here or wait in my apartment."

"You'd let me into your apartment without you?"

I shrugged. "Sure, why not? It's not like you'd steal anything from me, *would you*?"

He grinned. "And face your fiery, redheaded temper? No thanks. With it getting dark, I'd rather keep you in eyesight. I think I'll get a beer and wait for you here."

I tossed my head. "Whatever. What do you want?"

"The house pale ale."

I put my hand on my hip and leered. "And here I took you for a stout man." I spun around before he could answer, but I heard his laughter when I went inside.

I had to work about ten minutes later than scheduled, but Collin sat on the patio, drinking his bottle of beer and watching the crowd. His shoulders were tight, and I knew him well enough to know that he was on edge. I suspected it had nothing to do with what happened between us earlier and more to do with the fact that I was fair game to vengeful gods.

Marlena, who had seen the whole incident on the patio, was beside herself. "While I don't usually encourage that type of behavior in the workplace, I can't say that I'm sorry it happened. Please tell me he's waiting for you so you can take him home."

"Yes, I'm taking him home." I was sure I'd later regret telling her, but it gave her momentary happiness. Who was I to take that away from her?

Collin stood when he saw me come out, ever the attentive date. Hardly anyone was around to pay attention so I wasn't sure who the show was for. We walked to his truck, the windows down as always.

"Aren't you worried someone will steal it or anything in it?"

"No. The beauty of driving something like this is that no one wants it or thinks anything worth stealing is inside it." He reached in the window and pulled out a shopping bag.

"Where are the henna supplies?"

"In here. Along with other things." He lingered on the words. What did that mean?

After we went upstairs and into my apartment and Collin began to pull candles out of his bag and set them on the coffee table. "Where do you want it?"

Why was he putting out candles? "Want what?"

"Your mark. Have you decided where you want it?"

"No. We were so busy tonight I didn't have much time to think about it. Why is yours over your heart?"

He stood several feet way. He simultaneously felt much too close and agonizingly too far away. "It's a reminder that the Curse Keeper magic flows within our blood, and that our hearts must be pure to carry out our duty."

Collin Dailey's heart pure? I wanted to laugh, but he was so close he was stealing my breath.

He studied me with a serious expression. "I've been thinking about it and I think the tattoo should be close to your heart. There aren't any rules about it, but the heart holds magical powers. The closer to your heart, the safer you'll be."

"I don't want to put it on my chest."

"You don't have to." How could he make four ordinary words sound sexy? Did he even know what he was doing to me, or was exuding pheromones as natural as breathing for him? "I don't want to put it there anyway."

"Why?"

His gaze dropped to my chest and he started to say something, then stopped. "I think we should put it on your back. If we put it on your left shoulder blade, it will still be over your heart."

"And the henna will be temporary?"

"Yes."

Why did this make me so nervous? "So what do we need to do?"

"I need to set everything up. Do you have to go to the bathroom or get something to eat?"

"Still concerned about my bodily functions?" I teased.

Again he started to say something and stopped. "So are you telling me that you're ready?"

"No." I disappeared into the bathroom and stared at my reflection in the mirror, caught off guard. I looked different. My cheeks were slightly flushed, my eyes brighter than usual. Had Collin done this to me? Was it the Curse Keeper magic?

I considered changing clothes. I was wearing a khaki skirt for work and my white blouse, the same one I'd worn all day. It was still dirty, but I hadn't had a clean white shirt to wear to work. Besides, I wasn't sure what one wore to a marking ceremony, and I didn't want Collin to think I cared about what I wore around him. Even if I did.

When I went back into the living room, the smell of lemons practically knocked me over. Collin was at the kitchen counter mixing a brown paste in a plastic bowl. He looked up as I walked in. "I'm mixing the henna."

"Okay." I reminded myself this was temporary. Claire had several tattoos, but they were too permanent to suit me. I couldn't even commit to a shampoo brand. How could I permanently mark my body?

When Collin finished, he set the bowl on the coffee table as well as a spray bottle and several wooden sticks. "I'm going to start now, so you can't talk, okay? We want this to work and we want the protection symbol to be strong. I'm going to do everything I can to make that happen. I'm going to add some elements that aren't in the normal ceremony. Usually the mark is just a symbol of our commitment. For the first time in four hundred years, its purpose is real."

I nodded.

"Stay over by the bar until I motion for you." He began to set white pillar candles in a circle around the sofa, lighting them while he chanted something in his ancient language. One candle remained unlit. Collin stood in front of it and reached a hand toward me.

I hesitated while Collin studied my face, his hand still extended. I was placing my life in his hands. He had the power to protect me. And the power to condemn me. Why should I doubt his intentions? He needed me just as much as I needed him. While I had no delusions that he cared about me, I also couldn't believe he wanted to cause me harm. In the end, it didn't matter. I needed this mark of protection. I was as good as dead without it. But I also realized that I could never go back to who I was before. I'd never be that Ellie again.

I reached my hand toward him but held back just inches away. Why did this feel so significant? So pregnant with possibilities and heartache? I looked into his eyes and saw a man I didn't recognize. He wasn't Collin Dailey, the man of questionable character. He was Collin Dailey, descendant of Manteo, Keeper of the Curse.

I put my hand in his and stepped inside the circle.

Collin bent over and lit the last candle, then led me toward the sofa. He stopped in front of it, his eyes on mine, his expression so stoic it made me nervous. Collin Dailey cared about nothing and no one, but Collin Dailey the Curse Keeper bore his responsibility seriously.

Then he began to chant, words I didn't understand, but power swirled around us. My mark tingled, and I closed my eyes. Collin began to unbutton my shirt, and I let him, my body alive with magic and lust. I wanted him to take off my shirt. I wanted him to do so much more.

His fingers brushed against the skin of my chest, and he slowly pulled my blouse open, lingering at my shoulders and sliding it down my arms. This must be what it was like to be seduced by Collin. Tonight, even if just for one night, I was going to let myself pretend he was seducing *me*.

My shirt fell to the floor, but Collin's hands remained on my arms, so feather light he gave me chills. Would he think my goose bumps were due to cold or desire? Did it matter?

His hands glided up my arms, to my neck and then my face, as he continued to chant. He cupped my cheeks, the heels of his palms resting on my jaw, his fingers barely stroking my skin. I opened my eyes, surprised at the intensity on his face. His mouth moved as the soft guttural sounds escaped, and I became mesmerized by his lips.

The words changed tempo and tone. Collin gently trailed his hands to my shoulders, his fingers pressing with tenderness as he pushed me down to sit on the sofa. He turned me gently, so that I faced the door. His fingers moved down my back, one hand sweeping my braid over my right shoulder with a softness I didn't expect. He inserted a finger under my left bra strap and slowly slid it over my shoulder and down my arm. Then Collin's chanting became louder and more insistent as his palm rested on my shoulder blade and a force surged in me, heat radiating out from Collin's hand.

My eyelids sank closed. Never had I felt this way with a man. It had to be the power that flowed through our veins. Magic and hunger stirred inside me, summoned by Collin, both through his words and his touch.

His hands were on my shoulders again, urging me forward so that my chest was on the sofa. His words changed again as his right hand left my body. And then I felt something wet touch my back, and Collin began to paint, my skin tingling with power with every stroke.

The design on Collin's chest was intricate, and I knew he was duplicating his own mark on my back. He spent several minutes drawing and reciting the ancient words. When the design was complete, he sprayed something cold on my skin, and the smell of lemons permeated the room. I suppressed the shiver that crawled up my spine.

His hands cupped my shoulders again and gently pulled me to my feet, turning me slowly, ever so slowly. When I faced him, he removed his hands. My eyes flew open at the loss. He took a step back and pulled his shirt over his head, dropping it to the floor. Then he moved toward me, until only inches separated us. Again we were face-to-face and shirtless. But this was different. So very different.

His right hand reached for mine, raising it and opening my fingers. He traced the mark on my palm before placing my hand over the mark on his chest, resting his heavy, strong hand over mine.

I looked up at him in wonder as his eyes closed. He still chanted the ancient words. My fingers stretched and flexed, the hair on his chest tickling my fingertips. Heat blazed through my palm, reaching out for the heat of Collin's mark. His muscles tensed, and he inhaled, his recitation louder and more intense.

Collin's eyelids eased open, and he moved my hand away, holding it between us. He released his grip, and his right hand rose to meet mine, pressing our palms together and lacing our fingers. As our marks aligned, the two halves of our power became one.

Then the universe opened and sang.

◡: CHAPTER SEVENTEEN :◡

The rush of power sucked my breath away. I was aware of everything at once, the Manitou of every living thing. Plants, animals, people. Bacteria, insects, fungus. The pulse and throb of their life force echoed around me. Inside me. Through me.

I was aware of the wind and the water, the earth and stars. The sand dunes in Nags Head, the ocean waves of the Atlantic, the storm brewing fifty miles away. I was in the center of the universe. I was outside the universe. I was everywhere at once.

What I experienced in the warehouse in Buxton was only a small sample of what I felt now. I wasn't just a Keeper of the Curse; I was a Keeper of the Manitou of every living thing threatened by the gods and spirits. I felt the loss of the dead birds we'd seen over the last two days, the unbalance it caused. And more I hadn't even known about. Deer in the forest. Cows on a farm on the mainland. Dogs, cats, raccoons. The Manitou cried for the loss.

It was up to me and the man before me to right the wrongs.

A magic more ancient than gods, as old as the birth of the world, flowed through our veins. Manteo hadn't simply used the power of the Croatan gods to create the curse; he'd appealed to a much older force.

The birth of the world began with the earth and the water. I was the child of the water, born of the sea. Collin was the child of the earth, born of the land. We were the yin and yang of the Curse.

I looked up at Collin, seeing the same rapture on his face that I felt. I could feel his heart beating in his chest. The inhale and exhale of his lungs.

The hair follicles on his skin standing on end. We were linked together by a force older than the world. By power that was strengthened with our union.

His lips parted in surprise as his gaze lowered to my face, and I realized that he'd stopped his chant. His fingers tightened over my hand, squeezing our palms tighter. His free hand wrapped around me, his palm pressing into the small of my back. We were skin to skin from the waist up with the exception of my bra, the rise and fall of our chests synchronized.

My skin tingled, burning with the ancient force and longing. I brought my left hand to his chest, the need to have every part of my body touch him overpowering all reason. His fingers moved higher up my back, flexing and gripping my skin as though he felt the same way.

I lifted my chin, looking deep into Collin's eyes. The blatant desire staring back at me made me want him even more. I slid my hand up his neck, my fingertips trailing over his pulse. His lips parted more, his breath coming in shorter gasps. I wanted to taste him, to nip his lower lip and run my tongue over it. To mingle our breaths in an attempt to join even more. Instead, I watched and waited. This was Collin's ceremony. I was only a participant.

He lowered his face, his hooded eyes concentrating on my lips. I stretched my neck, my lips drawn to his, but he stopped short, his hot breath fanning on my face. I breathed him in, wanting every part of him that he was willing to offer.

"Ellie." My name uttered by his tongue sent chills up my spine.

I needed him, more than the air that I breathed. I was his. He only had to ask.

His hand pulled away from my back and cupped the side of my head, tilting it upward. His breath was hard and fast. I felt the desire coursing through his blood, the proof of it pressed against my body. I waited for him to touch his lips to mine, but he remained agonizing inches away.

He moved closer in slow motion, our lips a hairbreadth apart.

I only had to stand on my tiptoes to reach him, but I wanted him to be the one to close the distance. To join with me.

And he did.

He kissed me with a gentleness I didn't expect, a hesitancy that surprised me. I kissed him back with more eagerness, and he released a groan before matching my fervor. His hand on my face moved around to the back of my head, holding me close while his tongue delved into my mouth.

Not only could I feel Collin's physical response, but I could sense his emotional one as well. He wanted me, badly. But he was also experiencing guilt.

His lips left mine, and he pressed my forehead to his chin. "Ellie." This time my name was tight and choked.

We remained like that, both of us catching our breath for several excruciating moments, until he removed his hand from the back of my head and retreated a step. Our joined hands were all that kept us connected. But I knew that was next.

His fingers uncurled but his palm still pressed against mine, the power between us too irresistible to release. His eyes, full of regret and hunger, searched mine. Whatever he found was what he needed. Resignation pulled his mouth into a frown and his hand lowered.

I stood in front of him for several shocked seconds, unsure what to do.

Collin took another step back. "You should be protected now."

The mark on my back might protect me from evil spirits, but what was going to protect my heart from Collin Dailey?

"Okay," I mumbled. My knees were weak, but I refused to show any sign of his effect on me, other than what I'd already displayed. Although if he was as aware of me as I was of him, he already knew.

Turning away from me, he scooped up his shirt and pulled it over his head. He began picking up the candles, blowing them out and putting them in his bag. The melted wax seeped into the brown bag, dark stains spreading outward. I wondered if I should help him, but I couldn't bring myself to do it. I couldn't bring myself to move from the spot where I stood. After throwing the bowl of henna and the stick into a small plastic bag and putting them in his larger one, he paused in front of me, uncertainty on his face.

"Tomorrow we should get my relic. It's down in Morehead City. If we're lucky, we'll get it right away, but if not . . . you should probably pack an overnight bag."

"Okay." Five minutes ago, that would have sent a thrill through my blood, but now it filled me with dread and regret. Still, it had to be done.

"While you were at work, I put fresh markings outside your doorway and inside around your window frames. You should be okay tonight, but if you need me, feel free to call."

I nodded, but his suggestion was worthless, and we both knew it. If I were to come face-to-face with a god or spirit, Collin would never get here in time, but what else was he going to say? *If a spirit sneaks in, good luck with that?*

"Your mark . . ." His voice sounded strained, and his eyes shifted to the corner. "Try not to sleep on it or do anything to smear it. The lemon-sugar juice I sprayed on it will help the henna set, but you need to leave it undisturbed at least until morning. The longer it has to set, the longer it will last."

"Okay."

There was nothing left to say so he moved to the door and hesitated. His mouth opened, his jaw working, then he shook his head and left.

I watched the door, standing in the exact spot where he pulled away from me, although I wasn't sure why on both counts. The last thing I expected was Collin Dailey to walk through my door again tonight. My head was a swirl of emotions I couldn't sort through, but one rose above the others, bobbing at the surface: rejection. Collin had screwed countless women, but he'd walked away from me.

It didn't make any sense, but if I let myself really think about him, nothing about Collin Dailey made sense. I knew he'd wanted me, I'd felt the physical proof, yet it wasn't enough. Why? I knew it wasn't honor—there wasn't an honorable bone in his body. So what had stopped him? Why had he felt guilt?

There was no sense dwelling on things I couldn't control. I was not going to get to the bottom of Collin Dailey's behavior tonight—as if I ever would—and I was curious what my henna tattoo looked like. I hadn't had a chance to peek at what he'd drawn on my back in his truck either, so I went to the bathroom and turned my back to the mirror.

The symbol Collin had just applied was as close to the one on his chest as I remembered. The stain on top of my skin was beginning to dry. On my other side was an ink pen drawing of a circle surrounding a square—the Curse Keeper mark on our palms—but also zigzag lines in the center and on all four sides. Underneath the ink was a faded mark, much more primitive. Three dark slashes that looked like claw marks at an angle. Above the marks was a crescent moon. It was hard to believe an ink drawing had saved my life, but I'd seen just as strange, if not stranger things over the last few days.

I needed to talk to Daddy again. The ceremony to close the gate was looming in the not so distant future and even though Collin knew how to perform it, I'd feel better going into the event with some inkling of knowledge. Maybe I'd have time to see Daddy in the morning. And hopefully he wouldn't mistake me for an evil spirit. There was no tempering the pain that went with that, no matter how much I prepared myself.

I'd also have to get time off from work, from both Myra and the New Moon. I sighed. I might have to end up selling more of Daddy and Myra's antiques. My only hope at this point was that the increase in tourists would boost the Dare Inn revenue. Still, it was so hopelessly in debt, I wasn't sure if anything could save it at this point. How ironic that the cause of the increased tourism that might save the inn was the curse that destroyed my family.

The wind howled outside my door with an eerie groan. Collin thought I was safe with the marks on my back and the symbols around my windows and door, but I was still on edge and didn't want to be alone. There was only one person who could help me feel better, and I knew she'd drop everything and run over if I asked. Especially if she thought she could get some details about Collin.

Claire answered on the second ring. "So what happened after I left?"

"At the restaurant or my apartment?"

"Collin went to your apartment?"

"Not only that, he took my shirt off."

"You're shitting me! I told you that the two of you had major chemistry. So why are you calling me now? Isn't he still there? Why not wait until tomorrow to catch me up?"

"He's gone. And I had to call you tonight because I'm going to Morehead City tomorrow, and I have a ton to tell you. In person."

"You've thrown me two things to latch on to: First, why are you going to Morehead City, and more importantly who with? And second, did Collin take off anything else besides your shirt?"

"That's three things, not two. Come over, and I'll tell you everything."

"I'm on my way."

She must have been sprinting out her front door when she hung up, because she knocked on my door in record time. In fact, she was still wearing her pajamas. "When was the last time we had a slumber party?" she asked, walking past me at the door and flopping on the sofa. "And yes, I noticed that you're still shirtless. Are you dying to show me a hickey? Because I have to tell you that hickeys are so high school."

"No." I pinched my lips into a frown. "I don't want to show you a hickey. Disgusting. Give me some credit, will you?"

"Then what's with the striptease?"

I turned around to show her my back.

"What the hell is that? You got another tattoo? The girl who would rather pierce her nose than get inked?"

"Yes, I mean no. I mean it's a tattoo, but it's henna, and technically, it's not *another* tattoo because the one on my palm isn't a tattoo."

"Where and when did you get it?"

"Collin did it. After I got off work."

She leaned back and crossed her legs. "Let me get this straight. Hotter-than-hell Collin came into your apartment, took off your shirt . . ." She paused, raising her eyebrows and waiting for confirmation.

I nodded.

". . . and then proceeded to give you a henna tattoo."

"Pretty much. Yeah."

"Okay." Her face twisted in confusion. "I think you need to start from the beginning."

So I did, telling her everything. About going to the pawnshop in Kill Devil Hills, going to Buxton, my run-in with Marino, breaking into the warehouse, Rosalina, Collin drawing on my back to counteract the god's hold on my soul, getting the cup back, and finally, my embarrassing situation with Collin tonight.

"I don't know why you're embarrassed," Claire grumbled. "You didn't do anything wrong. You can't help it if Collin can't man up."

"Oh, he manned up all right. I felt the proof."

Claire's eyebrows rose and she smirked. "See? That's an improvement over your last date."

"Little good it does me."

She folded her arms over her chest. "You're not giving up, are you?"

"*Giving up?* The man doesn't want to have sex with me, Claire. What is there to give up?"

"Of course he wants to have sex with you. But something is holding him back, which I admit, is incredibly hard to believe with that generic white bra you're wearing there." She faked a yawn.

I threw a pillow at her. "Shut up."

"Really, Ellie? That's the best you could do?"

"I never expected to be shirtless with him. He wasn't interested in me."

"Yeah, I got that in front of the New Moon when you two were practically dry humping."

"We were not!"

"Maybe not, but you were well on your way. I got so hot watching you two I had to go home and have sex with Drew within two minutes of walking in the door. I'm sure you can imagine his confusion."

"Yeah, poor Drew," I chuckled.

"The point is that while the flesh is willing, his spirit hesitates. We both know that he's not a man of principles when it comes to sex. It wouldn't take much to break him, so the question is do you want to?"

I shot her a look of surprise.

"You have to admit he isn't your usual type, Ellie. You go for dry, boring, and predictable. Collin Dailey is none of those things."

"Tell me about it. Collin Dailey is not boyfriend material." I still had no doubt that once we performed the gate-closing ceremony, I'd never see him again.

Claire leaned over her crossed legs and held her hand out. "Maybe you don't need a boyfriend. I mean, look how well that route has gone. You've spent your entire romantic life searching for the fireworks and romance you think your parents had, and you've barely lit a match with all those other guys. Maybe you should go for a fling and get the need for fire out of your system. Sometimes fire's not all it's cracked up to be."

I remembered Collin's hands on my skin and how alive I'd felt beneath his touch. He was like a drug I couldn't resist. But everything came with a price. "Sometimes people get burned playing with fire."

"But they sure have fun before they do."

I sighed.

Claire rested her hand on my knee. "Look, I'm not telling you to do it. I'm just saying think about it, but don't get your heart involved. You and I both know the most you'll get from a guy like that is a few rounds of hot rolling in the sheets, but sometimes there's nothing wrong with just a hot roll in the sheets."

I nodded. The wind howled again, and I tensed. "Did you mean it about having a slumber party? I really don't want to be alone. But I understand if you don't want to. Those things out there are real, Claire."

"What? And miss the chance to see a real live spirit? Pull out the chick flicks and pop some popcorn. If you're lucky, maybe I'll give you a pedicure. You never know, Collin might be a foot man."

I shuddered. I hoped to God he wasn't.

"But you're on your own with a bikini wax. I gotta draw the line somewhere."

"Not to worry. I don't want you anywhere near my bikini line."

Claire got off the sofa and patted my head. "Good girl. Playing hard to get just might be the way to get someone in your panties after all."

∽ CHAPTER EIGHTEEN ∽

Pounding outside my door and the sound of someone shouting my name woke me from my troubled sleep around four in the morning. I'd been dreaming of animals again, all of them crying out to me. *Curse Keeper, daughter of the sea, help us.*

At first, I wondered if the noise outside was Collin, although I couldn't figure out why he'd come back this late. I'd been sleeping face-first on the sofa, trying not to lay on my henna tattoo. I propped up on my elbows, checking on Claire who was stretched out on the overstuffed chair and ottoman, covered in an afghan.

Maybe I was imagining things. I started to lie back down until I heard it again.

"*Curse Keeper.*" The title was slurred as an insult, which could only mean one thing—an evil spirit was outside my door.

Shit.

The markings around the door would keep the spirit out, and the tattoo on my back would keep it from sucking my Manitou like a slushy from the Stop and Go, but that didn't mean it couldn't hurt me. However, I doubted ignoring it would make the thing go away.

I reached over and shook Claire's leg. "*Claire.*"

She startled, bolting upright. "What? What is it?"

"Listen."

Her eyes widened in the dark room, the only light coming from my closed bathroom door. I hadn't slept with a nightlight since a few years after Momma died. Maybe it was time to rethink that one.

We waited, our ears straining. The wind blew against my door and my windows. That was the only sound for several seconds until I heard it again. A banging on my porch and a voice. "*Curse Keeper.*"

Claire's eyes bugged even more. "*Shit.*" Her mouth hung open, and it took her a second to recover. She leaned toward me, whispering, "What are you going to do?"

"I don't know, but I don't think it will just go away. I should see what it wants." But I didn't want to see what it wanted. I wanted to hide in my room. Under the covers. With a flashlight. But I reminded myself that that wasn't what Curse Keepers did. They didn't cower in the dark. Dammit. Someone needed to rewrite the job description, whatever the hell it actually was.

Claire waited for me to do something.

Swallowing a lump of fear, I climbed off the sofa, realizing I was still wearing my bra and the short pajama bottoms I'd changed into earlier. I could put on a shirt but the last thing I wanted to do was screw up the symbol on my back, especially given what waited outside my door. I highly doubted it mattered what I wore to face an evil spirit.

I moved next to the door and leaned into it. "What do you want?"

"I wish to have an audience with you."

Didn't that sound polite and civilized? "No."

The wind beat against the door in a frenzy.

Was it a wind god or Okeus or his messenger or some other mean and nasty thing? "Who are you?"

"I am Kanim, the messenger of the rightful creator god!" it shouted with more wind effects.

The stupid thing was going to wake up my neighbors, and then it would probably suck out their Manitou. Did I want to be responsible for that?

"Can't we have this audience through the door?"

"*No.*"

I took a deep breath, working to steady my nerves. I had to face this messenger, but I wasn't dumb enough to just open the door. "I'll open the door, but I have to have your word that you won't hurt me."

I figured the request was pointless. Even if it said yes, could I really trust it? No honor among thieves, and all those other platitudes. But this wasn't a thief in the traditional sense, although I was sure you could count stealing people's life force and sending them to Popogusso as thievery. Even so, I was probably about to meet the messenger of a god, who probably had some sense of honor, if I could go on what little I knew of Greek and Roman mythology. Sure, the Native American pantheon wasn't the same thing, but I couldn't help but wonder if they all came from some god/spiritual motherland.

Claire jumped out of her chair and rushed forward, grabbing my arm. "Ellie, you can't be *serious*. What's to keep that thing from hurting you anyway?"

"I have to, Claire. If I don't face it, it will hurt someone else. I know it." Despite the Collin-centric portion of the ceremony there at the end, I'd been left with a bigger realization. It was my responsibility to protect other living beings—animals and humans alike—and that sense of duty was firmly embedded in my head.

"*You have my word*," the spirit answered.

"Claire, stand out of the doorway."

"Ellie!"

"Look, you wanted this thing to be real and it is. So step aside and let me do what I have to do."

She backed up a couple of feet, moving to the side. I knew part of it killed her. She was dying to see what was behind the door.

I took another deep breath. Collin had faced the wind god yesterday and sent it away. I could protect myself from a messenger if I needed to. Of course, Collin knew the Manteo line words of protection. I knew two words of the Dare portion. That wasn't going to me any good. I shook my head. No sense dwelling on the negative. I was going into this with a positive can-do spirit.

Boy, was that stupid.

The moment I opened the door, a gust of wind blew me backward, onto the sofa. I had to roll to the side to keep from smearing my mark.

"How dare you question the messenger of the god of creation!" the voice boomed.

The spirit shimmered, still a black fuzzy blob, but bigger and denser. I thought for a few seconds that I could see a human face and form.

"Ellie!" Claire screamed.

"I'm fine. Stay where you are!" I shouted, crawling to my knees.

"I warned you, pathetic Curse Keeper. Okeus's patience is thin."

The wind continued to blow, but I wasn't backing down to this egotistical supernatural asshole. I climbed to my feet, fighting to keep my balance against the blast. "Haven't you heard that patience is a virtue?"

The gust increased, but I bent my knees and grabbed hold of the chair.

"Have you made your decision?" Kanim boomed.

"What was the question?"

The wind screeched, an angry sound that made my skin crawl. Last night I knew that Kanim was too weak to kill me. Tonight I wasn't so sure, not after the wind god almost did me in at the warehouse. The gods and spirits were stronger at night, and I suspected this thing was responsible for a large portion of the animals that had been killed—and probably for the creepy birds on my porch the past two mornings. Still, I wasn't going to let him think I knew that.

Kanim's form shimmered. "Will you keep the gate open?"

I lifted my chin in an attempt to look brave. "I haven't decided yet."

"Every night you refuse to accept Okeus's offer, a sacrifice will be made. Do you still refuse?"

A sacrifice? I didn't like the sound of that, but there was no way I would accept his offer. "Yes, I still refuse."

I had tried to prepare myself for his response, but I couldn't prepare myself for the blast that threw me back and sideways into my fridge.

"*Ellie!*" Claire shouted.

Pain shot through my right side, where I slammed into the appliance. *Goddamn piece of Croatan fucking god shit.*

I climbed to my feet, grunting with pain and anger. Moving on instinct, my right hand rose and I began to chant, words I'd never heard from my father or Collin, words as old as the earth, born of ancient magic. They rolled off my tongue as easily as water rolled down a hill. The primeval sounds made no sense, yet their meaning echoed in my head. "I am the daughter of the sea, born of the essence present at the beginning of time and the end of the world. I am black water and crystal streams. The ocean waves and the raindrops in the sky. I am life and death and everything in between. I compel you to leave my sight."

The spirit screeched and flew backward, disappearing into the night.

Claire stared from the open doorway to me, her eyes huge. "What just happened? What did you do?"

I didn't answer for several seconds, still in shock. "I . . . I sent him away."

"You sent away the messenger of a god?"

I focused on my palm, the mark still tingling from the power that lingered there. Where had those words come from? Had Collin's ceremony and the symbol on my back loosened some of my memories? "I'm a Curse Keeper, Claire. My job is to send the gods back to the spirit world." I moved toward the door and looked around to see if anything else lurked in the darkness. When I didn't see anything, I shut the door and turned to her.

Claire lifted her shaking hand to her mouth. "What can that thing do?"

I sighed. "I'm not sure. Collin thinks the spirits are still weak, but they are gaining strength. The spirits and gods are feeding on the life force of animals to restore their energy. At some point they will be strong enough to kill people."

If possible, Claire's eyes widened even more.

"I'm going to stop them, Claire. Collin and I will close the gate and send them back."

She nodded.

I couldn't believe she was so shaken up. Claire was one of the bravest people I knew, especially when it came to the spirit world.

She helped me pick up the photos and things the spirit had strewn about. Neither of us felt like going back to sleep so I used the last of my coffee grounds to brew half a pot. We searched the Internet to see how to deal with the henna paste dried to my back without disturbing the tattoo. To my disappointment, I couldn't take a shower until tonight at the earliest. I hadn't had a shower since the day before, and I'd been in the heat.

After Claire removed the dried stain with olive oil, I went into the bathroom to wash the rest of my body with a washcloth. When I came out, Claire had the coffeepot turned upside down over her cup. She glanced up. "Seeing how drinking alcohol isn't an option at six thirty a.m., I called Drew and told him to bring some coffee over along with some clothes for me."

"Drew didn't mind?"

"*Please.* After last night, he owes me."

Drew showed up fifteen minutes later, wearing sweatpants and a T-shirt, carrying a duffel bag. He stopped outside the doorway, taking in the symbols marked across the threshold and on the door. His eyebrows rose as he nodded toward them, then back over his shoulder. "Did you know you had dead birds on your porch? And they're in some kind of pattern. Do I even want to know?"

Claire pulled him through the door. "No. You don't. Please tell me you brought the coffee."

He reached into the duffel and pulled out a bag, handing it over to her. "You are an evil woman making me get up so early."

She planted a kiss on his mouth. "And you *love* me that way."

A grin spread across his face. "You know it. I can't wait for you to be Mrs. Drew Reeves."

She kissed him for several seconds. "Only one more month." She turned back to look at me. "You have a fitting for your maid of honor dress next week."

Thinking about trying on a maid of honor dress in the midst of *hell on earth* seemed laughable, but then again, no more so than me insisting that I go to work the night before. Life went on, evil spirits or not. Or at least, I hoped it did. "Yeah, I'll be there."

Claire poured the grounds into a filter and glared at me. "Maybe you'll have a plus one. And maybe he won't be a loser."

I sighed. "If you're talking about Collin, forget about it. He's not interested. Circumstances have just thrust him upon me."

She winked at Drew. "I bet soon she won't be complaining about someone being *thrust* upon her." Claire snickered. "Let's just say that Collin needs a little push to take some initiative."

"Claire!" I shouted. Good Lord, was nothing secret?

Drew plopped onto a barstool and rested his chin on his hand. "Really, Ellie. Oh? Do tell."

I shook my head with mock irritation. "Drew, sometimes you are such a girl."

Claire announced she was hungry.

"You know I don't have any food here," I said. "You're going to have to go get something."

"Seriously," Claire grumbled. "You're not even responsible enough to feed yourself. How do you expect to save humanity?"

"You have no idea how many times I've asked myself the same question."

Drew's face scrunched in confusion. "Why is Ellie saving humanity?"

Claire's mouth dropped.

"Umm . . ." I mumbled, my heart racing. I couldn't believe she'd been so careless.

Holding out her hands, Claire grinned. "Isn't that what she does at the New Moon? She saves humanity by feeding them."

Drew didn't look convinced, but he let it drop.

Claire disappeared into my room with Drew's bag and came out dressed several minutes later. "If you won't feed me, I'm forced to go get breakfast from Poor Richard's. Thank God they open at seven." She picked up her purse and walked out the door.

I followed her, coffee cup in hand, being careful to walk around the circle of birds. "You're going to get me something, right?"

She continued to descend the stairs, raising her hand to flip me off.

"I take it that's a no," I mumbled to Drew, who'd come up next to me.

"Nah, she'll be over having to leave the apartment to get food by the time she orders."

I hoped so. I was starving.

My porch was a mess. I had two flowerpots on either side of the door and both were toppled over, as were my two plastic chairs. Could I expect visits from evil gods every night? I might need to bring everything inside. We swept up the birds into a bag—three robins, three blackbirds, and a cardinal. I had three more nights to close the gate and we weren't any closer to accomplishing that than we had been when the curse broke.

The morning was beautiful. The sun was out, and it was warm, but not hot enough to cause a sweat. It was early enough that the tourists weren't out so the streets were still quiet. And while my porch didn't face the sound—in fact it faced the back of the shops on the next street—I could still smell the salt of the ocean in the air. I sat on a chair and took a sip of coffee while Drew sat next to me.

"So you and Claire had fun last night?" he asked.

I pursed my lips in an exaggerated pinch. "Yep."

"You do know that I know something is up, right?"

I turned to look at him.

He grabbed my right hand and opened my fingers. "A tattoo on your palm? And something as primitive as a circle and a square? Then the symbols all over your door. That's so unlike you." His eyes narrowed. "Have you joined a cult or something?"

"What? No!"

"Then is this some belated rebellion against Myra? Because we all know how much she hates tattoos."

"No, but it's a family thing. Let's leave it at that."

"Okay, but you know you can talk to me if you need to. You and I have been friends even longer then you and Claire."

I offered him a smile. "Thanks, Drew." Leaning my head against the porch rail, I cradled my coffee cup to my chest while Drew examined my palm.

I'd had little sleep the last several nights, and the way Drew stroked my hand was relaxing. I began to drift off.

"Well isn't this cozy?" Collin's dry voice startled me out of my doze.

I tried to pull my hand away from Drew's, but he held tight.

"Good morning," Drew said with a bit too much cheerfulness to suit me. He must have realized who our visitor was. Damn Claire and her big mouth.

"Is it?" Collin's gaze fell on Drew's and my linked hands, his eyes narrowing slightly. "You must be one of Ellie's many *friends*."

Drew caught Collin's tone and sat up. "As a matter of fact, I am. Drew." And that was it. No explanation that he was Claire's fiancé.

I still cradled my cup, slouching against the porch. I understood how bad this must look. I was in my short pajama bottoms and I'd put on a tank top after Claire had rubbed off the excess stain. Drew looked like he was freshly awake with his unshaved face, bed head, and sweatpants. The coffee mug in his free hand sealed the deal.

Collin tensed. "Collin."

Drew grinned. "Oh, I know who you are."

Collin turned his steely gaze to me. "I hope you didn't screw up your mark lying on your back half the night."

His insinuation was obvious. I pulled my hand from Drew's death grip and raised an eyebrow, giving Collin my own deadly gaze. "Don't worry. I prefer to be on top."

Drew choked on his coffee, but Collin and I continued our stare-down for several seconds. To my satisfaction, he broke first. "Are you ready to go to Morehead City or were you too busy to pack?"

I smirked. "Sorry. I didn't think you'd be here so early."

"Obviously."

"I still have work to do."

His mouth lifted in an ugly smile. "Is that what you call it?"

I wanted to tell Collin Fucking Dailey to kiss my fucking ass. Who the hell did he think he was? And did he really think so little of me? He was the one who ran out the night before. He'd made it perfectly clear that he wasn't interested. So what did he care who I slept with? He'd already admitted that he'd screwed more women than he could count.

But instead, I smiled up at him like I had a secret, just to piss him off more.

Drew, on the other hand, had had enough. "I think you better watch how you speak to her."

Collin raised his hands in surrender. "I'd love to tell you she's all yours, but she seems to have a revolving bedroom door."

Drew was out of his seat, grabbing Collin's shirt with both hands.

"Drew!" I shouted, jumping to my feet.

"What the hell did I miss?" Claire asked, standing at the top of stairs breathless and holding a white paper bag.

I pulled Drew's hands away from Collin. Despite Drew's honorable intentions, I had no doubt that Collin would kick his ass. "Collin dropped by earlier than expected and is apparently surprised to see I have a guest this early."

Claire's eyes widened in understanding, her mouth forming an O.

"I was just about to tell Collin that my *revolving bedroom door* is my own business."

A frown covered her face. "Oh."

"I need to go in and pack." I reached for the door, refusing to look at Collin. "You do whatever the hell you want."

"Because you sure do," Collin said dryly.

"Damn fucking straight."

To my surprise, he followed me inside. I ignored him and went into my bedroom, shutting the door. I sat on the bed, a sick feeling washing through me. What just happened? Did Collin really think that I would have called some other guy to come in and pinch hit for him after we'd shared that kiss—that *connection*—last night?

The door opened and I jerked my head up, about to give Collin a verbal berating, but it was Claire with a worried look on her face. "Are you okay?"

My shoulders tightened. "Why wouldn't I be okay?"

Her brow knitted in confusion. "With Collin . . . and Drew . . ."

Pinching my mouth in disapproval, I shook my head. "Whatever."

She sat next to me. "I can go straighten him out."

Anger burned its way to the surface. "Don't you dare. If he thinks so little of me, let him. I deserve better than that."

"True." She paused. "But you know why he's so irritated, right? If you really want him, that's a good sign that he cares."

"Ha! Cares about *me*? As if." I scowled. "He jumped to conclusions be-cause he has double standards. He probably went out and got his friend with benefits to come over, and he thought I did the same thing."

Claire giggled.

I glared. "What the hell is so funny?"

"Thinking about you and Drew—together."

I shuddered. "Eww. That would be like doing it with my brother. If I had one. I've known Drew since preschool."

"But Collin doesn't know that."

I stood and grabbed my small suitcase out of my closet. "I don't care what he knows or doesn't. I still say if he's so willing to believe the worst of me, let him. I'm not going to set the record straight." Claire started to say something, but I pointed at her. "And neither are you."

Sighing, she stood and froze, then turned to me. "Why don't you get ready and I'll pack for you?"

"Don't you need to get to work?" Claire worked as a maid at the Tran-quil House Inn, but her boss was pretty lenient with her frequent tardiness.

She waved a hand. "I'll be fine. Drew brought my uniform. What do you think you need?"

"I don't know. A couple of days of clothes. And a dark pair of jeans and shirt." I shook my head at her questioning look. "Don't ask." I grabbed a skirt that matched the black tank top I already wore, clean black lacy underwear, and a matching bra, and went into the bathroom. Collin might not see what I was wearing underneath, but I'd know what he was missing and gloat.

Claire saw what I grabbed and an amused smirk crossed her face, but amazingly enough, she didn't say a word.

Feeling vindictive, I decided to make Collin sorry he'd passed this op-portunity by. I put more care into my makeup than usual and took down the braid I'd worn since yesterday morning. My long hair rippled with waves and I fluffed it with my fingers.

When I walked out of the bathroom carrying my cosmetics bag, Claire gave a low whistle. "You sure look like a woman who doesn't care what he thinks." She took the bag from my hand and tucked it in the suitcase.

"Shut up."

"I'm not complaining."

I took a deep breath. I was about to spend more alone time with a man who was pissed at me. But then again, half the time we'd spent together had involved him being pissed at me so what was new?

I called Myra and told her I wouldn't be in for a few days. I expected her to ask questions, but the only thing she asked was if I was okay. Unfortunately, Marlena wasn't as understanding.

"What do you mean you won't be in for a few days?"

"I've got something to take care of."

"I've got something for you to take care of too. Your shift."

"Marlena, please. You know I don't ever ask for special favors. I always pull my weight. This is important."

"This is the worst possible time, Ellie," she sighed. "The number of tourists grows every day."

"I'll be back soon. I promise." And hopefully, everything would be right again.

"You better or I can't guarantee you'll have a job."

Great.

I grabbed my bag, none too eager to see Collin, but Claire held onto it, searching my eyes.

"He's angry because he's jealous."

I released a wry laugh. "Collin Dailey? Jealous over me?"

She nodded.

"You're crazy."

"Look, you two are going away together, and who knows what will happen. I'm just saying if you want to play with a little fire, the kindling is already smoldering."

"You suck at this metaphor stuff."

"Shut up." Claire pulled me into a hug. "Just be careful. With your heart. And everything else."

"Thanks." I gave her a squeeze. "I love you too."

I broke away and walked out into the living room. Collin and Drew were locked in some manly display of cold stares. When the bedroom door opened, both men turned their attention toward me.

Collin stood, his mouth parted as he watched me walk out with my bag. I grabbed my purse off the kitchen counter and checked my wallet to make sure I still had nine hundred dollars. I spun around and gave him a grim smile. "Okay, let's get this over with."

Claire leaned into my ear. "That smoking kindling? It's blazing."

"Shut up," I said, but damned if I didn't hope that Claire was right.

∼ Chapter Nineteen ∼

Collin followed me to the truck and reached for my suitcase when I got to my door. To my surprise, he opened it for me. I stood in silence and shock.

"What?" he asked, irritated, but his earlier anger seemed to have eased.

"Opening doors, Collin? One would think I wasn't a slut."

He sighed, guilt straining his face. "I was out of line. What you do is your business."

"That's right. Just like what you do is yours. Now let's go."

He set my suitcase in the truck bed and climbed in, driving out of town, heading for the bridge to the mainland.

I should have been prepared for the dead animals, but I wasn't. I wasn't sure I'd ever be prepared for such a sight. Especially since twice the day before I'd felt the Manitou and the loss from the animals' presence.

Collin must have felt it too. His grip tightened on the steering wheel, his knuckles turning white.

"What happens if we don't close the gate?" I tried not to look at the side of the road. The sight of all the carcasses made me ill. "Will the spirits kill every living thing?"

He sighed. "No. They coexisted for thousands of years with animals and people. I think it's because they've been locked away for so long. Like I told you, they need the energy. But I have to wonder if part of it is for show. To let the world know they are back."

"That's not scary at all."

He shrugged. "If the gate doesn't close, I think they would eventually settle down."

"After they killed half the population of every living species."

"You have to look at it from their perspective. They were jailed for hundreds of years for no reason. I'm not surprised they're pissed."

My mouth dropped open. "Are you seriously defending them?"

He sucked in a deep breath and stared at me for several seconds before turning back to the road. "No. But I am saying that everything and everyone has a reason for what they do. If someone hurts you, and you understand why they did it, hopefully that understanding makes the hurt easier to accept."

"I don't give a rat's ass why a wind god wants my Manitou. I'm still going to be cursing him when I'm stuck in hell for eternity."

He cleared his throat. "They found a body in the botanical gardens this morning."

I sat up, the blood rushing from my head. "What?"

"I wouldn't necessarily think anything of it, but it was propped against the statue of Queen Elizabeth. A man, no visible signs of trauma. The police said he was from out of town."

"Maybe it was a coincidence. A drunk who got locked in the gardens and died of a heart attack."

"Ellie, he was frozen solid. In June."

I took a deep breath, worried I would pass out.

"I think this was a sign. To you."

"Why do you say that? Why me?"

"To scare you." He cast a worried glance in my direction.

My heart thudded against my chest. I needed to tell Collin about the visits from the spirit messengers. Yesterday I didn't trust Collin, and while he wasn't completely forthcoming, now I had no reason not to trust him with this. Especially after the ceremony and the mark of protection he'd given me.

"Collin—"

His phone rang, and he scowled as he pulled it out of his pocket. He answered and listened for several seconds before responding. "Why do you think I have the map? Are you saying it's gone?" He was silent, anger furrowing his brow. His free hand tightened on the steering wheel. "If he wants the Ricardo deal taken care of, he needs to back the fuck off and let me do it." Another pause. "Ellie's not any part of this. That was all a coincidence." He shot a glance in my direction. "I don't give a shit what Marino wants."

My stomach tightened. Somehow with everything that happened yesterday afternoon and last night, I'd forgotten about Marino. How could I forget about Marino?

Collin ended the call and shoved the phone in his pocket.

I took a deep breath and released it. "Marino still wants me."

His face taut, Collin kept his eyes on the road. "He's convinced you have some inside information and he wants it. *Shit*." He ran a hand over his head.

"Is there any way to convince him that I don't?"

"No."

This was bad, very bad. "And if he finds me?"

"He won't." He shifted in his seat, staring straight ahead. "We need to talk about last night."

More horror rushed through me, as if that were possible. Which part of last night was he referring to? I didn't want to talk about any part of last night, but especially one particular part of last night. I was stuck in a moving truck with this man, and I was pretty sure he wanted to rehash my humiliation. "No, we don't."

"Ellie. I want to talk about your mark and how I strengthened it."

"Oh." *Is this better or worse than talking about how he rejected me?* I wasn't sure.

"I meant to check it this morning." He paused. "Did it get smeared or smudged?"

Something inside me coiled tight. Before he sounded angry about the fact I might have slept with Drew; now he sounded like he was asking me about the weather. "Not to worry, Collin," I said in a snotty tone. "I told you I like it on top."

His jawed tightened and he swallowed. "Ellie."

"Too much information for you, Collin? Maybe this is my way of sharing so you'll share more information with me. Lord knows you keep most of it to yourself."

He looked as though he were counting to ten in his head. Finally, he said, "I simply want to know if your symbol is intact. If it's not, I want to fix it before tonight."

Weary of fighting, I rested my elbow on the window, placing my forehead in my hand. "When I checked it this morning, it looked fine."

His hands twisted on the steering wheel, barely enough to notice. "I realized that I never told you how to care for it. That's why I was there so early."

"I looked it up on the Internet. I saw you could remove the dried stain after five to six hours with olive oil."

"How did you reach it?"

I laughed, short and ugly. "You have to ask? I had help. And I was shirtless."

"Ellie, I was out of line—"

"Shut up, Collin." God, this was going to be a long couple of hours.

He was silent for several miles, before he started again. "When I was marked at eighteen, I had a ceremony, but it was only to cleanse my soul to receive the symbol. I had the actual tattoo done by a tattoo artist."

"Is that what you did last night? Cleanse my soul?" What we'd done last night had sullied my soul more than cleansed it. I hoped the stupid mark took.

"Some, but not most of it. We have a power now, individually and together. I hoped using that power would increase the strength of the protection symbol."

It did more than that. The entire ceremony had stirred some ancient power in my blood, but I wasn't sure I wanted to confess that to Collin yet, especially when lusting after him seemed to go hand in hand with it. "So how will we know if it worked or not?"

"I guess if you get attacked and a spirit or god tries to take your Manitou."

"Yay," I mumbled. "I can't wait."

Collin turned toward me, his face serious. "I'll be with you, Ellie."

Something about his expression and the huskiness in his voice set my stomach aflutter. Damn him. "What? Are you going to be with me every minute of the day until this thing is done? And then what about Marino?"

"Marino won't care about you after the Ricardo deal is done."

"And how long will that take?"

"A few weeks. Maybe a month."

"What the hell *is* the Ricardo deal?"

He shot me a glance. "The less you know about it the better."

"Easy for you to say. If I'm being hunted by some criminal, I'd at least like to know what it is that I'm supposed to know."

"Seriously, Ellie. In case Marino does find you somehow, the less you know the better. If he thinks you know *anything*, he'll assume you're lying about the rest."

My anger exploded and I clenched my fists to keep from hitting him. "Why the hell didn't you take me to Oscar? Why did you take me to Marino?"

"I told you to stay in the car!"

Tears burned my eyes, but I'd be damned if I'd cry over this.

Collin released a sigh. "Marino doesn't know *anything* about you. You live a quiet life in Manteo. There's no chance he'll find you. You'll be fine. I promise."

There was no way he could guarantee that, and we both knew it. "Be careful what you promise, Collin. I don't tolerate broken promises very well."

Marino was a situation that couldn't be fixed at this moment, so I decided to focus on a situation where I had some control, even if it was very little. I had to feel like I was in control of *something*. "When you placed your palm on my back, just before you drew my henna tattoo, you were infusing me with your power?"

"Yeah."

"What about when you put my hand over your tattoo?"

"It was the same thing. You have power, Ellie, whether you realize it or not."

I realized it now, but I couldn't help wondering if there was more to the power infusions. Collin had said he thought I could send lesser spirits back to the spirit realm without his help. Where and how would I learn how to do that? Would the ability just come to me like the words of protection had last night? Did I really want to chance it to find out?

"And our power together?" I asked. What I'd felt with our palms touching, with our marks connected—it had been unlike anything I'd ever experienced.

He looked at me again, still serious. "True magic."

"Do you know how to use it to close the gate?"

He nodded, but shifted in his seat. "Manteo performed the original ceremony so I'll perform this one. I'll tell you what I need you to do."

"When we touched last night . . ." I refused to bring up the surge of desire we'd both obviously felt, but there were other things I needed answers to. "I was aware of things I didn't know before. In fact, things I don't think were even told to me when I was little."

"I didn't know some of it either."

"But you knew about the Manitou?"

He frowned. "Yes, but not that we'd be aware of its presence." Why did that bother him? Other than getting answers and additional power, experiencing the Manitou was the best part of this entire job.

"Did you know I was the daughter of the sea and you were the son of the earth?" Which I found ironic, given that Collin was the fisherman.

His jaw dropped as he shot me a quick glance. "You found that out last night when we were connected?"

"Yes, and that the curse was born of an ancient magic that flowed through the universe before the birth of the world."

He scowled. "What else did you find out?"

"Did you know this stuff already?"

"It's part of our stories, Ellie. It's our tradition." The hint of arrogance wasn't lost on me.

"But you didn't experience those things last night? You didn't feel . . . connected to everything, or like all the origins of the universe were right in front of you?" His grimace was my answer. "So what did *you* feel last night when we touched hands?" It was a loaded question, and I hesitated to ask, but he was surprised I'd found out what I had. I knew he'd felt something, experienced *something*. The expression on his face last night had told me so.

"I felt the Manitou."

"But did you feel everything else?"

"We need to talk about what happens in Morehead City."

"Okay." He'd dug his feet in and wouldn't answer any more of my questions. I might as well let him change the subject.

191

"We'll go to the museum and check out the security measures as well as the location of the exhibit with the bowl."

"We're just going to walk in as us?"

"Sure. Why not? When the bowl goes missing, who would suspect that you or I took it?"

He had a point.

"Do you have a plan to get it?"

"I need to check the situation out first."

We drove the rest of the way in silence. Collin's damned unair-conditioned truck was hot as hell. If I'd been thinking straight, I would have offered to drive my car. It wasn't in the greatest shape, but it had air-conditioning and it couldn't be much worse than Collin's Red Death mobile.

The last few hours of the drive had been hot in other ways. Sitting next to Collin, my mind kept drifting to the night before. The more I tried to refocus, the more my mind latched on and refused to let go. The breeze lifted my gauzy skirt a few times, and I had to put my hand on the fabric to keep it from showing my sexy lingerie, although some deep and sinful part of me wished that I didn't take the precaution.

Collin's face pinched with irritation. "Do you ever wear pants?"

"Do you ever shave?" Not that I was complaining, despite my irritated tone. My traitorous mind thought about his five o'clock shadow under my fingertips the night before. I needed to think about something else. Anything else. Like scrubbing toilets.

We stopped for lunch in Morehead City before we went to the museum. I realized this was the farthest I'd ever been from Roanoke Island and not felt the debilitating pressure on my chest. If the feeling was curse related, Collin was sure to know about it.

"You're right." He nodded after I asked, looking down at his plate of food. "It was a way to make sure the Keepers never got too far away to fix the curse."

"But if they lived hundreds of miles apart, there was little chance the curse could be broken."

"Checks and balances, Ellie. The curse locked away the spirits, but there was a price to be paid."

"Steeper than the colony disappearing?"

"The gods needed a chance to be free."

"But who set the rules? Obviously, not the gods or they wouldn't be locked up."

"Not all of the gods were locked away."

My eyes widened. "What?"

"Ahone rarely dwelled on the land. He lived in the heavens. He escaped the curse, but tradition says he lent his power to it. *He* made the rules."

"He wanted the gods and spirits locked up. Why?"

"Jealousy? Pride? Who knows. But the other gods are liable to seek their own revenge."

So did that mean Ahone's messenger couldn't be trusted? Was Ahone really trying to save humanity or was he trying to save himself? "But that doesn't explain why I can get so far from Roanoke Island now. With the curse broken, you'd think I'd feel the pressure now more than ever."

His mouth lifted into a soft smile. "Isn't it obvious, Ellie? You can leave because we're together."

It was early afternoon when we got back into the truck to drive to the museum, and I was tired after two nights with little sleep. I dozed, my head leaning back on the headrest. When I realized the truck had stopped, I opened my eyes, surprised to find Collin watching me with an amused grin.

I sat up and smoothed down my skirt. Was he grinning because he'd seen my panties? I frowned. "What?"

"You snore."

"*What*? I do not!"

"You do. I never would have guessed." He opened his door and hopped out.

I grabbed my purse and followed him. "I do not snore!"

He laughed and pulled out his phone. "I have a video if you'd like proof."

"*You didn't!*" Livid, I ran for him, reaching for his phone. "Give me that!"

He stopped and held it over his head. "Why? It's cute."

Growling, I grabbed his arm and tugged. "You delete that right now!"

A wicked grin spread across his face. It was a challenge. "Make me."

I had multiple options. Most of them involved some type of kicking or striking him in the groin. I could only come up with a handful of other ideas after that. But it wasn't lost on me that we were in the parking lot of the museum we planned to rob. It was probably a good idea to keep a low profile and not cause a scene. My hands dropped, and I put a hand on my hip. "Fine. Keep it."

His grin never wavered. "Giving up so easily, hotheaded Ellie Lancaster?"

I lifted my chin and gave him a haughty glare. "I've decided to be the bigger person."

Disappointment flickered in his eyes for a half second before he smirked. "Suit yourself." He lowered his arm and I darted for the phone, catching him off guard.

I got a good hold on it but he held tight, my hand over his.

"If you wanted to hold my hand, Ellie, you only had to ask."

That was the second time he'd said that to me. I gave him a saucy grin. "Fine. I want to hold your hand."

His eyebrow arched. He shoved his phone into his pocket, then took hold of my left hand with his right. He tugged me closer so my chest was against his. "Happy now?" he teased.

I stared into his face, trying to catch my breath. This was ridiculous. I was getting hot and bothered holding Collin Dailey's fucking hand. No, I wasn't happy now. There was only one thing that was going to make me happy at this point, and it involved his hands touching intimate parts under my clothes.

Collin's grin faded as his eyelids lowered slightly, his pupils dilating. His grip on my hand tightened, keeping me next to him as his dark eyes searched mine. And he seemed to be struggling to breathe normally.

A car horn blared, and I jumped. We were standing in the middle of the parking lot. What the hell was wrong with me? I needed to get myself together.

Collin pulled me out of the way, then dropped my hand. I regretted the loss instantly. Damn. I was in so much trouble.

He started for the museum entrance, leaving me to trail behind, and I was glad. I couldn't face him. What was he thinking? He had to know that I wanted him. I hadn't hidden my desire, practically offering myself to him on a silver platter. There was no way he missed it. He read people. He knew.

But I was pretty good at reading people too. Especially when a guy was interested in me. Collin Dailey was interested, yet he held back. Why?

I didn't have time to dwell on it. Collin had already entered the building, leaving me on the sidewalk. Watching him disappear inside, I realized he wasn't necessarily rejecting me. Whenever we got close, he ran away. Could it be that Collin Dailey was afraid of getting close to me? I nearly laughed. Talk about delusions of grandeur. He probably worried I'd be some clingy chick, and he'd be stuck with me until this thing was done and for some time after.

When I entered the lobby, Collin had already purchased two tickets and waited for me with mock impatience. "For someone complaining about the heat, you sure were reluctant to get out of it."

If he only knew.

He lingered in the lobby a few minutes more, pretending to look at a map of the exhibits. I caught his eyes wandering around the room, cataloguing the locks on the doors, the sprinklers in the ceiling, the sleepy-looking guard—wearing a blue volunteer vest—and where he was positioned. Then Collin looped his arm through mine and grinned. "Time to go inside."

Watching the way he took in everything filled me with awe. A strange reaction to nefarious activities, and a true sign that this guy had crawled under my skin. Still, while I'd seen him in a few shady situations, I'd never seen him in full action. I pretended to check out exhibits, but my focus was too much on Collin. I wasn't sure how closely he wanted me to stick to him, but when I stopped at an exhibit about colonists in the eighteen hundreds with genuine interest, Collin moved ahead of me, out of sight. Once he realized I wasn't close, he came back and whispered in my ear, "We need to stick together."

I nodded, but it was a waste of time. He'd already taken off again.

The museum was bigger than I expected. We hadn't yet found the exhibit that displayed the wooden bowl, and I was beginning to wonder if the stupid thing was here. Several exhibits later, Collin's shoulders tensed ever so slightly. No one else would have noticed but it was obvious to me since obsessively watching Collin Dailey had become my new hobby. I *really* needed to get a new one.

I stood next to him, staring into the case about Powhatan Indians and artifacts from the time of Pocahontas.

"It's not here," he hissed in my ear.

I tried not to visibly react, but this was my worst nightmare come true. Well, second worst. The first was what would happen if we didn't get the bowl and close the gate in time.

He walked around a glass case. An empty platform at one end had a placard that read, SIXTEENTH-CENTURY CEREMONIAL BOWL, POWHATAN TRIBE.

I squinted in confusion. "I thought the bowl was Croatan."

"It is. They're fucking idiots who don't know *shit*." Good to know he was as worried about the bowl's absence as I was. His head jerked up and he searched the room until his gaze landed on a volunteer moving toward us. He plastered on a smile. "Excuse me." He gestured toward us. "We have a question."

The elderly man wearing a blue vest stopped next to the case. The top of his head was so bald it was shiny, but the hair on the sides of his head was long and swept over the top in an attempt to hide it. "How can I help you?"

"Actually," Collin said, "I was wondering about the piece that's missing there." He pointed to the empty spot. "Do you know where it's gone?"

The volunteer smiled. "Oh, good question, and it's a shame you're going to miss it. The bowl was sent for cleaning, but will be back on display in two days. Some experts believe it was used in John Smith's cleansing ceremony, before he was presented to Pocahontas's father."

Collin grinned, his mouth lifting higher on one side. "You don't say. My girlfriend here is *obsessed* with anything to do with Pocahontas." He wrapped an arm around my back and pulled me close to his body. "Aren't you, Myrtle?"

Myrtle? "I'm not sure I'd call it an obsession . . ."

Collin cocked his head and leaned toward the man, lowering his voice into a conspiratorial tone. "Don't let her fool you. She told me it all started when she saw the Disney movie when she was a little girl. She pretty much devoted her life to anything to do with the story of Pocahontas and John Smith after that. She has an entire room filled with anything to do with the topic and, I swear, she has over a hundred Pocahontas dolls."

The volunteer's eyes widened as he shot a concerned look at me. "Oh, my."

"She even has a tattoo on her butt cheek. A heart shape that strangely enough resembles the princess herself, with a flaming arrow shot into it with the words *John Smith* trailing behind in smoke."

"Oh. My."

I turned slightly and grabbed a handful of my skirt. "Would you like to see it?"

The man swallowed, his eyes now on my legs and my slowly rising hem.

Collin tensed. "She really should be on one of those hoarder shows, but what are you going to do?" Collin asked with a half shrug. He squeezed me tighter. "I love her."

"Those dolls are collector's items, Fred, and you know it." I gave the man a nod. "You can't put a price on history, now can you?"

The volunteer looked confused. "That's true."

"And as for the tattoo . . ." I lowered my voice. "Sometimes I just have to be *naughty*." I gave a little shudder.

The volunteer brushed a long strand of hair out of his eyes to get a better look at me.

"Myrtle, behave," Collin grumbled.

"Do you think Pocahontas *herself* touched the bowl?" I asked in a half whisper. "I'd give *anything* to see that."

The man shook his head, checking out my legs again. "Unfortunately, it won't be on display for two more days."

"But is it here? In the museum? Just knowing I might be in the same space as something Pocahontas touched would be like . . . the *best* experience of my entire life."

Collin's fingers dug into my waist. "Even better than me, Myrtle?"

I pinched my lips together and shrugged, waggling my eyebrows.

"It's due back tomorrow, and they'll put it back on display the day after."

I touched the man's arm. "But it used to be in the case? *Right there?*"

He nodded, looking down at my hand.

I closed my eyes and took a deep breath. "OMG. To breathe the same air that surrounded an object an Indian princess touched." I released a groan.

"Are you all right, dear?"

"*Myrtle.*" Collin's tight voice spurred me on.

My eyes flew open, and I pressed my hand to my chest. "Oh . . . to think . . ." I moaned again. "Pocahontas . . . touched something . . . here." I slid my hand down to my stomach in a slow sweep.

Other visitors began to stop and stare.

Collin released my waist and grabbed my arm. "Myrtle, I think we need to get your medication."

"But Fred . . ." I moaned, long and loud. "John Smith . . ."

Collin pulled me to the exit, looking over his shoulder at the volunteer. "Thank you for your help."

When we went into the next exhibit room, Collin released his hold. "*What was that?*"

"I found out that the bowl is coming back tomorrow, right?"

"I'm talking about the rest of it."

"Payback's a bitch."

"Now we're going to be suspects after your suspicious *display.*"

"Oh, please. Like my hundred-strong Pocahontas doll collection and the tattoo weren't enough?"

"After your Enrique act, I couldn't resist." He grinned and shook his head. "That was quite the show. If I hadn't stopped you, where was that going?"

I looked up at him, and stroked his jawline with my fingertip. "Ever seen *When Harry Met Sally?*"

His body tensed.

I gave him a wicked smile and spun around, heading for the exit. Let him think about *that* for a while.

~ Chapter Twenty ~

After we got back in the truck, Collin watched the museum, his hands folded over the steering wheel, deep in concentration.

"So do you have a plan?"

"Yeah."

I waited several seconds. "Are you going to tell me?"

He grinned that wicked smile he got when he knew he had something I wanted. But to my surprise, he answered. "I'd staked this place out before. I wanted to see if anything had changed."

"You had? When?"

"About six months ago, after my brother gave the bowl to the museum."

This surprised me on so many levels. First, although I knew Collin had a brother who didn't believe, I found it amazing that he disbelieved enough to actually give the bowl away. And two, that Collin had the nerve to get mad at me for pawning my cup. I smacked him on the arm.

He shrunk back in surprise. "What was that for?"

"There are too many transgressions to list."

He narrowed his eyes in confusion, then shook his head. "Do you want to know the plan or not?"

"Yes," I grumbled.

Again he looked confused before he shrugged it off. "My biggest concern before was how to get the bowl out of its glass display, so the fact that it's already out and not due to go back in until tomorrow is a godsend. What we need to do is get it tomorrow night, after it's been returned to the museum, but before it's put back on display."

"How in the world do you plan to break into a museum? They have alarms."

"I told you, Ellie. I've scoped this place out. I know how to get past the alarm system."

My mouth dropped open in disbelief. "You're kidding me, right?"

"Oh, Ellie. When will you learn to trust me?"

"When hell freezes over."

I expected him to make some sarcastic comment, but instead, he turned serious and studied me for several seconds. "Good girl."

What did that mean?

He moved on before I could ask. "We'll break in tomorrow night around midnight."

"But won't they consider us suspects?" I now regretted my earlier performance. I had no desire to do jail time for stealing some old bowl.

"You don't know the beautiful part of my plan." A shit-eating grin spread over his face.

"Are you going to sit there grinning like an idiot all day or are you going to explain your genius idea?"

"We'll make a switch."

"Excuse me?"

"I have a nearly identical bowl. They'll never realize that it's not the original—or at least not for a very long time. I hope. By then, we'll be ancient history, no pun intended. They'll never associate the theft with us."

"Do I want to know where you got the replacement bowl?"

"Probably not." I suspected this fell into the same category as the Ricardo deal. The less I knew about criminal activity, the better. "So why didn't you get it sooner? Why leave the bowl here for six months?"

"If I stole it and my brother found out, he'd just give it to someone else. The safest place for the bowl was behind a glass case until I needed it."

My suspicion went on high alert. "Wait. How did you know you'd need it? This curse has been in existence for hundreds of years. Why would you need the bowl?" He claimed he didn't know who I was when he'd come into the restaurant. What if he was lying?

But why would he *want* to break the curse? It didn't make sense, and I was too paranoid.

His face hardened. "Was I supposed to tell the next Keeper he or she could find the bowl in the museum? I'd have to retrieve the relic sometime, in order to pass it down along with the responsibility of being Keeper."

I scoffed. "The only way you were passing down the Keeper title was if you had a kid. You don't seem like the daddy type."

"You never know, Ellie. People change."

I'd like to think that. For some reason, I harbored a small, secret desire that Collin Dailey would denounce his life of crime and become a responsible citizen and then, just maybe, I'd have a chance with him. But that was irrational and stupid, and I'd better not forget it. If I wanted a fling with him, fine. But I could suffer no delusions that a relationship with Collin could be anything more. "So what do we do until tomorrow night?"

He turned back to face the museum. "It's a long drive back to Manteo, just to turn around and come back tomorrow. We could stay here for the night."

Butterflies squirmed in my stomach. "That was why we packed clothes, right?"

He grinned. "Okay." Then he turned out of the parking lot and drove down the Outer Banks.

When he pulled into the parking lot of a motel on the beach, I gave him a suspicious glance. I knew his financial situation. He didn't have eight hundred dollars to buy back my cup.

"How can we afford this?"

He shrugged and opened his door. "I know a guy."

I followed him out. "You know a guy? What the hell does that mean?"

"I've got it covered, Ellie."

I was sure he did. The question was did he have it covered by legal or illegal means?

We walked into the lobby, and I realized from the nineties décor that the motel was older and a little run-down. Nevertheless, beachfront property was premium. Run-down or not, I was sure Collin couldn't afford it.

Collin rested his forearm on the registration desk counter and smiled his one hundred megawatt death-by-sex smile. I could see the girl on the other side of the counter turn to putty in his hands. I decided to sit back and watch the master work his magic.

"So, sweetheart." Collin leaned closer and lowered his voice. "What's the best room you've got?"

"Um. They're all the same." She cast an ugly look in my direction before returning her gaze to Collin, batting her eyelashes. "They all face the ocean. But there are three levels and the rooms on the third floor on the north side have a better view."

"And how much is one of those rooms?"

She told him, and despite his financial straits, he didn't flinch. "Is Tommy here?"

She blinked in surprise. "You know Tommy?"

"Tommy told me that porcelain is king."

She tilted her head and looked at him with more awe.

What was up with the "porcelain is king" crap?

She handed him a room key. "You're in Room 326. It has the best view."

Collin slid the key card off the counter in one smooth movement. "Thank you"—he looked at her name tag—"Tammy."

"You're welcome, Mr. Pressley."

Mr. Pressley?

He started to walk away, but turned around and smiled again. "Is there anything to do around here for entertainment, Tammy?"

"I'd be happy to show you a good time."

I gave a little shudder, sure I'd heard her wrong. *Did she seriously say that in front of me?*

Collin leaned closer and shrugged a shoulder toward me, lowering his voice as though I couldn't hear him. "I'm a little preoccupied at the moment, but you never know when things will change." He winked and a slow smile lit up her face. "In the meantime, is there anything else I can do?"

"Sapphire Cove, the next town up, is having a street fair tonight."

He scowled. "Anything else?"

"There's a go-cart track with mini golf a half mile down the highway."

He obviously liked the sound of that even less. "Thanks," he grumbled as he ushered me out the door and back to the truck.

"Porcelain is king? Mr. Pressley? What was all of that?"

He spun around with a grin. "Think about it long enough and you'll get it." He grabbed my suitcase and two duffel bags out of the truck bed and headed for the stairs.

"Do I even want to know about your tête-à-tête with *Tammy*?"

"Insurance."

"*Excuse me?*"

"Ellie, when you've been in my line of business long enough, you learn to make friends whenever possible."

"And what exactly is your line of business?"

He shot me a grin. "Getting what I want."

At least he was honest about it. I wondered how much time he spent fishing on his boat and how much he spent on shady activities.

We climbed two flights and walked along the outdoor walkway to our room. While Collin opened the door, I stared out into the ocean, the rhythmic sound of waves drawing my attention.

Collin stood behind me, enclosing me with his arms as he braced his hands on either side of me on the rail. "You feel it don't you?" he whispered huskily in my ear. "The call of the water."

I nodded. "Do you feel it too?"

He swept my hair off my shoulder, his face close to my neck. "I'm the son of the earth, Ellie. You're the daughter of the sea. The call is for you."

What was he up to? I couldn't imagine that he was trying to start anything. Once again, I wondered if he couldn't help himself. The Collin Fucking Dailey charm was as natural as the air he breathed. He probably had to purposely suppress it.

"You feel a call from the land."

"Yes."

"So is it hard for you when you're on the water? Does part of you ache for the land?"

"I'm sure it's no different from how you feel when you're on the ocean."

"I've never been."

His body tensed, ever so slightly. "Never been what?"

"On the ocean."

"How is that possible? You live less than a hundred feet from the sound."

I shrugged. "Momma was deathly afraid of water, and my obsession with it didn't help. So she purposely made sure I never went on a boat."

"And later? After she died? Was that some desire to please her since you felt responsible for her death?"

Collin was dangerous. He was much too intuitive to suit me. "Partly. The other part was the few times a friend had a boat and offered to take me out on the sea. But they weren't the most trustworthy of people, and I decided it wasn't worth risking my life."

"Good call, but you need the water, Ellie. It feeds your own Manitou."

I stiffened at the thought of dead sea animals. I could never steal life so callously.

Collin sensed my horror and ran a hand down my arm. "Not like that. This is different."

It was a lovely thought, but I didn't have access to a boat. But perhaps that explained why Collin seemed so much stronger than me.

We stayed like that for several minutes, me watching the ocean and resting against the balcony railing, Collin pressed against my back, his arms on either side of me. I knew I should be thankful for this moment with him, but I was greedy. I wanted more of him, not just this.

Collin's arms dropped and he turned around and went into the room. When he left, it was as though a piece of me went missing. Just as I was about to chide myself for being overdramatic, I realized the truth of it: Collin and I were equal halves of a whole. Perhaps we could have simply done our job, combining our power when needed in the ceremony, but last night had bound us in a way that I was sure Collin didn't anticipate. Did he feel it too? If he did, why did he fight it so?

I not only needed Collin Dailey, I *wanted* him. I could try to ignore it for the rest of the time I had left with him and regret until my dying breath that I never seized this opportunity. Or I could go through it and have my heart broken when he left, because I knew beyond a shadow of a doubt that he would.

My heart would be broken no matter what choice I made.

The door to the room was still open, but I wasn't ready to face him yet. Besides, I wanted to see if he had a point about the water. I headed down the stairs and kicked off my shoes, carrying them in my hand as I trekked across the fifty-foot beach toward the water. The closer I got to the water's edge, the stronger the pull. When my feet hit the wet sand, I curled my toes and waited for a wave to wash over me. My knees almost buckled at the rush of power and I gasped out loud.

My eyes sank closed as I absorbed both the power and what it meant. As well as the potential disadvantage it gave me. Collin was a fisherman, but he spent a lot of time on the land. The ceremony would most likely take place on the land, possibly miles from water. There was nothing I could do about that. Would I be strong enough to be useful?

I decided to ignore what I couldn't control—Collin, my power or lack thereof—and enjoy this moment. The realization that I *did* have a purpose: Elinor Dare Lancaster, Curse Keeper. I walked deeper into the waves, the water crashing into my legs as I tilted my head back, my face absorbing the sunlight. My skirt flapped, the hem soaking up saltwater, and my hair blew around my face. I could almost feel the Manitou of creatures around me, just a tickle of their presence. I had been right the day before in the warehouse. This wasn't just a curse. It was a blessing.

I wasn't sure how long I stayed there, straddling both worlds, but it was long enough to become cold from the water and the wind. My long hair had become hopelessly tangled, and I reached up to brush it out of my face as I turned around to go back to the room. I stopped mid-turn, surprised to see Collin standing ten feet behind me. The raw desire in his eyes stole my breath. Collin Dailey wanted me as much as I wanted him. The knowledge knotted my stomach and caused an ache inside, an ache that I needed him to touch. To fill. I took a step toward him and stopped as he backed up several paces, then turned around and returned to the room without me.

∴ Chapter Twenty-One ∾

Collin didn't say a word when I returned. He sat in a chair by the window and watched a game show on the television.

On the walk back to the room, I decided I could go about this one of two ways: I could sulk the rest of our time together or I could figure out a way to break Collin Dailey. The second option held much more appeal. On so many levels.

I flopped on the bed next to him. "What are we doing tonight?"

He kept his attention on the television, an obvious ploy to get me to leave him alone. There was no way Collin was that interested in a tampon commercial.

"I don't know. I guess eat dinner."

"I want to go to the street fair."

His eyebrows slowly rose as his mouth parted. "You're kidding, right?"

"Nope."

He shook his head. "No. No way."

We'd see about that. I stood up and walked toward the bathroom. "I'm going to take a shower."

That got his attention. "That's not a good idea. You might screw up your mark."

I gave him a saucy look. "Then I guess you'll just have to redo it."

"*Ellie.*"

I set my bag on the bed and unzipped it enough to pull out my cosmetics bag. "I haven't had a shower in days, Collin. I'm sure the mark has set by now.

Have mercy on me." But I didn't want him to show me mercy. I wanted—I stopped the thought before I attacked him. I had no doubt he would eventually cave, but there was also no doubt that Collin was stubborn. Too bad for him he'd met his match. But I didn't want to smell like sweat and lemons when I seduced him and that meant I needed a shower.

He slumped in the chair, rolling his eyes in disgust. "Do whatever you want. You do anyway."

The sooner he accepted that, the better off he'd be.

I was in the bathroom long enough to steam up the mirror. I had to make sure I was ready for shenanigans with Collin Dailey and that included shaving. Plus I hoped he was out there thinking about me. Naked.

When I opened the door, he jerked upright, purposely trying to ignore me and shifting in his seat. He cast a glance my way, which turned into a double take when he realized I'd come out wrapped in the flimsy terry-cloth robe. His eyes stayed on me. Collin Dailey looked like a starving man, and he wasn't hungry for food.

"Do you want to check my back? To make sure I didn't screw up my mark?" I partially turned my back toward him, dropping my robe off my shoulder.

He looked away. "No," he responded more gruffly than necessary.

I almost chuckled and went back into the bathroom. I towel dried my hair and found a blow-dryer to help with the rest. When I was done, it was a frizzy mess. I sighed.

Since Claire had packed my bag, I wasn't sure what she'd included. Thankfully, she'd had more foresight than I had. I pulled out a black lacy shirt and a gauzy skirt, along with a lacy black bra and panties buried underneath.

I dressed and put on a little makeup. It was too hot to wear much more than blush, eye shadow and mascara, and lip stain. Next I plaited my hair into a soft, messy braid over my shoulder that reminded me a bit of Rosalina's. That gave me pause. I didn't want to remind Collin of Rosalina. I stared at myself in the mirror to get the full effect. I'd never be the beauty that Rosalina was, but I could manage pretty. Tonight I wore slightly more eye makeup than usual. I still passed for pretty, but with a bit of maturity.

When I emerged from the bathroom, Collin was pacing the floor. He turned toward me, and froze.

"Do you need to get ready?" I asked.

He nodded, then swallowed.

I smiled. Imagine that. A speechless Collin Dailey. Someone needed to mark that down for posterity.

He pulled a set of clothes out of his bag and moved past me. I purposely made it difficult. He looked like he was in pain when he closed the bathroom door. The sound of the shower soon followed. Collin didn't linger under the water long. He was in and out of the bathroom in less than ten minutes.

He picked up his wallet and truck keys off the dresser. "No street fair," he growled, stuffing the wallet into his back pocket. *Lucky wallet. I'd love to be that close to Collin's ass.* Good Lord. When had I become this person?

He glanced up and saw where I was staring and got flustered. What was Collin afraid of? Was he as worried that I'd break his heart as I was that he would break mine? What a joke. It was more likely he worried I'd pull some hysterical woman freak-out when he left.

Collin opened the door and held it for me. "You look very handsome," I said in a slow, sexy voice as I walked by him. He was more than handsome. I couldn't imagine how *People* magazine hadn't put his picture on their cover as the sexiest man alive.

Even though Collin had tried to keep his distance in our room, outside he fell in step beside me, his hand on the small of my back. I hid my smile. I didn't want to spook him. When we got to the truck, he opened the door for me. Unlike that morning, I didn't comment. I realized this wasn't something Collin did—open car doors for women. What exactly did it mean that he did it for me?

It took us less than ten minutes to get downtown. The streets were crowded and several were blocked off. Collin parked on a side road and was over on my side of the truck as I got out. I loved that Collin had told me no street fair, but then drove us there anyway. The boy was breaking.

"What are you hungry for?" I asked in a husky voice.

It took him several seconds to answer. "I don't care."

"Do you want to walk around and see what's here?"

"Sure."

I almost felt badly for him. Almost. I still hadn't figured out why he was resisting me so hard, but at least I wasn't making a fool of myself. He wanted me. Bad.

We stopped at a bar and grill and sat in the patio area on the sidewalk, watching the people pass by. Collin leaned back in his seat, uncharacteristically quiet. It occurred to me that if he had a reason for not acting on his feelings toward me, maybe I should respect that. He was clearly uncomfortable.

"Collin," I said, putting my hand on the table surface in front of him.

His eyes darted to mine.

"I didn't sleep with Drew last night. He's Claire's fiancé."

"I know."

That caught me by surprise. "You didn't look like you knew when you showed up this morning."

"Not at first I didn't, but the minute Claire arrived, I saw the way they looked at each other." He still scowled.

I thought clearing our misunderstanding would make things better. "We can go. If you want to get something to go, we can just take it back to the room."

He watched me for several seconds, then shook his head. "No. I want to be here."

I released my breath.

"I need a beer." He motioned for the waitress to come over and ordered a pale ale.

"I'll take one too."

He smirked.

"What?" I asked when the waitress left.

"I thought you preferred men who were stout."

I smiled. My Collin was back and had accepted my challenge. "No, I said I took you for a stout man." My eyebrows rose. "Was I wrong?"

A slow sexy grin spread across his face. "I'll let you figure that out for yourself."

My body flushed.

He leaned forward and waited for my response. Score one for Collin. He slid his hand across the table and reached for my hand, slowly turning it over. His fingertip traced the lines in my palm and I shivered. He grinned at the small victory. "Did you know I can read palms?"

I shook my head.

His finger traced a long line from my thumb to my wrist. "This is your life line." He bent over it. "Yours is quite long and bold. You'll live a very long and very large life." He found a line that ran down the middle of my hand. "This is your fate line." He studied it and grinned up at me. "You are destined for the best night of your life, Ellie Lancaster."

I wasn't sure how it was possible, but this was the second time Collin had got me hot just holding my hand. I could only imagine what it would be like when we finally slept together. There was no doubt we would. At this point it was a game of who would cave first.

His finger moved to a line on the other side of my hand. "This is your love line. It, combined with your fate line, says you will meet a dark, handsome man who will make you beg for mercy for toying with his principles."

I lowered my voice. "And does it say where I'll meet such a man?"

He lifted my hand to his mouth and licked the tip of my ring finger. "The Romans thought there was a direct connection from the left ring finger to the heart. But I think it goes somewhere else."

I tried to suppress a moan as my eyelids fluttered. Oh God. I wasn't sure I'd make it through dinner.

A languid smile lit up his face. Collin was in his element and our roles had been reversed.

Collin sucked on my fingertip. "Do you want to read my palm?"

The feeling shot right to my groin and I sucked in a breath. "What?"

He chuckled. "You seem distracted, Ellie."

"No." My voice wavered. "I'm fine."

He opened his left palm and traced his love line with my finger. Dear God, even that turned me on.

"This is my love line. Do you know what it says?"

"No."

"It says an incredibly sexy, but totally infuriating redheaded woman will barge into my life and drive me insane."

His sentence made me pause. "But insane in a good way?"

His smile was genuine. "Insane in a way I never thought possible." Then his wicked look returned, and he moved my finger to his fate line. "See how long and bold this line is? It's an indication of my sexual prowess."

I burst out laughing.

He leaned away, taken aback. "What's so funny?"

"Your sexual *prowess*?"

His eyes narrowed. "Is that a challenge?"

I grinned. "Oh, you have no idea."

The tables had turned again, and he was the one who looked like he was about to strip me naked right there on the table.

His voice lowered, and he leaned close. "You said you like it on top. I spent all day imagining it."

Oh. Shit.

The waitress came back with our drinks and asked to take our order. We hadn't even looked at the menu yet. Dear God. We still had to sit through dinner. I'd be begging Collin to screw me in the bathroom at this rate.

"I just want an appetizer." I shoved the menu at the waitress.

Collin grinned, keeping his eyes on me.

"Which one?" the waitress asked.

"Uh . . ."

"How about crab cakes?" Collin asked. "And the grilled shrimp."

I nodded. I'd eat raw carrots if it would speed this up and get us back to the motel, and I hated raw carrots.

She took the menus and left.

"Where were we?" Collin asked.

Torturing me for playing with your principles.

He continued his torture until the food arrived. As the waitress started to leave, Collin called her back, asking for the bill. I was glad to see I wasn't the only impatient one.

We'd barely eaten the last shrimp when Collin stood and reached for my hand. He pulled me into the crowd, his right hand wrapped tight around my left as though I would disappear. The sounds of a live band in the street caught my attention.

"Collin, I want to dance."

He shook his head. "I don't dance."

I pulled him toward the music, making our way through the crowd. He didn't resist, in spite of his protest.

I stopped a comfortable distance away so that we could hear the music but still converse. I swayed in time to the beat. "Why don't you dance?"

His gaze wandered to my hips. "I dance. Just not this kind."

"You know another kind?"

A wicked smile lit up his face. "How about you teach me how to dance your way, and I'll teach you how to dance mine."

Oh. Shit. "Deal."

He looked amused. "So tell me what to do."

I hadn't eaten much at dinner and the beer had gone straight to my head. I gave him a sexy look. "You don't strike me as the kind of guy who likes to be told what to do."

"You'd be surprised."

I took a deep breath. *Focus.* "We can either stand apart or we can be together."

Collin's hands settled on my waist. "Always together, Ellie. Always."

I placed my hands on his chest, but kept several inches between us.

"Now what?" Collin asked.

"Now you move to the music."

We danced, a slow seductive swaying of our hips. Collin's heart beat fast under my hand. I searched his eyes, finding evidence that Collin Dailey wasn't immune to me. "So far I don't think our dances are all that different."

Collin pulled me flush to his body, his hands still on my waist. "I need you closer."

My stomach fluttered. "I thought I was teaching this dance."

"From what I've seen, mine is *so* much better."

"You're not giving mine a chance."

"I've been giving yours a chance for hours." Collin slid his hands underneath the hem of my shirt, his fingertips skimming my back above my waistband. "Are you a witch, Ellie Lancaster? Have you cast a spell to entrance me?" He looked half serious and leaned his forehead down to mine, then whispered, "Or are you an angel sent to save my soul?"

I closed my eyes. If he didn't kiss me soon, I would combust.

His hands slid up my back, outside my shirt, his hands splayed and digging in as they moved. "You have *no idea* how much I want you."

"I want you too."

He groaned, and one of his hands found my neck, traveling up to cup the side of my head, our bodies moving to the slow tempo of the band. His mouth leaned close to mine, so agonizingly close. "Don't trust me, Ellie. You can't trust me." His voice cracked with pain.

How many times had he told me that? "I know who you are, Collin. I'm going into this with eyes wide open." I reached for the back of his head, trying to bring his mouth to mine, but he held back. What was he waiting for? What did he need from me? "No man has made me feel even a fraction of what I feel with you, Collin. I *know* this is short term. I know you'll be gone once the gate is closed. But I still want you."

His eyes closed, and his hold on my head tightened.

"What do you want from me, Collin? Do you want me to beg?" God help me, I was willing to do it.

"I'll hurt you, Ellie. I don't want to hurt you."

"I know you won't stick around. You'll hurt me so much more if you reject me, Collin. *Please.*"

He groaned again.

I stood on my tiptoes, pressing my lips to his. He stood still, his chest rising and falling against mine. My tongue ran along his bottom lip, finding an opening, then exploring his mouth.

His shackles fell off and he took over, his tongue joining mine, giving me what I wanted, but it wasn't enough. Not nearly enough. He pulled away, his breath coming in tight bursts. "Time for my lesson."

I nodded, but he was pulling me through the crowd toward the truck. He lifted me up and shoved me through the driver's door, following close behind. I lay on my back on the seat, and Collin leaned over me. His mouth was on mine, his hands up my shirt. I pressed my hips to his, needing more.

He growled, his body rising and denying me his mouth. I reached for him, intending to pull him back down. *Dear God, please don't let him change his mind.*

"Ellie, I'm not going to fuck you in this truck like a couple of high school kids where anyone can see us."

Good point.

He sat up and started the truck, throwing it into reverse. The drive to the motel took half the time it took to get downtown. From the look on Collin's face, a couple of times I wondered if he was going to change his mind and pull over to the side of the road anyway.

When he pulled into the parking lot, he had the door open, sliding me out the driver's side before the engine died. He shut the door and pushed me against the side of the truck. "I'll never make it upstairs if I don't kiss you now." His mouth found mine before I could answer, kissing me so thoroughly my knees buckled.

His arm wrapped around my waist, snugging me close. "Ellie, what the hell have you done to me?"

His mouth continued its onslaught, his tongue giving me a preview of what was to come. I moaned. I needed more.

He broke away, his breathing labored. "Upstairs. *Now.*"

∴ Chapter Twenty-Two ∾

He wrapped his hand around my wrist and he dragged me toward the stairs, practically running up the steps. His legs were longer than mine and I had trouble keeping up. "Collin, wait." This Collin Dailey surprised me. I always took him as a man in total control, even with sex. Especially with sex. To see that I made him this way made me even hotter.

He stopped on the first landing and pulled me against his chest, his mouth on mine again. "You're too slow."

I slid my hand up the back of his shirt, my fingertips soaking in the feel of him. "You don't like it slow?"

"I love it slow. Right now I want you fast." His lips and tongue worked a magic on mine I never thought possible. When he stepped away, my legs trembled before he grabbed my wrist again, pulling me up the next flight of stairs to the third floor. How did he expect me to run up stairs when I could hardly stand?

We'd barely reached the landing when he pushed me against the wall of the building, his lips and tongue paving a path from my ear to the pulse point on my neck. I grabbed the back of his head, resisting the urge to push him lower.

"Our door is less than fifty feet away," he growled against my chest, "yet I want you so much I'd fuck you right here if I thought no one would see us."

My stomach tightened and I groaned, urging his mouth back to mine. "Collin." I took control with my tongue, showing him how much I wanted exactly the same thing he did.

He leaned back, and he glanced around with a worried expression. "It's dark. I need to get you inside." He led me toward our room, his hand trembling with the plastic card key.

When he pushed the door open, I took the lead, yanking him inside and stripping my shirt over my head and tossing it to the floor.

He pulled me in his arms again, his lips over mine, his hands roaming my back and shoulders. "Wait." He moved away from me and toward the dresser, picking up a piece of what looked like charcoal and returning to the door.

"What are you doing?"

"Protecting you." He began to draw symbols around the door as fast as his hand would move.

That was the sexiest thing anyone had ever done for me.

"What do they mean?" I asked, standing behind him in my skirt and bra.

His hand paused, then his sketching resumed, slower this time. "The stars and moon ask the ancient force of night to protect you. I put them in each corner to make sure every side is sealed. On either side of them is a sun." He sketched out a sun with an arrow. "The sun is asleep, but its power is far reaching. This asks the sun to join with night, adding its power."

Next he drew a lightning bolt on the left side of the suns and something that looked like raindrops on the opposite side. "The air which is ruled by the wind gods. Placing them between the power of the sun and night, prevents the wind gods from using the air to harm you."

Tears filled my eyes. I had no idea.

"The mountains represent the land." He drew a zigzagged line. "My power." His voice was husky as his hand etched the symbols eight times on the door. "All forces join together to protect that which should be protected above all else."

He drew waves in the center of each side. "The sea."

I studied the door and symbols, speechless. "What protects you?" I finally choked out.

He turned around to face me, raw lust in his eyes. "Nothing can protect me, Ellie. I was a goner the minute I met you." He tossed the charcoal on the dresser as he took two purposeful steps toward me, his hand reaching for my waist. "Are you sure? Are you really, really sure?"

How could he ask me that after what he'd just done? My heart was forever lost to this man. "I've never been more sure of anything in my life."

"Then you have too many clothes on." Collin quickly unfastened the button on my skirt. It puddled to the floor as I lifted the hem of his T-shirt and pulled it up. Collin tugged it the rest of the way over his head and let it drop. He gaze wandered up my legs, over my black lacy panties, lingering on my bra until settling on my face.

"God, you're beautiful."

He reached for my face and brought it to his, his earlier frenzy seeming to have dissipated. Mine had settled into a deeper level. A primeval concoction of lust and need and something more significant, a feeling I couldn't name, but that was stronger than the other two combined. I knew I'd never experience this with anyone else ever.

His tongue sought out mine, a slow dance of heat and desire. I pressed my body to his, needing to touch him. Every part of him. I reached down and pressed against his crotch.

Collin released a long groan. My other hand fumbled with his belt, but he brushed it away, making quick work of the belt, button, and zipper.

I pulled him to the bed and sat on the edge. I slid my fingers into the top of his waistband and eased them down over his thighs. A thrill ran through my blood at the sight of his dark briefs. His jeans hung at his knees as my hands skimmed his outer thighs, moving toward the bulge in his underwear. Within a few strokes, Collin grabbed my hands and pushed me back on the bed, kicking his jeans off in the process. He used his body to pin mine, his hands holding mine over my head.

"You drive me crazy." His frenzy was back as his mouth devoured mine, then moved down to my chest, licking the tender skin over the top of my bra. "You still have too many clothes on." His hand reached under my back, unsnapping the bra strap with expert fingers. He pulled the straps down my arms and had barely tossed it aside when his mouth found my breast and his hands reclaimed mine.

I arched, wanting every part of me closer to him. I wrapped my legs around his waist, rolling my hips into his.

A low rumble filled his chest as he moved to my other breast, my hands still pressed to the bed. "Collin, I want to touch you."

He released my hands and shifted positions, sitting back on his knees and staring down at me.

"I can't reach you now." I propped up on my elbows.

"I want to look at you." His gaze landed on my panties. His fingers hooked the lace on my hip and dragged down, his face lowered, his lips planting kisses in the silk's wake.

My head dropped back as I released a moan. "Collin, please."

His mouth moved up to my breast, his eyes on mine.

I grabbed his head and pulled his mouth to mine. "I want you."

He was frenzy and fire again, his hands and mouth everywhere. He rolled us over and I was on top, straddling a key part of him still covered by underwear. I sat up and trailed a finger down his chest to the band of his briefs, giving him a sexy smile. "You have on too many clothes."

"What are you going to do about that?"

I loved seeing him like this, flat on his back, hunger in his eyes, the sign of his desire for me hidden only by a piece of fabric.

I reached for his waistband, but moved too slow to suit him. He sat up, pushing my legs down around his thighs. He kissed me long and slow, one hand finding my breast while the other delved lower. I gasped and he leaned back, his eyes dark with wanting. "I see the appeal of you being on top." He kissed me again, his hands working a magic that had nothing to do with the curse or the power in our blood.

"Collin, please." I pleaded.

"Don't move." His hands left my body and he leaned forward to pull his jeans off the floor, digging in his pocket to remove a foil package. He grabbed my hips and pulled me up to my knees, giving him enough room to remove his underwear and put on the condom.

We sat there for several seconds, staring into each other's eyes, indecision flickering in his.

"Collin, I've never wanted anyone as much as I want you right now."

He grabbed my hips again and guided me over him and slowly pulled me down. We groaned together as he filled me, and when he was sure I was okay, he began his dance. He was the puppet master, and he controlled my every move. I was climbing, climbing, so close to the edge, and we'd only just begun.

"Not yet, Ellie. Wait for me." He stopped and kissed me thoroughly, his tongue showing me what the other part of him waited to continue.

He released my hips, and my body found its own rhythm. His hand slid up my bare back, his fingers digging, claiming. Didn't he know I was already his?

"Collin," I gasped.

"Not yet." His hips began to move against mine, and we began a new dance, his movement more hurried, needy.

"*Collin*." I was wound so tight I wasn't sure I'd ever become untangled.

His left hand grabbed my right one, placing it over his mark and his hand found mine on my back.

I cried out, shattered to pieces at the assault of power and sex. Collin pushed deep, using his free hand to pull me closer, releasing a loud groan as he arched up.

We fought to catch our breath. I opened my eyes to see his face inches from mine, his eyes still dark with lust and need. "Are you an angel or an enchantress, Ellie Lancaster?"

I kissed him long and slow, nipping his lower lip and licking behind it. "I'm whichever you want me to be."

I felt him stirring again.

"You must be an enchantress. You have me under your spell."

He kissed me this time, making my pulse rise.

"And what does that make you?" I teased.

"Yours."

Collin had to be joking. There was no way he'd say that to me. Unless he was playing me, but why would he? I'd already told him I expected him to leave when the gate was closed. I didn't have time to think about it because he kissed me again, and I lost all conscious thought except for what he was doing to me at that moment.

We made love again, Collin on top this time. Afterward, he lay next to me, bringing the side of my body flush with his stomach and chest. He propped up on one elbow and brushed several strands of hair plastered to my cheek and forehead. "I'd suggest we take a shower, but it would probably be a waste."

Just the mention of having sex with him again made my body flush.

Collin grinned. "You are insatiable, Ellie Lancaster. You'll kill me with sex." His mouth lowered to mine, placing soft kisses at the corners. "Maybe you're a succubus."

"Those aren't real," I murmured closing my eyes.

"Don't be so sure about that." The tone in his voice told me he meant it.

My eyes flew open. "You're serious."

He stared into my eyes.

"What else is out there?"

"I'm not sure. Everything. Anything. But just like there are good and bad people, there are good and bad spirits. The bad ones will seek you out specifically. You're a Curse Keeper and you have a pure soul. Tomorrow we have to work on teaching you to protect yourself."

I laughed. "I think I just proved I don't have a pure soul, Collin."

"What we just did had nothing to do with the pureness of your soul, Ellie."

He was serious. I scooted backward and propped a pillow under my head. "Why do you think I have a pure soul?"

"The first time we linked, in the warehouse, I felt it. Your aura shined many times brighter than all of those around me. Honestly, I didn't expect it. Pure souls are rare."

"You see auras when we're linked?"

"You don't?"

"No. I feel their presence. Almost like omnipotence. Do you?"

"No." His eyes darkened with worry. "But the Manitou gives each person their own gifts."

"So what makes a pure soul?"

"Everything and everyone has a Manitou. When a being dies, its Manitou returns to the collective, if you will, and gets recycled. Unless it's consumed by a god or demon and then it's lost forever. But sometimes something or someone is born with a fresh Manitou. That makes them a pure soul."

"So why would someone be born with a fresh Manitou?"

"The world becomes tired and stale. So the larger forces release beings with pure souls. People and animals. Often around the same time or same life cycles, usually hundreds of years apart. According to the legends of my ancestors, anyway. My grandmother said that the Manitou of pure souls were present at the creation of the universe."

"By larger forces, you mean like night and day? Like the symbols you posted on the door?"

"Yes, and water and land. Everything has a counterpart. A yin and yang."

I picked up his left hand, lacing our fingers. "Like you and me."

His eyes darkened. "Yes, like you and me." He sounded so serious. And worried. Why would that worry him?

"Does the fact I'm a pure soul have anything to with the curse and closing the gate?"

His hand tightened around mine, his voice even tighter. "No. It's a coincidence."

"But the gods will know that I am a pure soul?"

His eyes were full of regret and worry as they looked up into mine. "Yes."

"You said I need to learn to defend myself, but why would I need to learn if we close the gate? Won't they all go back? Won't I be safe?"

He pulled his hand from mine and began to stroke the skin on my abdomen with his fingertip. His mouth followed his fingers.

My stomach tightened, and I released a low moan. "You didn't answer my question."

"Learning to defend yourself is a fail-safe." He found my breast, and I gasped. "In case we don't close it."

"Why wouldn't we close it? We're getting the bowl tomorrow night."

He captured my mouth with his, sending me into a dizzy tailspin. How could this man set my body alive? Would it still be like this without the magic in our blood? His face hovered inches from mine. "You're a pure soul, Ellie. I don't want to take any chances. Humor me."

If humoring him included what we were doing right then, I'd humor him the rest of my life.

∽ Chapter Twenty-Three ∾

I woke to sunshine and Collin's mouth on my face and knew immediately this had to be a dream. My bedroom window faced west. When I opened my eyes, Collin was planting kisses along my jaw and working his way down to my neck. I closed my eyes again. "I had the most wonderful dream."

"Oh, yeah?"

"I dreamed that I had wild, mind-blowing sex with the most gorgeous man alive."

"And who might this sexy, gorgeous man be?"

"Oh, I never said he was sexy."

"The two usually go hand in hand. And you didn't answer my question."

"I think his name was Collin." I grinned. "Colin Firth. I love a sexy British accent."

He threw a pillow at me and I laughed.

His eyes widened. "*Colin Firth*? You really think that old man is capable of giving you what we had last night?"

I sat up. "Well, to give an accurate answer, I'd have to give the old man a chance."

"Or I could give you another demonstration."

"Careful, Collin. I'll think you're an incubus."

His smile fell, and he cupped my cheek, leaning close to kiss me. "I'll do everything I can to protect you."

My shoulders tensed at his sudden change in mood. "You already do, Collin."

He shook off his frown. "There was a purpose to your wakeup call. I was going to give you a surprise, but now I'm not so sure if you're going to insult my sexual prowess."

I giggled. "It's hard to take you seriously when you use that word."

He raised his eyebrow in an exaggerated waggle. "I believe the stories of my sexual *prowess* are known far and wide."

I leaned back on my elbows, letting the sheet drop to my waist. "Oh really?" I shook my head. "I never heard a one of them."

He got to his knees and pulled me to mine, our naked bodies flush against one another. "I don't remember any complaints last night, Miss Lancaster." His hands slid slowly down my back and down to my ass. "Do you need a demonstration?" He lowered his head to my neck and nipped the tender skin.

"That might be necessary."

"Maybe later."

"I'll break you down, Collin Dailey."

He turned serious. "You already did." He kissed me again, a toe-curling kiss that left me lightheaded and dizzy. Then he got up and left me kneeling in the middle of the bed. "Maybe you'll think next time before you try to besmirch my reputation."

"Come back. I'll apologize." I lingered on the last word.

"No, first your surprise."

"You really have one? I thought you were kidding." Collin didn't seem like the kind of man who gave surprises.

"I really have one." He tossed some clothing toward me. "You'll need to put this on."

I picked it up and realized it was my bikini. "Do I want to know *how* you got this?"

"It was in your suitcase. Put it on."

"We're going to go lay out on the beach?"

"Later, if that's what you want to do. My surprise first."

I couldn't imagine what surprise he could possibly have that involved a bikini. Collin didn't seem like a frolicking-at-the-edge-of-the-ocean kind of guy either. But I got up and went into the bathroom to brush my teeth and put it on. When I walked out, Collin was in his swim trunks. If my surprise included seeing a shirtless Collin all day, I could live with that.

I held out a bottle of sunscreen. "Can you help me? I take it that we'll be outside?"

He took the bottle, and I turned around as he swept my loose braid over my shoulder. He kissed the back of my neck. "I liked your hair last night."

"Thank you," I murmured. This Collin was so foreign to me that he took some getting used to. When he finished, I put on the coverup Claire had packed. What had possessed her to think of my swimsuit? Probably wishful thinking.

Collin held the door open, holding several towels. "After you."

Outside the door, we encountered a rude reminder of the curse: two dead blackbirds, four robins, and a cardinal. Collin turned back to me, his face expressionless. "Is this what you find every morning?"

I nodded. "You don't?"

"No." His voice was hard. He kept his eyes on the birds as he kicked them out of the pattern. He went back into the room and called the front desk, asking them to send someone to clean them up.

Would there be another sacrifice today? The messenger had said there would be a sacrifice every day I didn't choose to side with Okeus. The guilt was overwhelming, but I knew if I pledged my loyalty to him, things would become so much worse. "Collin, something happened a couple of nights ago—"

He kissed me. "No. We're not going to talk about that right now. The sun is out and you're safe. We're going to enjoy the morning and deal with everything else later."

A new panic flooded my senses. "But the body in the botanical gardens yesterday, you said you thought it was a message to me." I grabbed his arm, my nails digging into this skin. "What if they go after my father and my stepmother? I have to go back!"

His hand cupped my cheek as he gazed into my eyes with reassurance. "Relax, Ellie. I already thought of that. After I heard about the body, I realized your family might not be safe. I poured salt across the doorways to the bed and breakfast."

My hold loosened. "How did you know about the bed and breakfast?"

His eyes wrinkled in confusion. "You told me you were helping keep your father's bed and breakfast afloat. Your last name is Lancaster. It wasn't hard to find out which place was his."

"But why would you do that, Collin? What made you think to protect them?"

"Because I know they are important to you." He kissed me gently. "I meant to tell you yesterday, but then the phone call from Marino's guy threw me off."

"Thank you." Those two words seemed so inadequate to express how much what he'd done meant to me, but the look in his eyes told me that he knew.

With Collin, I really felt we *could* be okay. Collin knew how to handle the spirits and the gods, but I also brought power to the union. We were stronger together than our two separate selves. We were getting his bowl tonight. We'd close the gate in time.

The morning was beautiful. The sun shone bright and the waves crashed onto the shore. I leaned against the railing, and Collin put his arm around my back. "Is it calling to you now?"

I nodded. "Yeah."

"Then let's answer it."

We went down the stairs to the beach. I couldn't help thinking about climbing those same stairs last night. I still couldn't believe how quickly things had changed. Collin must have been thinking the same thing because he gave me a wicked smile on the second-floor landing.

At the bottom of the staircase, Collin stopped next to two surfboards propped against the motel. "I take it you've never surfed."

My stomach tingled with excitement. "Are you serious?"

He grinned and handed me one of the boards. "So that's no?"

"What are you doing? We can't just take these."

"Relax. A friend of mine dropped them off."

I cocked my head. "Let me guess, you know a guy?"

He winked. "I always know a guy. I called him before you woke up." He picked up a bag and his board and we walked to the water.

"Shouldn't we be doing something more important?" I asked. "Like preparing for tonight? Or teaching me to defend myself?"

"Trust me."

A girl could get whiplash with his trust me/trust me not flip-flopping. He'd proven that he cared about me and my well-being. I trusted him. My stomach twisted with both excitement and nerves. "I take it that *you* surf."

"Any self-respecting boy growing up in Buxton surfed." He dropped the towels on the sand. "Drop your board on the sand first."

I did as he instructed and stripped off my coverup, tossing it on top of the towels.

Collin had that hungry look in his eyes again.

"I thought you were teaching me to surf."

"I got distracted by the view." He grinned. "First you need to learn how to stand on the board. Move to the center with your left foot forward."

I placed both feet on the board. "Now what?"

"Now bend your knees, keeping them over your toes. Then squat slightly and hold your arms out from your body."

I did as he instructed and winced. "Someone gave my inner thighs a workout last night."

Collin moved closer, his voice husky. "You're distracting me again."

I shrugged sheepishly. "Sorry."

His hand skimmed my bare waist. "No, you're not."

"You're right."

"Do you want to learn to surf or not?"

It was a tough decision. "I do. Now what?"

"Now we're going to practice getting up on the board."

He explained how to paddle into the waves and how to get to my feet once I was in a wave and ready to surf. After he showed me how to wax the board and we strapped the boards to our ankles, his face glowed with excitement. "I think you're ready."

We walked into the water and the first step in, I gasped and froze as the rush of power swept through me. Collin turned around.

When I caught my breath, I shook my head. "I've walked in the ocean before but never had this happen."

"It's because of the curse. Now that it's broken, you need the power of the sea. You probably felt it before but at a much lower level so you didn't recognize it." He turned serious again. "Ananias Dare traveled to the new land by the ocean, so he represented the sea in the creation of the curse. Manteo needed forces more powerful than the gods in order to contain them. Ahone wasn't enough help on his own. Whenever you feel weak, you'll need to return to the sea to recharge. Not fresh water. It has to be the sea. That's part of the reason we're out here."

"And the second part?"

He didn't answer.

I'd never needed the sea before. Intrigued by and drawn to it, yes. Why would I need the power of the sea if the spirits were all contained when we closed the gate? "Collin, doesn't closing the gate send all the spirits back?"

He paused. "Yes."

"Then why do I need to know this?"

He took my hand in his. "There are no guarantees. I want to plan for a worst-case scenario, okay?"

The surge of power had stabilized so we walked deep enough into the water to slide onto the boards and paddle out to the waves. After we got far enough out, Collin taught me how to sit on the board and find the right wave.

I was really going to do this. While I was nervous, my nervousness was outweighed by excitement. "What if I fall off?"

"You probably will at first, but try to fall off the back."

"Anything else?"

"Have fun."

The first few attempts, I did fall off, but then I found my balance and rode out several small waves. Collin, of course, was not only good, but all kinds of sexy. When I wasn't concentrating on staying on the board, I was watching him.

He caught me several times and grinned. I was sure I only added fuel to the massive Collin Dailey ego. He paddled next to me. "Let's go out a bit farther. I want to try something."

When we got out far enough to suit him, we both sat up, our boards parallel. "I want to touch our palms together out on the water. I'm curious to see if it does anything for you since we're in the sea."

"Do you think it will?"

"There's only one way to find out." He paused. "We sometimes lose ourselves when we do this. If I think you're in trouble, I'm going to break the connection, and you do the same."

My hands were jittery. "Okay."

"Ready?"

I lifted my palm and held it forward. Collin stretched his hand and grasped mine, linking our fingers.

The jolt was stronger than before, but the sensation was the same. Awareness of every living thing flooded my senses. The pulse of their life force throbbed within me. Surrounded me. Saturated me. The fish around us. The plant life in the sea. The microbes not seen by the human eye. Raw power danced across my skin, soaking through my pores, permeating every cell in my body.

My consciousness exploded, racing backward, through time and space to the birth of everything. And it was familiar. I'd been there, not just now, but there to witness the miracle when it happened. A primeval memory buried deep in the structure of my DNA.

A massive explosion of gas and energy filled the void of nothingness, rushing through my head. Power, so much power, engulfed me and swallowed me whole, as I raced through the creation of time and space. Stars burst into life, violent explosions of light and wind, fire and ice. Reds and blues and greens. Bright balls and gaseous clouds. The cosmos ruptured into life, reaching out into the far corners of the universe, carrying me along with it.

My trajectory slowed, circling around another explosion of orange and yellow light, a dying star, swirling in vortex, spinning, spinning, spinning until a giant ball of yellow light filled the black void. The light blinded me and the energy seared my core as the new star imploded. The sun.

I slingshotted off, caught in the debris spewed out from the implosion.

Particles of dust and rocks clumped together to form a molten mass, twirling on an axis, circling the star.

Earth was born.

Trillions and trillions of rocks carrying droplets of water bombarded the cooling mass. An outer crust covered the earth while the water released from the meteorites formed oceans. In steaming springs of boiling water, created from the union of land and water, an essence rose from the water and the Manitou was born.

Life.

And the birth of the gods.

Ahone, creator god, emerged from the dust of the land. He held his arms wide and called plant life into being. And when he saw the beauty before his eyes, he created animals of every kind. But still he wanted more. He put pieces of land and sea into a bag and shook them in it, creating man and woman. Humanity was his most prized creation, and he loved man and woman too much to set them free.

The four wind gods, angry and covetous beings, lacked the power to create, only able to destroy. They swirled around the earth becoming more and more angry at the beauty Ahone had made, but it wasn't until they discovered men and women that they rebelled.

Jealousy burned hot and fierce in the winds, and they decided to punish the creator of all life. They chose Ahone's greatest source of pride and threatened to destroy humanity if he refused to give up his power before the dawn of the seventh day.

Ahone loved his children and refused to kill them, yet he didn't want to hand his power to the hateful wind gods. His tears fell and flooded the earth, wiping out half of his creation. The earth, sympathetic to Ahone's pain, returned the tears to the air, creating clouds to foil the winds.

But still, Ahone did not turn over his power. On the eve of the seventh day, in his misery and despair, Ahone split himself in two, giving the majority of his power to his twin, Okeus.

While Ahone kept empathy and compassion, Okeus only knew greed and anger, receiving the ugly parts of Ahone.

The wind gods railed at Ahone's trickery, but were forced to concede. They swore they would leave humanity unharmed unless man performed a transgression worthy of retaliation. So Ahone shook out his bag and placed man and woman of all races in all four corners of the earth.

Jealous of his brother's creation of man and woman, Okeus made creations of his own. But Okeus lacked the love and compassion that filled Ahone, and Okeus's creations were abominations. He set them far and wide upon the earth to hunt and stalk man.

Ahone and Okeus sculpted the shells of their creations, but the land and sea's gift of Manitou gave them life.

The gods, spirits, man, and Okeus's creations reached a balance, coexisting for thousands and thousands of years until the white man invaded the land of Ahone's people, throwing unbalance back into the world.

Manteo, son of the Croatan chief and friend to Ananias Dare and his people, called upon the parents of the gods—land and sea—to contain their power and spare humanity in his desperate attempt to calm the chaos. Ahone stepped forward to add his now weakened power of creation. A gate was formed at the threshold of Popogusso, and the gods and spirits were sucked from the earth and locked away, where they cursed man and especially the Curse Keepers. All the gods except for Ahone, who watched for centuries, while the Curse Keepers waited for the seam dividing the realms to unravel.

The wind gods remembered their vow to Ahone and spent over four hundred years plotting their revenge.

Finally, two Keepers met and the gate was opened, but only by a crack, and two spirits and a god escaped. Aposo and Kanim, messengers for Ahone and Okeus, and Wapi, the wind god of the north.

The three other wind gods remained locked behind the gate, their anger and hate oozing through the crack in the gate to Popogusso, along with a host of Okeus's abominations.

They seethed, waiting for the gate to open the rest of the way.

They sensed my presence outside their gate, the threshold to both worlds. They cursed me with multiple tongues and multiple languages, reaching arms and legs, tentacles and tails through the crack in their desperate attempts to reach me.

"We are coming for you, Curse Keeper, daughter of the sea, witness to creation. In the dead of night, we will be watching and waiting. We will come for you, and we will make you suffer in retribution for the misery your people caused. You will curse the day you were created a thousand times over." Hundreds of tongues echoed the chant, my title on their tongues. "Curse Keeper, daughter of the sea, witness to creation, we are coming for you."

I was ripped back to my world, still choking on their hatred and gasping for air in a vacuum of nothingness. But I clung to my lifeline—my palm melded to Collin's.

"Ellie!" he shouted my name, terror in his voice, as a wave crashed over my head, dragging me down and severing my hold.

I was underwater, the current around me a mass of chaos, but there was no panic.

I was the daughter of the sea.

My palmed burned, and not from my connection to Collin. Wapi, the wind god of the north, was here, churning the water with his gusts. The fish in the water tried to escape, but the current created by the wind pulled them closer to me.

My connection with Collin had been broken, but I could feel the wind god stealing the life from the fish around me. They swam against the current, frenzied, and then went still. The temperature of the water dropped and sent a chill to my bones. The fish were being frozen like the tourist the day before.

The wind god was toying with me, sucking their Manitou as he spun around me and moving in tighter and tighter in a spiral.

During my first encounter with the wind god, I had been terrified. I was still scared, but I told myself I had knowledge and power this time. I had to trust the Curse Keeper magic. Suddenly, instinct, buried millions of years, burst free.

My head broke the surface, and my burning lungs sucked in a deep breath before the wind god's tentacles pulled me down again. I had the power to send him away. I only had to stay above water long enough to do what I needed to do.

My eyes burned from the salt water as the waves sent me head over heels and I slammed into a wall of dead fish. Panicking, I fought the urge to scream—a scream would be disastrous under water, especially when I didn't even know which way was up. Collin had marked me so the wind god couldn't steal my Manitou, or at least I hoped. That theory hadn't been proven yet.

Something tugged on my ankle, and I remembered the surfboard strapped to my leg. Reaching for the strap, I pulled myself toward it, my lungs aching for air.

My head bobbed above water. I grabbed the board and lunged over the edge, coughing and gasping. Collin was over fifty yards away, frantically swimming toward me. Another wave rushed toward me, but I was the daughter of the sea. The water gave me power.

"You have discovered your true self," the wind god hissed.

I spun my head around, trying to find him. How could I fight him if I couldn't see him? "I know the gate is only partially open, and your brothers are trapped inside."

The god laughed, a high-pitched sound that pierced my ears. "So you know when the gates are opened, they are coming for you."

Terror crawled along my spine. How could I face hundreds of spirits who were out to get me? But I didn't have to face them, not if we sealed the gate. I only had to face this one. "Then why are you trying to kill me now?"

"Stupid human, I'm not here to kill you now. I need you. We seek our revenge and it's much too early for that."

"Then why are you here?"

Collin was twenty yards away, desperation and fatigue straining his face.

The wind god created a vortex of air, circling around me, blocking out everything in sight.

"*Then why are you here?*"

"To make you fear me." Cold tentacles wrapped around my arms, icy cold seeping into my body. I shivered violently.

The vortex closed tighter, lifting the board—and me along with it—a foot into the air.

I held up my palm, the nerve endings at the edges of the mark burning with power. "*I am the daughter of the sea, born of the essence present at the beginning of time and the end of the world. I am black water and crystal streams. The ocean waves and the raindrops in the sky. I am life and death and everything in between. I compel you to leave my sight.*"

The vortex disappeared, as did the wind god. I collapsed on the board, my heart pounding furiously against my chest.

Collin reached me within seconds, his eyes wild with fear. "What did you do?" He leaned over the opposite side of the board, grabbing my arms as though if he let go, I'd get attacked again. His eyes widened in shock when he felt how cold they were. "*Ellie, what happened?*"

"I sent it away."

"How?"

"I remembered."

"Remembered what?"

"Everything."

~: Chapter Twenty-Four :~

Collin stiffened, his face tight. "What does that mean?"

I searched his eyes, hesitating. "I remembered the words of protection. I sent the wind god away."

"What else?"

No, I wasn't imagining it. He was worried about what I'd discovered. "I remembered the birth of creation. I was there."

His mouth dropped and awe replaced his anxiety. "The memory of a pure soul." His hand reached for my face, and he pulled my lips to his. "You scared the shit out of me. Don't ever do that again."

"What happened?"

"You completely zoned out, and I couldn't pull our hands apart. It was as though they were magically sealed."

"After my vision ended, I was aware that I was still melded to you. Then my hand broke free. When did the wind god show up?"

"Right before you broke free."

This was the second time I'd encountered him. Two of the three times Collin and I had pressed our palms together, the wind god showed up. The third time, we'd been behind Collin's protective symbols in my apartment. "He was here for me. He told me that he was."

Collin's face paled. "What did he say?"

I shivered. "That he wanted to make me fear him."

Fear filled Collin's eyes as he turned from side to side to see the dead fish floating on the surface of the water. "Did he try to take your Manitou this time?"

"I felt a tendril curl around me, but he told me he wasn't going to kill me. That he needed me."

Collin took a deep breath. "He's grown in strength. He's out in the daylight. You're not safe anymore."

Did Collin know that the gate was only partially open? And why was I always the target? "Why doesn't he come after you?"

"What are you talking about, Ellie? We were together. Both times."

"Exactly. We were together both times. The first time he only attacked me. This time he said he specifically came for me."

"It's because of your pure soul, I told you that last night."

"Why did you wait to tell me that I had a pure soul? Why didn't you tell me when you found out?"

He gave me a grim smile. "This isn't something I want to discuss hanging off a surfboard in the ocean while we wait for gods or spirits to return to finish you off. Let's go back to our room and change and get something to eat."

"Why are you evading my question?"

Collin's eyes hardened. "What part of trying to get you to safety constitutes evading your question?"

"You could have answered it already, Collin."

"Fine. I didn't tell you because I figured we'd close the gate, and you'd never need to know. Happy now?"

He was lying. Everyone else in the world would have believed him, but the slight twitch of his left eyelid told me he wasn't telling me the truth.

I nodded, but I was far from happy. Collin was still hiding things from me. In fairness, there were things I still hadn't told him. But there came a point when it was difficult to say, *Oh by the way, I forgot to mention I saw the gates of hell in a vision.*

"Let's just go back, and I'll tell you anything you want to know. We were lucky this time. I don't want to take any chances."

He was right, and I was too suspicious. Collin had done everything within his resources to help me and protect me, even before when I had annoyed the hell out of him. How could I expect less of him now? Especially now.

Collin had unstrapped his surfboard to reach me faster, so he retrieved it and we made our way to the beach. He handed me a towel and watched me dry off, but our earlier playfulness was gone. Collin was on edge.

We left the surfboards where we found them and went back to our room. I stood by the bathroom door and watched Collin lean his arm against the wall, staring out the window with an anxious look.

"I'm going to take a shower."

He looked up in surprise, almost as though he were so deep in thought he'd forgotten that I was there. Worry etched lines across his forehead, drawing down his mouth.

I moved to him, pressing my chest to his, and stroked the side of his face. "Don't worry. We'll get the bowl tonight, and then we'll close the gate. We'll be okay." I stood on tiptoes and drew his bottom lip between my own.

He released a deep sound in his chest and brought me closer, his tongue plunging into my mouth.

My tongue joined his as my heart pounded, lust coursing through my blood. His hands cradled my head, tilting it back to give him better access for his demanding exploration.

How could this man have this effect on me? I'd only known him a few days, but I wanted him more than I'd ever wanted anyone in my entire life. My hands dug into his back, pulling him closer. I needed him closer.

He kissed me—wild and desperate as though if he'd let go, he'd lose me. One of his hands dropped from my face and found the string to my bikini top at the base of my neck, then the one below. Collin backed up to the bed, pulling me with him, his mouth still possessing mine. He stripped off his swim trunks and my bikini bottom. He spun us around and pushed me down on the bed, his body over mine in seconds.

He was between my legs when he stopped, breathless, staring at me with such intensity it was amazing I could still think straight.

I reached my hand to his face, my thumb running along his stubble. "We'll be okay."

His eyes glassed over. "Are you an angel or an enchantress, Ellie?" His voice broke and he leaned his forehead against mine.

What did he need from me that I wasn't giving? I remembered the first time he'd asked. Was I a witch who enchanted him or an angel sent to save his soul? Collin had been involved in a whole host of unscrupulous activities, most of which I hoped to never know, but that man contradicted the man I knew. Why? Was this the real Collin, the man he refused to show the world? He'd been forced to take care of his mother and brother since he was ten years old. Who was I to judge him for what he'd done to make ends meet? But the deeds he'd done were burned deep within his soul. Maybe he thought things could be different with me. Or maybe I was fooling myself and he'd be gone in two days. He'd break my heart one way or the other, but I'd known that going in. At this moment, he desperately needed something and I was the one he wanted to give it to him. "I'm an angel, Collin," I whispered. "I'm an angel."

His mouth found mine as he entered me, both possessive and demanding. Wrapping my legs around his waist, I struggled to keep up, but Collin slowed, smoothing back my hair. "I'm sorry."

I kissed him and began to move. "It's okay."

Collin lifted his head, his eyes burning bright. "Ellie, you're the best thing that's ever happened to me. I can't lose you."

His words shocked me and made me want him more. This man, who never committed to anyone or anything, claimed to want me.

"I'm not going anywhere." It was my turn to kiss him with possessiveness. Could I hope for this to last more than a few days? I refused to let my mind dwell on it as my body responded to Collin's touch.

My response rekindled his desire. We made love in a frenzy of need and fear. Collin cried out my name, his arms around my back, pulling me as humanly close as possible, and yet it didn't seem to be enough.

I grabbed his hand, pressing our palms together.

The now-familiar jolt rushed through my body, every nerve ending alive. I gasped at the sensation. While I was still aware of the Manitou of the living creatures around us, this experience was more centrally focused.

Collin stilled, his mouth opening in surprise.

I laced our fingers, holding tight, and slowly lifted my hips to his.

Euphoria replaced his anxiety as he began to rock against me, more controlled and purposeful. He pressed my hand to the mattress, over my head.

I felt his beating heart, and the blood rushing through his veins, the surge of hormones. The smell of him intensified, sweat and musk and sex filling my nose. I felt his desire as though it were a force of its own. Emotions, thick and heavy, settled over my body. Collin might have other secrets but he couldn't hide this. Part of his soul was laid bare for me to examine. I'd never wanted anyone as much as I wanted Collin Dailey, but he felt the same way about me. His fear was real. He was terrified he'd lose me.

His breathing slowed, and he rolled us so that I was on top again. I pressed our joined hands to the bed, leaning over to kiss him, needing him to fill every part of me as I began to slide against him, every movement intensified. Every nerve ending tingled.

He sat up and moved to the edge of the bed, and I straddled him like the night before, our two joined hands resting against his chest, his other arm wrapped tight around my back. His mouth lowered to my breast, and I arched back to give him better access as my hips began a new rhythm, gasping for breath as my body ached for more.

The son of the land and the daughter of the sea.

Collin's head lifted, and his mouth found mine as we joined our bodies and our souls with forces older than the gods themselves. I had no idea of the consequences when I joined our marks together, but the rightness of this suffused every part of me, and my connection to Collin told me he wanted it too. We performed our own ancient ceremony, both aware of the reverence.

I lifted my free hand to the back of his neck, staring into Collin's eyes. Naked desire laid bare. We couldn't hide our feelings. Not with this. We were two halves to a whole. Water, the mother of creation. Land, the father who supported it. We were forever joined, our souls tethered. In this moment, the truth came to life: Whether the gate closed or not, I would never be whole without this man by my side.

My passion climbed to dizzying heights, and urgency took over, Collin's pace matching my own. My lips sought his, our tongues joining the dance. I pressed my palm closer to Collin's as I pushed hard onto his thighs, needing more. And as I teetered on the edge, I truly became one with Collin, losing track of where I ended and he began. A fusion of flesh and soul.

When I fell, nerve endings exploded as wave after wave of ecstasy overtook me.

"Ellie!" Collin's hand dug into my back, and he followed behind me.

I rested my forehead against Collin's as I fought to catch my breath, our hands still linked. I unfurled my fingers, but Collin held tight, holding my hand to his chest.

"Not yet." His husky voice whispered in my ear.

I kissed him lightly. "Am I an angel or an enchantress, Collin?"

His free hand rested on the side of my neck. "Angel. I hope to God you're an angel." He kissed me, then slid his hand from mine. "Ellie, do you know what you did?" Fear colored his eyes again.

I nodded. I'd burned our souls together for eternity. "I'm sorry. I didn't know."

He shook his head. "No. Don't be sorry. Not now. Not for this."

"I didn't realize . . . it wasn't until—"

His mouth stilled mine. "I didn't know it would happen either until it was too late. It's okay."

I smiled, thankful he wasn't angry.

Collin lay down and pulled me with him, our bodies curling together. I rested my head on his chest and dozed off, his arm around my back in possession and comfort. My entire life I'd been searching for my purpose and here it was in my arms. Collin and being a Curse Keeper.

"Collin, why did you come to the restaurant that day?"

He released a chuckle. "I was hungry."

"Very funny. You live in Wanchese, right?" I looked up into his face, and he nodded. "So why were you in Manteo?"

"I heard the New Moon had a great beer selection." The words were smooth and believable. So why did his eyelid twitch?

"Did you know who I was when you came in?"

He grinned. "If I remember correctly, and I admit my memory might have been addled from the air vacuum, but I found out your name from your name tag." He paused. "And it was on a very lovely chest."

I propped up on an elbow. "Collin, I'm serious."

His smile fell. "Ellie, how would I know who you were?"

I shrugged. Although I knew the likelihood was nearly impossible, I couldn't help but wonder.

"My turn." He propped up on his side so that we were face-to-face. "Why didn't you tell me that you lost all your memories of the curse after your mother died?"

"I did. Yesterday. In the truck."

"Why didn't you tell me sooner? Why did you let me accuse you of being irresponsible?"

"It didn't seem important why I'd lost my memories. I just had."

"But I thought you'd purposely been irresponsible, when in fact, you had no control over it."

"But I did have control over relearning what I needed to know. I purposely chose not to learn it again. That was irresponsible."

His mouth pursed, and I knew he disagreed, but he didn't press the issue. "Okay, your turn. What else do you want to know?"

"Why didn't you tell me I had a pure soul?"

He sighed and rolled on his back, staring up at the ceiling. He raised the arm he had around my waist over his head. He was pulling away from me. "It was in the warehouse when we joined hands, and I was intent on getting the map, Ellie. I still didn't trust you. I thought you'd blatantly disregarded everything to do with the curse while I was the one who made sure to memorize every detail, make every preparation." His arm lowered and his eyes found mine. "I was the worthy one, yet you were the one who received the gift. I guess I thought you didn't deserve to know."

I was sure that was the most honest answer Collin had ever given me. Perhaps given anyone.

"And then the god attacked you, and when I realized what he had done, I knew others would come after you. *Of course* they'd come after you, but now they'd be more zealous. You were a rare prize. I had to make sure you were protected. It was my responsibility. As a Curse Keeper."

"What happened in my apartment didn't feel like responsibility."

He pulled my mouth to his, kissing me long and slow. "It wasn't. I can assure you of that. By then I'd figured out why you'd forgotten. And after everything that day . . ." He kissed me again. "I wanted you more than I'd ever wanted anyone in my life. But you deserved better. You still do."

"Isn't that for me to decide, Collin?"

Fear and pain filled his eyes. "Ellie, you don't know what I've done."

"Shhh." I leaned over him, my hair brushing his chest. "Your past? I don't want to know. Let's start over."

"How many times can we start over?" He was throwing my words from that day back at me.

"Does it matter? As many times as it takes."

"We're bound together, Ellie. I'm sorry." His voice broke. Did he regret what had happened minutes ago? He'd just told me that he didn't, and our connection told me that wasn't a lie. He tilted my head back, searching my eyes. "One day you'll hate me, and you'll curse these past few moments. When that day comes, just know that I wish I could do it all over again. From the beginning."

What was he not telling me? I knew his past was ugly. Our encounter with Marino was all the proof I needed. Part of me knew I should ask, but I didn't want to lose this moment with him.

I gave him a soft smile. "Your turn. What else do you want to know?"

He shook his head. "I know everything I need to know."

I licked his bottom lip. "Too bad. I was going to tell you that I had almost decided you were a better lover than Colin Firth."

He laughed. "Oh really? What about your research?"

"I'll need to do continuous research with you to make sure you maintain your standards, but you're safe for the next few hours."

His eyebrows lifted playfully. "Only the next few hours?"

"Not to worry. I'm sure you'll prove your *prowess* all over again."

Collin rolled me over onto my back. "I caught that dig at my skills. You'll pay for that Ellie Lancaster."

I smiled. I was counting on it.

∽ CHAPTER TWENTY-FIVE ∽

Collin was worried I'd get attacked again, and he refused to leave the room until he thought I was prepared. He ordered a pizza while I took a shower and we ate, sitting cross-legged on the bed while we discussed strategy.

"I think you should get the symbol on your back permanently tattooed. Today."

My mouth dropped open. "You're serious?"

"Yes."

"Why would I do that? We're going to close the gate. Isn't that being pessimistic?"

"It's called preparing for the worst-case scenario, Ellie. I told you that already."

I leaned over and gave him a kiss. "What about hope?"

His serious eyes studied mine. "Sometimes hope is not enough."

Collin was really spooked, and that made me nervous. He was the one who knew how to perform this ceremony. I sat up. "What aren't you telling me, Collin?"

"I'm telling you that even with the best preparations, we may not be able to close the gate. Manteo was sure he had the ceremony right the first time and look what happened. There's no guarantee this will work. You need to be prepared for that."

"Don't you mean *we* need to be prepared for that?"

"Of course, *we*. But you're the pure soul."

"There's something you're not telling me."

He climbed off the bed and dragged his hand over his head, refusing to look at me.

Fear burrowed in the pit of my stomach. "Collin, you're scaring me more by keeping whatever it is from me. I need to know."

His mouth contorted as he wrestled with what to say. Finally, he sighed and sat on the bed. "I think I've forgotten part of the words for the ceremony. It's been nagging at me for several days. I thought the words would come back, but they're not."

My eyes widened. "What does that mean? That the ceremony won't work?"

"No, I think we'll be fine. I changed the cleansing ceremony when I marked you. Before it was much more about preparing the Keeper's Manitou, but yours is pure so I focused more on infusing it with power. And the protection mark works. The wind god didn't try to take your Manitou this morning."

"Because he didn't want to kill me. He very well could have killed me for all we know."

He shook his head, worry puckering his mouth. "Maybe. All I know is that I've never been more scared in my life."

He was opening up, so I decided I needed to as well. "What if I told you that the door to hell wasn't all the way open?"

He turned rigid. "What are you talking about?"

"I saw it. When you and I were together on the ocean. I saw the gate to the spirit world. Only three beings escaped—messengers for Ahone and Okeus, and the wind god. The rest are still behind the gate. Waiting. If we don't close the gate before the seventh day, they'll all go free."

Collin's face paled, and he looked terrified. "Only three? We always assumed the gate would open entirely, and we'd have a week."

"There are hundreds more waiting to come out. We have to close that gate, Collin."

He nodded, looking like he was about to throw up.

Should I tell him the spirits and gods threatened me? He was already freaked out and worried about my safety. Besides, he already knew they'd want me specifically. Telling him about the threats seemed like overkill.

"Did you see anything else?"

"I saw the birth of the gods. I saw Ahone cry a flood when the wind gods threatened to kill humanity. I saw Ahone split himself in two to create his twin, Okeus. I saw Okeus create his own children—demons. And then I saw the gate." I wrapped my fingers around Collin's hand. "We *have* to close the gate. I refuse to consider the alternative."

"Do you realize what an incredible gift you were given?" he asked in awe.

I nodded. More than he knew.

He took a deep breath. "Only three beings? You're sure?"

"Yes."

"You're not safe."

"Enough of that. Teach me how to get through the next two days."

He swallowed and nodded his head. "You know the words to protect yourself? You said you remembered?"

"They came to me the other night, after you marked me with the henna tattoo. In the middle of the night, Kanim, the messenger for Okeus, came to see me. For a second time."

"*Second time*?" His eyes hardened.

I shook my head. "The first night was after we'd gone to Rodanthe and you told me not to trust you, which wasn't hard. I *didn't* trust you. The messengers for Ahone and Okeus both visited me that night. In fact, Okeus's messenger was the one who broke my window."

"Why would you keep that from me?"

"I didn't trust you. You were hiding things from me. Okeus's messenger told me that I needed to side with him."

"And Ahone's?"

"Ahone's messenger told me that I needed to make sure the gate was closed. That he'd sacrificed to save humanity before and he'd do it again."

"And the second time? Did Ahone's messenger come?"

"No, just Okeus's. He told me that there would be a sacrifice made for every night I refused to accept his offer." My chest constricted. "Do you know if there was a sacrifice made last night?"

"I don't know Ellie. Maybe the hundreds of dead fish today were enough."

We both knew that wasn't true. I stood up and grabbed my purse, digging through it.

"What are you doing?"

"Checking on my family."

I called Claire. I was pretty sure Collin hadn't protected her.

"Hey, Ellie. Are you still out of town?"

My eyes sank closed with relief. "Yeah."

"And how's it going?" Something in her voice was off.

"Great, but I need to check on something." I paused for a second. "I heard there was a man found dead in the botanical gardens yesterday, by the statue of Queen Elizabeth. Do you know if there was anything like that today?"

"Yeah . . ." Something was wrong.

Fear washed through me, and I sank to the bed. "Is it my dad or Myra?"

Collin's hand gripped my shoulders from behind me.

"No. No. They're fine." She tried to sound reassuring, but she was holding something back.

"Then who, Claire? Just tell me."

"It was Lila. They found her in front of the restaurant this morning."

"*Lila*?" My voice cracked.

"I'm sorry."

The first guy was some random guy, but Lila was someone I knew. We weren't exactly friends, but her death upset me, especially if she were dead because of me.

"There's . . . one more thing." The way she drew out the words told me it was as bad as Lila, if not worse.

"What?"

"The guy they found in the gardens was Dwight."

"*Dwight*?"

These people were sacrifices made because I wouldn't side with Okeus. Collin was right. Their deaths were a message. There were two nights left. Who was next? A good friend and then family?

Oh, God.

I swung around to face Collin.

He reached for me as his forehead wrinkled with concern. His fingertips lightly stroked my arm. *Collin is worried.*

I jumped off the bed. "Claire, you're not safe!"

"What are you talking about?" But there was fear in her voice.

"They're coming for you next." I pinned my gaze on Collin. "We have to go back."

His face tightened. "No. We need the bowl first."

Tears filled my eyes. "They're going to go after Claire next, Collin. I *know* it."

He pulled the phone out of my hand. "Claire, listen to me. I need you to get sea salt and pour it across every opening to your house—doors, windows, chimneys. Everything." He paused. "No. You can't tell Drew what's going on. Just tell him that something on your ghost tour spooked you." He was silent and relief covered his face. "Good, now I need you to do something else. Can you go to Ellie's parent's and do the same thing there? Ellie's right. I think they'll target you next. But the salt *will* keep them out. Even so, stay inside as much as possible. Especially at night. Call Ellie back if you have any questions." Collin handed the phone back to me.

I pressed the phone to my face. "Claire, I'm so sorry."

"Why are you apologizing? This is not your fault."

But it was and I didn't know how to stop it. "Thanks for taking care of Dad and Myra."

"Not to worry. I'm working there for you this afternoon. I'll take care of it then."

"Thanks, Claire. I love you."

"I love you too."

Collin pulled me into a tight embrace. "They'll be fine, Ellie. We'll get the bowl and head back tonight."

"Salt? Will it work? Why not use salt for my place then? Why mark the doorway and windowsills with symbols?"

"I promise it will work, and the marks are because you're different. The marks are insurance."

"We could tell Claire how to mark the doors."

"It wouldn't work, Ellie. Our Curse Keeper magic makes the symbols work."

"I suppose my words of protection only work for me too."

"Yes, just like mine only work for me. What are your words?"

"*I am the daughter of the sea, born of the essence present at the beginning of time and the end of the world. I am black water and crystal streams. The ocean waves and the raindrops in the sky. I am life and death and everything in between. I compel you to leave my sight.*" I shrugged, self-conscious. I felt like I was back in high school English class reciting Shakespeare. "When I say them to a god, I hear the words in English in my head, but the sounds coming out of my mouth are definitely not."

"You're probably saying them in the ancient language. Legend has it the ancient language was created by the gods. Your words are a lot like mine, which is what I expected."

"What are yours?" The bits and pieces I'd heard him use in the warehouse were in the ancient language.

"*I am the son of the earth, born of space and heaven. I am black earth and sandy loams. The mountain ranges and the rolling hills. I am the foundation of life and the receiver of death and everything in between. I compel you to leave my sight.*"

"So that will send a god away, but not lock it away?"

"Right."

"But you said we could send lesser spirits back on our own."

"That requires more than words. You need symbols too. The symbols themselves are meaningless unless you ask the force or spirit to help. To protect you from the gods, I used forces greater than them, as well as my Keeper power. The lesser spirits are tricky if we are on our own. We need to find their weakness, and we might need to hang around the spirit awhile to figure it out. We can send it away with our words of protection, but not permanently."

"And demons?"

"They're like gods. Some mimic man, others animals. The problem is that they can masquerade as another creature and you might not know it."

"Great."

His hand covered mine. "Ellie, just remember that these beings spent thousands and thousands of years roaming the earth before our ancestors banished them. If the gate stays open, I think they can coexist with the rest of creation."

I couldn't believe what he was saying. "You're kidding, right? They eat people and animals."

"It's just like *The Lion King,* the circle of life. No one faults the lion for hunting prey. They are simply existing."

"They fault the lions when the lions are hunting people."

He leaned his head back and groaned.

"Fine," I said. "Let's say the gods and spirits are released and let loose and they learn to coexist in a magical, ideal circle of life. You're forgetting one key piece here, Collin. Me. They want me."

He slowly shook his head. "No. I haven't forgotten you."

I patted his leg. "So we focus on getting the bowl, then closing the gate tomorrow night."

Collin turned his head toward the window and nodded. Why did that upset him?

I started to ask when Collin's cell vibrated on the dresser.

He looked up, startled out of his musings, and reached for it. I realized the entire time I'd been with Collin I'd only known his phone to ring once.

"Yeah," he answered. Whatever he heard on the other end hardened his eyes. He disconnected the call, then opened the door and peered out. "Fuck."

"What?"

"Marino's men. Shit." He took two deep breaths.

"Where are they?"

"Here. The only exit is the staircase and they're in the parking lot." His jaw tightened. "Ellie, we can't get out, and they're coming up."

My chest constricted. "What are we going to do?"

"They're looking for you. We only have to keep them from finding you."

"How are we going to do that?"

The skin around his mouth blanched. Squaring his shoulders, he picked up the motel phone. "Hey, Tammy, this is Mr. Pressley. Did two men come to the front desk looking for me?"

Tammy. The front desk clerk who threw herself at Collin while I was standing there.

Collin lowered his voice to a husky drawl. "I'm needing some fresh towels. I wondered if you could bring some up right away." He paused again. "I know you're covering the desk, sweetheart. But it can't wait. I needed those towels up here like five minutes ago." His voice was heavy with innuendo.

My mouth dropped open.

"Go out the back. And hurry, sugar." Collin hung up the phone and bent down, lifting up the bed skirt.

"What the hell was that?"

He dropped the fabric, cursing. "Marino's boys know I have a woman up here, but they haven't been inside the lobby. My friend came back to pick up the surfboards and saw them. He's stalling them as long as he can. When they get up here, if I have Tammy here instead of you, they'll leave."

It was brilliant and disgusting all at the same time. "What exactly do you plan on doing with Tammy?"

"Whatever it takes for them to think you're not here."

"I don't like the sound of that."

"*Ellie.* I need you to cooperate." He opened the door to the closet, and a low sound of frustration rumbled in his throat "This is so fucking obvious, and the second place they'll look. I'm going to have to make my performance stellar so they don't search at all."

"Where's the first place they'll look?"

"The shower." He grabbed my arm and shoved me inside.

I glanced around the room. Evidence of what Collin and I had been doing for the last twenty-four hours was everywhere. My chest tightened. "What will they do if they find me?"

Fear flashed in his eyes before they hardened again.

I heard a knock on the door, and I seized his arm, terror clawing at the back of my head. "*Collin.*"

He pressed his lips to mine for a quick kiss. "I'm not going to let them find you, Ellie. Trust me." He turned to the door and then back at me. "Whatever you hear out here . . ." He swallowed and looked nervous. "Just keep in mind that I'll do whatever the hell I have to do to protect you."

I nodded as he shut the door.

A few seconds later, Collin's voice floated through the shuttered slats of the closet door. "Hello, sweetheart." His voice was low and sexy. "I thought you'd never get here."

"Where's the girl you were with?" The receptionist's voice was pouty.

"Who knows? She knew I was interested in you, and she had a hissy fit and left. And now it's just you and me." I could see their feet through the slanted cracks, hers tripping toward Collin as though he'd pulled her to him.

"What about the towels?"

"Sweetheart, I don't give a fuck about the towels. It's you I want."

"Why's her stuff still here?"

"I bought it all for her and she left it behind. Why are we wasting time talking about her?"

I strained to hear what they were doing. About thirty seconds later, I realized the sounds I heard were Collin making out with the receptionist. I swallowed my disgust and my nausea, reminding myself that he was doing it to protect me.

"You feel good." Collin mumbled.

A few articles of clothing fell to the floor, and I squeezed my eyes shut. *He is doing this for you.* I'd been with him enough to know that this was his con voice. It still didn't help when I heard the sound of the mattress dipping as they dropped onto the bed.

Several seconds later, I heard pounding on the door. "Dailey! We know you're in there!"

"Who's that?" Tammy asked.

"My bookie." Collin grumbled, then yelled, "Keep your pants on while I find mine."

He took off his pants?

"Open up this fucking door or we'll knock it down."

The door creaked open and Collin asked, "What do you want? As you can see, I'm busy."

"Where's the girl?"

"Uh, open your fucking eyes." Collin's smartass tone was clipped. "She's mostly naked on the bed."

My stomach rolled. He'd gotten her *mostly naked*.

"Not that girl. Ellie."

"Who's Ellie?" the receptionist asked.

I forced my breathing to slow down. I'd be damned if they found me in the closet because I was hyperventilating.

"Ellie . . . Ellie . . ." Collin drawled, then laughed. "I think she was two women ago. Or was it three?"

"How many women do you sleep around with?" Tammy screeched.

"When was the last time you saw her?" Marino's guy asked.

"Which one?" Collin asked.

"Ellie, smartass."

"It's hard to remember. After I helped her sell her candlesticks, I dropped her off back in Greenville."

"What the hell was she doing in Buxton if she's from Greenville?"

"Boys . . ." Collin's voice took on his sexy tone. "I don't know why women do what they do. I'm only glad they do it."

"What's her last name?"

"I rarely ask. It gets too complicated."

"Let's hope, for your sake, you asked this time."

Collin sighed long and heavy. "Let me think. I'm pretty sure it was Mitchell. Ellie Mitchell."

"And she lives in Greenville?"

"Hell if I know. That's where we hooked up, and that's where I dropped her off. At a dive motel off of Highway 43. "

"What were you doing in Greenville? It's a little out of your usual range."

"I heard there was a poker game I didn't want to miss."

"You get around, Dailey," the man grumbled.

"You have no idea. Now if you don't mind, boys . . . I was in the middle of something."

"Marino's not done with you yet."

"He never is."

The door shut and Collin sighed. A few seconds later, his hardened voice asked, "Where were we, Trixie?"

He's going to finish what he started?

"It's *Tammy.*" Tammy sounded irritated.

"Trixie. Tammy." Collin sounded bored. "What's the difference?"

"*What's the difference?*"

"You're here to fuck me, right? You're not here to hear me say your name."

"Are you serious?" she screeched.

"*What?*"

The bed groaned. "I'm out of here."

"I don't get it. What's the problem?"

She cursed, and I heard a thump on the floor. "If I get fired for this, I'm coming back up to beat the shit out of you."

"Take a number, sweetheart."

The door slammed, but I stayed in the closet, unable to go out and face the room. To see the bed where I'd experienced the most intimate moments of my life, cheapened by Collin laying on it with that girl. While I was in the closet listening.

But that wasn't fair. Collin hadn't enjoyed a minute of it. I'd heard it in his voice. Nevertheless, I still wanted to vomit.

I opened the door and a shirtless Collin sat on the bed, his elbows on his thighs, his face buried in his hands. At least he'd had his pants on. He looked up, fear in his eyes, waiting.

We stared at each other for several seconds, until my eyes drifted to the head of the bed. She'd laid there. With Collin.

He must have seen the horror on my face, because he jumped off the mattress and reached for me.

I held my hand up and turned away. "Don't."

"Ellie, please don't do this. I did it to save you."

My chin trembled. *I will not cry. I will not cry.* I believed with all my heart that he did it to save me, yet I still couldn't make the sick feeling in the pit of my stomach go away. I took a deep breath. "I know. I believe you." I looked into his eyes. "I just need a minute, okay?"

He nodded, looking defeated. I hated that I was doing this to him. He'd tried to set up the scene so Marino's men wouldn't search the room, and it had worked perfectly. But I couldn't get the mental image of him kissing someone else out of my head. Or taking off her clothes. And instead of thanking him, I was hurting him. "Collin, I'm sorry. I know you did it for me, but I just . . ." My voice broke, and the tears I'd held back broke loose in a sob.

"Ellie, I'm sorry." He wrapped his arms around my back, and I buried my face in his chest. "This is all my fault."

"I can't do this, Collin. I can't be this person, fighting for my life." I pulled back and searched his face. "This isn't me. I'm a waitress from Manteo whose idea of an exciting night is sneaking onto the Nags Head sand dunes after the Jockey's Ridge State Park closes."

"I know."

"In the past few days my life has been in danger countless times. I've been attacked by supernatural beings and chased by some goon who has a grudge against you." I smacked his chest with my hand. "I told you I wanted to go to Kill Devil Hills! I wanted to go see Oscar."

"I know. I'm sorry."

"But this. This." I pointed to the bed. "I know I should be grateful. Thankful." I hiccuped a sob. "I'm so mad at *me* right now."

"*You?* Ellie, you didn't do anything wrong."

"I knew exactly who you were going into this. I knew you wouldn't stick around. I knew you'd replace me with some other woman, but I'd hoped to God you would wait until after you left me. I'd convinced myself I could live with a short-term thing. But that was a lie. I knew you'd break my heart."

"Ellie." His voice sounded strangled.

"But I thought that I could survive the grief. I knew I'd found what I'd been looking for with every fucking man that's walked in and out of my life. Goddamn my luck for finding it with a guy who wouldn't stick around. But I didn't care. I wanted you so bad that I fucking didn't care."

Collin's eyes searched mine.

"How could you treat that girl like that, Collin? How could you be so cold?"

His chest heaved. "I . . . I had to get rid of her."

I shook my head, disgusted with myself. "I'm no different than that girl. I threw myself at you just like she did."

Horror filled his eyes. "God, Ellie. No! You are nothing like her!"

"How can you say that? All I can hear is you telling me 'You're here to fuck me, not hear me say your name.'"

"No! Ellie, you're a thousand times better than any woman I've ever been with. I'd never do that to you."

"Why? Why wouldn't you?"

His hands grabbed my arms. "Don't you feel it when we're together? How we're two halves of a whole. We truly are the children of the earth and the sea. We belong together, Ellie. God fucking knows I don't deserve the chance to be with you. You've only seen a small part of my life, and it's ugly. But you make me want to be someone worthy of you. When I'm with you, I think maybe I can be."

"Collin." Why was he telling me this?

He grabbed my face. "I want you. You. You *know* this Ellie. You saw it when we were linked. Our souls are bonded. Do you think I'd just throw that away?"

I shook my head. "I don't know. I don't know anything anymore."

"I need you, Ellie. *I need you.* Please believe that."

Tears rolled down my face.

"Please, just give me a chance. Please don't give up on me." His mouth found mine, and I fell into him, unable to resist his pull on my heart.

Everything he said was true. I needed him too. I'd only known him five days, but my life would be empty without him. I knew who he was going into this. How could I punish him for that?

∾ CHAPTER TWENTY-SIX ∾

We packed up and left soon after our discussion. It was early evening and we still had several hours before Collin planned to break into the museum. We grabbed some fast food and ate dinner on the beach closer to Morehead City, watching the waves crash onto the shore.

I'd calmed down after my breakdown, and now I was embarrassed. I'd confessed things I'd never intended, but instead of pushing Collin away, my revelations brought him closer. He seemed relieved that I was still with him. At the moment, I was more worried about breaking into the museum. "What's your plan to get past the security system?"

"I have the code."

"You're kidding. How could you get the code?"

He grinned.

"Let me guess. You have a friend."

Tilting his head with a cocky gleam in his eye, he stuffed a fry in his mouth. "You're learning."

"So we use the code, break in, switch the bowl, and leave?"

"After we find the bowl. That might take awhile."

"Are there guards? Cameras?"

His eyebrow rose, amused. "Listen to you. One would never guess this was your first in."

"Shut up, Collin. And technically, it's my second."

"It's no to both of your questions. It's a bare-budget museum."

He'd been trying his best to go back to the way things were before. Before I caught a glimpse of his real world in our motel room earlier. The way he watched me now, he knew I was thinking about this afternoon.

"Ellie, this morning . . ." He paused "We didn't use a condom earlier, and I presumed, since you didn't mention it, that you're on birth control."

"I have an IUD."

His mouth pinched and he nodded. "That's not why I'm bringing it up. I trust you to be responsible in regards to that. The last thing either of us needs is for you to get pregnant. I brought it up because of what happened this afternoon." He bit his lip and stared out into the water. "I've slept around. A lot. That's no secret. But I want you to know I always used a condom until this morning. Always. You weren't exposed to anything."

I gave him a soft smile. "Thanks."

He was silent for several seconds. "I'm worried about bringing you into the museum. If for some reason we get caught, you're looking at felony charges. I don't want to put you in that situation. But at the same time, I don't want to leave you anywhere. Especially at night. So I'll leave the decision up to you. If you don't want to come, I can either put you in a motel somewhere and mark up the door. Or I can take you home now and drive back and break in."

"You'd really drive over six hours round-trip, just to take me home if I wanted?"

His anxious eyes found mine. "Yeah. If that's what you want."

"Do you really think my family and Claire are safe?"

He nodded. "Honestly, as long as they have salt guarding the thresholds to their houses, they're probably safer if you're *not* with them."

That was hard to hear, but not unexpected. "I want to stay with you."

"Are you sure?"

I knew what he was really saying—that I wasn't stuck with him. That I could try to lay low for a day, show up for the gate closing ceremony, and then go back to my life, alone. There was no way that I could do that even if I didn't want to be with Collin. I'd shirked my responsibilities for too long. I might not know as much about the curse as Collin, but I wanted to share equal responsibility. Besides, with us getting so close to the deadline, I could only imagine what the gods would do to stop us. We were safer together. Just like my family was safer without me.

I nodded. "I'm sure."

"Okay." He grinned, his eyes dancing. "Let's plan a break-in."

Shaking my head, I chuckled. "I think you're enjoying this just a little too much."

"Oh really?" His eyebrows rose in mock surprise. "And you're telling me you didn't enjoy breaking into Marino's warehouse?"

"I did not."

"You did. I watch people, Ellie. I notice things."

What else had he noticed about me? "That was different. He's a crook who stole your map. This is a museum."

"A museum that stole my bowl."

I narrowed my eyes in confusion. "I thought your brother gave the bowl to the museum."

"He did, but it's my bowl. Which means they should have given it back when I requested it."

"You actually asked them to return the bowl?"

"You're damn right I did. It's mine."

I shrugged. "Possession is nine-tenths of the law."

"Which is a fucking lie. But I'll get it back tonight."

Collin had somehow gotten a layout of the back rooms of the museum and although he didn't know for sure where the bowl would be, he had a general idea. The museum was relatively small so even if we had to search the entire employees-only area, it wouldn't take more than an hour.

Collin turned serious again. "I want to talk about tomorrow night."

My stomach did somersaults. I knew we needed to discuss it, but to do so would make it more real.

"The map is old and doesn't have any familiar landmarks, but from what I've determined, the original ceremony took place next to an oak tree. I think it's the big oak tree in the Elizabethan Gardens, next to the Fort Raleigh visitor center."

"So we have to go to the botanical gardens?" Was that the reason Dwight was found there?

"Yes, and we have to complete the ceremony before sunrise. Like Ahone giving up his power to Okeus, the ceremony has to be performed *before* the dawn of the seventh day."

"Why can't we do it during the day?"

"Because the powers we need to invoke are stronger at night. Not to mention we'd attract all kinds of attention during the day. It's a public place."

"So our next date is another break-in, this time at the Elizabethan Gardens. Collin, you know how to show a girl a good time," I teased, nudging his arm with my shoulder.

"No easing into a life of crime for you." But his voice was strained, like he hated involving me.

I leaned over and kissed him long and slow. "We're in this together. I know what I'm getting into."

He nodded, but he didn't look so sure.

"So we break in to the botanical gardens tomorrow after dark?"

"I want to wait until the early hours of the morning to decrease our odds of getting caught. We should have time to get everything set up and make sure the ceremony is complete by sunrise." He looked away. "But right now we need to concentrate on the current break-in."

We stayed on the beach for another hour, both of us reluctant to leave. We would head back to Manteo after we got the bowl, and draw that much closer to the ceremony that would either save humanity—or doom humanity forever.

Collin drove into the museum parking lot, parking in the back. I was nervous, even if I didn't want to admit it to Collin. He didn't seem very worried about getting caught, despite his offer to keep me uninvolved. Still, I had no desire to add my fingerprints to the national data bank so Marino could track me down.

I wasn't wearing the all-black outfit I'd had Claire pack. Instead I wore a pair of denim shorts, a tank top, and my Vans. "I don't feel appropriately dressed for a break-in."

"Not to worry, Ellie. It's not black tie."

"Very funny. You know what I mean."

"There's no dress code for breaking in. You're fine."

"Easy for you to say." He wore dark jeans and a T-shirt.

He leaned over and kissed me. "Look at it this way: If you get arrested, you'll look gorgeous in your mug shots."

"You think I look gorgeous?" I asked in surprise.

"Of course I think you look gorgeous. Let's go before you start wanting to discuss how you should have worn your hair." He opened his door before I could answer, pulling his bag out of the truck bed.

I met him at the side of the truck, my stomach flopping like a fish.

"I only have one pair of gloves, so don't touch anything."

"Got it."

He looked up with a grin. "And try to stay out of trouble this time."

"Me? You're the one who left me with a wind god and as a result, I almost got my Manitou sucked out."

He stood, his jaw squared with determination as he handed me one of the two flashlights in his hand. "That won't happen again."

"It better not or I'll kick your ass."

"I have no doubt you will." I heard the grin in his voice. "Let's go." Collin picked up his duffel bag full of thievery tools and we headed for the back door. "There are two codes. The first gets us *in* the door. The other lets us *stay* inside. I've been told the second security keypad is in an office down the hall, and we have thirty seconds to enter the code before the alarm goes off."

I took a deep breath. "Okay." We were really doing this.

He grabbed my waist and pulled me to him, studying my face. "Ellie, it's not too late to change your mind. If you want to wait in the truck, we can roll up the windows and I'll mark them up."

I shook my head. "No. We're in this together."

Lifting my chin with his fingers, Collin's gaze hardened. "I know what I'm doing. If I think we're in any danger of getting caught, we're out of here."

"What about the bowl?"

"We can't perform the ceremony if we're in jail, can we? We'll cut our losses and hope we can make something else work."

For some reason that made me feel better, even though I was terrified the ceremony wouldn't work. If we were in jail, we'd never be able to protect ourselves. And the last thing I wanted was to be vulnerable to the hundreds of spirits whose entire exit plan centered on torturing me.

Collin pulled out his phone and checked his texts. He punched a code into a keypad on the side of the door and within seconds, the door popped open. Collin shot me a smile before he headed in, motioning for me to stay close to the door.

He moved down the dim hall, his flashlight bouncing around and searching open doorways. He disappeared in one room and came back out in about ten seconds. "We're good."

I closed my eyes for a moment as I sighed in relief. "Where do we look?"

"There are three possibilities. We'll search those rooms, then go from there."

"Will it be in a case or something?"

"Probably." Collin continued down the hall to a locked door. "If they keep the bowl under a glass box in the museum, it stands to reason they'd lock it up back here." He pulled out his lock-picking set and told me to point my flashlight at the lock.

"I sense a déjà vu moment," I whispered, my stomach rolling.

"We're fine. I told you we won't have a repeat of last time."

I cringed. "I hope not."

Collin tripped the lock and opened the door to small storage room filled with shelves. Most were empty, but a shelf by the door held a small metal box.

Collin headed straight for it. After he jimmied the lock, he opened the lid and grinned ear to ear.

I stood on my tiptoes, shining my flashlight into the box. It contained an almost flat, dark wood bowl with a thick lip. "It doesn't look like much."

"Neither does your cup." He handed the bowl to me and removed the fake one from his duffel bag. I had to agree that to my nonexpert eye, the bowls looked similar. Collin put the new one in the box and reset the lock.

He removed his relic from my hands and stuffed it into a cloth bag, then into his duffel bag. "See? I told you. And in record time."

"Okay, let's go," I said, heading straight for the back door. This all seemed entirely too easy.

Collin reset both alarms, then grabbed the handle to the exterior door.

"I suddenly have a very strange feeling that something bad's about to happen."

"Don't say that. We're almost home free."

And we were. Until we opened the back door and came face-to-face with Marino's men. The two guys I'd seen in the convenience store the other day stood ten feet from the museum's exit.

"Fuck," Collin mumbled, grabbing my arm and dragging me back inside.

"You disappear in there and we'll set off the alarm and stick around to make sure the police pick you up." The tall guy grinned. "And we all know you don't want that."

Collin slung his bag over his shoulder and held his hands out from his body. "No need for that, boys." He walked out the door.

I stayed in the doorway, unsure what to do. Getting arrested might be preferable to going with these guys. One thing was sure: If I didn't shut the door within seconds, the alarm would go off. But Collin was outside, and I'd already decided that I was sticking with him. I stepped through the opening, shutting the door behind me.

"I was just tellin' Tony here that it was a good night for a break-in. And lo and behold, look who we run into. Isn't that right, Tony?"

The short guy chuckled. "You know it, Vinnie."

Collin moved in front of me. "What a coincidence."

"Not really, once Marino figured out you took the map. It wasn't hard to put together where you'd go next."

"Changed your woman already?" Tony asked, and Vinnie laughed.

Collin's gaze made a slow sweep of the parking lot. "Yeah, I told you. I get around."

"Marino doesn't like liars, Dailey."

Collin titled his head. "Then why did he hire you two?"

"Smartass, huh? Good thing we're not here for you." Vinnie's gaze turned to me. "You're a hard woman to find, Ellie. Why don't you come on out and join us."

Leaving the sanctuary of the shadows, I lifted my chin, refusing to let them know I was scared, even though I was terrified. "I'm not surprised. I don't spend much time in gutters, and I'm sure that's your natural habitat."

"Ellie," Collin growled under his breath.

Vinnie laughed. "Ho boy. I can see why Marino wants her, but she doesn't seem your usual type, Dailey."

"You know I don't have a type. I'm not partial."

"Then you won't mind if we take her off your hands, and you can run along. We'll even let you keep whatever you have in that bag."

Collin's back stiffened. "I don't think so. I'm not done with her yet."

"Does she know about the woman you were screwing hours ago?" the other guy asked.

My skin crawled, but I put my hand on my hip. "I don't care who he sleeps with."

"Then you won't mind coming with us."

I swallowed the lump of fear in my throat. "Actually, I do. I came here with Collin, and I plan to leave with him."

Marino's man smiled, but the fake friendliness was gone. "Here's the simple truth of it, Ellie. You don't have a choice. So you either come along with us and ride to Marino's in comfort, or you do things the hard way." His eyes narrowed as he looked up and down my body. "And trust me, they will be *hard*."

Collin's hands fisted at his sides.

Terror flooded my head and I struggled to think straight. *How are we going to get out of this?*

Vinnie reached a hand toward me. "Now come here."

My feet froze to the concrete, my breath coming in uneven pants.

His voice lowered. "Don't make me come over there, Ellie."

Collin bolted toward them. "Ellie, run!"

I had a half-second delayed reaction before I ran toward the front of the museum.

Marino's men had already anticipated my move.

Collin intercepted Tony, tackling him to the pavement while the taller guy caught me quickly, his long legs making him twice as fast. Vinnie grabbed my arm and pulled me against his body. "That was a very bad decision."

Anger replaced my fear. "I'm warning you to let go of me."

He laughed loudly. "*You're* warning *me?*" His grip on my bicep tightened as he tugged me toward the sedan parked at the curb.

Collin and Tony had gotten to their feet. Collin pushed Tony's shoulder and tried to get around him, but Tony shoved him back. Collin stumbled, keeping his eyes on me.

I jerked my arm, but Vinnie's hold tightened. I kicked his legs and reached for his face to scratch him but got his neck instead. I got several blows in before he snagged my other arm and hauled me to his chest, excitement in his eyes. "You're a feisty one."

"Get your fucking hands off of her!" Collin shouted.

The guy holding me started to laugh. "You got it *bad*, Dailey." He turned his attention back to me. "No wonder Marino wants her so much." He dragged me to the car. I stomped on his foot, but he just laughed as he opened the back door. I leaned backward, anything to keep from being put inside, when birds began to screech and fly from the forest in a mass exodus, swarming over our heads.

The mark on my hand tingled.

Something fell from the sky, landing on the roof of the car with a thud.

A dead bird.

A new terror overtook me.

"What the hell?" Vinnie stood upright, confusion in his voice.

Two more birds crashed to the sidewalk.

I swung my head to look at Collin. His eyes were wild with panic as a slew of animals—deer, raccoons, rabbits, mice, and squirrels—fled in terror from the woods.

Hundreds of dead birds rained from the sky. Their frozen bodies landed on my head, on the car, on the sidewalk, and I screamed.

Vinnie dropped one of my arms to cover his head as he renewed his efforts to get me into the car. I was beginning to wonder if that wasn't the safest place after all.

I felt the spirit before I saw it. My hand burned and the smell of sulfur permeated the air, an oppressive blanket of evil following behind. A dark horizontal stream of smoke swirled toward us, aiming straight for me.

Collin regained his wits and struggled to get past Tony.

"What the fuck?" Vinnie growled, his fingers twisting into the flesh on my arm as I squirmed to get out of his hold.

The smoke stopped next to Vinnie and became a shimmering, silvery, charcoal-gray, dense mass. "Have you made your decision, Curse Keeper?"

Okeus's messenger. And Kanim was much stronger than before.

The man's hold on my arm loosened slightly. *"What the fuck?"*

"Silence!" The spirit's voice boomed through the air. A tendril of smoke shot out, covering Vinnie's face, wrapping black coils around his head and chest. His knees buckled, yet he still held on to me, pulling me down with him. The hand on my arm turned cold, and I screamed, unable to escape his grip. He fell to the ground, dragging me to my knees and trapping my right hand underneath him.

The guy blocking Collin had stopped fighting, his mouth open in shock. Collin stood next to him, frozen, watching in terror.

The mass now shimmered above the ground, next to Vinnie's body. "Curse Keeper, daughter of the sea, witness to creation. Join with your lord and master, Okeus, or suffer the consequences."

I struggled to catch my breath as I frantically tried to free my arm. The guy's hand had literally frozen around my bicep. I took a breath. "If you wanted me dead, you would have killed me already. Okeus needs me alive." I knew he wanted the gate opened, not left cracked. He needed me or it would be stuck.

The spirit howled and wind blew me back, but my arm was still trapped by Vinnie's frozen body. "Do not think to control Okeus or his children, human. You will curse the day of your creation."

I swallowed the bile rising in my throat. Vomiting right now would totally blow my tough-girl attitude. "Not if I shut the gate first."

Okeus's messenger laughed. "You are stupid and blind. You don't even know the truth."

"What truth?" Could I even trust anything this thing said?

"You will pay for your arrogance, Curse Keeper. I will search out the ones you love and send them to Popogusso like your predecessors locked us away."

The spirit's smoke swirled close to me, its tentacles stretching toward my chest, and my hysteria rose. What if Collin was wrong about the symbol he'd drawn on my back? What if I was wrong about Okeus needing me alive?

Collin's voice echoed through the night as he recited his words in the ancient tongue. His hand glowed, and determination tightened his face.

The messenger ceased moving toward me, then disappeared, howling. "You will regret this, Curse Keeper, son of the land."

Collin was next to me in moments, prying Vinnie's fingers from my arm to get me free. Collin grunted, then I heard the snap of breaking appendages.

My body rebelled and I vomited onto the sidewalk until I dry heaved.

The sedan engine started and drove away. Tony had left Vinnie and his fingers behind.

"Ellie, can you get up? We need to go." Collin's voice was gentle but insistent.

"Daddy." I had no doubt that Okeus would go after him. It was a matter of when.

"Let's get in the truck and you can call him, okay?"

I nodded but began to shake violently. I crawled to my knees and tried to stand. My legs wouldn't support my weight, and I collapsed as I tried to hold back my sobs. My forearm landed on a dead bird. I shrieked and scooted backward, bumping into Vinnie's frozen body.

I screamed.

Collin's hand covered my mouth, and I looked up at him in panic. His eyes were wild and I was relieved to see he was as freaked out as I was.

"I'm going to help you to your feet. First, I'll drop my hand, but you can't scream, okay?"

I nodded, tears flowing down my cheeks.

He let go of my mouth and grabbed both of my arms, lifting me up. I took a step, swaying as my vision began to fade. My knees buckled, but Collin bent and scooped me up against his chest while I fought the darkness invading my head.

Collin grunted as he squatted to retrieve the bag he'd dropped. He hurried us to the truck, fumbling with the door handle before setting me on the seat. He tossed the bag at my feet, shut my door, and ran around to climb into the driver's seat.

He tore out of the parking lot. "Ellie, can you roll up your window?" he asked while rolling up his.

I nodded and grappled with the knob, spinning it around. How fucking hard was it to roll up a fucking window? I let out a sob, then got upset and frustrated that I was crying. I hated crying. Crying was for babies, and I'd already met my crying quota for the next six months.

When I got the window up, I reached for my purse and pulled out my phone, calling Claire first.

"Claire, listen to me." I tried to calm down but my fear raised my voice an octave. "Whatever you do, do not go outside! Don't answer the door for anyone!"

"Ellie, what's going on?"

"They're going to try to hurt you, Claire. You and Daddy and Myra."

"Do you want me to go over to your dad's house?"

"*No!*" I took a deep breath. I needed to calm down. "No. You can't go outside. Promise me you won't go outside until the sun comes up." But even the daylight wasn't safe anymore. The wind god found me in broad daylight—twice. But the darkness was when they were strongest. "*Promise me.*"

"I promise. Are you okay, Ellie? What happened?"

"I'm . . . fine." I'd already freaked out Claire enough. No sense telling her what just happened. "I just need to know you're okay."

"I'm fine. Drew is fine, although he thinks I've gone bat-shit crazy with the salt. Your dad and Myra were okay when I saw them this afternoon. Your dad was even kind of with it and wanted to know if you were working on closing the gate."

"You're kidding?" While I was grateful he was lucid enough to protect himself, I was sorry I wasn't there to talk to him. Even though Collin had become forthcoming, Daddy probably had Dare Keeper answers I needed.

"I took a chance and told him that the spirits might be after him and Myra. He marked up the doors with the symbols Collin put on yours."

"He did?"

"Yeah, so see? He's safe. We're fine. Just take care of you, okay?"

"I love you, Claire."

"I love you too."

I hung up and turned to Collin. "My dad was aware of what was going on today. He marked his doors." My eyes sank closed. More than anything, I wanted to be with Daddy, for him to show me what he'd done. For him to hug me and tell me everything was going to be okay.

Collin pulled me toward him, putting his arm around my back. "See? It's okay. We're all safe."

But we weren't. Not really. We wouldn't be safe until that fucking gate was closed.

Ი Chapter Twenty-Seven Ი

To my annoyance, I cried for about twenty minutes. Every time I thought I had it under control, the dam I'd built up for my tears would crash open and I'd cry again. I tried to find my anger—that this was really happening, that I was the center of two life-threatening dramas—but it stayed buried deep, just like it had after my mother's death.

I hadn't seen a dead body since she died in front of me fifteen years ago. I purposely didn't attend funerals, even refusing to go to my grandparents' several years ago. I avoided hospitals. But tonight that man had died in front of me—holding on to my arm—and the shock and horror of the night my mother died raced into the void of nothingness in my head. I'd suppressed so much about that night. It had been the only way for me to survive, but now bits and pieces flitted around the edges of my thoughts.

The wind howled outside but my ears strained to hear other noises.

The grandfather clock. Tic. Tic. Tic.

A tree branch whacked the glass outside my bedroom window. Thomp. Thomp. Thomp.

I hid in my closet, my eyes squeezed shut. The door was wide open, but the room was dark and I huddled in the far back corner.

My mother's labored breathing came from the hall.

And another sound. The most terrifying. Drip. Drip. Drip.

I stared at the floor in front of me. Dark colored droplets splatted on the hardwood floor, forming a tiny pool. I lifted my gaze. A man with a hood held a big knife in his hand. Lightning flashed outside the window, casting him in an eerie white light. His clothes were dark, his face hidden. Every part of him was black and gray except for the crimson blood dripping from his hand and the knife.

I screamed.

"Ellie, it's okay. You're okay." Collin's voice interrupted the rush of images, his hand brushing my head.

I jolted upright, wiping my hair out of my face. I was sweating like a pig, and my hair was plastered to my cheek. We were still in the truck, which was like a sauna with the windows rolled up. "What happened?"

"You fell asleep. Did you have a nightmare?"

I nodded, looking out the windows. My hands shook again, and I took a deep breath. My limited memories of the night of my mother's death didn't include any part of what I'd just dreamed. Had it really happened that way? Or had my subconscious mixed with my fear from tonight and the last few days and added to my existing trauma? Did it really matter? I focused on the road in front of us, trying to think about anything else but the pictures in my head.

"Was it about tonight?"

I shook my head, but my fear made it exaggerated. I needed to get my shit together. "No. It was about my mother."

"Ellie—"

"I don't want to talk about it." I swung my head around to take in the scenery. "Where are we?"

"About five minutes from Manteo."

"I've been asleep that long? Why didn't you wake me?"

"I didn't see the point. Not until your nightmare. It took me several seconds to wake you up. Are you sure you're okay?"

"Okay?" I laughed, but my voice shook. I pressed my knuckle to my mouth, nipping the skin on the back of my finger. "*Okay?* How can I be okay? Dead birds rained from the sky. A man died right in front of me—holding my arm. He had his Manitou sucked out of him right there while we watched, and his body froze—*and he was still holding my arm*—until you broke his fingers to get me loose. *You broke his fingers, Collin.*" Nausea bubbled with my rising hysteria. "*How can I be okay?*"

Collin's hands tightened on the steering wheel. His jaw clenched, and I'd never seen him look so uncertain in the time I'd known him. So lost.

"I'm scared, Collin. I've never been more scared in my life."

His hand found mine and he encompassed it, squeezing tight as though I were his lifeline. And then it occurred to me that I was so busy going through my own personal freak-out that I'd never once stopped to think that Collin was going through this too. He was always so confident, so cocky. I never questioned that this might be just as hard for him. Sure, he'd heard all the stories and made all the preparations, but it was one thing to hear the tales and another to actually live through it.

"Are *you* okay?"

He turned to me, surprise on his face.

"Tonight had to freak you out just as much as it did me."

"Yes, but not the same way. I had to stand there and watch Marino's guy grab you, *touch you,* threaten you. I couldn't get past Tony to help you. I couldn't save you. The spirit did."

"What the hell are you talking about, Collin?"

"If Okeus's messenger hadn't shown up, you'd be with Marino right now."

"We would have figured something out."

He didn't answer, but he didn't look convinced.

"Saying Okeus's messenger saved me is like saying a lion saves a baby gazelle when the lion shows up to eat the hyena."

"Ellie." He swallowed and his fingers squeezed my hand tighter. "You told the spirit that Okeus needs you alive to open the gate the rest of the way. I think you might be right." He shifted in his seat and cast a glance at me. "What if his appearance wasn't a coincidence?"

"That would make Okeus omnipotent, Collin," I whispered. "Even locked behind the gate."

"He's a god, Ellie."

I couldn't let my head go there, thinking the gods were actually watching my every move. "No. I think the messenger showed up to ask for my decision. It was pure coincidence that he arrived when he did."

Collin turned down the street toward my apartment. Manteo was locked up for the night, all the good citizens asleep in their beds. Clueless to the terror outside their bedroom windows.

"He's angry, Ellie. But tradition says that he's a reasonable god."

I tried to jerk my hand from Collin's, but he refused to let go. "How can you say that?"

We had already reached my apartment and Collin parked in the empty space next to my car. He turned off the engine and turned to me, still holding my hand. He used his free hand to stroke the side of my face, his eyes imploring me to listen.

"Do you remember when I told you that they weren't meant to be locked away? That locking them up had thrown the world off balance?"

I nodded.

"Have you ever once considered that maybe we shouldn't close the gate?"

My mouth dropped open. Who was this man and what was he saying?

"Hear me out." He released my hand and cradled my face. "If we fail this, Ellie, Okeus *will* come after you. Maybe you should make a deal with him. To save you."

"*What?*" I looped my hands over his wrists. "At what price, Collin? At what cost? I save myself to doom countless others? How could I live with myself?"

"How can I live with myself if anything happens to you?"

"*I* am not your responsibility."

Tears filled his eyes and he started to say something before he cleared his throat and looked away. When he turned back, the raw emotion on his face stunned me. "You're my responsibility more than you know. More than *I* knew when I walked into the New Moon less than a week ago. One day, when you hate me for coming into your life, let alone letting you seal your soul to mine, when hearing my name fills your heart with pain, and you never want to see my face again . . . *even then*, you will be my responsibility."

My breath caught in my throat. "You're scaring me, Collin."

"It's okay." His lips were soft on mine. "I don't mean to scare you. I'm trying to let you know what you mean to me. I'm the reason for all of the chaos in your life. I walked into your restaurant and broke the curse. I took you to Marino. I'm the sole cause of the danger you're facing, but God help me, I'm not sorry." His eyes burned bright. "If it all goes away tomorrow . . ."

His voice broke and he swallowed. "I will never be sorry that I had this chance with you. And for that alone, you will hate me someday."

"Collin." Tears blurred my vision.

His mouth crushed mine, his hands tilting my head.

I pulled back, still holding his wrists. "Why do you think I'll hate you? Because of your past? I know about your past. I don't know it all, but I've seen an ugly glimpse, and I'm still here." I squeezed his wrists. "*I'm still here.*"

He shook his head. "You don't even know everything."

"I don't need to. I don't *want* to. This is a chance for both of us to start over. Together. After tomorrow night, we'll put all the ugliness in our past behind us and start over."

He nodded, still upset. Then his face hardened. "We need to get you inside." He opened his door and grabbed my hand, tugging me out the driver's door.

The night was silent. The only sound was the water lapping at the dock to the lighthouse. No birds. No insects. No dogs barking in the night.

My front porch was littered with dead birds. A calling card from Okeus. I squeezed my eyes shut, then opened them again. This was real. I couldn't close my eyes and pretend it wasn't. It was time for Elinor Dare Lancaster to grow up.

Collin kicked the lifeless bodies to the side, making a path to the door. The symbols drawn there were faded and he paused. "I need to redo this. I'm not sure it will hold."

"*We* need to redo it. *Together.* Teach me how."

He nodded and pulled a piece of charcoal from his bag as I unlocked the door. He drew the same symbols he'd made in the motel room, explaining them again, questioning to make sure I understood. When it came time to put his mark on the door, he looked down at me and kissed me. "This part will be different."

He drew a square intersecting a circle, the marks on our hands. Earth containing spirit. He placed his land symbol in the center of the square, diagonally, then handed me the charcoal. "Now draw your wave on the opposite angle and call upon the water force to add its protection."

I took Collin's position, stretching my arm to reach the top of the door, but I wasn't tall enough. Collin wrapped his arms around my waist and lifted me. I drew my water symbol, asking the ancient force of the sea to lend its protection to its daughter as well as the son of land. When I was done, Collin eased his grip, allowing me to slide down the front of his body. Such a simple movement, yet so highly charged with desire and need.

"Now the other three." Collin's voice was husky in my ear, and my body tingled.

I tried not to hurry the remaining symbols, giving them the same reverence as the first one. When I finished the last symbol, I moved to hand the charcoal back to Collin but his arms were around my waist, pulling my body to his, his mouth finding mine. The door opened behind me and he dragged us inside and shut us in, his mouth still on mine, claiming.

I stood on my tiptoes, my hands buried in his hair. Collin looped his hands around my thighs and lifted me to straddle his waist. His hands skimmed the backs of my legs, finding my ass and snugging me close. My legs wrapped tight around his back, and he lifted the hem of my tank top with impatient hands. I unfisted his hair to let him pull the shirt over my head, my impatient mouth finding his again.

He turned and pressed my back against the door. "Ellie Lancaster, my enchantress. You'll be the death of me."

Before I could ask what he meant, his mouth was on mine, his tongue demanding attention. I ground my pelvis into his, aching for him.

He moved us to my bedroom, laying me down on the bed. He stripped off his clothes while I watched, the perfection of his body highlighted by the streetlight that glowed through the gauzy curtain over my repaired window. Claire must have gotten it fixed while I was gone.

I got to my knees on the mattress in front of him, wanting to touch him, to seal this memory of him into my consciousness. My hands landed on his chest, the hair rough on my fingertips, his hard muscles sending waves of desire through my body.

He reached around me and unhooked my bra, then slid the straps over my shoulders, his mouth following on my right arm. He lifted my right palm to his mouth, kissing and licking the mark in the center.

I leaned back my head and moaned.

"You are the most beautiful thing I have ever seen." His silken words washed through my body, making me hungry for him. His hand combed through my hair. "I like your hair long and loose." He bent down and his mouth found my breast and I gasped. His hand fisted the hair at the nape of my neck, arching my back to give him better access.

Molten desire shot to my core. "Collin."

His free hand found the button on my shorts and then my zipper. Bringing his face to mine, he released my hair. Both of his thumbs hooked the sides of my waistband and slowly tugged. His palms circled my hips, sliding my shorts down the rest of the way to my knees, my panties following behind. His hand reached between my legs as he kissed me, his other hand in my hair again.

I reached for the evidence of his own desire, and he groaned, then pushed me down on the bed, pulling my shorts and panties off the rest of the way. He lay beside me, his hands and mouth everywhere, driving me into a frenzy.

"I want you to remember this. What you feel with me." He kissed my mouth again, then met my gaze, his eyes bright with lust and need. "Remember that I am yours for now and forever. And no man will ever give you what I can."

I grabbed the sides of his head. "No man has ever made me feel a fraction of what I feel with you. I'm not going anywhere."

His knee nudged my legs apart, and he positioned himself between them, balancing himself on his forearms. "Tell me what you want, Ellie."

Was he wanting me to talk dirty to him? I didn't think so. This was deeper than that. I gazed into his searching eyes. I lifted my right hand to his cheek, and as I said the words, I realized how true they were. "I want you, Collin Dailey. I've always wanted you."

His right hand grabbed mine, pressing our palms together and bringing them over my head as he entered me.

Bombarded with two extraordinary sensations at the same time, my mind scrambled to make sense of the rush, but my body followed instinct, matching Collin's every move. I was the swirling dust in the beginning of the universe. I was the explosion of a supernova. I was the energy of the sun.

He started slowly, driving me crazy with need, the strain on his face betraying his own struggle to not quicken the pace.

I was the bee drinking nectar from flower. I was the blade of grass on a sunny meadow. I was the deer in the field.

I wrapped my legs around his waist, offering myself up to him, an ache so deep I knew he was the only one to fill it. To ever fill it. "Collin," I begged. "*Please.*"

His pace quickened, his free hand reaching underneath me so he could get deeper.

I was the rain droplets in a storm cloud. I was the rushing water in a mountain stream. I was the vast, deep ocean.

I was climbing, climbing, climbing past the tallest mountaintop. Past the edge of the solar system. To the very edge of the universe.

I released a loud cry. My left hand circled his back and urged him deeper.

I was the first drop of water in the meteorite that hit the hot liquefied earth. The union of land and water.

And for one brief moment, I was whole.

⌁ Chapter Twenty-Eight ⌁

Collin was gone when I woke up. I had a moment of panic when I realized he wasn't in bed next to me, but I found a note on his pillow.

I have to prepare for tonight. You were too beautiful to wake up. No matter what happens tonight, know that I am always yours.
Collin

I hadn't seen Myra since the morning I'd stolen the candlesticks. And I hadn't checked on Daddy either, other than through Claire. I was eager to make sure they were okay.

Okeus had promised a sacrifice.

With trembling fingers, I called Claire, who whispered into the phone that she and Drew were fine, but she was going to lose her job if she didn't get off the phone. Next I called Myra, who was cheerful when she answered.

"I overslept but wanted you to know I'm coming in this morning. Is Daddy okay?" I asked, already knowing the answer from her tone but needing to hear her say the words.

"He's fine. Becky's here helping, but I'd love to see you before I leave for the visitor center."

If the people I cared about had been spared, then what did that mean about the sacrifice?

It was already after nine, but I was scheduled to work at the New Moon at four if Marlena let me come back. That meant I had the day to fill. My apartment didn't have a washer and dryer, so I'd even have time to do some of my own laundry.

I took a shower and dressed in a pair of capri pants and my last clean T-shirt. I packed all my laundry and found my car keys since I had too much to carry four blocks. When I opened the front door, I prepared myself for the birds, expecting to see the macabre countdown, but the bodies were gone.

Collin.

I smiled to myself on my way to load the laundry into the back of the car when I noticed the crowd on the sidewalk in front of the New Moon.

Oh, God.

Dropping the over-piled basket onto the parking lot next to my car, I ran through the opening between the buildings, toward the street. Pushing my way through the dense crowd, I tried to keep my fear from spilling out into hysteria. I needed to see what was going on before I panicked.

I spotted Bob, the manager of Kitty Hawk Kites, standing in the middle of the throng. "Bob! What's going on?"

He turned his pale face toward me. "Ellie, I'm so sorry."

My terror broke loose. "*What*? What happened?"

"Marlena."

I sucked in breath, fighting the blackness hovering at the edges of my vision. I was not going to pass out. "What happened?"

"They found her here. Outside the restaurant. Like Lila." Bob grabbed my hands. "The sick person doing this is targeting this restaurant, Ellie. You're not safe."

I choked on a sob. No, the people around me weren't safe. I stumbled to the curb and sat down, cradling my head between my hands and crying.

Bob sat next to me. "I think the police want to talk to you."

Of course they would, and I'd have to lie. Would they be able to see that? Tilting my head back, I drew in a deep breath, forcing myself to calm down. Sitting here crying on the curb wouldn't help Marlena, and it wouldn't help anyone else I loved or cared about. "I'm going to the Dare Inn to help Myra. If they ask about me, tell them they can find me there."

"Okay, but be careful Ellie."

Marlena. She was married with three kids. The most loving, giving person I'd ever met. Sure she could be pushy with my love life, but she loved me and now she was dead. Because of me.

I drove the few blocks to the bed and breakfast in a daze. What the hell was I doing? I was about to go inside and do my laundry and change linens and pretend that everything was okay.

Everything was so not okay.

The messenger had promised a friend and my family would be sacrificed. He'd stolen Marlena—who was next? Should I cave to Okeus's demands? It would keep the people I loved safe.

But would it really? Ahone had warned that the gate needed to be closed, and he was a god. But I couldn't ignore the fact that he alone had escaped the curse. Still, I knew deep in my gut that this was nothing compared to what would happen if the gate was opened all the way. I only had to make sure that Daddy and Myra were protected and get through tonight, and then this nightmare would be over.

I hauled my laundry to the back door of the residential house. Claire was right. Daddy had marked the doors. His symbols were a little different than Collin's but for the most part, looked to be the same. That gave me some comfort. After I started a load of my darks, I went to the guesthouse and found Myra on the phone in the office. She smiled and waved when I walked in and made my way to the small kitchen.

Three couples sat at the tables in the dining room.

"Ellie." Myra's worried voice greeted me. "I've been worried about you. I heard about Lila and Dwight."

My eyes welled with tears. "And now Marlena. They found her dead outside the restaurant. Just like Lila."

Myra's hand covered her mouth as her eyes widened. "Who's doing this?"

I didn't want to lie to Myra, but I knew she didn't want the truth. "I don't know."

"Are you safe? Three people you know have been killed. Maybe you should stay with us."

That was the last thing I should do. "That's not saying much, Myra. We know half the people in town." She started to protest, but I interrupted. "How's Daddy?"

She shook her head, trying to jump conversation streams. "He was better yesterday and still is today. I'm glad you're here. You should go see him."

"Thanks, Myra." I picked up a blueberry muffin to take with me and headed for the back door. I wasn't very hungry but I needed all the strength I could get.

"Ellie?"

I turned back to her.

"I hope you know that this house and everything in it is yours too."

I was confused for a moment until I remembered. The candlesticks. They seemed so long ago now, but it had only been a few days. I dropped my gaze. "I'm sorry."

She grabbed both of my arms and stared into my face. "No, Ellie. There's nothing to be sorry about. I'm sure you had a reason, even if you don't want to share it."

"I love you, Myra."

"I love you too. Go see your dad."

I found Daddy sitting in the living room watching television. His caregiver sat in a chair in the corner, knitting.

Daddy looked up. Confusion flickered in his eyes before he smiled. "Elliphant."

A soft smile warmed my cheeks. "Hey Daddy." I turned to the woman. "You can take a break while I sit with Daddy for a bit."

She nodded and left her knitting in the chair before she left the room.

Daddy watched her go, then turned back to me. "The curse . . ." Worry knotted his brow.

I sat next to him and held my palm toward him. "I have a surprise for you." Why had I been so stubborn and not showed it to him the day I'd gotten it?

He picked up my hand, and his mouth dropped. "It's real."

"It's very real."

Tears filled his eyes. "After so long . . . so many years of waiting . . ."

I felt so unworthy and so unwilling all at the same time. "I have a title. The gods call me Curse Keeper, daughter of the sea, witness to creation."

His brow furrowed with confusion. "I knew about daughter of the sea, but witness to creation?"

"I have a pure soul. My Manitou was part of creation. When Collin and I touch our marks together, I can feel it. I feel the essence of every living creature. It's so beautiful, Daddy. I wish it had been you. I don't deserve this."

"Shh . . ." He pulled me into a hug, resting my cheek on his shoulder as he stroked my hair. "Don't say such things. I confess, I would have given anything to be the Curse Keeper, but I'm proud of you. I'm glad it's you."

I blinked away my tears. "One of the times we touched, when I was in the ocean, I saw the birth of creation."

He pulled back, looking into my face with wide eyes.

"My Manitou was a witness to the creation of the universe. In a vision, I relived my ancient memories. I saw the birth of the world, and Ahone arise from earth and create man. I saw him split himself and create his twin, Okeus. Collin says pure souls are very rare, but the gods and spirits will want my Manitou even more."

He shook his head. "Ellie, I don't understand."

"Daddy, have you seen the dead birds and animals?"

He nodded.

"The gods are weak after being locked up for over four hundred years. Taking the life force of other creatures increases their strength. Did you know about that part?"

He shook his head. "No."

"A pure soul has more energy than multiple Manitous and they want mine. I was attacked by a wind god, and Collin put his symbol on my back to protect me. It works." At least, I chose to believe it did.

"They've attacked you?" He fidgeted with agitation. "Didn't you remember the words of protection?"

"No, Daddy. You know I forgot everything, the words of protection included. But I remembered them after Collin gave me a symbol of protection."

"What is this symbol of protection?"

"Do we not have one?"

"No."

I turned around and lifted the hem of my T-shirt.

"I don't recognize this, Ellie. Is this a real tattoo?"

"No, Daddy. It's only henna. Collin has a permanent one on his chest. Are you sure you don't remember it?"

"No. I recognize the symbols, but not the mark itself."

"Collin says the Manteo line has information and traditions they passed down in preparation for the breaking of the curse. It's probably something they came up with."

His finger traced the symbols. "The circle represents the spirit world. The squares mean the earthly plane. I recognize the symbols for the sea and the land. But this one . . ." His finger stopped and stiffened.

My back tensed. "What is it, Daddy?"

"Ellie, this one represents Okeus."

Icy fingers of dread crawled up my spine, and I shivered. "It's a symbol of protection, Daddy. It's to protect me against Okeus and the winds gods."

"The symbols are typically used to invoke the Manitou or other forces. The marks call upon the forces you're asking for protection, not the forces you need protection from. Like the symbols I put on the door. You wouldn't include the mark of the thing you were protecting against." He grabbed my shoulder and turned me back to face him. "Ellie, are you sure this man has your best interests at heart?"

Fear jostled with reason as I tried to sort through Daddy's information. If he had asked me about the Collin I met that first and even second time in the New Moon I would have questioned Collin's motives, but the last few days had proven time and time again how much Collin cared about me. The fear in his eyes was real. His concern for me genuine. There was no disguising our hearts when our palms were linked. When I bound our souls, his fear of losing me was undeniable. "Yes, Daddy. I trust him with my life."

"You said he has the symbol tattooed on him?"

"Yeah, Collin says when the Curse Keeper in the Manteo line turns eighteen, they have it tattooed on their chest."

He wrung his hands, becoming more agitated. That was a bad sign and often meant his dementia was creeping back in. "You say the entire line gets this tattoo? It could explain the Okeus symbol. There's a lot of duality with the curse. Land and the sea were evoked."

"Yes, because they are forces older than the gods. The land and the sea gave birth to the gods. Collin uses the symbols of the moon and the stars and the sun to represent day on my door to protect me from the gods at night."

Daddy rubbed his forehead, concentrating while he directed his gaze to the floor. "The story I was told said Manteo was quite distraught that they'd locked the gods away, and he knew that the gods would seek revenge when they finally broke loose. It could be that Manteo's line chose to appeal to Okeus for mercy when he was freed. He's the most powerful and the most vengeful of them all."

I nodded.

"You say the other Keeper, Collin, has protected you multiple times. The symbol must be what he says it is." He patted my hand. "Just be careful." He kissed my forehead, fidgeting more. He got to his feet and began to pace.

I sucked in a deep breath. If he followed his usual pattern, he'd become incoherent soon.

He stopped pacing and looked at me. "Do you have the cup?"

"Yes, and we retrieved the Manteo bowl last night."

"When's the ceremony?"

"Tonight. In the middle of the night. In the botanical gardens at the big oak tree. Tomorrow's the seventh day."

"Already?" He rubbed his forehead, pressing hard.

"Yes, but I don't remember anything of the ceremony. I forgot it all, Daddy." My voice broke. "I'm sorry I didn't let you teach me it all again."

"The ceremony . . . the ceremony . . . The Manteo Keeper performs the ceremony."

"What do we do with the cup and the bowl? Do we drink something at the ceremony?"

"Yes . . . I think it's tea . . ." He pressed harder on his forehead. "I wrote it down. I wrote it all down somewhere."

"You wrote down the Curse Keeper information?" I wasn't sure if I needed it now, but it would be nice to have the information for the ceremony, even though Collin knew what to do.

Daddy began to mumble as he paced.

I grabbed his arm and led him to the sofa. "Sit down, Daddy. You're getting worn out."

He shook his head, confusion replacing the clarity that had been there only moments before. I hated this stupid disease that stole my father.

I rubbed his arm and began to hum the old lullaby Momma used to sing me when I was little. It always calmed him down. He squinted. "Amanda?"

My heart sank. "No, Daddy. Momma's gone."

He looked around. "You look just like Amanda. Where did she go?"

I kissed his forehead. "I love you, Daddy. I'll try to make you proud of me."

Clarity flashed in his eyes for a brief moment before confusion returned. "Blood. No blood, Ellie."

My chest tightened. No matter how many years passed, I'd never get over my mother's murder. And neither would my father.

I sent Daddy's caregiver back in to sit with him and returned to the inn to start changing linens. Myra had already gone to work at the visitor center, and her friend Becky was in the office when I got back. "Becky, I'm sorry I haven't been around to help the last few days."

"Don't worry about it, Ellie. You work too hard."

I forced a grin. "No rest for the wicked."

She laughed. "Then why are *you* working so hard?"

I had plenty of time to dwell on what Daddy had told me. I had to admit that having Okeus's mark on my back concerned me, except I knew that Collin had the exact same mark. And the mark had protected me. Why was I questioning him?

But Collin telling me over and over again not to trust him played in my head. And his surety that I would hate him. An uneasiness crept up my neck. I shook my head. I was nervous about tonight. That's all this was. Nerves.

I decided to call Collin anyway for reassurance. He answered on the second ring, his voice panicked. "Ellie? Are you okay?"

"I'm fine."

I heard his sigh of relief.

"Why did you think something was wrong?"

"You don't seem the phone call type."

"Why do you say that?"

"I never saw you make a phone call when we've been together except to check on Claire and your family."

"True." I paused. "I just needed to hear your voice. I'm nervous."

His voice tightened. "I won't let anything happen to you. I'll protect you with my life."

Those didn't sound like the words of a man who had ill intentions toward me. Why was I doubting him? I felt slimy and unworthy of his concern. "I missed you this morning."

"I missed you too. When this is over, let's go away somewhere for a week, just you and me, a hotel with room service so we never have to leave." He sounded sad and wistful.

"I'd like that." I paused, my voice catching in my throat. "There was another body today. My boss, Marlena."

"The woman who seated me both times I came in?"

"Yes." My voice choked. "But she was more than my boss. She was my friend."

"Ellie, I'm so sorry."

"Okeus wants me to pledge my loyalty to him. I protected Claire last night, but I didn't protect Marlena. Who will he kill tonight?"

Collin was silent.

"Has Okeus sent anyone to you? Has he sacrificed people you care about?"

I heard his breath in the phone. Finally, he answered, "Yes, he's hurt someone I love."

I felt so incredibly selfish. I'd done nothing but whine for days, and he never once complained. And I never asked. "Your brother?"

"It doesn't matter, Ellie. It will all be behind us tonight."

"But Daddy and Myra."

"Redo the marks on their door after it gets dark and make sure they stay inside. They should be fine."

Should be wasn't what I wanted to hear, but I knew it was the best he could offer.

He cleared his throat. "I have to go. Promise me that you'll be careful until tonight, especially after it gets dark."

I smiled. "I promise."

I hung up and finished my work, shuffling my own laundry before starting the linens for the inn. I searched Daddy's office, looking for the information he might have written down about the curse. He didn't use the office much anymore, but Myra kept it as it had always been for when he had his clearer days. But my hunt turned up nothing. Where could he have kept it? Did it even exist?

Claire was waiting on my porch when I got home. She pointed to the door. "New artwork, I see."

My eyebrows rose. "Aren't you the observant one?"

"I heard about Marlena."

Pressing my lips together, I nodded.

"That was supposed to be me, wasn't it?"

Inhaling a deep breath to steady my nerves, I shrugged. "The spirit said a friend, Claire. Marlena was a friend too."

Claire pulled me into a tight hug. When she dropped her hold, tears brimmed her eyes. "And you know what she wanted most in the world? For you to find a fine-lookin' man." She flashed an ornery grin even though her chin quivered. "And you did. At least you made her happy."

I shook my head and snorted. "I guess you could say that. She nearly peed her pants when I told her I was taking Collin home the other night after work."

She swiped her eyes. "You're positively glowing when you talk about him. How *was* he?"

"Claire!"

"Come on, Ellie, give me something."

I unlocked the door and pushed it open. "Let's just say he was better than Dwight," I said without thinking. I'd momentarily forgotten he was dead and guilt flooded my head. Dwight was dead because of me.

"Please, a jellyfish is better than Dwight." But Claire's usual sarcastic bite was missing. "Give me something else."

She followed me in and shut the door while I set my laundry on my bed.

"Fine," I said with a smug smile. "Nothing I've experienced has even come close to what we shared." Little did she know.

She clapped her hands, happiness replacing her melancholy. "See? Didn't I tell you? Say it. Come on."

I forced a cheesy grin. "Fine. You were right. Happy now?"

"So what's going on with the curse stuff?"

My smile fell. "The ceremony is tonight."

"Are you two ready for that?"

"I think so. We have the cup and the bowl. Collin is preparing everything else today. We'll beat the deadline. We should be good." I hoped so.

"So what are you going to do after that? Are you going to join Match.com like I suggested?"

I squinted in confusion. "What are you talking about?"

"Now that you are back in the saddle and riding again, we want to keep it that way. You've tapped out the dating pool on Roanoke Island. Time to broaden your horizons."

I tilted my head. "Claire, Collin doesn't want this to be a couple-of-days thing."

"What are you talking about, Ellie? You know that Collin is not a commitment-type guy. That's why he was so perfect. Hot guy who fucks you blind—"

"Claire!"

"—and gets your confidence back so you can move on to someone more reliable." She narrowed her eyes. "Oh, my God. You're actually considering keeping him around."

"He's not what you think he is, Claire."

"A womanizing man-whore? You're really telling me that he's not?"

I didn't answer, trying to find the words to explain it.

She laughed, but it was bitter. "Let me guess, Collin told you that you're different than any other woman he's ever met, and he's going to change for you."

How did I answer that? When she put it that way, it sounded like a flat-out lie. But I'd seen a deeper Collin than he showed the world. Or was that all an act? No, I'd felt his bond to me through our marks. He couldn't lie to me, not when we were connected like that.

"Please, dear God, tell me you haven't fallen for him? I thought you were smarter than that."

I turned my back to her and looked out the window.

"Ellie." The disappointment in her voice hurt.

"Shut up, Claire."

She sighed and sat on the bed, crossing her legs. "What the hell do I know? Maybe he will."

I pulled my laundry out and started putting it away. "Yeah." I hated myself for letting her make me doubt.

"Ellie."

I turned to look at her.

"I hope for your sake he does. You deserve to be screwed by a guy like that every night and make babies so gorgeous that human eyes can't look upon them."

I grinned in spite of my worry, unsuccessfully hiding my chuckle. "I love you too. Now go home and get ready for your wedding next month." I paused. "Claire, when it gets dark, I want to mark your door."

"Seriously? The salt worked."

"Thank God, but the spirit threatened to hurt someone I love. I want to make sure you're protected. Just in case."

I needed all the insurance I could get.

⌁ Chapter Twenty-Nine ⌁

The restaurant had reopened after Lila's death, but it remained closed after Marlena's. She was the heart and soul of the New Moon. I wasn't sure I could even face working there without her.

The police showed up at my apartment mid-afternoon. The marks on my door threw the two officers, but they recovered before they sat down on my sofa. One of the officers was familiar. I was sure the middle-aged man had been in the restaurant before. But the other I'd gone to school with, Tom Helmsworth.

The older officer took the lead with the questioning. "Do you know anyone who has a personal vendetta against the restaurant?"

I shook my head, pressing the back of my knuckles against my teeth. "No."

"Have you ever felt unsafe working there?"

The only time I'd felt unsafe was the first day Collin showed up. "No. The New Moon is one of the best jobs I've ever had."

"Do you have any idea who could have done this?"

Tears filled my eyes, and I shook my head.

Tom shifted his weight. "What's with the door, Ellie?"

My breath caught. "You mean the marks?"

"Yeah."

"Protection."

His eyes narrowed. "What do you need protection from?"

Shit. Why did I tell him that? "I heard about the tourist and I heard about Lila. That they were frozen solid. That doesn't exactly sound natural, now does it? I'm protecting myself from evil spirits."

I expected Tom to laugh and call me crazy. Instead he kept his gaze on me, his face expressionless. "Why do you think these evil spirits would come after you?"

I swallowed. What did Tom know? This didn't sound like idle curiosity. "It's insurance. Just like the deadbolt on my door. I hope to God I'll never need it, but it's there in case I do."

Tom didn't seem satisfied, but he didn't press for more information. He stood, and the other officer stood with him. "Well, thank you for your time, Ellie."

I nodded. "Sure." I walked them to the door and the older man started down the stairs, but Tom stopped on the porch and stared at my door.

"You know what I don't get?" His eyes pierced mine.

My heart lurched. "No. What?"

"Where a woman white as Wonder Bread learned Native American symbols, and why she thought to put them on her door."

My mouth dropped open, but I wasn't sure what to say.

His voice lowered. "You can talk to me, Ellie. I can protect you. Is there something you have to tell me?"

I shook my head. "No."

He knew I was lying, but there was nothing I could do about that right now. I only hoped he thought I had information and didn't consider me a suspect.

Around seven, Collin sent me a text telling me he'd let me know when we'd go to the botanical gardens. Since the gardens were in the same complex as the Lost Colony grounds, Collin was smart to wait until the wee hours of the morning. So much activity was happening at the new excavation site—I still couldn't believe they called it that when it was so obviously not excavated—that three or four a.m. were probably the safest hours, and still gave us enough time before the sunrise.

He sent me another text around nine telling me to be ready at two.

Why didn't he call? Worry churned in my gut, fueled by doubt and fear.

I went to Claire's around ten. I was on edge and conscious of my surroundings while I fisted and flexed my right hand. My fingertips brushed the raised edges of my mark, giving me small comfort. I could protect myself and the people I loved. I wasn't helpless.

I wanted to wait until later to start on Claire's door, when hopefully no one would see me, but I was afraid to wait too long. While Claire was eager to let me mark her entrances, Drew, on the other hand, took some convincing. Especially since I refused to give him an adequate reason.

She stood back as I made the symbols Colin showed me, leaving out his symbol and substituting mine instead. For the center symbol, I put Claire and Drew's initials and prayed it was enough.

"That is so cool," she said after I finished.

"Let's just hope you don't need it."

When I left, I drove to the inn. Myra was an early-to-bed person, so I knew I wouldn't run into her close to eleven thirty. Daddy had marked the doors, but some of the symbols Collin used were missing. I'd feel better if I redid them all, but the inn had a lot of exterior doors, and it would take me awhile.

I made my way around the building, putting Myra and Daddy's initials in the spot that designated who needed protection, hoping it covered the guests too. But I put a fresh line of salt in all the openings for added insurance, even the windows I could reach. If the gate didn't close, I'd ask Collin if there was something more appropriate to use. I chided myself for my pessimism, but I couldn't shake the heavy dread that had settled around me.

I saved the front door that led out to the screened porch for last. I opened the screen door slowly to ease the creak in the hinges and nearly screamed when I saw Daddy in the corner, mumbling.

"Daddy! You scared me to death! Does Myra know you're down here?" I knew for a fact she didn't. There was no way she'd let him out here by himself.

Daddy ignored me, still mumbling, but I caught a few words. *Black water, son of the sea.*

He was saying the words of protection, but in English.

I took several steps closer. "Daddy?"

He stood in the darkest of shadows, probably the least safe place he could be. My palm began to tingle.

Shit.

My heart pounded against my ribs. I knew I could protect myself, but could I protect Daddy too? Did I have time to mark the front door?

"Curse Keeper." A shimmering white-grayish light appeared on the porch out of thin air, and I stood in front of Daddy to shield him. "Daughter of the sea, witness to creation. The hour is close at hand. Do you intend to close the gate?"

Since this spirit wasn't threatening me, he must be Ahone's messenger. "Yes, but I'm not sure how."

"Because you do not believe."

"I believe now."

"Yet you still have no faith."

"It's not a matter of faith. I just don't remember." Frustration welled in my chest. Were the memories buried deep inside, or had telling Claire wiped them away? Not that it mattered at this point. I had no hope of learning them in the next few hours.

"A sacrifice must be made to close the gate."

I gasped. I expected something like this from Okeus, but not Ahone. "What kind of sacrifice?"

"You are safe tonight. From Ahone."

I swallowed to keep from throwing up. "Okeus?"

"Okeus is not your greatest enemy tonight."

"What does that mean?"

My father's mumbling grew louder, and I glanced over my shoulder. Daddy had his hand up, muttering the words of protection in English. Would it work for him since he wasn't the Keeper now? I doubted it, fear spreading through my body like a cancer.

"The curse was flawed from beginning to end. Alpha and Omega. The beginning of time to the end the world. The universe tends to chaos but thrives on balance. Gods were not meant to be contained, nor can they be commanded. A price must be paid for the arrogance of man. Each line must pay a price and the retribution is steep. A sacrifice must be made."

My blood rushed in my ears. My palm burned, and I held it at my side, ready to send the spirit away, but he was here for a reason, and I hoped to find out why.

"What about Ahone? He was part of the curse."

"He has suffered many times over, and he will suffer again. The son of the land has already made his sacrifice; now it is time for the daughter of the sea."

What did Collin sacrifice? "Do you mean I must die?"

"Not tonight. Not by Ahone."

Daddy's mumbling stopped.

And then I knew, my eyes widening as my heart raced. "No! I've sacrificed one parent to this terrible curse already. I won't give another."

"Ahone will not close the gate without a sacrifice." Then the spirit was gone.

A sacrifice? I forced myself to calm down and think rationally. I couldn't sacrifice Daddy. I wouldn't. The gate could stay cracked for eternity for all I cared. But if gods were after Daddy, I had to protect him.

"Daddy! You have to go inside." I ran to the door, writing the symbols as quickly as I could. I'd made it to the symbol for air, when a wind blew me across the porch and sent me crashing into the wicker furniture.

"*Curse Keeper.*" My throat tightened at the derogatory tone. Okeus's messenger. "It is time to make your decision."

"Tell Okeus to go back to hell."

"If you refuse, you must make your sacrifice."

"What is up with you gods and your fucking sacrifices? *Go to hell!*"

Daddy stepped forward from the shadows. "I am ready to pay the price."

"No!" I screamed. "No! He doesn't know what he's saying!" I scratched the next symbols.

Daddy turned to me, his eyes clear and coherent. "Your mother died for you, Ellie. Now it's my turn."

"No! I'm not going to lose you too!" I grabbed his arm and dragged him across the porch and toward the front door.

The spirit sent a blast of air toward us, but I held onto Daddy's arm and managed to get the front door open and push Daddy inside.

"DO NOT DEFY OKEUS, CURSE KEEPER!" The loud voice shook the porch.

"*Fuck you!*" I shouted, lifting my palm and shoving it toward him, shouting the words of protection.

The spirit howled, screaming into the night as he disappeared.

I scratched the last of the symbols on the door as Myra appeared in her nightgown, bleary-eyed and frightened. "Ellie? What's going on?"

"Daddy was outside, and he was almost attacked."

Her eyes bulged, and she swung her gaze out to the yard. "Attacked by what?"

"Myra, the curse is real. It's all real. Okeus, the dark creator god, has marked Daddy as a sacrifice, but as long as you keep him inside and behind the marked door, you'll both be all right." The gods might have marked Daddy, but I'd do everything to protect him.

Myra tilted her head. "Ellie, listen to yourself. What are you saying?"

I searched her eyes, pleading with her to understand. "I know it sounds crazy, Myra, but it's real. Please. *Please*, keep Daddy inside. Hopefully this will all be a bad dream tomorrow. I have to go." I ran toward the screen door.

"Ellie!"

I turned around to face her.

"I believe you."

Those three words meant so much. I ran back and hugged her. "Thank you."

"Ellie, be careful."

I rushed to my car and drove back to my apartment, tightly wound, my thoughts a scrambled mess. Ahone's messenger said that he and Okeus weren't my biggest threat tonight. So what was? Collin? I just couldn't believe it. I knew he wasn't the most honorable man, but our link didn't lie. It wasn't Collin. Maybe Ahone's messenger was warning me that the gate wouldn't close if I didn't make a sacrifice and I'd face my nightmare. Hundreds of spirits intent on torturing me. I fought to catch my breath. That definitely seemed like the biggest threat.

Both gods demanded a sacrifice, so what were my options? The way I saw it, I had three: One, I accept Okeus's offer and pledge myself to him and save Daddy's life. Two, I provide a sacrifice of some kind to Ahone to close the gate. Three, I do nothing. If I chose one, I'd save Daddy but lose the world, and most likely myself, to evil. If I chose three, I'd most likely spend the rest of my life constantly on guard, protecting Daddy and myself and watching the world be overrun with spirits. I only had one option I could live with, the second. But I could never sacrifice Daddy.

I would sacrifice myself.

A surreal calm settled over me. I thought my decision would freak me out more, and while I was terrified, I was more worried about what would happen if I didn't follow through with it. What would Collin say? What had Collin sacrificed?

Unbelievably, I fell asleep on the sofa and woke up to my cell phone ringing.

"Ellie, I'm setting up here," he said after I answered. "I'm worried that we'll run out of time. I need you to meet me at the botanical gardens."

"You're already there?"

"Yeah."

"Why didn't you bring me with you?"

"I've been here for a couple of hours and didn't want you out here out in the open."

"But *you're* out in the open." I didn't intend for my tone to sound so accusatory.

"What are you saying, Ellie?"

What was I doing? "Nothing. I'm sorry. I'm on edge."

His voice softened. "I am too. It will be over soon."

"I'll be there in about fifteen minutes." I hung up and grabbed my purse and keys, so nervous I thought I'd throw up. I looked around my apartment, wondering what would happen to all my things. Maybe I should have made a list of what I wanted done. But what did it matter? It was just stuff. The important thing was that I was saving the people I loved and everyone else in the world with them. Panic washed through me when I thought about how I would accomplish my own sacrifice, but I took a deep breath. *Calm down. You can do this.*

I was scared to be outside this deep in the night, but none of the gods bothered me. They were probably waiting to put on a show.

When I drove into the Lost Colony complex and pulled in the botanical gardens parking lot, I climbed out of the car and found Collin waiting for me in the shadows.

"Ellie." He stepped out and held a hand toward me. He was shirtless, only wearing jeans and his shoes, but his body was covered with markings. As I stepped closer, I saw that his eyes shone bright with excitement and nervousness.

I took his hand, and he turned to walk to the back gate. He was so quiet. So solemn. Should I tell him about my decision? I couldn't imagine he'd go along with it, not after all his protests of doing everything to save me. "Collin, I'm scared."

He stopped and put his hands on my waist, bending over to kiss my lips gently. "I'm scared too, but we can do this. I believe in us. I have faith."

Ahone's messenger told me that I believed but I lacked faith. Is that what he meant?

He kissed me again, more possessively this time. When he pulled back, his eyes had changed, and held fierce determination.

He opened the back gate and we walked hand in hand toward the giant oak tree. Hundreds of pillar candles circled the tree trunk. It would have been beautiful if it wasn't so serious.

"How long did it take you to set this up?"

"A few hours."

"I would have helped you, Collin."

He squeezed my hand. "I know, Ellie. I didn't want to risk you being out in the open."

Why did he always say that? Why didn't he worry about himself?

When we got closer, I saw markings carved into the ground, intricate patterns dug into the grass. I recognized only a few. "What do they mean?"

"They're like the symbols on your door. Calling upon the ancient forces, listing the gods and spirits that I know. The rest is a prayer of a sort."

Inside the large circle was a smaller circle with a small round table and Collin's bowl. "Did you bring the cup?"

I nodded, pulling it from my purse and handing it to him. I tossed my purse to the ground outside the ceremonial area. My legs shook.

"Are you ready?"

"What if this doesn't work, Collin?"

"Have faith."

Yet you still have no faith.

Was that the key to closing the gate? That, along with my sacrifice? I had to at least address this with Collin, even if I didn't tell him my decision. "Collin, Ahone's messenger told me I needed to make a sacrifice to close the gate. He said you'd already made yours."

His eyes hardened. "You don't have to sacrifice anything tonight, Ellie. I've made sure of that."

"With your own sacrifice?"

"We need to get started." Collin's hand tightened on my mine and he led me into the smaller circle.

What had Collin sacrificed? I couldn't imagine him sacrificing someone in his family. But I had two choices: either I trusted Collin or I didn't.

Is there really any choice?

I stepped inside the circle and the entire world hushed, as though we'd stepped onto hallowed ground. I looked up into Collin's face for reassurance.

He placed me in the middle of the smaller circle, next to the table. Then, standing in front of me, he leaned down to give me a gentle kiss. "It's time."

Collin began to chant in the ancient language. The sounds hung heavy in the air. Everything felt slower. Louder. More meaningful.

The moon floated full in the cloudless sky. The stars shone so brightly I felt like they would rain down upon us.

The veil to the spirit world was close. The air grew thick, and I dragged it into my lungs with each slow breath. Magic was heavy and oppressive here, and I felt helpless and weak in the face of it. I closed my eyes. I wasn't helpless and weak. And I wasn't doing this alone. I had Collin.

Collin stood in front of me, pouring a dark brown liquid from an old pot into the bowl and the cup, chanting his melancholy tune. I lifted my eyes to the heavens. We were but specks in this vast and infinite universe. I couldn't be a pure soul for nothing. The gift that I carried meant *something*. Something other than food for the spirits.

Collin grabbed my face in his hands, devotion and determination in his eyes as his song continued. My soul was older than anything here. I carried an ancient history deep inside me. What did it mean? For what purpose?

I believe now.

Yet you still have no faith.

Collin pulled my shirt over my head and his hands skimmed my shoulders, his right palm landing on the symbol on my back. My back arched with the rush of power, and he brought me to his chest with loving arms.

Okeus's symbol was on my back.

The symbols are typically used to invoke the Manitou or other forces. The marks call upon the forces you're asking for protection, not the forces you need protection from . . . You wouldn't include the mark of the thing you were protecting against.

Fear gripped my heart. Why was I frightened? Collin wouldn't hurt me. Was this what Ahone meant? That I didn't have faith in Collin?

Collin picked up a rope from the table, placing one end in my left hand. Then he put my right forearm against his right one, wrapping the rope around our arms, binding us together.

"*Ellie, do you know what you did?*"

I nodded. I'd burned our souls together for eternity. "I'm sorry. I didn't know."

He shook his head. "No. Don't be sorry. Not now. Not for this."

When he finished, he took a deep breath, and his eyes darkened with desire. His free hand found my cheek, sliding down to my neck as his words filled the night. The air grew hazy and some part deep inside me recognized it as magic. How could I know that? Did I need to have faith in the magic inside *me*? I had to admit that something felt off. Collin was supposed to be performing a ceremony similar to what Manteo and Ananias Dare had performed. Yet somehow I knew this wasn't the same as theirs. Collin was using the union of our souls to strengthen the ceremony. That had to be a good thing. The first ceremony failed.

I changed the cleansing ceremony when I marked you.

My heartbeat pounded in my head. It all boiled down to trust. Did I trust Collin or not? This man I'd seared my soul to, regardless of what he was doing now.

Collin picked up a knife from the table.

Don't trust me, Ellie. You can't trust me.

No. I refused to believe Collin would hurt me. He'd sworn time and time again he'd protect me. When we were joined with our marks, I saw into his soul.

One day, when you hate me for coming into your life, let alone letting you seal your soul to mine, when hearing my name fills your heart with pain, and you never want to see my face again . . . Even then, you will be my responsibility.

Tears streamed down my face, yet still my heart refused to believe. I thought Collin meant I'd hate him for his past, but the ancient wisdom borne in my soul told me I was wrong.

Collin knew I'd hate him for his betrayal.

I want you to remember this. What you feel with me. Remember that I am yours for now and forever. And no man will ever give you what I can.

He held the knife above our heads and I watched, mesmerized and in too much shock to fight him as he swiped the knife across my palm and then his. My hand was numb when he tilted our hands over the bowl and the cup, our blood dripping into the vessels. Smoke rose from the surface of the liquids, rising and joining together as it floated toward the tree.

Blood. No blood, Ellie.

I cried out in pain and shock as Collin pressed our marks together.

The world around me faded, and the spirit world burst free.

⌁ Chapter Thirty ⌁

The knot in the giant oak tree began to glow and a bright light suffused the air, blinding me. But when I closed my eyes and blinked them open, I could see. The gate to hell swung open, the shouts and cries of three wind gods, the demons and other spirits, clung to the molecules in the air.

The wind god of the north appeared in the shape of a bird with a human head and flowing white hair. "Come my brothers. You are free!" Three large birds with human heads flew out of the tree and circled over Collin and me. They dove and pecked, but bounced off an invisible dome that surrounded us. They grimaced and shrieked. "We promised we would come for you Curse Keeper, daughter of the sea, witness to creation. We will make you pay. We will be lurking in the night for you."

Okeus appeared next, moving through the gate toward the tree, in human form. He was handsome with raven hair, long on one side and short on the other. His eyes were black as the night. He held his arms open wide. "Come, my children! You are finally free!"

Grotesque creatures spilled out of the tree like ants, crawling over one another in their rush to freedom. They circled Collin and me. Collin stiffened and his free arm snaked around my back and pulled me to his chest. The creatures sniffed at the edge of our circle, clawing at the invisible shield. Hundreds covered the ground in the garden, knocking over the candles and trampling the marks in the grass. "We will hunt you in the night Curse Keeper, daughter of the sea, witness to creation. You will rue the day you came into existence. We will torture you for four hundred years as your people tortured us."

Then they disappeared into the darkness. All but Okeus, who walked toward us, wearing a wicked smile. "Well done, son of the earth. You have opened the gate, and while I can give you continued protection, your reward will not be granted. You defied me by protecting the daughter of the sea." Okeus turned to me, his finger piercing the shield. A sharp talon extended from where he should have had a fingernail. The tip touched my right arm and his claw sank deep, dragging across my skin and cutting a jagged design. His symbol.

I screamed from the pain, and my knees collapsed. Collin held me up, horror in his eyes.

"Until the day you die, you carry the mark of my curse."

My vision swam as Okeus disappeared. Collin and I were alone with the open gate before us.

Ahone came next, descending from the sky, wearing a white robe and a long white beard. "Witness to creation, you believe, but do you have faith?"

Tears fell down my face. I didn't know what to have faith in anymore.

"There are forces greater than the strength of the gods. You are witness to creation. You have seen this with your own eyes. You have been present in all of time and space. You were chosen for a reason, Curse Keeper, witness to creation. You must have faith."

Anything we send back right now won't stay there. The gate to the spirit world is open and it would only return. They will only stay locked away if the gate is closed.

The only chance humanity had at survival was if we shut the gate.

"I don't know how."

"You will when you have faith."

"After I make my sacrifice?"

Ahone nodded.

Did I need Collin for this? I doubted that he'd even help, not that I wanted his help. I tugged the rope around my arm free and pushed Collin's arm off of me. I held up my throbbing right hand, blood dripping down my wrist, and walked toward the gate. Ahone said the answer was there if I had faith.

What was the difference between belief and faith? I believed this was real because I'd seen it with my own eyes. But faith meant believing without proof.

Ahone interrupted my thoughts. "The sun is rising, witness to creation. When the sun touches the surface of the earth, the gate is sealed open forever."

No pressure.

"Ellie," Collin called behind me, panic in his voice. "What are you doing?"

Anger rose hot and scalding, and I turned and pointed my finger at him. "You shut the fuck up *right now*."

Pain swam in his eyes. I turned to face the opening.

How was I going to do this? I didn't know what to do, but I realized that was the point. Wasn't that the purpose of faith? Trusting in something even when you didn't know what to do? But how did I sacrifice myself and still close the gate?

"Daughter of the sea, the universe strives for balance. You are only half of a whole."

As much as I abhorred the thought, I needed Collin's power to help me do this.

"What is your sacrifice?" Ahone asked.

"Myself."

Collin gasped. He moved next to me, grabbing my arm, his eyes widening in terror. "Ellie. *No*."

Ahone shook his head. "You must give something of great value that will cause you pain to lose. You cannot sacrifice yourself."

I swallowed a sob. I couldn't close the gate without a sacrifice, and the sun would be up soon. What was I going to do?"

Daddy stepped out from behind the tree, still wearing his pajamas. "I am the sacrifice."

"No!" I shouted. How did he get here? How did he know where to go? Horror magnified my panic. *I told him.* I turned to Ahone "He doesn't know what he's doing."

Daddy smiled, his face full of love and pride. "Ellie, I *do* know what I'm doing. I've lived my life so proud to call myself the Curse Keeper and now I get to be part of history in the making. Now I will live on in the legends."

My legs shook. "Daddy, no. *Please*. Don't leave me."

"You and I both know I left you years ago." He turned to Ahone. "I'm ready."

I started to run to stop him, but Collin wrapped his arms around my stomach. "Ellie, don't."

"Get your fucking hands off me."

But Collin's grip tightened as Ahone reached a hand to Daddy's chest. Ahone's fingers turned to white smoke, which spiraled around Daddy's body. Daddy's head fell back and his legs grew limp.

The smoke gently lowered Daddy to the ground, then retreated to Ahone's hand.

"Both of your sacrifices have been accepted. You may close the gate."

Sobbing, I shook my head, leaning forward, but Collin's arms kept my back pressed against his chest. I didn't want to close the gate. I wanted Daddy.

"Ellie, don't let your father's death mean nothing," Collin's voice broke, whispering in my ear. "He wanted you to close it."

I spun around to him, my sorrow exploding into rage. "You did this! You betrayed me! You *opened* the gate, Collin. How could you?"

He shook his head, tears in his eyes.

"It's your fault my father is dead. I will never forgive you for betraying me, Collin. *Never.*"

"I know." He sucked in a breath. The sadness and pain in his eyes were nearly my undoing. He took my hand and pushed his palm into my own.

In an instant, with the jolt of power, I was directly in front of the wide-open gate, searching deep inside my being for the ancient force. I realized my agonized soul was the key to finding it. Great sacrifice was needed to save the world. Ananias Dare had sacrificed his entire village, including his wife and child. Perhaps he'd done it inadvertently, but he'd done it all the same. I needed to feel deep pain to uncover the ancient magic. Didn't Ahone realize that Collin's betrayal was sacrifice enough?

I leaned my head back, my mark still linked to Collin's, opening my left arm wide and summoning the force. A black hole filled the sky overhead.

"Collin, you opened the gate. You have to close it."

He stood at my side, his eyes wide in confusion.

"Push the gate closed, Collin, or I will kick your fucking ass."

He looked around as though he were in the middle of a dream, but he grabbed a thick iron spindle with his left hand and pushed the gate closed.

I pressed our still joined hands onto the metal bars. "We are daughter of the sea and son of the earth. I am witness to the birth of the earth and the birth of the sea, magic more ancient and powerful than that of the gods. Our union gave rise to their birth and our union will give rise to their death. I call upon our primordial power to seal the gate to hell."

Sparks flew from the melding of the gate to the wall of the spirit world.

When I was sure it was sealed, I dropped Collin's hand, and we stood under the giant oak tree, on trampled grass and overturned candles. The sun's rays had begun to peek over the horizon.

Ahone stood next to the tree, Daddy's body at his feet. "The universe strives for balance. The son of the earth has paid his sacrifice. The daughter of the sea has also paid hers. Daughter of the sea, you may now bear my mark." Ahone disappeared into mist.

I rushed to Daddy and dropped to my knees. I reached a tentative hand toward him, terrified he'd be frozen. *"Daddy,"* I wailed as I stroked his face, thankful to find it still warm. He looked so peaceful, as though he were asleep. "Daddy. Wake up. *Daddy!*" I shook his shoulders, leaving bloody smears on his cheek and his pajamas. "Wake up!"

"Ellie, he's not asleep." Collin's voice cracked behind me.

I pressed my cheek to Daddy's chest, listening for the dull thud I'd hear when I was a little girl. The only sound was my own ragged breath from my sobs.

"Ellie, we have to get out of here." Collin squatted behind me and gently gripped my shoulders.

My body stiffened. *"Get your fucking hands off of me."*

His fingers slid slowly off of my arms, and he rose, but remained inches behind me.

I stood, spinning around to face Collin. "What was *your* sacrifice? Was it your brother?"

A hint of anger mixed with the pain etched on his face. "No. God, no."

"What? What did you give Okeus?"

The morning hung pregnant with pause. "My soul."

I gasped. It all made sense.

Are you a witch, Ellie Lancaster? Have you cast a spell to entrance me? Or are you an angel sent to save my soul?

"Why would you do that, Collin? Why would you sell the devil your soul?"

"You don't understand, Ellie."

I shook my head in disgust. "You're right. I don't understand. I thought I knew you."

His eyes hardened. "I told you not to trust me."

"That's the only thing I should have believed." The cool morning air hit my flushed skin and I shivered, then spun around, looking for my shirt.

"Ellie. I swear to God I didn't mean to hurt you."

"Don't you mean you swear to Okeus?"

"Ellie, *please.* Just let me explain."

I ignored him as I bent down to pick my T-shirt off the ground. Dizziness swamped my head as I stood back up, and I realized how much blood I had lost. My right arm was covered in it.

Collin reached for me, but I slapped him away with my left hand. "Don't you touch me. You lost any right to touch me."

"Ellie, please." The pain in his voice almost broke me. Almost.

I tugged my shirt over my head. "You lied to me. You endangered my life. You endangered humanity for what? *You sold your soul.* What did Okeus promise you, Collin?"

"Ellie."

"You *knew.* The day you came into the restaurant, you knew. You did this. *You did this to me.* The contents of hell have spilled upon the earth and every single creature has vowed to hunt me down and make me pay for their imprisonment. All for your selfish greed." I found my purse on the ground and picked it up, pushing through another wave of dizziness. "I hope you're happy, Collin. I hope it was worth it."

"If I could do it all over again—"

My heart twisted with pain and grief. "You'd do the exact same thing. You told me that last night." My voice caught on a sob, but I swallowed it. "You wouldn't change any of it."

He held out his palm toward me. His mark was there, covered in both of our blood. Hours ago it was a symbol of hope; now it was reminder of my idiocy. "I didn't know, Ellie. I swear I didn't know."

"And now you do. But it doesn't change a fucking thing."

I turned around and took a deep breath. I was about to walk away from the one person in all of eternity who could make me whole. My literal other half. The pain was excruciating, a thousand times worse than any physical pain I had ever felt. I choked back a sob. Could I do this? Could I walk away from him?

How could I not after what he'd done?

I took a step, nearly collapsing from the pain of separation.

"Where are you going?" Collin called after me, his voice broken.

I stopped and looked over my shoulder. "I'm going to do what my father raised me to do. I'm going to save the world."

Author's Note

The idea for *The Curse Keepers* came to me in March 2012. The end of my urban fantasy series—The Chosen—was on the horizon and I was looking for a new project to start on when the series was finished.

Although I wasn't sure what I would write about, I *did* know that I wanted to write another urban fantasy without vampires and werewolves. My friend and critique partner, Trisha Leigh, suggested I base it on the Lost Colony of Roanoke. In my version, the colony disappears because of a curse.

This story is based on historical events and figures. Manteo is real. He was a Croatan Indian who befriended the English when they first arrived in what is now North Carolina, years before the colony landed onshore. Manteo sailed to England with Wanchese, another Croatan Indian, and spent several years in England before he returned to the New World on the ship with the first colony. A ragtag band of 118 men, women, and children determined to create a new life free of religious persecution landed on Roanoke Island on July 22, 1587. Their governor was John White, but he soon returned to England to get more supplies, leaving behind his daughter Elinor/Eleanor (both spellings found interchangeably), newborn granddaughter Virginia, and son-in-law, Ananias Dare, along with the rest of the colonists, less one man who was murdered by a neighboring Native American tribe.

John White returned three years later to discover the colony had disappeared. Nothing was left behind, not even the buildings. While many wild speculations have been made—including my own, even if I know mine is fictional—the reality is that the colony, which faced constant threats from angry Native American tribes, probably moved either inland or farther down the coast to live with friendlier tribes.

Although information about the colony is hard to find, searching out information about the Croatan tribe has been even more difficult. I have never researched a book or series as much as I have *The Curse Keepers*. Nor have I found so few results from my searches.

Sadly, much has been lost about the Native Americans the first English settlers encountered. The English were far more concerned about converting the Indians to the English way rather than preserving the Native American history. I have spent months and months reading books, e-mailing professors of North Carolinian Native American history, and surfing through information on the Internet to come up with a spirit world for *The Curse Keepers*. I've pulled stories and gods from several coastal, early Native American tribes to come up with my own creation story.

The story of the Great Hare god and the jealous wind gods is recorded in several books. I also found belief in two creator gods, Ahone and Okeus (pronounced Ok-ee), one good and one evil. However, the story of Ahone splitting himself into two so he could save humanity is my own fabrication. I have also searched early Algonquian languages to come up with authentic Native American words for the names of the wind gods since no names are recorded. I found no record of a flood story, but so many beliefs share this story, I decided to include it in my own creation myth.

The Manitou is part of Algonquian belief. So is the spirit world hell, Popogusso. The idea of pure souls is my own creation. I have uncovered many other demons and monsters in ancient Native American folklore. They will make appearances in future books.

Manteo is a real town on Roanoke Island. Writing about a real town that is relatively small presented a challenge. I visited Manteo in April 2012 but only spent two days exploring the town, Roanoke Island, and the visitor center at the Fort Raleigh National Historic Site. I have a weeklong trip planned for July 2013 to research more of the island, including Wanchese, a fishing village, and the surrounding area, both on the Outer Banks and inland.

When I wrote *The Curse Keepers*, I wanted to capture the character of the town as much as possible, but I couldn't keep everything exactly the same. I've changed the names of many real establishments. If you visit Manteo, you'll probably be able to figure out most of them.

The Curse Keepers is rich with history, and it's my hope that my respect for lost Native American tribes comes through in this book as well as future books.

Acknowledgments

If it weren't for my best friend and critique partner, Trisha Leigh, *The Curse Keepers* would never exist. When I was brainstorming a new urban fantasy series that didn't include vampires or shape-shifters, Trisha suggested I come up with something based on the Lost Colony of Roanoke. Two hours of Google Chat later—despite the fact we live ten minutes apart and talk on the phone every day—the plot for *The Curse Keepers* was born.

Thank you to my awesome editor, Alison Dasho, who has worked with me on multiple books and helped me tweak the series synopsis and world building for *The Curse Keepers*. She always believes in me, even when my confidence wavers.

Thanks to my beta readers—Rhonda Cowswert, Wendy Webb, Becky Podjenksi, Marsha Norlock, Christie Timpson, Pamela Hargraves, and Emily Pearson. Rhonda is the best beta reader an author could hope for. She understands the number one rule of beta reading: Friends don't let friends look stupid in print.

A huge thanks to the citizens of Manteo who answered questions about life in their town when I visited in April 2012. Also thanks to Becky Smith, a resident of Manteo who shared information through e-mail. I tried my best to get life in Manteo as accurate as possible. What I did get right is because of the generosity of the Manteo residents.

And finally, I want to thank my children, who have learned to accept the fact their mom has a different life than most moms. Between the multiple trips, the crazy sleep schedule, and the fact I work every day, Christmas included, they've not only accepted the changes in their lives but also give me their full support. They see that I'm living my dream. They can make theirs come true too.

ABOUT THE AUTHOR

Denise Grover Swank was born in Kansas City, Missouri, and lived in the area until she was nineteen. She then became a nomad, living in five cities, four states, and ten houses over the next decade before moving back to her roots. She speaks English and a smattering of Spanish and Chinese. Her hobbies include making witty Facebook comments and dancing in the kitchen. She has six children and hasn't lost her sanity. Or so she leads everyone to believe.